'Alina, the bab... family. I can't—I *won't* permit this child to be born illegitimate.'

Somewhere out in the real world a driver beeped his horn. She sensed Ethan studying her, could imagine his brain churning with arguments to reinforce his demand. For him, her full compliance was essential. He'd accept nothing less.

'How long is it supposed to last?' It came out wrong. She hadn't meant to sound so cold, so detached. She certainly wasn't prepared for the pained look in his eyes.

'We've got seven months to sort out the future. No one will be surprised if our sudden marriage doesn't survive long-term.' His hand left her stomach and cupped her chin. 'I won't force you to stay, and I swear you won't lose from this arrangement.'

He was right—because she'd already lost everything worthwhile. She'd bought a new gold ring because she hadn't been able to bear the sight or the feel of the original.

'You give me your word that I can leave when I decide?'

'Yes.' It was blunt. His body was rigid, his features unreadable.

'All right. I'll marry you.'

BOUND BY THE UNBORN BABY

BY
BELLA BUCANNON

First Published in Great Britain 2016
By Mills & Boon, an imprint of HarperCollins*Publishers*
1 London Bridge Street, London, SE1 9GF

© 2016 Harriet Nichola Jarvis

ISBN: 978-0-263-92001-7

23-0716

Printed and bound in Spain
by CPI, Barcelona

Bella Bucannon lives in a quiet northern suburb of Adelaide with her soulmate husband, who loves and supports her in any endeavour. She enjoys walking, dining out and travelling. Bus tours or cruising with days at sea to relax, plot and write are top of her list. Apart from category romance she also writes very short stories and poems for a local writing group. Bella believes joining RWA and SARA early in her writing journey was a major factor in her achievements.

Deepest thanks to my husband and soulmate, who claims that inside my head is the scariest place on earth but loves me unconditionally anyway. Special thanks to the generous, supportive South Australian Romance Authors for their encouragement and steadfast belief in me.

And to Flo Nicoll, who saw beyond my raw writing and gave me the courage to drastically cut and revise and produce a story worth telling.

CHAPTER ONE

THIRD DOOR ON the left. Why the hell hadn't he given in to his original instinct, phoned the hotel with a refusal, then binned the short letter hand-delivered to his office? He'd never heard of Alina Fletcher—didn't have the time or energy for enigmatic invitations.

Except one phrase, vaguely referring to his family, had captured his interest five weeks after his sister and brother-in-law had died in Barcelona, less than two since his second trip to Spain regarding their estate.

He felt drained. Flying overseas and coping with local authorities while handling the glitches regarding his latest hotel acquisition had been exhausting. The basic Spanish he'd acquired on other trips had helped; deprivation of sleep didn't. He desperately needed a break to enable him to grieve for Louise, and for Leon, who'd been his best friend since primary school. Any additional angst was definitely unwelcome.

The open doorway allowed him a clear view of the woman facing the window. Slim build. Medium height. Short dark brown hair. His gaze slid rapidly over a sky-blue jacket and trousers to flat shoes. Unusual in this time of killer heels.

'Ms Fletcher?' He was curter than he'd intended, influenced by a hard clench low in his abdomen.

She turned slowly and his battered emotions were rocked even more. Pain-filled eyes underlined with dark smudges met his. Widened. Shuttered. Reopened, clear and steady. Whatever had flickered in their incredible violet depths had banished his lethargy. His dormant libido kicked in, tightening his stomach muscles, accelerating his pulse.

Inappropriate. Inexcusable.

'Ethan James? Thank you for agreeing to meet me.'

No welcoming smile. Did he detect a slight accent? He'd have to hear more—wanted to hear more.

He cleared his throat. 'Did I have a choice?' Moving forward with extended hand, he frowned at her hesitation. *She* was the one who'd requested the meeting.

After a cool, brief touch she gestured to the seating. 'Coffee? Black and strong?'

His eyes narrowed at her assumption of his preference, flicked to the wedding ring she wore. Married. Why did he care? The perfume she wore didn't suit her. Too strong. Too exotic. He wasn't thinking clearly—hadn't been since that devastating early-morning phone call.

'What do you want?' No games. Either she told him the reason they were here or he walked. 'You've got two minutes to convince me to stay.'

She met his glare unwaveringly. 'Then you'd better start reading.' Perching on the front of an armchair, she pushed a buff-coloured folder along the low table before pouring coffee into a cup.

His muscles tensed. She appeared confident, was counting on him thinking he'd always wonder if he left without an explanation. He grudgingly picked up the unnamed folder and sat, stretching out his long legs.

Once she'd placed the drink in front of him she took a book from the bag by her side and settled into the chair to read.

He pulled the file out, glanced at the front sheet—and his already shattered world tilted beyond reality. He flipped the pages, studied the signatures. Scowled at the seemingly composed female ignoring him. A fist of ice clamped his gut. His heart pounded. Not true. Not believable. Though the signatures were genuine. He'd seen enough of them in the last few weeks to be absolutely certain.

Why? There'd been no indication.

He reached for his coffee, drained the hot liquid in one gulp while glancing at Alina Fletcher. Not so serene on further scrutiny. The fingers on her left hand were performing a strange ritual. Starting with the littlest, they curled one by one into her palm, with her thumb folding over the top. Dancelike, the movement was repeated every few seconds.

Nervous? She damn well ought to be, hitting him with this out of the blue. He gave a derisive grunt. He'd have been blindsided however she'd informed him.

Reverting to the opening document, he meticulously perused every paragraph.

Alina automatically flicked the blurred pages of her book, her fingers trembling. Her thoughts were in turmoil. This encounter ought to have been straightforward. She'd come to Sydney, acquaint the brother with the situation, and then they'd discuss options in a businesslike fashion. Instead she'd tensed at the timbre of his formal greeting, been slow to take his hand, shaken by her quickening heartbeat.

Please, please, let it be hormonal.

The best scenario was that he'd concur with the logical solution. She'd return to Europe and they'd communicate amicably via email or phone. Living alone would be no hardship. She only shared accommodation when it was required by an employer and rarely maintained friendships, even those forged from seasonal reunions. No roots. No ties. Liking co-workers was a plus. None had been able to break through the wall staying sane had compelled her to build.

She still wasn't sure what had drawn her to Louise on their early irregular meetings. Perhaps an empathy that had enabled her to see behind the sparkling personality and glimpse the hidden sorrow? A feeling that she was a kindred spirit? Seeing the loving relationship Louise had shared with Leon? She'd often thought of them while travelling. Four months ago fate had brought them together at a critical time for Louise, a soul-searching one for her.

She'd stayed away from the funeral service in Barcelona for her own sake, needing time to decide what to do. Contacting Ethan James while he was arranging for his relatives to be transported to Australia for burial would have been insensitive. It was, however, the honourable thing to do now. In the end the only thing she believed would ensure her future peace of mind.

Until she'd looked into those cobalt eyes with their thick black lashes—so like Louise's, except dulled with sadness and fatigue. Unwarranted, almost forgotten heat sensations had flared low in her belly. Immediately squashed. *Never again.* She'd barely survived before—sometimes felt she hadn't.

During the last year she'd slowly, *so* slowly, begun to open up a little to people. Now she was caught in a different nightmare, with far-reaching consequences. It all depended on the man intently scanning the papers she'd given him.

She approved of his neatly trimmed dark hair, his long fingers with well-shaped clean nails. His no-frills attitude to her letter. Leon had described him as astute, pragmatic, and extremely non-sentimental in business. Personally reserved. The very qualities she needed right now.

She sipped her mint tea, praying her guest would agree to her suggestion. Her skin still prickled from his oh-so-fleeting touch. A hint of earthy cologne teased her nostrils every time she inhaled. Unusual and unfamiliar. Definitely not one of the brands she'd sold working in a department store in Rome last summer.

The tension in the room heightened. She looked up, encountered cold, resolute scrutiny, a grim mouth and firmly set jaw. Did he intend to dispute her claim? In October he'd have all the proof he'd require.

Ethan saw fear chase the sadness from her eyes, swiftly replaced by pseudo-cool detachment.

'You're carrying their child.' He didn't doubt the validity of the documents. They were legal, watertight contracts—somewhat alien to his carefree relatives. 'Why?'

'Three early miscarriages with no medical explanation. No trouble with conception. Surrogacy offered them a way to have a baby of their own.' She spoke precisely, as if she'd rehearsed every word.

He swore quietly, fervently. Why hadn't they told him? There'd been no hint of a problem on any of his visits. Or had he been too focused on his growing business empire to notice?

Anger at lost opportunities gnawed at him. Guilt at missing any change in Louise's demeanour flooded him. The urge to strike out was strong. Pity the only one in the firing line happened to be the messenger.

'Why the secrecy? Why *you*?' He ground the words out violently.

She didn't flinch, though faint colour tinged her cheeks. Crossing her arms, she lifted her chin. 'I offered. My choice. My reasons.'

Something in her tone warned him not to pursue the subject. Fine—he'd accept the simplified statement for now. Coming to terms with being uncle to an unborn child conceived by his dead sister and her husband, carried by a stranger, took precedence.

'When's the child due? Did they know?' A myriad of questions buzzed in his brain, making it impossible to prioritise.

'Late October. I'm nine weeks. We did a pregnancy test together.' Her lips trembled. Her gaze shifted to the wall behind him. 'They were so incredibly happy for a few days. Until that goods van smashed into them at that outdoor café.'

Her tortured eyes met his. Anguish ripped through him on hearing those mind-numbing words spoken in her tremulous voice. He knew. He'd received the international call, read the reports. Seen photographs of the mangled wreckage.

Suddenly he craved solitude. And space. He wanted to run from this woman, escape from her predicament. Forget everything and crawl into a cave like a wounded animal to lick his wounds and recover.

Not going to happen.

He ought to stay, talk more. Get more details. How could he? She exacerbated his torment.

Jamming the file into the folder, he stood up. Alina stayed in her seat, her eyes a mixture of sorrow and perplexity, making him feel like a louse. He pulled his mobile from his inside pocket.

'I need time to take all this in. Give me your number. I'll phone you tomorrow.'

She told him, including the Spanish code. 'You can leave a message at Reception so you won't get charged international rates.'

Ethan let out a short, half-choked laugh. She appeared genuinely concerned at the thought of him paying the fees—something his company did every day. 'I can stand the cost.'

A soft blush coloured her cheeks. His gut twisted in remorse.

She rose to her feet, proudly defiant, tightly clasping her book. 'I appreciate what a shock this is. If there'd been an easier way to tell you, I'd—'

'There wasn't. Goodbye, Ms Fletcher.' He spun round and strode out.

The tension drained from Alina's muscles, to be replaced by frightening awareness. Alien. Alarming. His aura still filled the room, surrounding her, challenging her resolve. Threatening what little stability she had.

She tried to equate this barely held together man with the sharp, on-the-ball tycoon described to her. The one who'd always managed to extricate the two friends from escapades usually instigated by the younger one. The one who'd transformed a failing local travel centre into the multimillion-dollar Starburst hotel and tourism empire.

The man she'd just watched hurriedly exit seemed to be operating on stretched nerves.

Pouring another cup of tea, she reproached herself for bringing more trauma into his life, but knew she'd had no choice. The realisation that she'd been banking on him taking charge, relieving her of all major decisions, hit home. She squeezed her eyes shut, stemming the tears. He hadn't rebuffed her completely. There was still hope.

She pictured Louise sobbing in the café the day after the specialist had advised her that any more pregnancies might be detrimental to her health. She recalled walking her home, talking with her, learning about her society-obsessed parents' rigid attitude to social status.

Her sympathy for Leon's and Louise's plight, and her strong desire to help had been understandable; the solution that had popped into her mind had been astounding. And terrifying.

After two days of intense soul-searching she'd offered to be a surrogate. Their initial refusal had given way to grateful acceptance in light of their limited options. Over a supper of fruit, cheese and dips, washed down with local wine, they'd conceived the perfect plan. Almost foolproof. They hadn't counted on brake failure destroying their hopes in the cruellest way possible.

She stroked her stomach. *Their* baby—not hers. She was simply a cocoon. In October she'd have given birth to their son or daughter and then stepped away, allowing them to experience fully the delights and dramas of parenthood.

Ethan *must* consent to her plan. This tiny new life inside her deserved the love and happiness its new family would have shared. Ethan, rather than his parents, was her preferred choice. If they all chose not to… Well, then she'd have to confront and conquer her demons.

Gathering up her belongings, she went to her room, hoping the television would prevent her thoughts from straying to tomorrow's call. And its maker.

She was window-shopping along George Street when her phone rang late the next morning.

'Alina?'

Spoken with a slightly different emphasis, as if personal to him. Silly idea. He'd given her the impression he considered her an intrusive dilemma.

'Sorry I didn't call earlier. I've been juggling my schedule. Are you free tonight?'

'Yes. I came to Sydney for the sole purpose of meeting you.'

'And if I'd refused?' he asked brusquely.

'I'd have posted you a detailed letter with the file and caught the next available flight to Spain.'

'And wha—? No, not now. A hire car will be outside your hotel at five-thirty. I've booked a table. Goodbye, Ms Fletcher.'

He hung up, leaving her startled by his broken-off question. Understanding his scepticism, she swore to be honest—though she'd keep her past to herself unless it concerned the baby. Last night as she'd fallen asleep she'd sensed an elusive unidentifiable memory skip through her mind. Didn't want any more.

Ethan drummed his fingertips on his desk. He'd meant to ask why she wore a ring—if there was a husband or partner in the picture. He'd been distracted by her impassive replies and had accidentally activated an email from Brisbane requiring an urgent reply. Hence his regrettable abrupt ending to the call.

His back ached…his brain spun. An evening on the internet researching surrogacy had raised more questions than it had answered. It hurt that they'd gone through so much heartache alone. Why hadn't they reached out to him? Surely they'd known they mattered to him more than anything?

He'd supported Louise's marriage to Leon against his parents' wishes, happily standing as best man. He had never doubted their love for each other, had admired their courage and steadfast defiance of the demands to wait until they were older. Louise's declaration that they'd have a park wedding in front of a few friends had provoked his mother into grudging agreement. She had then proceeded to turn it into a flash affair for her own social gratification.

From what he'd seen, growing up, those two had been the exception in a world of duplicity and the façade of wedded unity. His own memories of being brushed aside, of days seeing only nannies or cooks, still rankled.

Knowing he carried the genes of two people with no apparent parental feelings had determined his future. Swearing there'd be no children, even if he married in the future, he'd resolved to be the best uncle to any nieces or nephews. Now that vow would be tested in a way he'd never imagined.

Lying awake, contemplating options, he'd finally decided on the best solution for the child and his family. It all depended on that gold ring. Alina Fletcher might not concur with his decision. She was the one who'd offered the use of her body, the one who'd travelled to Australia to meet him. The one who'd spun his world out of orbit with her revelation. She'd committed herself by contacting him.

He'd been disconcerted by his physical reaction to the stranger with the inconceivable news. An effect he blamed on fatigue, combined with his almost celibate life for months. So he'd run—hadn't stayed to find out what *she* wanted, what she expected from *him*.

He'd finally slept restlessly, risen early, and reshuffled his work diary.

Alina spotted Ethan immediately: tall, head-turningly handsome, impossible to miss among the people milling outside the luxurious hotel. His sister had been spontaneous and cheerful; her dinner companion tonight exuded an aura of deliberation and sobriety.

Blaming the prickling sensation down her spine on stress, she steeled herself as she unbuckled the seatbelt. Her door opened, giving her a view of a solid torso clad in an elegant designer suit. She was glad she'd impulsively packed her black dinner dress, bought four years ago in rural France. Rarely worn, it was simple in design, chic enough to give her confidence a boost. Loose enough to conceal any hint of her condition.

She swung her leg out and his fingers curled around her elbow, taking her weight as she alighted. Holding on longer than necessary. As it had yesterday, his touch generated tingles, radiating across her skin.

'Thank you for being so prompt.'

His deep voice sounded less dynamic. The shadows under his eyes were darker. Another too-full day after too little sleep?

Why the let-down feeling at his mundane comment? Quickly followed by a zing of pleasure when he put his arm around her to escort her through the crowd? Heat flared in places that had been winter-cold for years, shocking her into silence.

He released her the moment they entered the elevator

for the short journey up to the restaurant, taken in silence. They were greeted by the maître d', who led them to a window table set apart in a far corner, secluded by greenery. Alina followed, acutely aware of the man behind her and the limited number of diners in the room. She sat, staring in awe at the North Sydney high-rises across the harbour.

'This is incredible,' she said, and sighed, turning her head to take in more. Too far. Their eyes met; warmth flooded her cheeks. He must think her so gauche. To her surprise he glanced out, then smiled at her for the first time, transforming his features, making him less forbidding.

'I guess it is. Over time you get used to the skyline being there.'

'Not possible,' she declared vehemently. 'And it's going to get better as all the lights come on, isn't it?'

CHAPTER TWO

ETHAN'S FATIGUE LIGHTENED at her enthusiasm for something he took for granted. Her eyes gleamed, darkened to the colour of the flowers of the plant on his PA's desk.

His jaw firmed as she returned the smile from the young waiter who offered her a menu. The curt nod he gave him on accepting his was unwarranted, and instantly repented.

Her delightfully intense expression as she carefully read each item restored his good humour. She finally looked up and gestured, palm out.

'How on earth am I supposed to decide? I'm not even sure what some of them are. You choose for me.'

'The lemon sole is particularly good. Or the chef's special if you are in the mood for lamb.' His gaze dropped to her pink, unenhanced lips. Forget food—he wanted to taste *her*. She'd be sweeter than any dessert coming out of the kitchen tonight.

Her voice cut through his inapt thoughts.

'I'll bet they're all delicious. Nothing too spicy or strong-flavoured.' Putting her menu on the table, she laid her arms on top, unintentionally drawing his attention as she leant forward. 'And small portions for me, please.'

The taut fit of the material over her breasts intrigued him. Had being pregnant enlarged them? They'd been hidden under her loose jacket yesterday. Tonight they'd been the first thing he'd visually noticed when she'd stepped from the car—preceded by that perfume so not right for her.

What the hell was wrong with him? The woman opposite him wore a wedding ring and was pregnant. He tamped down his libido, concentrated on selecting their meal.

'Oh, wine...?' Alina's hands fell to her sides as a young

woman carrying a bottle placed an ice bucket and stand next to their table.

'Non-alcoholic,' Ethan hastily reassured her, before addressing the waitress. 'Please allow my guest to sample it.'

She savoured the tangy fruit flavour, drank a little more, and smiled. 'It's very refreshing. Thank you.'

She gazed around while he ordered their meals. A screen of plants, plus a larger than standard space, separated them from the adjoining tables. Little chance of being seen—none of being overheard. Had he asked for it? Or—oh, this upmarket hotel must be part of his Starburst chain.

The waitress left. Alina raised her glass, let the tangy liquid slide down her throat. Her curiosity overrode tact. 'Are these plants and extra space always here?'

He shrugged. 'On request. Some couples find the seclusion romantic. Some men aspire to an elaborate setting with privacy for a proposal.' He paused, a glint of amusement in his eyes. 'In case of rejection.'

She understood the need to keep her presence a secret. An icy shiver ran down her spine. What if he rejected *her* proposal? She had to persuade him it was best for everyone involved.

'Doesn't it invite curiosity from people who might recognise you? Who'll wonder who I am?'

'Few people dine this early. I believe you'll feel more comfortable eating here, then we'll go somewhere quieter to discuss our situation.'

'You're right. Thank you.' Her gaze wandered from the silverware, the fine cut-glass, and the decorative light fittings to the amazing panorama outside the window.

'Fine dining. Romantic setting with harbour lights. They create a wonderful memory for any couple,' he commented.

Like a sandy beach with rippling waves at dawn. Her eyes misted. She bit the inside of her lip. *Don't go there. It's all gone. Gone for ever.*

Ethan wasn't about to let her attention stray. He had too much to learn in too little time. Her history. The reason she'd agreed to be a surrogate. Why she wore that ring. Why a simple piece of jewellery rankled so much.

'Alina?'

Too sharp.

She started, blinked twice, and refocused. 'I'm sorry. I was miles away.'

'I noticed.' He leant an elbow on the table, rested his chin on his hand, and scrutinised her. He sensed her superficial demeanour was a defensive shield, preventing her from revealing anything personal. It was one he aimed to breach for his, and the child's, benefit.

'Relax. Enjoy your meal. You like seafood?'

'Love it.'

Her words coincided with the appearance of their appetiser: creamy pumpkin soup with croutons. They ate in silence, apart from her praise for the country fresh flavour. He signalled for the empty dishes to be removed, requested their mains be held for five minutes.

Once they were alone, he leant forward. 'How long had you known Leon and Louise?'

'Oh. Um… I guess casually for more than three years. If there was a position vacant I worked in a café near their house whenever I was in Barcelona.'

'A waitress?' His eyebrow quirked. *Whenever she was in Barcelona? She was not a resident?*

She bristled at his inference of her pursuing a lowly profession. 'Be careful, Mr James. You're demeaning your staff, who are giving us excellent service tonight.'

He acknowledged her rebuke with a nod. She looked gratified and continued. 'It's a useful skill for a working traveller. I rarely stay anywhere for long.'

'Any other *useful* skills?' This was getting worse by the

minute. Casual worker. Temporary. No profession. Why had they chosen *her*?

Alina fought the urge to challenge his condescending attitude. He was the baby's uncle—ideally its future guardian.

Her choices had been determined by her need to have limited social contact. She toyed with the stem of her glass, drew in a steadying breath. 'Any office work, translating or bar tending. Plus anything seasonal or transient, such as crop harvesting. I have references, if you're interested. It's been my life for seven years—my choice.'

'Not any more. Your foreseeable future will be governed by what's best for the child you are carrying. And I will have an input in every decision.'

His low, inflexible tone added to the challenge in his piercing eyes. She matched him, picturing his relatives' joy—so short-lived.

'The baby *is* my main priority. I'm taking care of myself, eating healthily, exercising sensibly.'

The bite in her voice shamed her. She'd never been confrontational, had always tried to get along with others, even in short-term work environments.

She gulped, tried for conciliation. 'Everything I do is to maintain their dream.'

Their dream—not hers. Talking with Ethan James raked up memories best left forgotten.

'What nationality are you? Where are your legal documents? Birth certificate?' He topped up their wine glasses as he spoke, then watched her as he drank.

Hands hidden in her lap, her spine rigid, she refused to show any sign of weakness. 'I'm Australian, born and bred. Is that good enough for you? For your parents? My passport's in the safe at the hotel.'

She'd done it again. She'd anticipated his questions, prepared herself for suspicion, even rejection. So how did he manage to wind her up so easily?

He waited. His unfathomable dark blue eyes revealed nothing. Inexplicably, she found herself wondering how those firm full lips would feel pressed against hers.

No. No. No! She let out a loud huff of air. Had to be hormonal. Couldn't be the man. It was vital for him to think the best of her.

She tried again. 'Anything not needed regularly is with my solicitor in Crow's Nest.'

'Good. Easily accessible.' He nodded, smiled as if her reply pleased him. 'Here comes our main course.'

He'd chosen grilled lemon sole served with lightly sautéed vegetables and a side salad. It was melt-in-the-mouth scrumptious—the best meal she could remember. Her tension eased as he kept the conversation neutral and light. Because he was satisfied with her answers so far?

Dessert was an unbelievably good strawberry soufflé. She sensed his perusal as she scraped the last morsel from her dish. Didn't care. It was heavenly.

Putting down her spoon, she smiled at him. 'Mmm. Mouth-watering food. Great service. Do you eat here often?'

'I'll pass your approval on to the chef. Apart from dining here, with or without guests, I find it convenient to ring in an order and have it sent to my office or apartment.'

'They home-deliver? Like pizza?' She stared at him in amazement. He regularly ate personally delivered gourmet meals. She occasionally ordered takeaway, saved money by picking it up.

His throaty laugh skittered across her skin. 'Hey, we cater for twenty-four-hour room service. My meals travel a little further in a taxi, that's all.'

'Wow. We *so* live in different worlds.'

His eyes darkened and bored into hers. She couldn't move, couldn't look away. Her lighthearted words had shattered the mood.

Ethan pushed his empty dish aside, annoyed at her emphatic statement. She made it sound like an insurmountable division between them. Although their life in Spain might have been simpler, more casual than his ambition-driven existence, basically his core beliefs were the same as his sister's and brother-in-law's.

He'd enjoyed every moment of the regular visits he'd made to Barcelona, including the noisy, fun-filled meals lasting well into the night. There had always been friends around. So why hadn't he met *her*? Bad timing?

He drank the last of his wine, dropped his napkin on the table. 'Are you ready to leave? We'll have privacy to talk upstairs.' Where he'd be able to override any dissension to his proposition.

'Upstairs?'

Apprehension shaded the striking colour of her eyes, and a strong urge to reassure her rocked him.

'Company suite for family or friends. Leon and Louise stayed here twice; usually they came to my apartment.'

She didn't answer. He came round to hold her chair while she retrieved her bag from the floor and stood, head held high. Courageous. Beautiful.

Taking her elbow respectfully, he guided her towards a door in the side wall. The ever-alert maître d' was there before them. Ethan thanked him, adding praise for the attending staff. A moment later they sped upwards in an exclusive elevator.

They stepped out into a foyer, not the corridor Alina had envisaged. Colourful modern art complemented the light sand-coloured walls between two white doors. He used a key card to open the one on the right, gestured for her to enter.

Her remark rang true as she stared enviously at her surroundings. Different worlds nailed it. She'd cleaned rooms, never luxury suites. And for him this was the norm, his everyday existence.

Floor-to-ceiling windows afforded a spectacular view of the city on two adjoining walls. Perfectly situated to take advantage was a dark wood dining setting, with a centrepiece of bushland flora. A matching coffee table stood in front of a luxurious dark blue three-piece lounge suite, facing a wall-mounted television. Two large bright blue and red abstract paintings hung on light grey walls.

Her companion shrugged out of his jacket, tossed it onto a chair, and gestured towards a hallway. 'The bathroom is the third door along if you need it.'

He walked across to a fancy coffee machine, reaching for two mugs from the cabinet above. She watched the play of his muscles under his navy shirt, chided herself for the sudden appreciative clench low in her belly.

'If not take a seat. Tea? I assume your condition is the reason you didn't drink coffee yesterday?'

He'd noticed. Totally focused on the documents, reeling from shock, he'd still been aware of what she'd drunk. Had he mentally sized her up, judged her, as well?

'Herbal, if you have any, please.'

'No problem. Make yourself comfortable.'

So solicitous. So hospitable. Would his attitude change if they couldn't come to an agreement?

She moved to the settee, kicked off her shoes, and curled into a corner. 'Could you make it fairly weak? Just in case.'

He glanced round, his brow furrowed. 'In case of what?' His face cleared. 'Ah, having trouble with morning sickness?'

She appreciated the concern in his voice, even if it was more for the welfare of his niece or nephew than for her.

'I've been lucky so far—occasional nausea from strong aromas, nothing too bad.'

This polite, bland conversation had no reason to irritate

her—however, it did. There was no one around to hear them. *Let's get on with it.*

'What else have…? Never mind.'

Ethan tamped down his curiosity regarding her history. The current situation had priority. He put the two mugs on the coffee table and sat down beside her, inadvertently too close for detachment. Close enough to smell the fragrance he'd determined to change at the earliest opportunity. Close enough to notice the faded scar almost hidden by her hair. Close enough to inadvertently touch her. He linked his fingers to prevent impulsive movement. To keep it impersonal. *Huh, she's having Louise's child. Can't get much more personal.*

Clearing his throat, he returned to basic facts. 'Has the pregnancy been confirmed medically?' A natural question to open the conversation.

She flicked a non-existent lock of hair from her forehead. A recent change of hairstyle? Cut shorter than she normally wore it?

'No. We did an early home test on February the seventh. Although it showed positive, I repeated it before booking my flight.' Her voice was clear, with no hesitation.

He nodded. 'We have an appointment at eleven-thirty next Monday with Dr Patricia Conlan—reputedly one of Sydney's leading gynaecologists. I've been assured she'll give the best care to you and our baby. She's had a cancellation, otherwise we'd have a longer wait.'

Her pupils dilated, making a stunning display of her violet irises. Her hand moved swiftly to cover her abdomen, triggering a surge of possessiveness in him, alien and disquieting. An instinctive action? Had he imagined the flicker of awareness at his deliberate use of a certain adjective?

'You need your own proof that I'm pregnant. I'll be ready.'

'Not proof. Confirmation that everything is okay.'

She sampled her tea, smiled approvingly. 'It is. Apart from mild nausea, I'm fit and healthy. What else do you want to know?'

All your secrets. She'd been in his thoughts all day, disturbing his concentration at inopportune moments. Every time he'd walked past his PA's potted plant the flowers had conjured up a picture of stunning, sorrowful violet eyes. He'd never been drawn to any woman so fast, so powerfully. Telling himself it was because she carried Louise's child didn't cut it. His body had responded to her on sight, when he'd still suspected a scam.

'I've made frequent trips to Barcelona in the last three years. I don't remember your name being mentioned. How come we didn't meet?' There'd always been noisy gatherings at his sister's, available women and obvious attempts at matchmaking. 'I flew over for a week in January. They were excited and secretive, so I'm guessing it happened around then.'

'I deliberately wasn't part of their social group. Louise and I were casual friends who'd have a chat over coffee sometimes. Occasionally Leon would join us. I'd never been to their home until the day she confided in me. Again, my choice. The embryo was implanted on the twenty-eighth—after you'd left.'

Her gaze drifted to the window, as if she were picturing something from her past. She raised her drink and swallowed. As he watched the movement of her throat his fingers itched to caress her lightly tanned skin wherever it was exposed. Wherever it wasn't.

Draining his mug, he set it down with a sharp clink.

Startled by the noise, she swung round to confront him. 'I told you I travel a lot—mostly Europe. I'm not good at socialising or small talk.'

Merely lack of practice, to be rectified by the new circles he intended to introduce her into—a world involving business dinners and networking. She'd have his support and protection as long as she stayed with him. In return he'd expect her to accompany him to various functions when a partner was invited.

He'd been completely absorbed in her during their meal. Her eyes, her lips, the graceful curve of her neck as she bent her head, even the way she used her cutlery, all fascinated him. The plain gold ring on her left hand—the only jewellery she wore—niggled at his gut.

She still hadn't mentioned a husband or partner. It had always been 'I'. His curiosity had to be satisfied prior to revealing his intentions.

He fisted his fingers on his thigh, braced himself for her reaction. Spoke as she leant over to put her mug down. 'You wear a wedding ring. And my research informs me surrogates are invariably women who have had at least one successful pregnancy.'

She sat immobilised, one arm outstretched, her face in profile.

He couldn't stop the next words forming. 'Where's your child? Your husband?'

Her mug dropped to the table's edge, broke in two. Fell to the floor. Her skin drained of colour. Wide, tormented eyes met his. The truth hit him like a king punch to the solar plexus a split second before she replied.

'They died.'

Flat. Expressionless. Heartbreakingly poignant.

No movement. No sound. Then without warning she erupted from the settee, her desperate eyes swinging towards the door. She took one step. Ethan sprang to his feet and caught her elbow, twisting her round. Her stricken face shook him to the core. He let go.

'I didn't think. I'm sorry, Alina.'

She gulped in a deep, staggered breath that raked her body and silently walked to the hallway.

CHAPTER THREE

THEY DIED. WHY HADN'T he realised? The travelling. The solitary lifestyle. He hadn't connected the facts. Instead he'd acted like a bastard, without consideration for her feelings. An echo of his father.

Somehow he had to make amends, persuade her to stay. The child's acceptance of him depended on her conceding to his proposition. In every way. Alina the woman as much as the child-bearer. *Oh, Louise, what have you started? Why didn't you tell me?*

He picked up both mugs, dropped hers into a bin, washed his, and waited.

Alina sat on the toilet seat lid, hugging herself, rocking rhythmically, trying to quell her shuddering breaths. The cloud in her mind began to clear, leaving behind a mixture of fear and shame. She'd blown it—been ambushed by a question she ought to have foreseen. Ethan James was a man who'd check the information he'd been given—investigate until he knew everything. Or believed he did. And instead of calmly answering, she'd panicked.

She cringed, dreading what his opinion of her would be now—a neurotic female with serious hang-ups who claimed to be pregnant with his niece or nephew. It was essential he be convinced of her emotional stability, so he'd trust her to take proper care of herself and the baby until its birth.

Dampening a cloth from the rail with cold water, she pressed it to her face, ashamed of her abrupt reaction. Her reflection in the mirror was pale and strained—not the composed image she'd hoped to project. *For Louise and*

Leon. She recited her mantra, squared her shoulders, and returned to the main sitting area.

Ethan leant on the counter by the coffee machine, watching her with sympathetic eyes. Guilt also flickered in the cobalt blue, stirring her conscience.

She gave an awkward shrug. 'You surprised me. I anticipated a doctor asking about my history, but I guess I'm not as prepared as I thought. Add my hormones acting crazy, and jet lag—'

'My fault. I didn't mean it to come out so brutally.' He moved forward, gave her plenty of space. 'My only excuse is I'm still trying to come to grips with it all. Forgive me?'

She empathised—had been there. Heck, she was *still* there. Shock upon shock robbed you of lucidity. In the last twenty-four hours, she'd delivered a bundle to him. Not having any option didn't ease her remorse.

She managed a twisted smile. 'Time heals is a furphy. Developing a façade to get through each day is the only way to survive.' And hers threatened to crack with every look, every touch from this man. Her mouth dried; her throat constricted. 'It's not right. They deserved to have their baby. Life *stinks.*'

Fierce and heartfelt.

Ethan concurred that life wasn't always fair, but refrained from admitting it. 'Life's what you make it. Are you up for talking a little longer? If not I'll take you to your hotel and we can continue in the morning.'

'I'll stay.' She ran her tongue over dry lips. 'Could I have another tea, please?'

'Thank you for agreeing. Same flavour?'

With a brave attempt at smiling, she curled into the corner of the settee. When he sat he left a bigger gap between them, avoiding accidental contact.

Space didn't help. Yesterday he'd attributed his reaction to her as the combined effects of disbelief, weariness,

and self-enforced celibacy due to his business commitments. Problems with the expansion of his hotel chain into
Queensland—on top of his regular heavy workload—had
left him little time for a personal life even prior to the accident.

Tonight the desire for physical contact had been—*was
still*—much stronger. He'd resisted with effort, knowing it
was essential to allay her doubts and resolve some of the
essential matters. Every day counted in the agenda he'd
formulated.

She drank thirstily, colour gradually returning to her
cheeks. Unsure eyes met his and he thought he'd have given
almost anything to appease her by bringing the evening
to an end.

'That was the reason you kept moving? No ties? No
commitments?'

Relief washed over him when she merely nodded before
placing her mug down carefully.

'We need to discuss certain issues—the main one being
protection for the child. It wasn't random curiosity, Alina.
I have a genuine motivation for everything I ask.'

Her jaw firmed, her shoulders hitched. Bracing for
what? The sight of her teeth giving a quick tug to the side
of her mouth gave him a moment of regret, determinedly
squashed. He needed facts.

'What did you imagine would happen when you requested a meeting?'

To his surprise she relaxed, as if she'd feared a different query.

'Springing a newborn niece or nephew on you didn't
seem right, even though I don't think you can get DNA
proof till then. I figured you'd appreciate time to get used
to the idea—time to decide if your family wanted to adopt
the—'

'*If* we wanted to adopt Louise's child?' In a second he

was towering over her, six feet of instant fury directed solely at the woman recoiling from him.

A range of emotions flickered across her features. Resentment. Anger. Guilt?

She pushed herself upright, causing him to step back. 'Yes—*if*. You expect me to believe your parents will *welcome* this? Even *with* DNA proof?' She glared up at him, delightfully incensed, daring him to contradict her.

Stunned at her outburst, he felt his temper abate. His mother's perception of social standing… His father's snobbery… Their disapproval of his sister's marriage… All probably the reason Louise's miscarriages had been kept secret.

He spun round to the window, running agitated fingers into his hair. How much more angst was a man supposed to endure?

'Options were limited because of their attitude.'

Her tone was gentle, conciliatory. He turned.

'Louise knew they'd consider adopting a failure, although it *was* to be their last resort.'

'I'm not sure they'd have accepted a surrogate grandchild either,' he grated.

'They weren't going to find out.'

It had slipped out, and Alina couldn't retract the declaration.

A predatory gleam flared in his eyes. He moved quickly, trapping her against the settee, his breath fanning her face. She stood her ground, holding his gaze, hoping he couldn't sense her trepidation.

A long moment later he inclined his head. 'I suggest we sit, so you can explain exactly how the three of you intended to hide it from us.'

She didn't sit. She flopped, desperately trying to regroup. Extremely perceptive, he had a reputation for dealing strictly on the level. Though he might accept his parents' rigid viewpoint had been the incentive for all their secrecy and deception, he certainly hoped the trio hadn't broken any laws. That would definitely test his principles.

He also had a way of undermining her defences, honing in on sensitive secrets. Some were not for sharing.

She watched him settle, folding one leg onto the settee. His features indicated that he was cool, calm, and collected. His right fingers lightly drumming on his thigh proved otherwise.

Crunch time. Next week she'd probably be back in Spain, managing alone until October. She'd learned life's lessons the hard way, already had a plan worked out. There was the trust account Leon had set up, plus an Australian bank account she'd never accessed.

Wriggling into the corner, she tucked her feet up and challenged him. 'Then I can go to my hotel?'

'Yes. Tell me the basics. We'll discuss the rest later.' Milder tone. Persuasive.

He laid his arm along the back of the settee. A normal gesture, yet she had a sudden urge to slide into its embrace, lay her head on his shoulder, and let him take care of everything. Crazy notion. Not for her. *Ever.*

'They made a generous donation to a clinic that caters to low-income couples. The procedure was done under fictitious names, with Louise and me using the same one. We planned to travel around, avoid people we knew. As a patient, I'd use her name.'

She stopped, reluctant to continue as his posture changed. He'd jolted upright when she'd mentioned fictitious names, slowly shaking his head in disbelief. Now he sat still as stone, an incredulous stare in his dark blue eyes. Icy chills ran down her spine; cold sweat formed on her palms. He didn't approve—couldn't comprehend all they'd been through.

'We didn't hurt or cheat anyone. In fact the money we donated gave other couples a chance to realise their dream too.'

His lips compressed. 'What about doctors and scans? The birth? What if something had gone wrong? How many people did you intend to lie to?'

Alina's grip tightened till the ring she wore dug into her flesh. Damn fate and to heck with life. She'd finally found the courage to confront her dark solitude; to try and help someone else in despair. And now she'd been left with the fall-out on her own. *Again.* She curbed the tears threatening to fall. He'd probably dismiss them anyway.

'As few as possible. There was no reason to suppose this pregnancy and birth wouldn't be normal.' Apart from the fact that this tiny person growing inside her belonged to someone else. 'You can't possibly understand. You weren't there.'

He froze. She couldn't even detect any movement from his breathing. His black eyebrows were drawn together, his cobalt eyes dark and fathomless. He was justifiably shaken. Right now she didn't care. She wanted this night to end.

'No, I wasn't. They never gave me the chance to be.'

They were both silent for a moment, then he startled her by reaching out and taking her left hand in his. His thumb stroked over her gold ring.

'How old are you?'

'Thirty.'

'I'll turn thirty-six in December. You're not involved with anyone?'

She shook her head warily.

'No one else is aware of your surrogacy pact?'

A more emphatic shake.

His next words were spoken in a clear, resolute tone. 'Then as far as everyone's concerned, Alina, this child is ours.'

Her heart began to thump wildly. He was claiming the

baby as his own. *Ours. Our baby.* She stared at their joined hands and remembered his earlier words. The best solution of all. More than she'd dared hope for. No need for adoption.

'And it's credible because you were in Spain at the right time.' A whisper...barely audible.

Ethan had still been struggling to make sense of it all even as he'd made his declaration. His sister and his best friend had been prepared to lie, even commit fraud, to become parents. He'd have done everything possible to help. They hadn't asked.

Instead, whatever their original intentions had been, he would now be the father of their child. His tenacious, practical persona, the one that had achieved corporate success, kicked in. He refocused on Alina. He'd give her no choice. She had to accept the optimum scenario he'd envisaged last night.

Her drawn face and drooping eyelids mirrored his own exhaustion. They'd both been bombarded with emotional stress since the accident. Maybe if he carried her into the bedroom they'd sleep peacefully, continue their conversation in the morning. Maybe if he cradled her in his arms they'd find comfort.

Bad idea. He swung his leg off the settee, stretched as he stood. Glanced at his watch.

'It's been gruelling for both of us.' *Like a manic rollercoaster.* 'And tomorrow won't be any easier. This suite has three bedrooms. You can sleep here or I'll escort you to your hotel.'

'I'd prefer my hotel.' She hesitated, bit her lip before resuming doggedly. 'We weren't being reckless. We'd have gone straight to the nearest medical facility at the slightest hint of any problem.'

Her eyes begged for understanding, and she held out her hands, palms up, in supplication. 'I'm not lying. We'd never have risked the baby's health. *Never.*'

'I don't doubt it.' He didn't. They'd concocted a crazy scheme, with holes you could drive a truck through, and yet he found himself believing that with luck on their side they might have succeeded.

He phoned for the hire car. She put her shoes on and went to the bathroom.

A little later Alina stood quietly in the doorway, watching him replace the mugs. For seven years she'd befriended few men, always kept things casual. From the moment they'd met, Ethan James had stirred feelings she tried not to acknowledge. She prayed it was a fleeting thing, caused by her condition. Gone after the birth. Entrusting her shattered heart to anyone would be too great a risk.

So how come that stupid organ was beating faster at the sight of his muscles tensing as he stretched up to the shelf? Why was she gawking at his broad shoulders? Why was she remembering the feel of his hand on her spine?

He turned, as if sensing her presence, smiled reassuringly. She smiled tentatively back. He walked to the door, picking up a laptop bag from the dining table and his jacket on the way.

'Driver's waiting. We'll discuss tomorrow in the car.'

They exited the elevator into an underground car park, where a flashy silver limousine waited. Ethan gave their destination to the chauffeur before joining her on the plush seat. She loved the texture of the soft leather, breathed in its potent aroma, enhanced by her escort's earthy cologne. The brush of his thigh on hers as he twisted to buckle himself in caused her to shift towards the door.

Talk. Any subject. Anything to distract her thoughts from the vitality of the man by her side.

'What happens after I've seen your doctor? Do I leave?' she asked, striving for a casual tone.

The glance he gave her was enigmatic. 'No.' Removing

the computer from the bag at his feet, he placed it on his lap and activated it.

Was he crazy? Her staying would bring embarrassment to his family, cause conflict with his parents. Better she go, returning later in the year. No matter what agreement they made, this baby would be born in Australia.

'You stay with me. You signed a legal contract to carry and give birth to this child. The purpose of your scheme was to prevent that child from suffering any repercussions from its origin or circumstances. Nothing's changed.'

Corporate-speak. Direct. Uncompromising.

He turned the laptop, enabling her to see the document displayed. An insane impulse to laugh shook her. It was an application for a marriage licence, with the groom's details already entered on the left, her name and his address on the right.

She bit back a negative retort. Ethan James didn't play games. He dealt with every situation shrewdly, sweeping aside opposition with logic and unwavering perseverance. And that was what she was to him—a *situation*, to be processed with tact and practicality.

He set the laptop aside, turned towards her. She flinched as his hand splayed across her abdomen, sending a warm glow sliding from cell to cell. She couldn't tear her eyes from his touch.

His voice was honey-smooth, adamant.

'Alina, the baby you carry is my family. I can't—*I won't*—permit this child to be born illegitimate.'

She sympathised, but he had no idea what he was demanding from her. The warmth faded, replaced by a cold chill. Another hand, so like his, had lain there, eagerly anticipating the movement of an unborn baby. Caring. Sharing. Taken from her with no warning.

Somewhere out in the real world a driver beeped his horn. She sensed Ethan studying her, could imagine his brain churning with arguments to reinforce his demand. For him her full compliance was essential. He'd accept nothing less.

His words might come from an innate sense of duty, but the passion in his voice proclaimed a deep brotherly love. She'd been a willing party to the covert plan to protect the baby's name. It was as essential now as it had been then. She consigned her memories to the deep pit where they belonged.

'This explains your interest in my papers. How long is it supposed to last?' It came out wrong. She hadn't meant to sound so cold, so detached. She certainly wasn't prepared for the pained look in his eyes.

'We've got seven months to sort out the future. No one will be surprised if our sudden marriage doesn't survive long-term.' His hand left her stomach and cupped her chin. 'I won't force you to stay, and I swear you won't lose from this arrangement.'

He was right—because she'd already lost everything worthwhile. She'd bought a new gold ring because she hadn't been able to bear the sight or the feel of the original. Wearing it discouraged male attention. He offered a marriage of convenience. No intimacy. No permanency. An expedient arrangement, lasting long enough to convince everyone he was the father.

She couldn't tell him—couldn't tell anyone about the darkness. Remembering the past tore her apart. Speaking of it out loud was unthinkable. His way made sense. If they married, his paternity would be undisputed. He'd give this baby the love she was incapable of feeling.

'You give me your word that I can leave when *I* decide?'

Being nomadic, with no involvements, was the only way to prevent her life from being devastated again. Last year she'd occasionally been drawn into small-town activities. And she'd connected with Louise and offered her help, completely breaking her basic rules. Look where *that* had landed her.

'Yes.' It was blunt. His body was rigid, his features unreadable.

'All right. I'll marry you. When will it be?' So impersonal, so soulless. Why did that worry her?

'Tomorrow morning we'll collect the documents we need from your solicitor for a one o'clock meeting with the celebrant. She'll check the application, lodge it immediately, and the wedding will be a month later.'

He packed the computer into its bag.

As soon as legally permitted. Eleven years ago it had seemed to her like an eternity to wait.

CHAPTER FOUR

ETHAN CONTINUED TALKING as he unbuckled his seatbelt. 'I'll be here at eight-thirty in the morning.'

With a start she realised they'd reached her hotel.

'I'll be in the lobby.'

How did you say goodnight to the stranger you'd promised to marry? The day after you'd met? A man you'd never even kissed.

That last thought rattled her, and she tripped alighting from the vehicle. Ethan steadied her with an arm around her waist. She trembled from his touch—or her own agitation. She wasn't sure which.

'I'll see you to your room.'

He guided her through the foyer towards the elevators.

'It's quicker to walk up one flight,' she said, grateful no one else was there. His aroma mingled with hers, filling the space, heightening her already taut nerves.

He followed her into her room, his sharp, narrow-eyed appraisal of the decor rankling. To her dismay she sensed him making mental note of the mundane fixtures and colours. Her accommodation, definitely lower standard than his hotel, faced the rear of an office block. It was simply somewhere to shower and sleep for a few days.

'It's clean and comfortable,' she retorted. 'It suits my budget. So, if you've finished being critical, I'd like to get some sleep.'

'I'm not judging, Alina. By contacting me you have placed yourself and our child under *my* protection. That's the reason you can't stay here.'

He reached out to her. She stepped back, holding up her hand. She didn't have the inclination to pack even the few belongings she'd brought for a short stay. In addition, she needed some physical space between them to reinforce mental distance.

'Not tonight. I'll check out in the morning.'

His expression disheartened her.

'Please, Ethan,' she begged. 'Give me one night.'

He relented, let out a rough grunt. 'I've been pretty hard on you, haven't I? No more than on myself, I swear.'

He touched her cheek gently. 'I'll see you in the morning. May I have your mobile for a moment?'

He took it and programmed his number in.

'In case you need to contact me. Sometime tomorrow we'll transfer your phone to an Australian plan.' He brushed his lips on her forehead. 'Sleep well, Alina.'

She locked the door behind him. Leant her brow against it, her mind a fuddled whirlpool of everything they'd said and done, everything they hadn't, the way he'd looked, smelt and created minute fissures in her defences.

She filled out the breakfast menu, hooked it on the outside door handle, then sank wearily onto the bed, just for a few minutes. Tomorrow she'd need to be focused. Solicitor. Celebrant. Hazily she wondered what else he had planned.

He'd already booked the celebrant, arrogantly confident that she'd accept his proposal. Not that he'd actually *asked* her. She ought to…

Deep, dreamless sleep claimed her, held her despite the traffic noise. Held her through the alarm's whirl.

Ethan rested his head against the seat, staring unseeing at the city buildings on the drive home. He'd wanted to kiss Alina Fletcher. Not the soft-touch goodnight kiss he'd given her prior to leaving, but full mouth-to-mouth contact. Another unexpected jolt to his system, and the reason he'd let her stay at her hotel.

His primal instinct to relocate her and shield her from

any adverse action was logical. His nephew or niece—no, his *son or daughter*—deserved every resource at his command to ensure a safe and healthy start in life. The sexual attraction was another blindsider.

The women he dated would never settle for 'clean and comfortable' accommodation in any circumstances. The woman he'd coerced into marrying him was an enigma, hiding more than she revealed.

As he lay on his bed, reliving their conversation, the tight rein he kept on his emotions finally cracked. Images flickered through his brain like a movie screening: the secret signals between him and Louise at strict formal meals with his parents, late-night covert snacks watching clandestine television in his room. Her radiant face when she and Leon had confided they were in love. Boyhood games with his best mate, double-dating in their teens. Standing proudly beside him as best man at their wedding.

The dam broke. The tears flowed for his spontaneous, vibrant sister. For his brother-in-law, friend and confidant. For the beloved couple who would never hold and cherish their child.

He rolled over, buried his face into the pillow. Guttural, heart-wrenching sobs racked his body and soul.

Alina was already in the lobby when Ethan arrived fifteen minutes early the next morning. Her treacherous senses responded to his lithe movement as he strode across the pavement. She felt skittish, illogically animated, despite the stern talking-to she'd given herself as she'd showered and prepared to leave.

The delivery of her breakfast at seven-thirty had finally awoken her, still fully dressed on top of the bed. Years of routine had enabled her to shower, pack and be settling her account within an hour. Years of self-enforced solitude had her wishing she could hail a cab and run.

Stylishly dressed in tailored grey trousers and a short-sleeved dark green shirt, Ethan was halfway to the reception desk when he veered towards her. Her pulse skipped at the sight of his tanned muscular arms. Her cheeks flamed at the memory of his touch, his oh-so-light kiss on her brow. *Had* to be hormone madness. She refused to contemplate any alternative explanation.

'Good morning, Alina. You look refreshed. Sleep well?'

She recoiled from the full impact of the 'seduction smile' Louise had mentioned. Quickly recovered.

'Yes, thank you. I'm ready to go.' As she bent to collect her suitcase their fingers collided, adrenaline spiked. She jerked hers away at the same moment his body stiffened.

'Gentleman's prerogative,' he murmured, picking up both pieces of luggage.

She walked silently beside him to the street, where a chauffeur waited by the open boot of a limousine—same car, different driver.

'I'll programme the car hire number into your phone. Use it whenever you go out alone.' He glanced at her as he stowed her luggage. Quickly added, 'I appreciate you're used to being independent, but since Monday you and our child are my family. I take care of what's mine.'

For a moment she resented his over-protective attitude, before realising the baby took precedence. As it should. She'd agreed to live the Ethan James lifestyle so she'd have to adapt and conform.

'I'll try.'

'Thank you. We'll need your solicitor's address.' As they drove off towards the harbour tunnel he offered her his mobile. 'Call his office and arrange to have your papers ready for pick-up.'

'Already done. He'll see us when we arrive.' His surprised expression forced her to explain. More than she'd wanted to. 'I have his mobile number. He dealt with everything after... I was pathetically incapable of doing anything—couldn't make decisions, couldn't think. I...'

'Was reacting normally to grief.' His hand covered hers. 'I understand, Alina.'

'Um... He's a good man. His office is my Australian address.' *I shouldn't find your touch so comforting.*

'It might be expedient to change it to mine. You'll be living with me at least until next year.'

Living with him yet not together. Next year?

Too many decisions in too short a time.

'Can I decide later?' She met his gaze, found mild curiosity not censure.

'Of course. Speak up if you feel I'm rushing you.'

Like the leader of a stampede. Not an opinion he'd take kindly to.

She stared out of the window as the traffic crawled along, reliving the incident in the lobby. Ethan had been looking down when their fingers touched. Had he noticed she'd removed her ring?

From the stories she'd heard, and the photos she'd seen, she'd formed a vague, admirable image of Louise's successful brother—had had no interest in knowing anything more. The man at her side was flesh and blood, solid and real. She was learning to gauge the inflections in his voice, to interpret the messages in his expressive blue eyes. Her body involuntarily responded to him. The image had been far safer for her mental stability.

Ethan held back when the solicitor greeted Alina with a hug and soft words, allowing them privacy. The handshake he received was firm, the assessing gaze slightly disconcerting. Was he being compared to her husband? This man knew the full story of her bereavement, had been there for her when... What about the Fletcher family? Where had *they* been? Where were they now?

He noticed movement at her side as they were led to a

small office, arched his neck to confirm the nervous finger ritual. His heart lurched when her features crumpled at the sight of the archive box on the otherwise empty desk. Once they were alone she drew a long breath, before walking forward and lifting the lid with unsteady fingers.

On their return journey Ethan booted up his laptop. His gaze flicked from the screen to the box containing her life history, on the seat between them. Moved to her left hand. To her bare ring finger.

He was acutely aware of the toll the visit had taken on her. Her fumbling through the box's contents and forced shallow breathing had torn him apart. He still hadn't finished sorting the personal papers he'd brought from Spain.

Gently taking hold of her wrist, and letting what she held fall back inside, he had closed the lid. 'Not here. Not now.'

He'd lifted the box from the desk, then linked his fingers with hers. After speaking to her solicitor for a few minutes they'd left.

She hadn't spoken since she'd introduced him in the office, apart from a mumbled goodbye. Now, as their eyes met, she blinked, swiftly looked away. Primal instinct urged him to dump his laptop on the seat, wrap his arms around her and kiss her till the haunted expression in her eyes changed to—to what? Desire? Passion?

Get real, James. Where the hell is your head?

'I'm not being very helpful, am I? But I haven't needed to access them since probate was granted.'

He heard the slight accent in her trembling voice. Caused by deep emotion?

Putting his computer aside, he clasped her slender hands in his. 'Working hands. Not salon-pampered. Well-cared-for working hands,' he murmured. 'Seven years is a long time to be running and hurting. Finding yourself alone and pregnant so soon after you'd finally begun to connect again must have been traumatic, and yet you found the courage to confront me.'

She let out a tiny huff of a laugh. 'I considered you to be the approachable one in the family. I'd never have been brave enough to tackle your parents alone.'

'That will not happen,' he stated forcefully. 'I won't allow them to interfere, so we'll meet them together after the wedding. I have friends who'll be witnesses. Is there someone you'd like as yours? Family? Friend?'

She had an alluring, pensive air as she pondered his question. *Was* there anyone? There had to be relatives somewhere.

'I have no family. My mother left me with her parents when I was four. Never said who my father was. I haven't heard from her since. Grandma's cancer was quick and aggressive, the year after I finished school, and Grandpa had a heart attack three months later.'

Soulful violet eyes held his for a long, long moment; resolve flickered there, then glowed.

'There are a few people I've kept in touch with. I'll have to think.'

Her tension had eased and her voice was steadier. She appeared to have accepted the reality of their situation. His admiration for her grew, along with another indefinable impression.

'Our next appointment is at one,' he said hastily, not wanting to dwell on the effect she had on him. 'So we have plenty of time.' He released her, reached for his laptop. 'And I think you are brave enough for anything, Alina Fletcher.'

'Thank you.'

He was wrong, but Alina accepted his compliment rather than set him straight. He considered her courageous. Would he believe the same if he knew her decisions were driven by the conviction that she'd be unable to feel any maternal bonding ever again?

'I mean it. Coping with all this must be painful.'

He opened the box.

Excruciating. Like having old wounds ripped open with no anaesthetic. 'It had to happen sometime.' *And it must be now.*

She moved the box closer to her side. 'I'll find what we need.'

Her birth certificate and papers relevant to her mother were on the top, where they'd fallen. Nothing heartrending there. She passed them to him, willed her hands not to shake as she dragged a buff envelope from the bottom. She held her breath, forced herself to focus.

Concentrate on the two you need. Ignore the rest.

Icy fingers fisted round her heart. She clenched her teeth as she carefully removed two certificates. Tucking them under her hip, she waited until he'd finished entering information, then filed away the papers he'd used.

'I'll do the rest.' She heard the tremor in her tone, stubbornly persisted, needing to retain some privacy. Needing to keep the walls up and solid. 'It's *my* past.'

He studied her with an intensity that made her insides quiver. 'If you're sure?'

She wasn't. She had no choice. 'Thank you.'

He settled the computer on her lap, ensuring it was stable. 'I understand.' He paused. 'You haven't eaten a lot this morning, have you? Fancy an early lunch?'

How could he tell? 'I had toast and fruit—enough after that lovely meal last night.' Truth was she'd had to force the food down, and she still wasn't hungry.

His eyebrows twitched almost imperceptibly. His interest wasn't for her alone. She let him win.

'Chicken salad with crusty bread sounds tempting. Will the dining room be open?'

'We'll have Room Service.' He pulled out his mobile.

She tuned him out as she typed names, locations, dates.

She recited, *They are words, figures, nothing more* in her head. Her newly unadorned finger mocked the information she entered.

'Done,' he told her. 'We'll eat, then deal with the celebrant. Changing your phone supplier has to be done in person, so we'll combine that with a visit to the jeweller.'

She met the steely resolve in his eyes. He was locking her into her promise. There'd be no reneging allowed.

His mouth curved into a persuasive smile. 'It won't be so bad, Alina. You'll have time to adjust to life with me until the wedding. Any functions I ask you to attend during our marriage will be quiet occasions, with people I trust.'

'I made a list this morning.' That was better. Keep the conversation on standard stuff.

This time his eyebrows actually arched. 'What sort of list?'

'Things to do. Everyone who'll have to be notified that I'm relocating. Most of my official stuff goes to Crow's Nest.' She couldn't stop the catch coming into her voice. 'Louise used to check the mailbox in Barcelona for me sometimes.'

'We'll need to arrange for it to be redirected. Do you have a base there?'

'No, I rented rooms on a casual basis. When I was away the owner stored my stuff for a small fee.'

'We'll fly over later, so you can decide what to bring back.'

She gave a short, hollow laugh. He made it sound like a day trip to another state. 'Hardly worth a trip. There's just an old suitcase and two plastic boxes.'

His turn to be confounded. 'That's all you have?'

Shoot, she'd spoken impulsively to a very astute man. She pictured the cold steel unit she'd visited once, fought the hard clench in her abdomen. Couldn't lie. Couldn't look into those perceptive eyes either.

'Everything else I own is in storage. I don't go there.' Mentally *or* physically.

'Too painful.' He made it a statement.

Guilt tempered with empathy overrode her self-pity. His grief was new, raw, and he had to cope with the aftermath of the accident. He was processing the estate personally. She'd let her solicitor take charge.

'I'm sorry, Ethan. I haven't been very sympathetic to *your* loss. I've been too wrapped up in myself.' She covered his hand with hers. 'You've had so much to deal with and still managed to be patient with me.'

'That's easy.' His voice hummed with tenderness. He flipped his hand to enfold hers. 'You're carrying our child.' His sudden grin took her by surprise. 'Do you have a things-to-buy list?'

She responded with a light laugh. 'I've jotted down a few things. Why?'

'Just wondering. All done?'

She frowned, realised he was referring to the marriage application, and felt the lightness of the mood change.

'Not quite.' She returned to the keyboard and added the final data. When she looked up his head was averted, as it had been when he'd made the call.

'I've finished, Ethan. Thank you for giving me privacy.'

'No problem, Alina.'

The car pulled in to the kerb as he stowed the computer in its bag.

Their lunch was delivered to a family suite. Afterwards Alina watched TV while Ethan went to another room to take a phone call. She viewed without seeing or hearing. Was he *ever* off duty? Her guilt resurfaced. The time and effort he was devoting to her meant less for his expanding empire.

The telephone's ring made her jump. Should she answer

it? Thankfully Ethan came through and told Reception to send their visitor up.

Too late to change her mind.

She swallowed the lump in her throat, tamped down her qualms. Steeled herself to act like a newly engaged woman. For his sister and brother-in-law. For their baby.

The celebrant was friendly, bright and efficient. She guided them through the procedure, gracefully declined a drink and promised to lodge the paperwork immediately. The wedding was set for Sunday, April the twentieth at five p.m.

Within fifteen minutes of her departure they were on their way to his apartment.

CHAPTER FIVE

OPULENT WAS THE word that came to mind as Alina stood in her own lavish en suite. *This is my home until the end of the year.*

She ran her fingertips across the marble surfaces—pure, cool luxury—but felt wary of touching the shiny chrome taps in case she left marks.

Bright stunned eyes stared at her from the pristine mirror. Walls the palest of pale mint-green complemented darker green mottled floor tiles, the crystal-clear shower. Matching it all were the softest, fluffiest towels she'd ever snuggled her face into.

She washed her hands, massaged moisturiser into her skin, breathing in its mild perfume.

She loved the beautifully appointed bedroom too. Also with a green theme, nothing bright or glaring, and as tranquil as a country spring morning—including a painting of a clear stream flowing between banks of willow trees. It was her own calming space, where she might be able to achieve meditation.

Sitting cross-legged on the luxurious cream carpet, she rested her elbows on her knees. Shut her eyes. *Black terror.* They flew open. She concentrated on the rural scene. *Breathe in. Breathe out. Count slowly. Count the flowers in the grass. Count the trees or rocks. Block out everything else.* Her inner fears receded—a little.

She stretched, unravelling her legs to lie flat, gazing up at the downlights strategically recessed in the ceiling. By tucking her chin in tight she could see her toes. For how much longer? She rolled over to do twenty push-ups. Did the building have a gym? If she didn't work she'd need to start exercising more.

She brushed her hair and went to join Ethan in the spacious open living area. Too tidy. Too clean. To her, not lived-in. No magazines or books scattered around. No bowls of fruit or nuts. The only personal touches were two framed photos on one shelf of a too organised bookcase.

His dark hair showed over the top of the long red couch, his low, rich voice lured her forward. As if sensing her, he turned, spoke into the mobile held to his ear. 'Hang on a minute.' He covered the mouthpiece, studied her with reflective cobalt eyes. 'Okay?'

Her reward, when she nodded, was a full-blown lethal Ethan James smile that blew her composure sky-high. 'Give me ten minutes. If you're thirsty, I'll have coffee.'

The kitchen area was TV-cooking-show-perfection: black granite benchtops——including an island—with stainless steel appliances. It enforced her earlier assessment. His apartment contained top-of-the-range exclusives with a wood and leather theme. Had he given carte blanche to the same interior designer who'd decorated the hotel?

She hadn't cooked in a kitchen with an island since— since she'd sold the three-bedroom house, mortgaged to the hilt, that she still couldn't bear to see ever again. Not since hired contractors had packed up the contents and put them into storage arranged by her solicitor.

She clamped her teeth together and focused on the coffee machine—top-brand, naturally.

'Bronze pod for me. Biscuits in island cupboard. Top shelf.' His voice floated through the room, accompanied by soft clicks as he dialled another number.

Everything she needed, including a decorative wooden box with the word 'TEA' inlaid on the lid, sat on the bench. She activated the machine for his coffee, then opened the box. A delighted 'Wow…' whispered from her lips. Her blind lucky dip into one of the sixteen compartments of herbal tea—some quite exotic—produced lemon and ginger.

Ethan waited while his project manager verified figures, his eyes tracking Alina as she made two trips, carrying mugs and a plate of biscuits into the lounge. There was nothing hurried in her movements—hadn't been from the moment they met. Except when he'd challenged her about her husband and her child.

His eyes did a slow full-body scan, from the short wavy hair framing her pretty face down to the sleek white blouse, over her still flat abdomen, over slender shapely hips, ending at dainty bare feet. His own body enjoyed every second of the journey.

Quiet and unassuming, she'd have been overshadowed by the vibrant Spanish women he'd chatted up on his visits. Or would she? She disturbed him in a sensual way, new and puzzling, and definitely unwanted in their current circumstances.

'Ethan? You still there?'

The voice in his ear jolted him out of his daydream. Reality ruled.

He gave due praise to his colleague for an urgent problem solved and ended the call. Dropping his mobile by the files on the table, he took an appreciative drink of the strong adrenaline-reviving coffee.

'Thanks for this.' The object of his distracting thoughts was now curled up in one of the lounge chairs with a notebook and pen, completely oblivious to the effect she had on him.

'What's the title of the latest?'

Alina frowned.

He indicated her notebook. 'List?'

'Ah… Personal items. Clothes. What I have won't do for living *your* lifestyle.'

Her voice held an audible hint of resignation that sparked a twinge of sympathy. He understood her reluctance, but couldn't change his stance. He was taking the only course of action he'd be able to live with, irrespective of personal preferences or consequences. Those must be considered collateral damage.

'I've ordered a credit card for you.' He held up his hand to stop her interjecting. 'No argument. Having you here is my decision, so I'll cover any costs you incur because you're living with me.'

'I have money.'

Enticingly stubborn, eyes fiercely defiant, mouth so tantalisingly kissable...

He'd eventually win—just not easily. Every step was a walk in a minefield and they'd hardly entered the paddock. Knowing women as he did, he figured once she began to shop for her growing figure and new social commitments she'd realise he was right.

'Compromise? Accept the card. Use it at your own discretion.'

Her gaze shifted over his shoulder to the photos on the bookshelf. Leon and Louise on their wedding day. With him at a social event. Her eyes softened. She played it down but she'd cared for them too.

He watched neat white teeth bite into a chocolate-covered biscuit, inexplicably imagined them nibbling on his neck. Selecting a plain shortbread, he stretched his legs and crossed his ankles. Wondered what it was about her he found so fascinating.

'Compromise it is. I have final say,' she stated with determination, causing him to chuckle out loud. 'Is there a gym in the building? Or nearby. Until I find a job I'll—'

She stopped as if stunned when his body jerked forward. Coffee dregs splashed onto the table. His eyes narrowed.

A *job*? She wanted to *work*? Hell! He stood, drew in a ragged breath and quelled his exasperation.

'Wait.'

He strode to the kitchen, brought back a cloth and mopped up the mess. She watched him warily. How could he explain his world to a woman who'd depended only on herself for so long?

Sitting by her side, he took her hand in his, felt her resistance. Held on. 'In the social circles I grew up in few women worked. There was always a hint of condescension when my parents spoke of those who did—even those with a profession. My contemporaries are a mixture, mostly by choice. I make no judgement.'

He cupped and tilted her jaw until their eyes met.

'We are different. You've come to me two months pregnant, with limited work skills. Uh-uh.' He quickly placed his thumb over her lips as she stiffened. 'That was not an insult, merely a statement of fact. I admire the diverse ways you've supported yourself, but I'd like you to relax, indulge yourself while you are with me. Accept a little pampering. Let me take care of you both. Please.'

'I'm not sure I know how.'

Her wistful eyes confirmed her words. He waited, liking the way the violet darkened and her brow furrowed as she contemplated the idea.

'Does taking courses constitute work?'

Spontaneous laughter rose in his throat. She was adorable. He hugged her close, pressing his lips to her hair. Wanting to press them to hers.

Rising to his feet, he held out his hand. 'Come with me.'

She hesitated for a second, then accepted his offer. He led her through the kitchen into a short corridor, flicking a hand at two doors on the right.

'Storage and spare.' He opened the door on the left. 'But this is what clinched the deal for me.'

He watched her expression and wasn't disappointed. Her amazement duplicated his when he'd first walked into the not yet finished lap pool/gym area. One glance, one split second, and he'd contracted to buy.

She gawked at the neat array of exercise machines and banks of weights, at the long narrow strip of water. Her lips parted, but he quickly averted any speech with fingers over her mouth.

'Don't...'

Her eyebrows lifted as he spoke.

'Don't you dare say it.'

Her chin lifted defiantly. 'You have no idea what I was thinking,' she claimed into his skin.

He huffed. 'A comparison between our worlds and I refuse to listen to any more.'

She studied the equipment for a moment, then him, and damned if he could define the expression in her eyes. Though he sure as hell knew he wanted to change it.

'Our choices define us, Alina. This is one of my best. My sanctuary from long hours and constant electronic hassle.' He moved behind her, put his hands on her shoulders. 'Now it's yours too. I'll set up lighter weights on any of the machines you want to use. Do you have bathers with you?'

Bathers? Alina's eyebrows scrunched. She'd packed for one or two meetings with a workaholic businessman. The rest of her time would have been spent sightseeing. Depending on the sales, maybe she'd have bought a few bargains. At the last minute she'd thrown in her one evening dress.

She twisted her head to tell him she'd add them to her shopping list. Froze. Her movement had brought her lips close to his. Kissing close. Her legs became jelly. Her mouth as dry as autumn leaves. Her heartbeat a jungle drum message.

His earthy cologne, enhanced by the scent of musky male, encircled her. The hazel rims of his dilated pupils were clearly discernible. Hypnotic eyes drew her in. Heat from his body seared her back, even though their only contact was through his hands. Arousing warmth lured and yet frightened. Distantly familiar. New and alarming.

It was illogical to feel chilled and cheated when he abruptly let her go. Put distance between them.

'Use this area any time you like, though I'd prefer to be here while you do. If the water's too cold I'll up the temperature. Towels are in the cupboard by the door.'

General information, spoken matter-of-factly. He obviously wasn't bothered at all.

Illogical to feel disappointed that his main concern would be the baby's wellbeing. She vowed to make good use of the gym and pool whether he was there or not.

Ethan walked towards the door, berating himself for the rush of desire he'd felt when she'd turned to him. He had to find a way to block this impractical attraction. He chose his women carefully. No homebodies, no clingers. No romantics. Intelligent, beautiful; sometimes both. He shared pleasant evenings and satisfying nights with them. Nothing more.

Alina had no idea how she affected him. She'd probably fly back to Spain tomorrow if she knew what he'd been thinking. How he'd almost kissed her. How much he still wanted to.

Frustrating days, weeks, months loomed ahead. Enforced celibacy with Alina within reach. Limited touching. Yet making their story believable required getting personal, learning each other's personalities and habits. Fast. They had to present a united picture to everyone: a couple mutually attracted enough to have had an ardent fling. It wasn't happening at the moment.

He pivoted round, catching her elbows as she cannoned into him. 'You know something about me, courtesy of my sister. I'm still groping in the dark where you're concerned.

So it's imperative you talk to me, lighten up when we're together.'

He slid one arm around her waist; saw apprehension cloud her eyes.

'We'll let people assume we were lovers…they'll believe I'm the father.' He skimmed his fingertips lightly across her cheek, murmured softly as he lowered his head. 'A man and a woman who've made a baby should at least act as if they've kissed.'

He covered her mouth with his, giving her no chance to thwart him. And his barely restrained libido ran riot. His arousal was swift, unstoppable. Tangling his fingers in her silken curls, he anchored her head while desperately fighting the urge to deepen the kiss.

Willing her lowered eyelids to open, he moved his lips over hers. Pressed a little harder. Her soft lips tasted sweet. Didn't respond.

Nice one, James. Great way to gain her cooperation and trust.

Did he imagine the light tremor under his hands? The tiniest motion of her lips? He eased away. Her eyelids fluttered, opened. His breakneck pulse cranked up another notch at the bemusement in her incredible violet eyes. Lord, he ached to have her even closer, moulded to his hardened form.

Worst idea ever.

He shifted, let his hand slide over her shoulder, down her arm. 'We'll work on it.'

She eyed him with suspicion as she pulled away. 'Yeah, like you need the practice.'

Her offhand comment might have succeeded, if not for its delightful breathless timbre. Deny it all she liked, she'd been affected by his kiss. He rubbed his nape, wishing he could dive into the clear cool water behind him. A few laps fully clothed might diminish his ardour and help regain his sanity. Instead he had another trip in an enclosed car with her by his side. With that too-strong, not-for-her perfume assailing his senses.

With supreme effort he brought the conversation back to household routine. 'The pool is cleaned regularly. The apartment is serviced Monday, Wednesday and Friday mornings. They process any dry cleaning I leave on the kitchen island.'

She looked dazed for a second, then welcomed his change of topic. 'You have security. How do I enter and leave?'

'I've ordered another key card. You can have my spare.' He checked his watch. 'Time to go. Can you be ready in ten minutes?'

Alina wasn't surprised when they were escorted to an exclusive room on the fourth floor above a renowned jewellery store. Entrance to the secure area was gained by virtue of a buzzer and intercom system.

Ethan moved one of the four seats closer to hers, giving the impression of an attentive fiancé. She berated herself for tensing. How could they fool anyone into believing they were a couple?

An elegant, bespectacled man entered, offering congratulations as he placed two ring trays in front of them, another at the end of the cloth-covered table. Alina stared, stunned. Her body involuntarily tried to put distance between her and the brilliant array. The strong arm around her shoulders tightened as if Ethan sensed her agitation.

Dazzling gems in a myriad of colours and settings sparkled and gleamed. Too flashy for her…too many to choose from. There was no comparison to the small diamond in a heart setting that she'd chosen and been kissed over so long ago.

Don't think. Don't remember. This has nothing to do with reality and emotion.

Quiet words were spoken. The jeweller left with the two trays. He returned with a less ostentatious selection. She still couldn't choose, couldn't bring herself to touch.

Ethan caressed her cheek with his knuckles. 'Too much choice, sweetheart? May I?'

Noting his endearment, knowing it was for the benefit of their attendant, she managed a fleeting smile and leant back. She didn't dare speak in case the pain showed in her voice.

Without hesitation he selected an oval amethyst surrounded by tiny diamonds set in gold. Elegant, not showy. Her finger trembled as he guided it on, holding it firmly to stop it sliding off.

Raising her hand, he pressed his lips to her fingers. 'Perfect. Beautiful. *You.*' He kissed her gently.

She knew this was purely for show, knew she had a part to play. So she did what she'd struggled against by the pool. She returned his kiss.

Her heartbeat accelerated. Her body quivered. His hold tightened, his lips firmed. Her fingers crept up his neck, teasing the ends of his hair. She felt giddy, breathless. Cherished.

Until her stomach knotted and fear replaced the floating sensation. Heat flooded her cheeks; she broke away and bent her head to his chest.

Ethan framed her face with his hands, forced her to meet his gaze. Her warm blush was gratifying. Coupled with the soft glow in her violet eyes, it gave an idyllic image of a newly engaged woman.

His own feelings were elusive, and he had no inclination to analyse them here. They were new, overwhelming— might be caused by any one of the upheavals in his life.

He placed the ring to one side, before swapping the tray

for the one at the end of the table. 'Do you prefer a plain or patterned wedding band?'

He'd bet odds that the cross-cut patterned ring she chose was very different from the one she'd worn years ago—not the plain one she'd removed since yesterday. He selected a matching, broader one, then spoke to the jeweller.

'Mine fits. Alina's need to be resized.'

CHAPTER SIX

THEIR NEXT STOP, within walking distance, was his communications supplier. Somehow the end result was a new mobile for Alina with her account bundled with his. Ethan James had a charming way of overruling objections, leaving you feeling as if you'd done *him* a favour.

Like the way he'd cajoled her into an exclusive perfumery store after claiming that he'd noticed her spray bottle was nearly empty. When had *that* happened? Well aware that the one she wore, a Christmas gift, was too strong for her; she was delighted with the new delicate spring fragrance. She'd been aware of the surreptitious looks he'd exchanged with the assistant. What else was he planning?

The arrangements, phone calls, et cetera had all taken time and effort, yet he made it seem simple. To him it was. Decisions were made. Actions followed. Tangible proof of the attributes that had ensured his phenomenal success. Skill and diplomacy would ensure the optimum outcome: a healthy son or daughter.

On their way back to the apartment the car pulled in to the kerb and Ethan unclicked his seatbelt. 'Won't be long.'

He hopped out and the driver moved off. One lap of the block found him waiting to be picked up, now carrying two plastic bags containing rectangular objects with a delicious exotic aroma.

He laughed at her puzzled stare. 'Thai takeaway. Best in town.'

'But…' Of course—the call he'd made while the salesgirl had been demonstrating functions on her new phone.

'Nothing hot or spicy. And what we don't finish tonight

we'll have tomorrow. I've had many a breakfast of reheated Asian food.'

So had she—more from the need to stretch a budget than for pleasure. She laughed as her stomach rumbled. 'I'm hungrier than I thought. Thank you for remembering about the spicy.'

'I remember everything you've told me, Alina.'

His eyes caught hers, held her spellbound. She fought to break the hold, had to stay detached. Letting him in was a risk with too high a cost.

She was happy when he opted to eat in the lounge, claiming casual dining made takeaway taste better. Watching television would provide a break from personal questions and conversation.

At his request she carried two glasses and a carafe of iced water into the lounge, while he brought china, cutlery and the food.

'Tonight it's your choice—apart from reality shows,' he remarked, scooping special fried rice onto two plates.

'I haven't watched much at all these last few years. Hey, not too much on mine.' She stilled his hand, preventing him from overloading the second plate. 'The news is fine by me.'

During the ad breaks they discussed the events of the day—small talk which gave her invaluable insight into the man she'd committed her immediate future to. He wasn't as complimentary about the present government as she'd expected, and spoke sympathetically about lower income earners.

The latter didn't surprise her; she'd experienced his attitude to shop assistants and his own hotel staff. He did surprise her when he patiently explained the intricacies of a technology breakthrough. So she chose a documentary next, figuring it would interest him, knowing she'd like it too. His avid interest in the excavation of an ancient English church which had revealed a former king's remains proved her right.

Ethan's attention strayed during the advertising breaks. Alina would have plenty of time to watch anything she liked in the coming months. It suddenly occurred to him that she'd need something to occupy the hours while he was working. Even if she did sign up for a course or two.

How many people in Sydney had she kept in touch with? Was there anyone she'd confided in? He couldn't imagine how he'd have got through his teens, resisting his parents' expectations, without Leon to confide in. Even Louise, five years younger and flighty as a cuckoo fledgling, had listened and supported him.

Alina had stayed away from Australia. Did that mean there were no close friends here? It was obvious that she carried a deep-seated torment inside. *Damn*, he knew so little about her, but he couldn't bring himself to push too much. He was supposed to be good with people. If he earned her trust maybe she'd confide in him. When he knew the details he was convinced he'd be able to find a way to ease her pain.

Alina stretched as the final credits rolled, then carried their plates to the dishwasher. Ethan followed with the glassware and caught her yawning.

'Ready for an early night? It's been a full-on day for you.' Sympathy showed in his eyes, warmth in his tender expression.

A restful soak in the bath with an intrigue novel appealed more than bed. Did that seem rude? As if she wanted to get away from him?

As if sensing her confusion, he gently took her in his arms, hugged her and let her go.

'Goodnight, Alina. Thank you for being so cooperative. I know it wasn't easy. Sleep well.'

'I survived. Goodnight.' She walked away.

'Alina?'

She turned at the doorway.

'I swear I'll take care of you and our child. Believe me?'

She looked into sincere blue eyes and her doubts subsided. 'Yes, I do.'

This time he didn't stop her, and went back to the lounge. Trying to read reports was a futile exercise. A few strides along the hall was a beautiful woman who stirred him as no one ever had. A woman whose soul-destroying sorrow influenced every decision she made.

Today she'd begun to react naturally—the way he needed her to if they were to convince everyone they'd been lovers. Their supposed affair might have been short, but their mutual attraction had to be evident. On his part it was becoming less of a pretence every time she was near. And from her tentative responses he suspected her buried feelings were beginning to emerge.

Ten past nine. Past morning rush hour. Alina leant on the island, checking her notepad, and glanced down at her well-worn jeans. Added two items to her list. She drank her ice-cold juice, scrunched her nose. Pushed the credit card Ethan had given her in a circle on the granite. Having it didn't mean using it.

He'd knocked on her door early this morning to tell her he was going to his office. Drowsy, needing to use the bathroom, she'd barely acknowledged his remarks. When he'd leaned in to brush her hair from her eyes, his unique smell and the touch of his fingertips had blown her lethargy away, leaving her wide-awake, tingling.

She dropped the pen. This was ridiculous. What could be simpler than writing a list of clothes and accessories to be worn by the wife of a hotshot billionaire? Or was he even richer? Any woman he dated would have no problem filling the page. But she was a nomad, with a meagre pile of cheap, easy-care clothing. Her serviceable underwear would never grace a magazine page or stir a man's libido.

Hey, what was she thinking?

Focus. You only have to buy enough to be presentable for a few weeks.

As she put on weight she'd have to shop again. More expense.

For a second her mind flashed to the investment account. Another buried secret.

Sometime after twelve she sank wearily into a window seat of a busy café. Two bags containing the pathetic results of her attempted retail therapy took the chair beside her. This was hopeless. She'd chickened out every time she'd tried to enter any of the high-fashion boutiques she'd found. Embarrassing Ethan in clothes from the stores she normally frequented wasn't an option. At this rate she'd be in track pants and baggy jumpers right through autumn.

She needed help…didn't know who to ask. She was used to working; now she had all day with nothing to do. Or did she? She'd meant her reference to taking courses as a joke, but now she deemed them a plausible time-filler.

As the waitress walked past, carrying two plates of fish and chips, another idea popped into her head. Taking out her notepad, she began a new list, pushing it aside when her order arrived.

Indulging in a gooey cream-filled pastry didn't solve her wardrobe problem but it tasted good. Drinking Viennese hot chocolate while writing the final items lifted her spirits. Surely he'd give her plenty of notice before expecting her to meet his friends or accompany him to functions?

Ethan sniffed appreciatively as he entered the apartment—later than he'd intended due to an impromptu meeting with his second-in-command. The sooner he implemented the new changes in his workload, the better.

It was a surprise to find the table set for two, even though he'd called, asking her to order dinner from the hotel. There was a bowl of fresh garden salad in the centre, and a bottle of Shiraz waiting to be opened. His home was warm and welcoming—a pleasurable new experience. He shed the trials of his day and moved forward.

'Mmm, smells good. Mushroom sauce, if I'm not mistaken.'

'Hi.' Alina came around the island, carrying water and glasses. 'Dinner will be ready by the time you wash up.'

Placing his laptop on the end of the table, he moved nearer, breathed in flowers and sunshine—perfect for her, enthralling for him. If this were real...

It wasn't.

This morning she'd been dreamy-eyed, and he'd come close to kissing her. He hadn't thought, had merely acted, something he'd need to curb if they were to build a trusting relationship.

'Give me five minutes.'

Alina arranged steak with foil-wrapped baked potatoes on warmed plates, placed hot crusty rolls in a serviette-lined basket. Smiled with satisfaction. Everything looked appetising, hopefully tasted as good. If she could convince him to let her cook and clean she'd feel so much better about their arrangement. Support for the child was one thing— her being totally dependent on him another.

No way was she going to compete with his qualified chefs. She'd serve recipes she felt capable of, even if they weren't gourmet standard. The cookbook she'd bought was for inspiration.

Ethan had already poured his glass of wine when she set down his plate, along with the gravy boat. When she returned with her meal he was waiting by her chair, studying his food across the table. She held her breath while he took his seat.

The sparkle in his eyes when they met hers was unnerving. 'This didn't come from my hotel kitchen, did it?'

'No.' She broke eye contact, her heart sinking. Took a sip of water. If the difference was so obvious she'd already lost.

'Hmm…' He poured gravy, put sour cream on his potato and began to eat.

Her breath caught behind the lump in her throat. Her whole body felt primed for his reaction. She so wanted his approval.

'It's good.' His smile caused her lungs to deflate, the lump to dissolve.

'Not what you're used to?'

'Better.'

She bristled. She didn't need or want pseudo-compliments. 'You don't have to butter me up. I know there's no comparison.'

'I promise I will always tell you the truth, Alina. Since the accident I've ordered meals. They came. I ate often while still working, usually too focused on facts and figures to taste or enjoy it. At home I lived in a void. My way of blocking out the grief, I guess.'

That she understood. 'And I made it worse with my bombshell.'

'No—no way.' He dropped his knife, reached across and took her hand. 'It was as if nothing had real purpose. I avoided thinking about Louise and Leon because then I'd have to accept they were never coming back. I hated knowing I should have been there for them much more than I was.'

She laid her free hand on top of his, subconsciously acknowledging its male texture.

'You felt guilty? Oh, Ethan, there was never, ever, in any conversation I had with them, the slightest hint that you had been anything but a loving and supportive brother and friend. One who'd be there for them in a heartbeat if they needed you. I don't know why they kept their problem a secret. Maybe because shielding those you love from worry goes both ways.'

'Maybe. I keep wondering if there was anything else I could have done for them. All I know is that you've given my life meaning again. I wake in the morning knowing my sister and best friend aren't completely lost to me. I feel—'

He broke off, slowly withdrew his hand, as if unsure of revealing too much emotion.

'Best we eat while it's hot. What other culinary delights do you have planned?' He helped himself to a serving of salad.

'You mean it? You'll really need more than one meal to make a sound judgement.'

'Bring them on.'

His smile as he raised his drink ignited trails of heat along her veins, threatening the solid barriers she'd sworn to maintain.

'Here's to many more home-cooked dinners together.'

They clinked glasses. Alina let her water slide, cool and refreshing, down her throat.

'It's on the understanding that you tell me if it's not good or not to your taste. If I take over the housework as well it'll fill my days. I'm rethinking the courses idea.'

'I'm locked into a cleaning contract, so that's a different proposition. Anyway, in a few months you might be grateful for the help.'

And with the purchase he'd arranged today she might also reconsider.

She pondered his statement as she cut into her steak. 'You may be right. It's not easy work, but it pays the bills. Losing their hours here may cause hardship for someone.'

'You discuss what you'd like done with whoever comes. I'll notify the company that you have the authority.'

'Thank you.'

So she'd also done cleaning during her nomadic life, had not been too proud to accept domestic employment. Showed consideration for other manual workers. Every conversation gave Ethan more insight into her—thankfully without her realising how much she revealed.

'Are you a sports fan?' she asked. 'I know Leon and Louise were Sydney Swans supporters and watched the games on the internet. You don't appear to have much free time.'

'We never missed a home game when they were here. I'm still a fully paid-up member of the club, and get to go occasionally. It wasn't the same without them, and the Starburst Group has been growing, demanding more time. I often wind down at night watching whatever sport's being televised. Clears the mind.'

He asked which countries she'd been to as they ate fruit and ice cream for dessert. She revealed that she'd become fluent in Spanish, Italian and French, got by in other languages, and considered it no big deal. His Spanish was basic, so to him it was an enviable achievement.

He made hot drinks while she stacked the dishwasher.

Alina struggled to keep awake during the short late newscast. Had to stop herself from falling against his shoulder and nodding off.

'Do you mind if I go to bed? I'm not usually so tired… It has to be the change of environment or the pregnancy, so hopefully it won't last long.'

'We'll check if you need extra vitamins on Monday. You go and rest.'

'Thank you.'

Admitting her failure at clothes shopping when he'd been so complimentary about her meal seemed a backward move. She'd try again tomorrow.

She had no idea that her disappointment showed in her face, but Ethan noticed, and couldn't resist drawing her into his arms for comfort.

'Dinner was delicious, Alina. I know this isn't easy for you, but I promise we'll work out any problems that arise. Tell me if anything bothers you and I'll try to put it right.'

Her eyes were bright as she accepted his vow, and without conscious effort he bent his head to kiss her, moving his lips softly over her mouth. He felt a slight movement in her lips, heard a muted sound from her throat. Reluctantly raising his head, he encountered bemusement tinged with sadness.

He relaxed his hold, stepped back and tried to keep his voice stable. 'Sleep well, Alina. I should be home earlier tomorrow.'

Watching her go, he cursed himself for his lack of restraint. Tonight they'd really begun to connect, and he feared she might rebuild her barriers overnight. He cursed his parents for the hang-ups that governed his thinking, tainted his ability to feel deep emotion with others apart from Louise and Leon.

His short, raw, ironic laugh was spontaneous. Those two had had no qualms about showing their love—privately or in public. Eye contact, touching, kissing—all had been as natural to them as breathing. He'd never, ever seen either of his parents show any tenderness for each other, never seen a sympathetic gesture like the one Alina had given him tonight.

Not wanting to dwell on why kissing Alina made him feel less alone, he reasoned doing it when they could be seen would substantiate their story of a short and overwhelming passion. But it had to be believable—from both of them. No holding back, no tension. He was a grown man, well able to curb any sexual urges.

* * *

Today had been better. Alina placed her special purchases on the coffee table before carrying the other bags into her bedroom. She'd still avoided high-fashion boutiques and exclusive salons, but with her more positive attitude she'd had some success.

In a big department store she'd found two summer dresses and a lightweight jacket to go with either of them on cooler days. The shoes and bag she'd bought also went with both. She had limited her new underwear purchases, knowing she'd soon outgrow them.

After showering and changing she settled in the lounge to be productive. She had a cup of tea, a block of nut chocolate and a home renovation show on the television. There was plenty of time before Ethan was due home.

His consideration might be because of the baby she carried, his attention and kisses might be to make their relationship more believable, but she had to admit she found them nice. Nothing more. She hadn't been cared for since she'd fled from Australia, too cowardly to face anyone or anything that raised painful memories.

Mentally planning tonight's dinner, she opened her present to herself…

CHAPTER SEVEN

SUBDUED NOISES CAME from the lounge as Ethan opened the front door—the earliest he'd been home for months. Putting his briefcase and packages down, he strode in. He hadn't let Alina know he was on his way, meaning to surprise her. Instead he was the one who stopped short, spellbound by the vision in front of him.

Alina was ensconced on the settee, her eyes lowered, completely absorbed in the material in her hands, her tucked-up legs hidden by a flowing pleated floral skirt. He took in the sleek line of her neck, the satin glow of her cheeks, the sweep of her dark brown lashes. A perfect picture of natural beauty, and for the rest of this year she was his to admire.

He stepped forward, willing her to look up, anxious not to startle her. Her own subtle aroma enhanced her new perfume, making his nostrils flare, stirring his blood. She sensed his presence, gave him a shy glad-to-see-you smile that zinged straight to his heart.

With two paces, completely forgetting his mental declaration of self-control, he was beside her, his arms around her. He bent his head, glimpsed the reticence in her eyes and somehow managed to pull back. Couldn't stop his grip intensifying, though.

'Ouch.' His left leg jerked. He massaged his thigh and chuckled. 'I've been slapped a few times. Never stabbed.'

Alina paled, staring at the small metal needle in her fingers. 'I… I'm sorry. I…you… I was sewing. You made me forget I…'

He took the offending weapon and placed it on the coffee table alongside an array of coloured thread. 'My fault. I was distracted by the entrancing sight on my settee. Didn't allow for hidden danger.'

She blushed at the compliment. 'It's not sharp. Do you want to check if there's bleeding?'

The nervous tremor in her voice, plus the remorse in her eyes, acted like a dousing of cold water. He'd shocked her, shamed himself. This macho being, acting on impulse, wasn't him. He couldn't explain even to himself, didn't know why.

He moved away, dragging his fingers through his hair, trying to concentrate on the essential reason for her presence in his apartment. Five days ago he'd had no idea she existed. To her he was the preferred solution to a situation she didn't want long-term.

Boardroom strategy—that was what he needed. He had to get back to his original plan. Convince everyone they'd been lovers. Keep his distance in private. Best solution for everyone—especially the woman observing him now with dark, cautious eyes.

He picked up the cloth stretched over a round wooden hoop from her lap. Various shades of green thread had already been woven into the outline of a country cottage garden.

'Interesting. Pretty scene.'

'Small, light, fits into my backpack and challenging enough to keep me occupied in the evenings.' She took it from him and laid it on the table. 'It's absorbing—stops me from thinking too much.'

'And you have a weapon handy if you're attacked,' he teased, standing up and pulling her to her feet. 'New dress? Beautiful.' His scroll from head to foot was deliberately quick, yet he still felt an appreciative clench. 'Good shopping trip?'

Her smile faded. 'Not my favourite occupation. Having

no idea what size I'm going to be in a few weeks doesn't help. How was *your* day?'

'Busy. I received a delivery today. Let's sit down.'

She tensed as he reached into his inside pocket and brought out a small black box.

Taking her left hand in his, he slid the amethyst ring onto her finger. 'Perfect fit.'

She stared down at their joined hands. Her posture slumped.

'Alina.' Her head came up. He had a quick glimpse of sorrow, then it cleared. 'Remember why we're doing this. Who it's for.'

'I know.' She freed her hand then crossed her arms, hugging her body. 'It's… All this isn't what I expected.' Her mouth tried to form a smile. Didn't quite make it. 'I won't let you down.'

So brave, so determined to do the right thing, no matter how heart-wrenching her memories. So delightfully confused by her physical reaction to him.

Basic instinct urged him to hold her, protect her from more pain. But it wouldn't work for either of them. She wasn't going to stay. She had emotional baggage that his expectations of her were exacerbating. He had an agenda, an empire to build. He'd have a young child completely dependent on him.

He accepted he'd never be as approachable as his sister. She'd rebelled outwardly against their parents' attitude, defied them to marry the man she loved, and emigrated to escape their continued interference. He'd channelled everything into developing his company, determined never to emulate his parents and end up in a cold, loveless marriage.

Better to stay a bachelor, to enjoy female company without emotional entanglements. Strict rules and no pain when it ended. Becoming a single father at this stage might throw his life out of whack, testing him to the full, but he'd cope, adjust and succeed.

And on the topic of interference, Alina needed to be aware of a major factor.

'My parents won't be invited, so please don't wear the ring in public until after the wedding.'

She frowned, not understanding his meaning.

He explained. 'I've gathered Louise mentioned their attitude on social standing and—unbelievable in today's world—"breeding". They take snobbery to a new height. You're in or you're out, no middle ground.'

His gut clenched as he recalled their fights with Louise, their turning on him when he had defended her and Leon.

'They were never happy with Leon being my best friend because, although he was wealthy enough to give his children the best education affordable, his father had begun his working life as a bricklayer. His building firm is my main contractor, always will be. When Leon asked their permission to marry Louise they practically threw him out, forbade him from seeing her.'

'Which obviously didn't work. Couldn't they see how happy they were? How much he…he adored her?' Her voice faltered over the last few words.

'That didn't factor in their thinking. Our wedding may not be conventional, but I'd like it to be an occasion you'll remember fondly. There'll be no one there who might upset you in any way. Telling them afterwards gives them no choice but to accept that we're married.'

'I understand.' She began to slip the ring off. He stopped her.

'Keep it on at home. For me.' He brought her fingers to his lips for a second, then stood up. 'I've also got something to help occupy your time. Close your eyes.'

Alina had no fear of natural darkness. It was her own internal black world that tormented her. So, as soon as she sensed him leave she covered her eyes with her hands and opened them.

Shame at the way she'd swayed forward for his kiss, had almost succumbed to him, fizzed in her stomach. At the time she'd seemed to be weightless, floating, with no power over her limbs or her actions. She didn't resist. Didn't participate.

When he'd sprung away the bewilderment had had her blathering like a drunk, made worse by his shocked expression and deliberate retreat, putting distance between them. He'd recovered first, bringing normality back to the conversation, seemingly putting their embrace behind him.

That was what she had to do—act like a mature woman. She took long deep breaths, calming her stomach. Her defensive shields were solid. Mind you, if they began to crumble...

'Keep them shut.'

He'd returned.

'Or covered.'

Must be looking at her.

She heard some clunks, and the drag of the coffee table. The cushions dipped as he sat next to her. Now her stomach sizzled with suspense.

'This is for you.'

She stared in astonishment at the red laptop with matching mouse and butterfly motif pad. Alongside lay a hardcover notebook plus a boxed set of pens. Her hand flew to her mouth.

Grinning broadly, Ethan gently lowered it, then lifted the computer's lid. 'The password's "bluesheen" at the moment.'

'You bought this for me?' Her incredulous gaze swung from his face to the laptop. Twice. She'd never had a computer of her own. Not with the nomadic life she lived.

Though lately she'd been considering one of those light-weight notepads.

'All yours. Complete with bag so you can take it anywhere.'

She touched the keyboard cautiously, her fingers tripping across the keys. He caught one and pressed it on 'start'. The screen lit up and her eyes eagerly followed the process.

This was *hers*. Really hers. She turned to the man watching her with dark, hypnotic eyes. Swayed towards him again. Stopped. Touched his arm.

'Thank you.'

She was lost for words.

So was Ethan for a moment. His heart pumped and the lump in his throat threatened to choke him. He'd seen the intent to kiss him in those sparkling violet eyes, and perversely he rued her change of mind.

'You're welcome. Mouse or touch?' The connection for the wireless mouse was already in the port.

'I've always used a mouse. I'll have to learn to touch.'

Learn to touch him?

His chest tightened. He obviously hadn't listened to his own pep talk.

She quickly bent forward and began to type in the password; her hair only partially covering her reddening skin. He wasn't fooled by the action, and surmised she'd had the same thought.

'Why "bluesheen"?' The catch in her voice spoke volumes.

'Came out of the air.' *She'd been wearing blue the day they met.* 'Easily changed.'

'I love it. What are all these icons for?'

Her eyes shone with excitement, heightening his own pleasure.

'Finding out is part of the fun. I've added the internet, an email account and cloud backup.' He opened the notebook. 'All the passwords are written in here, plus relevant names with phone numbers—including my IT guy, who set it up. He's offered to give you one-on-one lessons if you like. I'm not too bad—he's brilliant.'

'Why? You know I won't be staying, so why are you doing this?'

He shrugged. 'Don't argue—just accept it. You can enrol for online courses…there's plenty to choose from.' He lightened the mood by joking. 'Imagine all the lists you'll be able to create. And you know you'll enjoy finding recipes.'

'You may not think so when you have to eat my weird concoctions.' She smiled back.

'I'll take my chances.'

His mobile rang. Bad timing. She was more at ease with him now than she'd ever been. Muttering a light curse, he wrenched the offending instrument out of his pocket, checked the caller. With a grimace he stood up.

'I have to take this. Do you have dinner planned?'

'Yes, but not started.'

'Save it for tomorrow. I'll book somewhere quiet where we can talk.' He got to the end of the lounge and glanced back, his dazzling smile sending heatwaves to every region of her body.

'You really do look exquisite, Alina.'

Another genuine compliment that gave her confidence another boost. It was hard to believe he'd bought her such a thoughtful gift she'd use in so many ways. The expense hardly registered with him. The time and effort he'd taken meant so much more.

Shutting down the laptop, she watched each process avidly, wanting to take in every little detail before carefully closing the lid. When she packed everything into the bag she found a charger and a set-up manual.

She'd intended to try shopping again tomorrow—now she'd rather stay home and browse. Anything she didn't understand would go on a list to be shown to Ethan. Although at least one session with his IT specialist was a must.

After putting her embroidery into a craft bag, she went to her room to give her minimal make-up a light touch-up.

As she walked along the hall the muffled mingling of running water with what sounded like a mistuned radio came through his door. Curiosity made her stop and press an ear to the wood. The slightly off-key singing persisted, too indistinct for her to recognise the vaguely familiar song.

The shower stopped. She scurried away, her cheeks burning. If he caught her would he be angry or amused?

She couldn't get that tune out of her head…couldn't remember the title. Couldn't ask him.

For Alina the family-owned restaurant with its discreet booth tables was ideal. She hadn't asked the name of the suburb; that would be making it a memory for keeping. Though, perversely, she knew she'd never forget the tasty meal, the restful music from the live band…her attentive escort.

Couples were moving on to the small dance floor and she watched them with envy. She had once known how it felt to be held tenderly, barely moving in a traditional lovers' slow shuffle. Without warning, images of all the women Ethan might have entertained here broke into her daydream. Stunning. Polished. Fashion connoisseurs who'd dance faultlessly.

'Hey.' His deep voice cut through her thoughts and she turned to meet his amused gaze. 'You're very pensive. Care to share?'

Not in a million years. The predictable warmth stole up her neck. 'Just enjoying the music. The meal was delicious. Is this a favourite haunt of yours?'

'A friend brought me here last year. I kept it in mind,

waiting for a special occasion.' He put his hand invitingly, palm up, on the table. 'Never found one until today.'

Mesmerised by his incredible dark blue eyes, she laid her hand in his. He began to stroke her knuckles with his thumb. She dismissed the danger signals in her head. Her skin tingled from his touch. Her throat dried up, and liquid wasn't the solution.

Had she been so sensitive to male contact before? Had her hormones gone this crazy ten years ago? Those memories were locked away, never, ever to be revisited.

Ethan had seen her wistful expression as she watched the couples moving around the floor, her body swaying in time to the music. She was in another world. A long-lost world? He wanted her in the here and now, totally focused on *them*.

She'd provoked an acute rush of satisfaction when she'd given him her hand. His heartbeat had spiked, unaccustomed yearning snaking through him. The eons-old urge of man to protect his child? Or primitive gratification that its mother trusted him to safeguard them both?

'Dance with me, Alina.'

She glanced across the room, shook her head. 'I'll embarrass you. I only do modern stuff with no touching. Nothing like this.' She gestured towards the dancers. 'They are so graceful.'

'No touching *ever*?' His eyebrows rose in disbelief. 'Or only since…?' He left his question unfinished, didn't need a reply.

She tried to free her hand, merely succeeded in twisting it so that his thumb pressed into her palm. Stopped resisting when he resumed his slow caress. Was he playing fair? Touching and kissing hadn't been mentioned when they'd first made their agreement. There'd been no reason in that emotionless civil conversation.

'You're denying something you really want, Alina. Trust me. You'll regret it if you don't.'

Cautious eagerness dawned in her sceptical eyes. 'Your toes might regret it if I do.'

He laughed, walked round the table without letting her go. 'Let's find out.'

Drawing her to her feet, he led her onto the dance floor. He placed her left hand on his shoulder, his right hand on her waist, then clasped her free hand in his, over his heart. Each movement was slow, deliberate. Non-threatening to her peace of mind.

'Look at me, Alina.'

Alina did.

'Trust me.'

She did.

'Let me guide you.'

He held her firmly, murmured in her ear and directed her steps with his thighs. His breath tickled her earlobe, his cologne filled her nostrils. Heat radiated from his touch as he compensated for her initial stumbling. She let her muscles go loose, giving him full control of her movements.

They glided round the room as if floating on air. Her eyelids fluttered. The music combined with the man to create an ethereal realm she wished she could stay in for ever. No more sorrow. No more loneliness. She gave a soft sigh, glanced up—into a searing wave of cobalt desire.

Their feet stopped moving; their bodies swayed in time with the rhythm of the music. She couldn't swallow, couldn't breathe, yet she felt his deep intake of air. Felt…

Guilt—as strong and shattering as when she'd been the only survivor.

The magic dissolved into stark reality. She began to shudder—couldn't stop. She tried to pull away, found herself being ushered to their table and gently settled into her seat. The strong arm stayed around her, supportive, grounding.

A moment later there were muffled words in a concerned tone, a deep reply. Deep as Ethan's voice but clipped, disconnected, not like him at all. She did know that it was his fingers lifting her chin, and hazily wondered why they trembled.

'Alina?'

She blinked, saw his pale face, his brow creased in concern. She bent her head, unable to find words to explain.

His hand dropped. 'Let's go home. We'll talk there.'

'No.' Plaintive, even to her own ears.

'We have to.' Soft-spoken. Decisive.

They drove home in silence. Alina counted cars as they passed, timed their stops at traffic lights—anything to keep from dwelling on the talk ahead. Could she feign a headache? Believable in the circumstances, but delaying the inevitable.

If Ethan James wanted to talk, they'd talk—sooner rather than later.

Wouldn't even care if the moment she'd accidentally met reading the last paragraph with the only intimacy ext----- lived at this point-----

This isn't easy for us, Alina, we are now. I've never had a problem with women before, but now I'm around-----

wouldn't force them to be in-----

CHAPTER EIGHT

ETHAN KEPT HER hand in his after locking the car, only letting go to allow her to enter the apartment first. How come she'd not only become used to that small intimacy but welcomed it? She dropped her bag onto the island, walked round to make hot drinks.

'Would you like coffee?' She reached for a bronze pod.

'Make it a black pod. I need a strong kick.' He was already walking towards the hall, discarding his jacket as he went.

Good idea. She picked up her bag and headed for her room to change. Jeans and a casual top were more conducive to a serious discussion.

In the few minutes it took her he'd returned, and their drinks were ready in the lounge.

'Biscuits?'

She shook her head. 'No, thank you.'

His lips twitched at the corners, just a tad. 'Chocolate?'

So he'd noticed the wrappers in the bin and her stash in the cupboard. Again she declined. Why the heck was she being so formal? Last night the atmosphere had been light and friendly. Today even better. Until that moment when the past had reasserted its claim on her.

She sat in the corner of the settee, drawing her legs up tight when he chose one of the armchairs, putting extra space between them. She stared at the mug in her hands, dreading the words she might hear, fearing he might be annoyed if she couldn't or wouldn't answer.

'We have to talk, Alina.'

The sombre tone of his voice brought her head up. His eyes had the sharp intensity she remembered from when she'd taken over filling in the marriage application. As if reading her inner thoughts was the only thing that mattered at this moment.

'This isn't going to work the way we are now. I've never had a problem with women before, but now I'm second-guessing what to do. For our baby's sake we have to convince everyone we've had a passionate affair.'

'And I'm failing miserably. I'm sorry, Ethan. I don't know how... There was only ever... I...' The words wouldn't come. She bit the inside of her lip, looked down at her white knuckles gripping the hot mug.

His hollow laugh snapped her gaze back to his face.

'I'm not doing much better, Alina. I never knew grief could be so overwhelming, so soul-draining. You brought some light into my dark world. Now you're here—so sweet and beautiful, so vulnerable.'

He leant forward, hands clasped between spread knees.

'I can't deny the physical attraction. Can't fathom whether it's linked with knowing you're carrying Louise's baby. Tonight—the music, dancing with you in my arms—I was in a new world. I frightened you, and I'm sorry—'

'No. It wasn't you,' she cut in. 'There've been so many first-for-a-long-times for me, it's bewildering. I feel like I've been thrown back into mainstream city living without a guidebook.'

She suddenly realised she was mimicking his stance, sharing his desire for their plan to succeed. Something shifted inside her, as if the extra tightening around her heart that had come when she'd heard about Louise and Leon had slipped a few notches. The old pain remained. She'd accepted only death would bring *that* to an end.

'It's only been four days. I didn't expect to stay in Australia—much less with you.' She smiled, watched as his eyes softened and his brow cleared. His answering smile lifted her heart. 'I'm rusty in all the social niceties of sharing a home and…and things.'

He shifted as if to stand, sank back. 'I don't have a good track record there. I've only had two live-in relationships, neither here, and neither lasting more than five months. Both confirmed my belief that I'm not cut out for domesticity. I'm too pragmatic—and, as one of them pointed out, I've no romance in my soul. Assuming I *have* a soul.'

'That's better for us, isn't it?' Although did she really want him to stop his gentle touches, his scorching looks? His kisses?

'No.' Sharp. Instant.

He came to sit at the other end of the couch, folding one leg up, spreading one arm along the back. She wriggled into her corner and listened.

'We need to create an illusion of instant attraction and overpowering passion. I've never been demonstrative with girlfriends in public. Little more than hand-holding and social greetings. So a good way to convince people our affair was different is to show affection in front of them.'

'You mean kiss if someone's watching?'

'Alina, we're implying that we had a short, tempestuous affair that resulted in your becoming pregnant. That you're here with me now will tell everyone you mean more than any other woman I've dated. Which is true in the nicest way. Our limited knowledge of each other doesn't matter—displaying our irresistible attraction does.'

'So somewhere between how we've been and how Louise and Leon were?' Not a hard task, considering the way she reacted to him each time they touched. As long as she kept her heart secure.

'Definitely less blatant—though I envied them their intimacy. I can't imagine having such a close bond with anyone. I'm aware I'll have to change the way I think and act, make it credible to friends and family. It's not only me who'll be affected by our success.'

She locked eyes with his. 'The baby.'

'*Our* baby. It's essential my parents believe that. You have to be comfortable with me as your partner, alone and in company.'

'I can.' She heard the slight tremor. 'I will be.' Better. Stronger.

Ethan slid his leg off the couch. 'Come here.'

That persuasive honey tone. Those compelling cobalt eyes.

She sidled along until there was barely a hand's length between them. His fingers lightly traced her cheek. His arm slid around her, loose yet secure.

'Any time you feel uneasy, tell me.'

His slow smile had her leaning in closer.

'Any time you feel like taking the initiative, go right ahead.'

He stroked her hair, laid her head on his shoulder and cradled her against his body. His heart beat strong and steady under her hand, an echo of hers. His voice, his cologne, everything about him was becoming familiar, safe. It was a feeling she refused to analyse.

'We'll keep to ourselves for a couple of weeks. When you're ready I'd like to arrange dinner with the couple I hope will agree to be our witnesses. If we're out and meet anyone I know I'll introduce you only by name. After the wedding I'll tell my parents, and then the whole world can know.'

'All at once?' she teased, liking the way his eyes crinkled at the corners when he laughed down at her.

She also liked the sound of the couple he went on to describe—friends he'd known for years, who'd also known and visited Louise and Leon.

They made small talk, sat in quiet contemplation, still in

an amicable embrace. When it was time to retire it was she who raised her face for his tender goodnight kiss.

Ethan leant against the wall, his gaze fixed on the light under her door, not quite sure what had happened tonight. A week ago he'd have claimed the scenario he'd suggested held no qualms for him, apart from the discomfort of their public displays.

He'd have bet his finest hotel that his romantic emotions would not have been involved, and still didn't quite believe they were. The trauma of losing his sister and best friend, the shock of Alina's pregnancy, plus his determination to take responsibility for the child were a formidable combination. It was enough to scramble anyone's senses.

He still believed his decisions had been made with logic and foresight, with the child's future wellbeing his main consideration. Main? He meant *only*. He'd be a single father, with all the problems that entailed. Public displays had to be kept objective—surface emotion only.

Yet he couldn't deny that Alina slipped under his guard whenever they were together, popped into his thoughts when they weren't.

The light went out. He whispered, 'Pleasant dreams…' and went to his big, lonely bed.

Alina woke early, had coffee brewing and the table set for breakfast by the time Ethan walked down the hallway dressed for work.

'Good morning.' He sat opposite and poured his favourite sugarbomb cereal. 'Do you want a lift anywhere this morning?'

'No.' Too quick. Too sharp.

Last night their decision had sounded plausible, simple to put into practice. This morning, as water had cascaded over her in the shower, she'd decided she wanted some alone time, to mull it over and fully accept its implications in her head.

'I'd like to practise on the laptop. I bet there are functions I've never heard of.'

'There are probably programs I've never used either. Any questions you have I'll try to answer later. With luck, and few interruptions, I might only need a few hours at the office.'

'Don't you usually work all day on Saturday?'

'Ah, that was the *old* me in the *old* days.' His sparkling eyes belied his self-critical tone. 'A pre-baby workaholic. Now I'm in training to be the best daddy ever.' His voice roughened over the last sentence, and the sparkle dimmed a little.

Alina covered his hand with hers. 'You will be, Ethan. You'll be everything they'd want their child to have in a father.'

'And mother.'

She jerked her hand away. He caught it.

'There won't be any other. I sure as hell won't marry again just to provide maternal comfort or for the public two-parent image. I've learned from experience how a marriage held together purely for society standing can influence a child.'

That was why he'd have no problem letting her go, would never try to persuade her to stay.

There was no justification for the dejection that washed over her. No reason for the retort that burst from her.

'Louise turned out fine. She was generous, warm-hearted and open. Even through her medical traumas there was always a genuine welcome for anyone at their home. You know how everyone loved her because she was…was… *she was Louise.*'

'And I'm not like her?' He released her hand, picked up his spoon.

'I'm sorry. That's not what I meant.'

'No, but it's true. She never changed from the sweet, wide-eyed creature the nanny at the time put into my arms when I was five. She grabbed my finger, gurgled, and I immediately forgave her for not being the brother I wanted.'

His light laughter was tinged with remorse.

'I wish I'd been as courageous as her—constantly rebelling against the rigid conformity of our upbringing, openly making friends with people she liked, whether they were deemed acceptable or not. My way was quiet avoidance rather than personal confrontation.'

'You kept Leon's friendship, and championed them when they wanted to marry.'

He huffed. 'My parents didn't like that. I don't think they've forgiven me for supporting Louise's declaration that she'd happily have a park wedding without them. Not the "done thing" in their circle. It would have been embarrassing, so they capitulated.'

'Do you see them regularly?'

'We have little in common—different standards. They'd like me to be more involved in their close-knit elite group. I dislike the way they boast about my success to elevate their own status. They are, however, the only parents I have, so we maintain a polite relationship.'

He ate for a moment, eyes downcast. Pondering. Then looked up and spoke with determination.

'Forget them for now. Cutting down my office hours is essential to my being available for appointments right now, and planning for our baby in the future. So I've been reorganising my staff.'

'You're delegating?

'Even better—I've promoted. My second-in-command now has two assistant managers. Between the three of them they'll take most of the day-to-day load off me. By the time our baby comes everything should be working smoothly enough for me to take paternity leave.'

'Decision made. Action taken. Problem solved.'

'You don't approve?' He sounded disappointed.

'I do. Very much. It's so much a part of who you are. And it's been a long time since I've felt secure enough to depend on anyone for anything.'

She was paying him a compliment, saying what he should want to hear. Ethan shouldn't feel aggrieved, but he did. She admitted to trusting and relying on him—both important to their relationship. But he wanted something different, something more. Something indefinable.

He pushed back his chair, picked up his bowl.

'I'll clear. You head off,' Alina said, buttering a piece of cold toast.

'Okay. I should be home early afternoon. Did you buy bathers?'

'Yes, haven't worn them yet.'

He hadn't used the gym since Sunday. Or the pool since Tuesday evening, after their talk. He was normally a creature of habit and liked his routine, which included daily exercise and swimming early morning or evening. The less disruption, the less stress. If she worked out at the same time he'd know she was okay. It would be a start to getting his life back in control.

'How about when I get home? We'll work out, then swim.'

Her face lit up. 'That sounds good.'

He went to his room, planning a positive day. A few minutes later he collected his briefcase from his study, and left.

Alina ate her toast and honey, mulling over her every encounter with Ethan. She'd developed a habit of deep thinking over people and situations during her solitary lifestyle. Sometimes she created fictional stories about them in her mind to pass the time.

This was real. The attraction between them was real—
had been since the moment she'd turned from that window. She could understand *her* reactions. Suddenly thrown
into enforced proximity with an attractive, virile man after
seven years alone... Pregnant, with rampant hormones
playing havoc with her emotions...

His puzzled her. She appreciated the need for them to
give the impression they'd been lovers, so kissing was essential. The first kiss had been experimental, to judge her
response, the second for show. The others... She wasn't
sure. Yet she'd sensed tension in him every time—right
from the initial touch of his lips on hers. As if he was keeping a tight rein on his actions. Or on emotions he claimed
not to have.

She sipped her camomile tea, pulled a face. Cold toast
was okay—cold tea was not drinkable. It was time to get
cracking.

She clicked on the kettle, cleared the table and set herself
up for a morning's exploration of the internet.

The sound of the front door opening had Alina's head
swinging round. A quick check of her watch surprised her.
Ten to three. How could it be that late?

'Hi, you've set yourself up pretty well, there. Good use
of the dining table.'

How did this man's smile make a good day seem brighter?

'Better than leaning over the coffee table. Did you get
what you wanted done?'

'Finally—it took longer than I'd hoped.' He leant over
her shoulder to check her screen. 'Agassi Falls? Planning
a trip, Alina?'

'Just having fun surfing,' she replied. 'I checked out
some courses, then spent some time finding out what all
the icons stand for.'

'I trust you've been taking breaks and eating properly?'

Banana peel lay in a small dish, alongside an empty mug on the table.

'Yes, sir. I've stretched every hour…done other stuff in between.' She arched her back and smiled up at him. 'This morning I went out for a short walk; this afternoon I went through your kitchen cupboards to see what's there before looking up some recipes. I found a few meals we might enjoy, but—'

'You can't print them out. We'll fix that on Monday, along with a desk and chair.' He held out a red USB. 'In the meantime copy and use mine.'

'Thank you.' She surprised both of them by rising up on her toes to kiss his cheek. 'This is all I need. You don't want to be left with excess stuff.'

Ethan opened his mouth to refute her claim. Changed his mind. Words weren't going to change hers.

'That's my concern. Right now I'm psyched up for the session in the gym we agreed on.' He took her hands, held her at arm's length. 'Hmm, nice tracksuit—you look as good in green as in blue. Give me five minutes.'

'I'll meet you there.'

He strode to his room, fantasising about the bathers she might be wearing under that outfit as he hastily pulled on T-shirt, bathers, track pants and sneakers. She was waiting for him, sitting on the press-ups bench. The lights were brighter than he usually set, the music a pleasant background sound.

'Bike or treadmill for warm-up?' she asked, offering him a bottle of water. 'I don't mind either.'

'I'll take the bike.' It was still set up for him. 'Twenty minutes okay?'

She agreed, and he selected a programme for mid-range difficulty. Settling into his normal pace was easy—resisting the temptation to watch Alina not so easy. She moved smoothly, gracefully.

'I promise I won't fall off.' She'd caught him checking her out.

'It's been a while since anyone's been here with me.'

Solitude in this special area had always been a plus. It was his private time, for releasing tension. Only occasionally had he invited anyone to join him. To his surprise, he didn't mind Alina being there at all. In fact he felt downright glad to have her running alongside him. A feeling that unnerved him a little, causing him to switch back to getting-to-know-you mode.

'What sort of keep-fit do you do on the move?'

'Depends on the current job. Crop-picking, dog-walking or waitressing are usually enough. If it's in an office I run, or do casual sessions at pools or gyms.'

'Whoa—back up. Dog-walking?'

Her laugh, the first genuine one she'd given, zipped through him. Musical and light, it was a sound he wanted to hear again. Often.

'It's fun, challenging or downright exhausting, depending on the size or number of pooches. And always available in any city, any country.'

'Ever lose any?' The more he learned, the more fascinated he became.

CHAPTER NINE

'NO. I HAD one Labrador who didn't want to go back to his owner, but I didn't blame him. The woman's perfume was so overpowering it clogged my throat.'

She blushed and bent her head. So delightfully embarrassed he wanted to jump off and comfort her.

'Hey, yours just didn't suit *you*. On another woman it'd be different.'

'Someone more flamboyant? More "out there"? It was a Christmas gift from a temporary boss, probably recycled. The box had been opened.'

'Now you have the perfect fragrance for you—delicate, reminding me of sunshine and flowers. Ethereal…' He chuckled. 'Maybe not the last one. Though sometimes you *do* drift off into another world.'

Alina was grateful for the distinct ping announcing the end of her programme. She stepped off as the machine slowed down. Moved over to the weights.

For the next thirty minutes they rarely spoke, each concentrating on their own exercises. She'd have been completely relaxed if she'd been able to block out the male effortlessly lifting weights alongside her, built well enough to play A-league football.

He smiled whenever their eyes met in the huge wall mirror, disconcerting her. His T-shirt moulded to his sculpted chest and muscular upper arms. Her breath hitched every time his biceps firmed as he curled or lifted weights. She felt hot, sweaty, much more than she ever had while exercising before.

Deciding she'd done enough, she walked over to the pool. Discarding her tracksuit, she used the ladder, shivering as she descended into the cool water. Made a mental note to ask him to up the temperature. Taking a deep breath, she ducked under, sinking to the bottom, then shooting up. She grabbed the rail, shaking her head, refilling her lungs... Found herself staring at a pair of slender feet attached to tanned legs with a light covering of black hair.

She tilted her head for a slow scan past firm calves to the muscular thighs that had steered her round the dance floor last night...and a pair of black swimming trunks that left no doubt as to his manhood.

Her mouth dried; her pulse raced. Her body heat over-rode the chill from the surrounding water. She didn't dare meet his eyes, chose the coward's path and swung into a freestyle stroke away from him. Quickened her pace at the sound of a splash behind her.

Ethan overtook her, touched and turned at the end. He was still below the surface as they passed again. She recovered her composure, slowed to her normal leisurely pace. This wasn't a contest.

Six laps were enough for her.

She sat on the top of the ladder, wrapped in a towel, her feet dangling. She ought to leave. Shower and dress. Think about dinner—no, too early for that. She stayed. Not sure why, except that it was mesmerising, watching Ethan churn through the water, hardly making a ripple. The way he went through life: single-minded, controlled.

He swam like a machine—clean, even strokes, power-ing along the pool, flipping like a seal at the end. She timed his push-offs. Always constant. So precise. So coordinated.

She frowned. He'd dipped in front of her on his last turn, hadn't resurfaced. Suddenly he burst upward from the water, making her jump. His chest skimmed her legs as he rose, catching hold of the rail for stability.

'Waiting for me?' He grinned, spraying her with tiny drops as he shook his head.

'Hey!'

He levered himself higher so they were on eye level. 'It's only water. Anything special you'd like to do tomorrow? We'll have all day.'

'Oh. No work or commitments?'

'None. I'm all yours. Stay home, and relax. Go for a drive. Walk on the beach. Your choice.'

How was she supposed to make an instant decision with him so close that there was a hint of his cologne in the chlorine-scented air? With his glistening muscled torso inches from her twitching fingers? With his appealing blue eyes offering her something she refused to name?

'A ferry ride.' Out of the blue. From somewhere in her past.

His eyebrows almost met his dripping hairline. 'You want to go on a ferry?'

She nodded. 'The Manly Ferry across the heads. I used to love it during the winter in rough weather.'

His smile shot into a scowl. 'No *way* are you going out in a storm.' Grated out. Possessive.

She laughed, recognising the over-protective tone. 'They don't cross in really rough weather. I don't get seasick. And it's spring.'

He relented, didn't look convinced. 'We'll decide at Circular Quay.'

He twisted, hoisted himself out onto the pool side and picked up the towel he'd left nearby. Alina stood, heading for the door as he patted excess water from his body. He caught her arm and took her towel from her.

'Stand still.'

He moved behind her, began to dry her hair, firmly yet gently. It was soporific, soothing. She arched her neck in pleasure, sighed when he dropped the towel and began to massage her neck and shoulders. Trembled when his hot breath teased the pulse under her ear.

'Your muscles are taut as a drum. A proper massage might help.'

From *him*? Considering he was the main reason for their tension, she doubted it, but his offer was tempting.

'There's a beauty parlour in the next block. Make an appointment.'

Why had it suddenly become less appealing?

After Alina had retired for the night Ethan turned off the television and dimmed the lights. Then, sipping brandy, his feet up on the coffee table, he tried to make sense of the mayhem his normally ordered life had become.

He was committed to becoming a short-term husband and a lifelong father. He was becoming attached to a woman whose heart and love belonged to a dead guy. Her response to him was merely physical. His carefully planned future was now a day-by-day unknown.

Ethan suggested they put light coats, plus anything else she wanted to take, into her backpack—which *he'd* carry. He deliberately lingered over breakfast, determined to use their outing to ease any tension between them, make this a day for light conversation with no conflict.

It was mid-morning as they strolled towards Circular Quay. After guiding her across the first road he linked their fingers, claiming it would prevent them from being separated by the crowds already building up. She didn't argue, seemed content to let him be protective. He was rapidly becoming more comfortable with the feeling.

Had to curb it when, while drinking water and watching the boats, she declared she'd love to do the Harbour Bridge climb.

Alina hadn't *forgotten* the sheer joy of crossing the heads to Manly on a windy day in choppy seas. She'd purposely blocked it from her mind. Now she realised how much she'd missed the city she'd lived in for so many years.

Today it was fairly mild, until they reached the gap leading to the ocean. She felt alive, leaning on the rail, facing into the breeze, letting it prickle her skin and tease her hair. Nautical toots and engine noise, calls from yachts as they sailed past, all combined with the sounds of circling seagulls to fill her world.

'There's nothing like this anywhere—nothing so exhilarating.' She twisted her head to smile up at Ethan, braced behind her, his hands on the rail either side of her.

His expression said he didn't quite agree. She turned back, leant well forward, as if searching, unsure how to express the way she felt. He repeatedly said that he owed her, but she hadn't expected him to show it so personally, to spend so much time with her. Covering her living costs would have been ample.

'Hey.' One arm wrapped round her. 'It's a long way down.'

'I'm looking for dolphins.'

'Wrong area for them. Wrong season for whales.'

Husky tone, hot breath fanning her ear.

'Some friends and I did a whale-watching trip along the coast a few years ago. Mid-June, I think. If you're feeling up to it, we'll go.'

'I'd love it.' She let him draw her back against his chest. Breathed in the salty air. And him. Let herself live in the moment.

Ethan wondered if she knew how captivating she looked. Genuinely happy, with flushed cheeks and sparkling eyes, she was irresistible. He made a mental note to arrange a day's sailing with friends.

He cupped her cheek, bringing her face round to his. 'Nothing like it. Definitely no sight more beautiful,' he murmured, dipping his head to capture her mouth. He saw her eyes darken. Felt her tremble. Silently agreed: it *was* exhilarating.

The ferry lurched, breaking them apart. He grabbed the rail again, trapping her safely between his arms. They rocked in unison as the boat ploughed through the rough swell. General conversation might be safer.

'I have to confess the only ferries I've been on for years have been for corporate evening events with catered food and drinks. My friends and I used to think day-old pies and cold cans of drink were the ultimate meal.'

He realised how many other simple pleasures he'd left behind as he built his Starburst chain. Pleasures Alina understood and still enjoyed. His adrenaline surged at the thought of her helping him rediscover them. Then she'd go, leaving him to share them with their child. He trembled at the challenge.

Alina felt it and looked round.

'That wind's cold. Do you want to go inside?' he said.

He wasn't lying. It went right through the jacket he'd put on before boarding. Hers wasn't much heavier.

'You're kidding? Inside is for sensitive people, small children or the wuss breed. There's hot drinks and delicious fish and chips waiting near the docks.'

She turned back to watch their approach into Manly.

Ethan nestled his head against hers. 'Okay, but if I catch a chill you have to nurse me.'

The sound she gave was suspiciously like a giggle. 'No chance. No virus would dare attack you without an appointment.'

He stiffened. Was that the impression he gave? Good humour won him over. A week ago she'd been wary of him, anxious about his reaction to her pregnancy. Ready with a plan to have the baby alone if he denied her. He felt a warm glow deep in his gut. If she liked him enough to bait him he must be doing something right.

So he had a reputation for being hardnosed in business? He also was known for being fair and trustworthy.

Late on Monday morning Alina walked through the foyer, trying to pep-talk away her apprehension. Exercising hadn't helped. The line between truth and tacit lies seemed so tenuous. She was not the biological mother—had to persuade everyone she was. She and Ethan had never been lovers, had shared only a few kisses—one long one for an observer's benefit. Were required to act as if they'd had a passionate affair.

Her trepidation had increased when she'd realised he'd been rescheduling appointments to accommodate her and the problems she'd brought him. This morning he'd left early for a meeting postponed from Wednesday. Thirty minutes ago he'd phoned to ask her to come down and meet the car as he'd be running late.

For the baby. For Louise and Leon.

Repeating her mantra silently, she went outside to wait in the shade, praying he wasn't stuck in a traffic jam. The vehicle pulled in to the kerb as if summoned by her plea. She hurried forward, not giving the driver a chance to alight. Scrambling in, she dragged the door shut, leaving Ethan leaning forward awkwardly with his arm extended.

'Oh, sorry.' She gulped in a quick breath, inhaled his distinctive cologne. Flicked him an apologetic grin. 'I'm not used to having someone take care of me.'

'That lesson I'm learning.' Cobalt eyes appraised her as the car moved off. 'You look anxious, Alina.' He caressed her jaw line, tilted her chin.

'What do you expe—?'

He cut off her rebuke by firmly pressing his lips to hers. Her heartbeat hiccupped, doubled in speed. Sent her blood racing along her veins.

The kiss lasted less than a moment. Or for ever. Too

long. Too short. She slumped against the seat and stared at him, too befuddled to think coherently. The piercing eyes holding hers hostage showed no sign of the turmoil he'd inflicted.

She consciously steadied her breathing. 'You should warn me.' It came out like a husky plea for more rather than a reproach.

Ethan gave a low chuckle that resonated over her skin and skittered down her spine. 'So it's okay to kiss you any time as long as I don't surprise you?'

His amusement stretched already taut nerves. 'That's not what I meant.' She scrunched her eyes and bit on her lip.

'I'm not insensitive, Alina.' He lifted his hand. Let it drop. 'Every time I touch you I'm very aware of how you feel. Remember we need to portray a couple who can't resist each other?'

For him it was all for public image, so his declaration should please, not disappoint. Stupid hormones. She *so* had to check with the doctor why they were affecting her this way. In private.

'I can handle the pretence.' *Liar.* 'I'm getting used to it.' *Double liar.* 'It's... The doctor might ask for information I can't...can't give.'

'Ah...'

As if he understood. She shook with frustration. 'No, you don't get it. I can give her the dates she'll need, fudge the method of conception. It's... She's bound to ask...'

It had been bad enough writing details on the clinic's patient information forms he'd accessed on Friday. She'd thanked him for his considerate action in allowing her to fill out her medical history privately. It was the idea of it being voiced out loud that was eating at her. There was no way to explain the dark place where she'd buried the unbearable pain and heartbreak.

He wrapped his arms around her, drew her into his warmth. His hands began a soothing caress over her spine.

His voice was gentle, as if speaking to a child. 'You're not alone, Alina. I'll be with you.' His hands stilled. 'Unless you *want* to see her alone.'

Of course she did.

'No, that's cowardly. I can handle it.' Her quivering voice proved otherwise.

'Are you sure?'

He meant it. And the compassion in his blue eyes and the generosity of his offer gave her strength.

'You may have questions too. Besides, the father has the right to be there.' With a jolt of amazement, she realised a simple truth. 'I'd *like* you to be there.'

'I am the father...' His large hand covered her abdomen. 'My baby. Our child.'

She didn't protest and he appeared satisfied. She'd never be able to use that phrase, never be able to care that way again. Hearing it resonate from him relieved her. He was going be a great father.

Ethan linked his fingers with hers as they entered the light, hospitable clinic. Her anxiety was palpable and he had no remedy. Give him a struggling business to rescue any time.

'Relax, Alina. It's only a preliminary examination.'

At least his words earned him a faint smile. He steered her into an empty elevator and pressed the button. The compulsion to comfort her and drive the shadows from her soulful eyes rippled through him.

'We're bending the truth for our child's sake, Alina. The book claims doctors need dates and medical history— nothing more. No one's going to pry into your personal history.'

Her eyes widened in astonishment. 'What book?'

'The one I bought Tuesday morning, specifically written for expectant fathers.' His mouth twisted. 'Very informative and downright scary.'

They stopped and he guided her out.

She handed in the forms and her obligatory urine sample at Reception and were directed to an empty waiting room. Light classical music played softly in the background. Alina sat idly flipping the pages of a magazine. Ethan filled two plastic cups from an orange juice dispenser and offered one to her.

She accepted it with a noticeably shaky hand and his heart sank. He noticed her agitated finger movements, half hidden by the bag on her lap, finishing in a clenched fist. Hoping their appointment wasn't delayed, he put his cup on the low table and wrapped steadying fingers around her hand.

'Patricia Conlan has a very good reputation.' He raised the hand clasping the cup to her lips. 'Now, drink. Slowly.'

Alina obeyed, emptying the cup. He drained his, took both cups to a bin, then returned to sit beside her, studying a poster on the wall opposite.

She kept her eyes downcast, wishing she had his self-discipline. He'd been predictably shaken by her initial bombshell, and angry a few times during subsequent conversations, but he'd rapidly recovered his composure every time. She, on the other hand, had trouble keeping any control over her emotions.

She glanced sideways, surprised to find him looking more nervous than he'd let on. The long supple fingers of his right hand thrummed on his thigh, and she recalled them spanning her stomach. The image of them sensuously exploring her body flashed into her brain, and she couldn't stifle a throaty gasp.

He jerked round. 'Alina, are you all right?'

'Alina Fletcher?'

She jumped up, willing her burning cheeks to cool,

grateful for the interruption from the uniformed woman in the doorway.

They were ushered into the consulting room.

'Dr Conlan will be with you in… Ah, here she is.'

'Alina, Ethan. It's nice to meet you.' The fortyish woman with slightly mussed brown hair and bright blue eyes clasped her hands, then Ethan's, in genuine welcome.

'Let's sit down and get acquainted.' She emanated compassion and invited trust.

'Thank you, Dr Conlan.' Alina took a seat, placing her handbag on the floor as a folder was opened and perused. Even Ethan's reassurance couldn't dispel her feeling of foreboding at the thought of queries about her past. An occasional note was written, an occasional 'hmm' mouthed.

She noticed a slight resemblance to her husband's Aunt Jean, triggering a pang of guilt. She'd only kept in token touch with everyone, had avoided personal contact. In a few weeks she'd have to notify them that she was living in Sydney. Remarried. Having another baby. The latter when Ethan decided to make the announcement.

Sneaking a peek at him, she met genuine concern. Whatever he saw caused him to take her hand, link their fingers and squeeze. He had no idea how calming those slight actions were.

Dr Conlan laid down her pen and glasses, placed her elbows on her desk and linked her fingers. She smiled sympathetically.

'I appreciate this must revive painful memories for you, Alina, and I sincerely hope your new baby brings you happiness.'

Ethan squeezed her hand again.

'The sample you brought in officially confirms your pregnancy. If you'd like to go into the examination area, I'll be in shortly. We'll talk after.'

Alina went to the open doorway indicated. The faint

murmur of voices drifted in as she prepared and lay down on the examining table. She stared at the ceiling, silently chanting her mantra.

CHAPTER TEN

NICE AS THE doctor was, Alina felt relieved as they left. A referral for an ultrasound and an appointment card were in her handbag. Ethan held the door open, his free hand clasping the pamphlets they'd been given.

She'd seen his surreptitious peek at his watch in the elevator. Catching his arm she stopped them both. 'You need to get back to the office, don't you?'

'There's always work to be done. We can—'

'Hail a taxi and I'll drop you off. The sooner you get back, the less chance of staying late.' And she'd have some quiet contemplation time to mull over the doctor's advice, read those pamphlets, and fully accept the path she'd chosen.

His cobalt eyes gleamed with gratitude. His fingers rested gently on her cheek for a moment. 'Spoken like a true corporate wife.' He looked round. 'There's a snack bar over there. I'll grab a sandwich to eat at my desk.'

He made one call during the taxi ride to his office, booking the ultrasound for Monday the twenty-first of April at ten. She wrote the date and time in her notebook as he repeated them for confirmation, realising it was the day after the wedding. When she would be recorded as his wife.

Ethan sensed a change in her. Was she too beginning to realise the enormity of their agreement, so simple in words, so complex and mind-boggling in reality? In front of the doctor he'd claimed to be the father of her child. He'd said 'our baby', 'our child' so easily. Now he had to fulfil the promises he'd made to Alina and his sister's memory.

His pragmatic nature demanded everything be put in place quickly, privately. Nothing left to chance, no hesitation that might give anyone cause to believe he doubted his paternity. Even before she'd agreed he'd set up appointments without considering the effect on her. Even after learning of her loss he hadn't deviated from his plan.

He hadn't allowed for the reality—hadn't understood the impact it would have on them both.

He reached for her hand, breathed in her sweet fragrance. She didn't react; lost in a world he had no right to access.

The taxi was nearing his office. He tilted her chin, took in her subdued expression and almost told the driver to keep going. What could he say or do? Nothing until she was ready to confide in him. A quick kiss on her forehead produced little response. He had no right or reason to be disappointed. Only a week ago he'd walked out on her.

Alina's head was inside the kitchen island cupboard when the intercom buzzed at about eleven the next morning. She'd just managed to reach the small can in the back corner and jerked at the sound, banging her head.

She walked over to the front door. Hesitated. Ethan hadn't mentioned anyone coming. Would he want her to answer? Another buzz. She pressed.

'Hello.'

'Good morning. Is Ethan at home?'

The hairs on the back of her neck lifted at the high-pitched, cultured voice. Her mouth dried. She swallowed twice, rubbed her neck. Finally managed a croaky reply. 'No, I'm sorry, he's not.'

'I'm Sophia James. May I come up?'

His mother—judgemental to the nth degree. Far worse than the ex-girlfriend she'd suspected. Should she let her in? What would she do if Alina refused her entry?

'Hello? Are you still there?' Slightly peeved.

'Please come up.' Denial only delayed the inevitable.

In three weeks Sophia would be her mother-in-law. For a short time anyway.

She raced to her bedroom to check her appearance. After brushing her already neat hair she went slowly back, taking long lung-filling breaths. Waited, slowly counted to nine after the bell rang before opening the door.

Sophia James was the epitome of a stylish, sixtyish woman with all the resources to fight any sign of ageing. From her coiffured dark hair to the handmade high-heeled shoes colours matched, everything fitted perfectly. There was nothing soft about her at all. Not a trace of warmth in her red lips or in her flat brown eyes.

Alina felt an irrational zing of satisfaction that both this woman's children had expressive blue eyes, clearly inherited from another family member.

'Please come in,' she said, standing aside.

Sophia walked in with an air of entitlement, scanning the area as if it were her territory. Scanning Alina as if she were an applicant for a lowly household position.

'You are not the cleaner. Why isn't Ethan here with you?'

Spoken as if she couldn't be trusted to be alone in his home. She felt a twinge of insecurity, then pride came to her rescue. She lifted her chin, squared her shoulders. *She's Ethan's mother. Treat her with respect. She's the baby's grandmother.* That last thought eased her resentment. This lady would *not* take kindly to any of the traditional titles given to a grandmother.

'I'm Alina Fletcher. Would you like coffee or tea? Ethan's at work.' She held back on saying, *But I'll bet you know that.*

'Mild coffee, thank you. White. No sugar.' As if she were ordering from a waitress in a café.

Alina watched as Sophia stopped before entering the lounge, giving the area a thorough scrutiny before selecting one of the armchairs. Giving the impression that she had never seen the decor before. After popping a pod into the machine Alina joined her, staying on her feet to attend to the drinks.

'You're the girl with Ethan in the photograph a friend texted to me. You were kissing in the street, and now you're acting like this is your home. Are you *living* with him?' Blunt and insulting.

She made a point of staring at Alina's bare left hand, made no attempt to hide her displeasure. Alina's attitude swung again. How dared this woman question and insult her?

'I don't discuss my private business with strangers.'

Sophia's lips thinned, almost disappeared. Her back stiffened. 'I'm his mother. I have a right to know.'

'Then perhaps you should ask *him*. Next time we're in contact I'll ask him to get in touch.'

It was a definite dismissal. Forget coffee. Alina wanted her gone.

The scathing look Sophia gave her was defused by the dull shade of red flooding her face. She rose stiffly to her feet.

'Be warned, Ms Fletcher. You don't fit. You may have him fooled for a short time, but his contemporaries will see through you as easily as I do.'

Her movement to the door was as near to a stomp as Alina had ever seen anyone do in heels. She followed, far enough behind so that Sophia had to open the door herself.

She turned for a parting shot. 'Even suitable girls don't seem to last long with Ethan. Your novelty will quickly pall for a man of my son's impeccable taste.'

She swept out, leaving the door open.

Alina closed it, shaking with disbelief. She uncurled her clasped fingers to enable them to rub the back of her neck, tilted her head to the ceiling. What had she done? Apart from insulting his mother, and practically throwing her out of his home, she'd given the impression she had authority here.

Ethan hadn't wanted his parents to know about her yet. A public kiss hardly equated domestic cohabitation. Should she have lied?

Her head reeled.

Should she wait 'til he came home to tell him, when she'd be able to see his reaction? What if Sophia rang him first with a distorted version of events?

Taking bites of some dark rich chocolate for courage, she debated the pros and cons…

'She *what*?' The outrage in Ethan's voice seared down the phone line. She'd got no further than telling him his mother had visited before he'd exploded.

'I'm sorry, Ethan. I didn't know whether to let her in. I—'

'She's never been there before—never been invited. What did she want?' Barked out, agitating her even more.

'Someone sent her a photo of us kissing. I didn't know what to tell her.'

She'd screwed up. No, he'd put her in that position by keeping her a secret. It was *his* family who had the issues.

'You should contact her. I… I… I'll see you tonight.'

She hung up.

'Alina?'

She'd gone. Ethan realised his knuckles were white from his grip on the mobile phone. His free fist ground onto his desk. She'd sounded distressed. What the hell had his mother said to her?

He'd never been so angry. Or so worried when Alina didn't answer his call back. He selected his mother's number.

'Ethan, we haven't heard from you for a while.'

Not since they'd criticised the wording for the gravestone. Lucky for her there was half a city between them else he'd be tempted to throttle her.

'So you thought you'd pop into my home when you knew I wasn't there?'

She spluttered. He gave her no chance to refute his claim.

'Don't bother denying it. My receptionist logged the same female voice yesterday, saying she might call in. Your voice is quite distinctive.'

It wasn't said as a compliment. Anyone who truly knew him would have been wary of his low, controlled tone.

'I was worried. I'd received a photograph of you with that girl I met in your apartment.'

He almost lost it at her throwaway reference to Alina. Gritted his teeth, needing to know how his mother had discovered she was there. He waited for a long, tense moment.

'Okay, I described her to an acquaintance who lives a few floors below you. She said she'd seen her—sometimes alone, sometimes with you. I'm only looking out for your welfare, Ethan. There's something not quite right about her. She just about ordered me out.'

'After, I'm guessing, you began to interrogate her. Listen carefully, Mother. You'll have no more contact with me at all if you bother Alina again. Understand?'

'Ethan, you—'

'Goodbye, Mother.'

He dragged his fingers through his hair. *Alina, sweetheart, you didn't deserve that. I made a mistake—should have known she'd start digging at the slightest rumour I might be dating.*

He tried the apartment. No answer. Tried Alina's number twice more. It went to voicemail each time.

There was no sound in the apartment, no sign of Alina. Her mobile lay on the kitchen island. *She has to be here. Has to be.*

Ethan strode to her bedroom. The breath he felt he'd been holding for ever whooshed out at the sight of her handbag by her dressing table. Her bathroom door was open. Not there. One place left to check.

The gym area was silent apart from the low hum of the water pumps. The lights were dimmed, giving him limited vision of the figure floating in the pool. The only movements were slight flicks of her feet, gently propelling her along towards him. A rush of relief swamped his body. He sagged against the doorjamb, his heart racing. He'd had no reason to think she would run, yet he'd feared she might.

Wiping his hand over his mouth, he wondered why this fragile, damaged woman stirred him as no one ever had. It went deeper than the embryo she carried. His anger towards his mother had been at her treatment of Alina. His concern had been solely for Alina's feelings.

He toed off his shoes, stripped to his boxer shorts, watching her slow progress through the water. Not wanting to startle her, he walked along the side, meeting her halfway. Felt his lips curl. How did she keep a straight line with closed eyes?

They flew open, though he'd swear he'd never made a sound. Her head turned. One look into sorrowful violet and he dived in, surfacing next to her. He hauled her into his arms, the anxiety he'd experienced giving his action more force than he'd intended.

He buried his head in her neck, his lips seeking her pulse, his heart rate lifting at the feel of its erratic beat. The feel of her hands clasping his shoulders, her legs brushing his as they trod water, the tantalising aroma from her skin—all heightened his senses.

Her wrists stiffened, preventing him from drawing her closer. He raised his head, meeting censure in her eyes.

'Alina, I…' Where the hell were the words he needed? 'You hung up on me. Didn't answer your phone.'

Indignation flared, making the colour of her eyes even more stunning. Her hands lifted and slammed onto his skin, clearing his mind. He huffed out air, drew in fresh breath, regained control.

'I'm not angry, Alina—not at you. You sounded so upset. When you didn't pick up I was…' *Admit it. Tell her how you felt.* 'I'm not sure what I felt. Just knew I had to see you, hold you.'

'Your mother—'

'Had no right to come here. If I'd even suspected she might I'd have told you not to grant her entry. I'm sorry, Alina—and, believe me, so is she right now.'

'You've talked to her?'

His chest tightened. Hadn't she believed him when he'd said he'd protect her?

'More like a short, angry lecture. Plus her one and only warning. I made it clear if she upsets you again I'll have even less contact with them.'

'That's a bit drastic. They're your family, Ethan. I knew about her attitude, so I shouldn't have overreacted—though she certainly lived up to her reputation.' Her tone softened with regret. 'I'm really messing up your life, aren't I?'

He shook his head. 'Quite the opposite, Alina Fletcher. You enrich my life every day. You and our baby have changed my world.'

Her hands relaxed, allowing him to tighten his hold, bringing them into full body contact. Her fingers traced a featherlight path up his neck, across his chin. A glimmer of desire flickered in her eyes. It was satisfying for a few seconds—until his body responded to the flimsy barrier of cotton bathers and silk boxers between them, to the press of her breasts on his bare chest. To the flesh-on-flesh contact of their thighs.

His mouth crashed down on hers. No preamble, no gentle brush of lips—this was need, satisfying a hunger that had been building for days. From that first gut-clench, that first look into her haunted eyes.

He tilted her head for better contact, took what she offered, his tongue caressing hers, tangling, tasting the sweetness he'd dreamt of. And she was an active participant, giving and receiving, her fingers weaving into his hair, holding his head to hers.

His heart thumping, pulses pounding at every point, his lungs screaming for air, he had never felt so gloriously alive.

Reluctantly breaking the kiss, still holding her close, he gazed into violet eyes as bright as the stars in a moonless night, stunned and bewildered by the ardency of their kiss. He'd crossed an unspoken boundary, knew he should apologise. Knew it would be a lie.

'Do you want another apology?'

How could Alina ask an apology of him when she'd willingly contributed to the kiss? When she'd seen the concern in his eyes as he'd surfaced beside her? When it had been him she'd been thinking of as she'd floated in the semi-darkness, lost in a hopeless fantasy?

There'd been no sound—only a crackling in the air surrounding her skin. She'd opened her eyes and dream had become reality. A splash and a moment later she'd been enveloped in strong arms, his lips nuzzling her neck.

As if nothing had happened. As if his mother hadn't treated her with contempt. She'd bristled, hit him in an effort to get away.

His sincere contrition had chastened her; his defence of her had quelled her resentment. His claim that she enhanced his life had spun her back into her daydream and his kiss had been everything she'd imagined and more. She could no longer deny that she wanted him—rampantly hormonal or for real. Where that took them, she had no idea.

'I don't ever want you to say sorry unless you truly mean it. I'm the one who ought to apologise, for acting like an immature schoolgirl. I should have kept calm this morning and placated her.'

She was blurting out waffle, keeping back the words she really wanted to say.

The incongruity of the situation suddenly hit her. She was in a dimly lit pool, treading water with an almost naked, definitely aroused man whose very presence threatened her safe, isolated, unemotional existence.

'Ethan, I… I can't… Oh, hell, I can't shop.'

Ethan's eyes widened when she swore. His hold loosened, giving her the chance to paddle backwards, putting distance between them. He caught her at the steps, his touch light yet compelling. His hand framed her cheek. His little finger lifted her chin, enabling him to study her face with the intensity she no longer found intimidating. Especially when the warm, caring gleam in his dark blue eyes said he'd wait as long as it took for her to confide in him.

She quivered: from his look, from his hold, from her fear of his reaction. From everything about him.

His lips curled in reassurance. 'If I let you go now, will you explain what that meant when you're dry and dressed?'

When she'd had time to rethink, time to decide to try again. When he'd be corporately attired, in his business persona again.

Her eyes blurred with tears. She needed help—the sooner the better.

'Of course I can shop—that's ridiculous. It's buying stuff to wear when I meet the people in your world that's so daunting. Those fancy boutiques scare me; even the upmarket department stores are discouraging if you don't follow the latest trends. Reading magazines doesn't help, because I have no idea what's suitable for what event.'

'I like you in blue.' Instant and believable. He gently wiped the corners of her eyes with his thumb. 'And your new dresses look great.'

'They were easy. Summer daywear. Once I start meeting people you know I'll be judged on how I look, what I wear. How I speak. I'm afraid I'll fail you.'

Her mouth stayed open, unable to form more words as her brain seized on her last thought. Failing Ethan, having her unsuitable image impact on him, was her number one fear. Perhaps an avoidable situation if one woman had behaved as a loving mother should.

'Why couldn't your mother be more like Louise? Then I'd be able to ask *her* for help.' As soon as the words were spoken she wished them back. Gave a choked snort of a laugh.

'Stupid question. If she were we wouldn't be having this conversation. I need to manage by myself.'

CHAPTER ELEVEN

ETHAN HAD LOST track of the number of times he'd been racked with guilt these last several weeks. There'd been days when it had been as prevalent as breathing.

He'd given Alina a credit card, assuming she'd enjoy shopping. A lot of the women he knew—including his mother—considered having unlimited credit their due right, an essential element in their pursuit of looking stunning on the arm of their partner at any public or private function.

Alina was different. No demands, no preconceived notions. Absolutely no idea how beautiful she was.

He placed his hands on her waist, lifted her onto the side of the pool, and checked his watch.

'We'll meet in the lounge in, say, thirty minutes?'

'For what?'

His pulse hiked at the endearing way her brow wrinkled and her eyes narrowed, as if she expected a reprimand.

'A shopping trip. If I'm the one you're dressing for, I guess I ought to help in the selection.'

His reward was a beaming smile and sparkling eyes—worth any amount of waiting outside changing rooms or carrying umpteen promotional bags. The single experience he'd had accompanying a female shopper had left him disinclined for a repeat, but this was for Alina.

'You mean it?'

He ran his finger down her cheek. 'I told you—I take care of what's mine.'

She was on her feet in an instant, grabbing a towel on the way to the door. He followed, hoisting himself from the water, giving himself a quick dry-off before retrieving his clothes.

* * *

It wasn't working. Ethan felt way out of his depth, wished he'd offered to find someone else to help her. He knew when a woman looked chic, understood the way it transformed her inner attitude. The selected clothes weren't having that effect on Alina. They were in the third boutique, and she'd modelled the tenth outfit.

The assistants had been helpful, yet there was an edge to their attitude he couldn't fathom. Was it him? His obvious antipathy to this environment? Was it sweet, shy Alina, who hadn't looked comfortable at all, posing awkwardly as if she'd rather be anywhere else?

If she lifted her chin, held her shoulders back and stood proud, the effect would be so much better. He groaned inside. He'd promised to help her—failure wasn't an option.

'This isn't working, is it?

Her voice echoed his thoughts as she came up behind him, wearing the dress she'd left home in. He swung round, ready to protest.

Alina stopped his words with two fingers on his lips, ignoring the tingles her action generated.

'You're uncomfortable with it all, and I'm as helpful as seagulls at a beach picnic. I can tell what clothes *aren't* right on me. Others…' She shrugged. 'I have pictures in my head of women attending special events, can't put myself there. Maybe if you lend me some of your confidence it'll solve the problem.'

He gave her a crooked grin and took her hand. 'Not such a good suggestion, huh? I overestimated my expertise with all this. Louise was never a fashion slave, she—'

His eyes lit up, and his smile turned into a heart-stopping grin.

'I'm an *idiot*. Though, in my defence, I've had a few distractions.' He brushed his lips over hers. 'You being number one. Wait here.'

He was back in a few moments, after talking to the head saleswoman. As they left he pulled his mobile from his inside pocket.

'Got your notepad and pen?'

By the time she'd found them, his call had been answered.

'Thanks, Tanya…we're getting there. How are you? Definitely—we'll make it soon. Right now, I need the names of a couple of boutiques Louise patronised. It's for someone special who's recently moved to Sydney.'

He repeated three names and numbers for Alina to write down, promised to arrange a foursome dinner soon, then said goodbye.

'Don't know why I didn't think of her earlier.' He gently flicked her chin. 'Like I said—distractions. She recommends the first one, says the woman there has an uncanny knack of finding the perfect outfit for her customers. Let's ring—find out if she can see us today.'

Maralena's displays were simple, yet very effective, with one model in an appropriate setting in each window. Alina's fingers gripped Ethan's as they entered. She had no doubt how she'd be perceived, how the sales staff would wonder what he saw in her, why he was with her. She received an encouraging squeeze. What she needed was a little of his innate self-assurance.

Inside, there was room to move easily around the minimal racks of clothing, or along the walls containing full-length gowns. The blonde woman who came to meet them was everything Alina wished she was: poised and perfectly groomed, yet clearly approachable. She dispelled any fears with her genuine smile.

'Welcome to Maralena's.' She held out her hand to Ethan. 'Mr James, please accept my deepest sympathy for your loss. Louise always brightened our day when she came shopping, whether she purchased or not.'

'Thank you, she's very much missed. Please, call me Ethan.' He drew Alina forward. 'This is Alina Fletcher, her friend from Spain.'

'I'm Marlena—I tweaked the name a little for business. I'm pleased to meet you, Alina.'

She shook hands, then stood back, giving her new customer a quick and thorough appraisal. Unlike Sophia's critical gaze, it was a professional assessment which didn't bother her at all. To her surprise, the eyes that met hers were approving.

'It will be a pleasure to help you, Alina. Do you have any particular style in mind? Any colour preferences?'

All doubt dissipated, as if Alina's whole body gave a sigh of relief. She'd found the help she so desperately needed.

'I have a list of what I *think* I need.' She sensed Ethan's lips curling. Was tempted to nudge him in the ribs with her elbow. 'I've been backpacking through Europe for a long time, so I'm out of touch with what's in fashion.'

'What suits you is more important. Do you have a time limit today?'

'No.' Emphatic from Ethan. 'Take all the time you want.'

A few minutes ago Alina might have begged him to stay. Now she had no qualms about placing herself in Marlena's hands.

She put her hand on his arm, drew him aside. 'Thank you, Ethan, this is just what I've been hoping to find. You can go back to your office now. I'll be fine.'

His eyes narrowed. He didn't seem convinced.

'Did you leave work unfinished and come home because you thought I was upset?'

'No, because I *knew* you were.'

'I'm not now. The quicker you get back, the earlier you'll come home.'

He grinned. 'Can't fight feminine logic. Okay, I'll go. Call the hire car when you've finished.'

'I promise.'

He kissed her, slow and tender, seemingly oblivious to anyone else in the shop. Her fingers tightened on the strap of her bag, her other hand lifted to cradle his neck. Her lips moved in unison with his.

She felt his muscles tense. Wasn't this a kiss for show? To her it seemed the perfect place. Maybe he didn't, so she broke away.

'I'll see you later.'

'Mmm…' He blinked and his head jerked. Still holding her, he nodded to Marlena. 'Take care of her.' With a final squeeze of her hand, and a husky, 'Tonight…' he walked away.

'Okay, Alina, let's see your list.'

She was escorted into a dressing room. Within minutes she'd confided her lack of success and doubts of her fashion abilities to an empathetic Marlena.

Ethan's mobile rang as he walked into the apartment building a few minutes before seven. Things were settling into place, with the agenda set for a breakfast meeting with his new management team in the morning. Once they were clear on their roles he'd be able to reorganise his working hours.

'Good evening, Father.'

'Ethan. I believe you have a new girlfriend?'

'Yes.' He wondered what spin his mother had put on today's events.

'We'd like to meet her. Does dinner on Saturday night suit you?'

'I'll check with Alina.'

'We'll look forward to seeing you. Goodbye, Ethan.'

He stood in front of the elevator, staring at his mobile,

his gut twisting in regret. He had more cordial conversations with the people he spoke to regarding aspects of renovation or trading with his hotels. Was he destined to be as impersonal as his parents, considering he had their combined DNA?

The idea appalled.

He stabbed at his floor number, tapped his thigh on the journey up and strode purposely to the door. Alina came through from the lounge as he dropped his briefcase on the floor. His mind registered her sweet smile in the same instant as he wrapped her in his arms, burying his face into her silken curls, breathing in their citrus aroma. He relished her warmth, her softness, the way she stood still in his embrace, her only movement being to slide her arms around his waist.

Seconds ticked by. Holding her wasn't enough.

He lifted his head. 'Hi.'

Their kiss was gentle, a mutual giving and taking. So soul-soothing he kept it short rather than risk pushing for more. This was new—something to build on. She was beginning to trust him as a man. He was beginning to reassess who he was.

She leant back in his arms to study his face.

'You caught up?'

Warmth radiated through him. This felt *right*. This was the way homecoming should always be. 'As good as. How did you go?'

'Two outfits which I love. One's here, the other needed some alteration, so I'll pick it up on Friday.'

'Only two?' He grinned down at the face she pulled and kissed the tip of her nose. 'Whatever you feel comfortable with, Alina.'

'The new season stock's arriving in a week or two. By then I'll be bigger. Common sense says to buy what I need as I need it.'

His laughter shook his body. 'Since when did common sense become aligned with fashion shopping?'

'Hey!' She swatted his arm playfully, then froze as she realised what she'd done, eyes widening in shock.

Alina couldn't believe what she'd done. One second he'd been teasing her, the next she'd reciprocated. Completely spontaneously. Without thinking, she'd hit him, as if they'd been friends for a long time. The incredulous look on his face made it worse.

'I…' She tried to break free, suddenly found herself being lifted and carried backwards, to be plonked unceremoniously on the kitchen island. His hands gripped the bench either side of her. His impassive features gave no indication of his thinking. It was like their first meeting, but without the angst filling the room.

'Ethan, I—'

'Alina Fletcher,' he cut in. 'I do believe you are starting to let your true self sneak out from its constrictions.'

She dropped her head. He lifted it with his finger, his thumb grazing her skin. His eyes sparkled with amusement, daring her to act again. The very fact that she wanted to scared her, holding her back. She trembled, held her breath. Then, as if of its own accord, her hand lifted, her fingers covering his on her chin.

The air around them seemed hot and heavy. She couldn't think straight His eyes darkened. His lips curled. Did his body sway closer? Did hers?

He abruptly withdrew his hand, pushing himself upright, shaking his head. 'A cool dip in the pool before dinner?'

Her body flopped. Gratefully, she seized on his suggestion. 'Yes. *Yes.*'

'Don't sound so eager to run, my sweet.' He swung her to the floor, keeping hold for a moment. 'And don't be afraid to show the woman you really are. I like what I've seen so far.'

Not trusting her voice, she gave a quick nod before turning away.

He stopped her with a gentle hand on her arm. 'My father's invited us to dinner on Saturday. I'm so angry with my mother I'm inclined to say no.'

'Delaying the inevitable? I think I'd rather face it now.'

'The way you did with me? I won't let them demean you, Alina.' A softly spoken declaration that demanded compliance. A firm hold she didn't want to break. Commanding blue eyes that enthralled.

'*You* were receptive,' she said. 'They're bound to think I'm trapping you. You're not the type to lose control and forget protection.'

Ethan never had. Even in his testosterone-driven teens he'd always been disciplined. Now, being with Alina every night, inhaling her essence, having her within easy reach, he appreciated how overpowering desire could be.

Anger ground in his gut. At his parents, who judged everyone by high, rigid standards and dismissed any contrary opinions. At himself for allowing them to influence his life, his behaviour. At the fates who had taken his sister's life when the best times were just beginning.

Yet those same fates had brought Alina and his future son or daughter to Sydney. To *him*.

Taking a short step forward, he manoeuvred her into his arms. In the simple act of holding her and stroking her hair he found solace as he reassured her.

'That's all the more reason for us to convince them of the undeniable magnetism between us. If we show them we're happy they'll have to accept it.'

'*Are* you happy?' A muffled plea into his shirt.

He tilted her chin to gaze into lovely despondent eyes and swore silently. Didn't she realise how much her being here meant to him?

'How can I *not* be happy? You've given me the most

precious gift I'll ever have. You are giving a part of Louise back to me. Her child. You had easier options, yet you came to me not knowing how I'd react. You *did* know how my parents would.'

She took a long, shuddering breath, drawing his eyes to her full pink mouth. His body vibrated in response. She had no concept of what she was doing to him. He wasn't sure himself.

'Can we go this week? I'd prefer less time to dwell on it.'

His mobile rang before he could answer her. He grimaced at the caller ID. 'I agree. I've got to take this, so I'll meet you in the pool.'

He walked to his room, trying to focus on building regulations instead of smoky violet eyes and full, inviting lips.

Alina walked away, didn't look back. His words had woven a soothing path through her mind, into her heart. Diminishing her qualms.

You've given me the most precious gift.

So similar to the phrase she'd heard from Louise when those two blue lines had materialised on that vital stick. Validation that she'd made the right decision to contact him now rather than after the birth.

Seven minutes to six on a Thursday evening and his desk was clear. Ethan felt pumped at an achievement he determined would become more routine than not. He conceded that the new promotions, which would become official at midnight on Sunday, made it possible.

He stopped on the way home for handmade chocolates to celebrate. Trying to quell the rush of anticipation, he entered the apartment, silently chuckling at the sci-fi epic music coming from the speakers.

Alina was preparing dinner at the kitchen counter. His eyes drank in her brunette curls, her enticing curves—soon to be curvier. Alluring. Desirable. This attraction was unlike any he'd ever experienced. Because of the situation? Her condition? His unexpected paternity? None of them explained that initial gut-clench when the only knowledge he'd had of her was her name.

She continued working, oblivious to his presence. How near did he have to be before she sensed him?

She had. The moment he'd opened the front door. Trying to quell her quickening heartbeat and ignore the prickling at the back of her neck was a futile exercise. There was nothing to account for her sudden heat rush.

Darn hormones. Why pick *this* pregnancy to play up? The first time—she couldn't prevent the comparisons surfacing—there'd been occasional morning sickness, a few cravings, and manageable backache in the last trimester. She'd been blissfully content, cherished, and pampered by...

She gripped the vegetable peeler till it stung, fought the tears threatening to spill.

His cologne seeped around her. Still no sound or greeting. Was he playing games, waiting for her to acknowledge him? She put down the peeler, pivoted.

Her lungs seized up. Her mouth dried. She sucked in her cheeks and swallowed, trying unsuccessfully to form moisture. Ethan stood there, gazing at her as if she were priceless, unique. When he walked round the island, smiling at her, she couldn't have moved if someone had tossed a grenade.

'You were so engrossed I didn't want to disturb you.' He cupped her chin, restarting her lungs in a short sharp gasp. He drew her to him as if their future was limitless and she leant into him, wanting to be closer. Wanting whatever he was offering.

He kissed her lightly, then deeper when her lips moved under his. When they parted of their own accord he accepted the tacit invitation. The tip of his tongue found hers.

Heat flooded every cell. She tasted a hint of wine, coffee, tightened her hold on his neck, hungry for more.

Her stomach lurched. She wrenched free, clapping her hand over her mouth. Holding an arm across her belly, she bent double, trying not to throw up.

'Alina, what's wrong?'

The anxiety in his tone penetrated her brain. The support of his strong arms steadied her.

'Alina?'

The nausea hit again. Breaking free, she stumbled to the bathroom, crumpled beside the toilet bowl and dry-retched repeatedly. Didn't have time to worry about privacy.

CHAPTER TWELVE

WATER SPLASHED IN the basin and then Ethan was kneeling beside her, offering a damp cloth. She pressed it to her skin, letting the coolness soothe the heat from her humiliation. He'd kissed her and she'd practically thrown up on him.

Why? She'd eaten nothing, done nothing to trigger it. She shivered, couldn't stop, couldn't stem the shame churning in her belly.

'Alina?'

She looked up into blue eyes dark with concern. For the child? A tiny pang of regret hit her heart.

'I'm sorry, Ethan—so sorry. I've no idea what triggered that.'

He gently removed the cloth, tossed it into the sink, then cradled her to his chest.

'Hey, I've got friends with children. Over the years I've heard plenty of stories about so-called morning sickness. Including the fact that it should be named any-time-anywhere-for-no-apparent-reason sickness. Feeling better?'

She touched the stubble on his chin, managed a rueful half-smile. 'I think so.'

He helped her up, waited until she'd rinsed her mouth, then aided her walk back to the lounge. Sat beside her, his arm around her shoulders.

'Do you want some chocolate to take away the taste? I brought a box home.'

'Peppermint tea with plain biscuits will be more settling. I can get them.'

'You stay put. You're sure you're all right?'

For his sake she nodded, forcing a smile.

His eyes narrowed as if he wasn't convinced. 'My book

contains a whole chapter on morning sickness, and its triggers. I think I'd better reread it.'

She put her hand on his thigh. 'Thank you for…for being there.'

'Always.' He kissed the top of her head. 'I'll be right back.'

Ethan went to the kitchen, turned on the kettle and sank against the bench, taut hands rubbing his face. He'd had to fight for composure in the bathroom; he still shook inside.

Seeing her sickly pallor as she'd hunched over the toilet had scared the hell out of him. Hearing the rasp in her voice had affected him in a way nothing had before. Because he'd feared for their baby? Or because Alina had been hurting? Both had ripped him apart.

On his return, he felt the taut knot in his gut ease at the tinge of colour in her cheeks. He gave her the tea and biscuits, scrutinised her as he drank his tea, the same flavour. If he had to he'd make herb tea his regular drink at home. Just in case.

'I feel better. Thank you.' She started to rise.

He stopped her, catching hold of her arm. 'You're sure?'

Her smile was steadier. 'I'm fine.'

Alina went to the kitchen, where the salad she'd been preparing waited, not realising he was behind her until he spoke.

'What can I do to help?'

Help? He hadn't offered before. She'd never been sick before. 'I can manage. You go do whatever you had planned.'

He hesitated, his cobalt eyes gleaming with an emotion she didn't dare try to decipher. The new upheaval in her abdomen had nothing to do with her being pregnant.

'Go. I can handle kebabs and salad.'

Why did it take so much effort to drag her eyes from him? She forced herself to concentrate on the half-finished carrot.

'I'll call you when it's ready.'

The grunt he made was unintelligible and utterly male. It tickled the edge of her memory. Was quickly relegated to the clouds, where it belonged. She sneaked a peek as he left, wished she hadn't.

His grey shirt was moulded to muscles toned to perfection from swimming and working out. Her gaze was drawn down past his trim waist to firm buttocks that flexed with each step. Her breath quickened. This was crazy. She was checking him out like a teenager.

Her knees shook. She flattened her hands on the benchtop for support, barely aware of the peeler handle digging into her palm. She craved ice-cold water, cursed the heat flooding her body. Daren't risk walking to the tap.

He spun round, catching her off guard. 'By the way...' His mouth stayed open. His eyes widened. He grinned—a conspiratorial I-know-what-you're-thinking grin. Moved slowly towards her, holding her spellbound with captivating blue eyes.

The music from the speakers reached a dramatic crescendo, heightening the atmosphere. It had hardly registered until then. Now it filled the space between them. The width of the room. The breadth of the kitchen island. The length of his arm.

She faced him, her brain in a quandary as warnings of danger sparred with reminders of his kisses. He halted at that arm's distance, his eyes now sombre, his features composed. A façade. She noted his rigid stance, the way he'd fisted his hands.

'Are you game to try again?'

She heard the caution in his voice. The kiss? He'd initiated it; she was the one who'd allowed it to become more intimate. This time there'd be no intoxicating flavour of wine or coffee. She guessed he'd used mouthwash, had seen him drink peppermint tea. Just in case.

Until Tuesday's highly emotional embrace in the pool

his kisses had been mostly tender—a gentle way of gradually familiarising her with his touch. Their intimate kiss, though interrupted, had been a giant advance in their relationship. A definite declaration that he found her attractive. Desired her.

There'd been no mention of their sleeping together, but she couldn't deny her body responded to his virility, couldn't stop his image invading her thoughts. Oh, Lord, had her nausea been triggered by guilt, by feelings of infidelity?

He quietly waited for her answer. They both knew there was only one way to resolve the issue.

'Yes.'

Her single husky word had him enfolding her and gently covering her mouth with his. The music faded. The air around them crackled. Time stood still. His lips moved slowly, persuasively over hers. His hands stroked unhurriedly, without pressure. He kept space between their bodies.

Her fingertips inched up his chest until they touched his skin. His body trembled. His earthy Ethan aroma filled her lungs, clouding her brain. Dominating her will. Freeing her will. Her fingers twisted into his hair. Her lips parted.

Ethan held his breath, every muscle tensed in a supreme effort not to sweep his tongue inside to explore the sweetness he'd sampled earlier. Being restrained with a woman was a new experience for him. Mutual attraction led to equally satisfying sex. No strings. No commitment.

This was different. For indefinable reasons. After the initial spontaneous jolt everything he'd done had been influenced by the fact she was pregnant. Or had it? When they were apart she was in his head. When they were together he couldn't stop looking, touching and inhaling her essence, fresh as spring.

He slowly traced a line with his tongue around the soft,

moist inside of her lips. She gasped, taking in his breath. Quivered under his roaming hands. His body hardened and he shuffled his feet, widening the gap. Sliding his tongue in deeper, he cautiously stoked hers, fully prepared to stop at the slightest hint of distress.

There was none—only a timid response that almost had him hauling her closer. There was no sense of time. It felt as if he were standing on the edge of a precipice, knowing there was something wonderful waiting if he'd just let himself fall. With a rough shuddering breath he lifted his head to gaze into clear, shining eyes.

'I guess it was one of those inexplicable pregnancy things, huh?'

Her spontaneous laugh zapped his already strained senses.

'Seems like it.'

To double-check, he kissed her briefly, firmly. 'So— you feel okay?' His pulse kicked up even higher when she flick-licked her bottom lip and smiled, as if she'd tasted something delicious.

'Go—or you won't be eating dinner tonight.'

He went, deeming it an option he'd happily choose.

On Saturday morning Alina paced restlessly round the apartment. Something was itching at her brain—wouldn't surface, wouldn't go. She'd booted up her computer. Closed it down. She'd changed, walked into the gym, turned, walked out. Changed back into jeans and a top. Curled up with her embroidery, packed it away after a few stitches. Every room was tidy; everything was clean.

She glanced at the kitchen calendar and the notation for tonight: *Dinner with parents*. An unavoidable ordeal to be endured. She was convinced they wouldn't be adding her to their regular guest list unless they wanted Ethan there too. And he'd given her the impression he'd happily miss most of their organised events.

A picture flashed into her head at the sight of today's date. She quickly blocked it out. She didn't do special days.

Tenuous, ghost-like memories nipped at the edge of her mind, wouldn't be dismissed. Tears welled in her eyes as memories crashed back. Her mother-in-law's birthday. *Mum.* Unlike Sophia, she'd welcomed Alina, drawn her into the family and loved her as a daughter. She'd be lucky if Sophia tolerated her for the time she was here.

Ethan had family and friends for support. She didn't begrudge him any of them; he'd need all the help available next year. She had no one. Unless…

You only have to reach out. There'll be no recriminations, only love and understanding.

Her thumb trembled as she scrolled through her phone for the name and number. A short tear-choked conversation later she grabbed her handbag and ran out the door, heading for the one person she could tell anything. Though she wouldn't reveal the whole truth.

Where was she? Ethan drummed his fingers on his office desk, forced himself to focus on the computer screen, rereading figures he hadn't taken in before. They were good. His mindset wasn't. He exited the program, scowling. Why hadn't she returned his calls?

He hadn't been concerned when she hadn't answered her mobile or the apartment phone at first, assuming she was in the gym area. Now, however… He checked his watch for the umpteenth time. Ten past twelve—over two hours since his first call.

He rotated sideways, staring at the city skyline, seeing only her face, wondering why she'd been so subdued this morning after they'd spent two enjoyable evenings together. Maybe it was one of the mood swings detailed in his book.

He grabbed his phone again, hesitated with his hand in mid-air. It rang, vibrating in his palm. Wrong caller ID. After quickly dealing with the matter, he went to the coffee machine. With refilled mug in hand he paced the floor, trying to convince himself it was normal trepidation given her condition.

In truth, she'd triggered something inside him from the moment they'd met—something incomprehensible. She didn't fit his long-term plan in any way. Grieving and haunted, she was determined not to stay in Australia. He wouldn't stop her leaving, though he'd give her support for as long as she wished. He wasn't perfect, but the child she carried needed a parent as hang-up-free as possible. And right now *he* needed her to answer her damn phone.

Grabbing a printed report on his Gold Coast hotel, he sprawled on the long sofa, his mug and mobile on the low table by his side. Normally he'd have been elated that the renovations were on schedule and under budget.

Startled by his ringtone, he almost knocked over his coffee in his haste to grab his phone. His adrenaline spiked when he saw the caller ID. He sucked in air, tried to project a calm he definitely didn't feel.

'Alina.'

'Ethan, I'm sorry.'

Her distressed voice chilled his heart. Feigned calm flew out of the window. He was on his feet, striding to grab his jacket as he spoke.

'What's wrong? Where are you? I'll come for you.' Hell, he felt as desperate as he sounded.

'No! It's nothing. I'm an idiot, that's all.' Breathless. Anxious.

He stilled. Wished he was there so he could see her face, read how upset she really was. 'Tell me.'

'I went to visit my husband's aunt. We sat in the garden and my bag was inside, on her sofa. I missed all your calls.'

Spontaneous laughter surged up his throat and burst out at the simple explanation. She was all right. She was safe. He perched on his desk, torn between pure relief and self-reproach for worrying so much.

'It's not funny. I've got six messages from you.'

Her slightly miffed tone was endearing.

'I'm just glad you're okay. Where are you now?'

'Sitting on a bus.'

He wanted her here, wanted to hold her. Wanted to shake her for scaring him. Kiss her until she melted in his arms.

'Why were you calling?' she added.

'My father rang, asking if we could arrive half an hour earlier tonight.'

She was always ready on time—he could have called when he left the office. Then he wouldn't have had two hours of angst. Or heard her sweet, apologetic voice.

'No last-minute reprieve, huh?'

'I'm afraid not. You're sure you're okay?' He sure as hell hadn't been, two minutes ago.

'I'm fine. I'm truly sorry for worrying you, Ethan.'

'Worrying me? You, my sweet, are putting me through emotions I can't even name.'

He ended the call, huffing the air from his lungs as he tossed his phone onto his desk. He wasn't normally prone to panic. If there was a problem he coolly and methodically searched for a solution.

Was this new apprehension going to be part of his future? A normality of being a parent? He'd probably be overloaded with advice and disaster stories once his friends found out about his impending fatherhood. Knowing they'd be there for him and his child, he'd take it all in the spirit it would be given.

Alina had said she had no family, and yet there was this aunt—her husband's aunt. And maybe other relatives? How close was she to them? Close enough to want to re-establish contact. Why deny them before? Why turn to them now?

Hell, he'd hardly learnt anything about her; she kept her guard up tight. That hadn't been an issue when they'd met and agreed to marry for the child's sake. Now she was real to him, she was special in a way he'd never felt before. *He* wanted to be the one she reached out to for support.

Alina wriggled uneasily on the bus seat. Unflappable, down-to-earth Ethan had been rattled until she'd explained. If that teenager texting with his head bent hadn't bumped into her, she wouldn't have thought to check her phone. An incident she'd skip mentioning. She accepted his reasons for being over-protective, preferred not to give him cause to be more so.

She replayed his words in her mind. He'd seemed genuinely concerned for her. The tenderness in his voice during that last remark had almost had her saying, *Ditto.*

Once he'd recovered from the initial shock of her pregnancy he'd been very supportive. He hadn't pressured her for the details of her life she'd rather keep private. And, while his physical attraction to her was obvious, his manner had been conciliatory, letting her set the boundaries.

It was parent confrontation time. Ethan glanced at the dashboard clock and eased his foot on the accelerator. Alina sat quietly, hadn't said much at all since he'd arrived home. There'd only been time for him to grab a quick shower and change before leaving. He'd still had the reality of her having relatives on his mind, hadn't wanted to talk either. Even if he could figure out how to bring up the subject, now was not the time.

He glanced over. She was staring ahead, pale and rigid, as if being driven to the guillotine. Her left hand was hidden but he'd bet it was doing that finger dance. His heart wrenched. Sweet, brave Alina, with demons he could only imagine, was prepared to confront his ultra-judgemental parents for *his* benefit, and he was jealous because she'd called someone who'd be on her side.

Jealous! No, he couldn't be. He flicked her another look, felt a deep surge of tenderness. Accepted the reality of that emotion, new for him.

Taking his hand from the wheel, he gently covered hers for a few seconds. 'You are beautiful, Alina Fletcher. I'm proud to have you by my side—any time, anywhere.'

His reward was a tentative smile. He wanted more.

Alina toyed with her hair, smoothed her skirt over her slightly rounded belly. Was it too late to ask him to take her home? Too late. Too cowardly. They were the child's nearest relatives, next to him. Maybe they'd mellow with age; grandparents often did. She'd be gone soon, so any adverse judgement on her shouldn't impact on Ethan or the baby.

The vibes she'd picked up from Ethan had exacerbated her tension, turning the butterflies in her tummy to turbulent judders. She wished she were anywhere else—like on the Manly Ferry, steaming across the heads, wind blowing her hair, spray cooling her cheeks. And Ethan surrounding her, his chest at her back, arms at her sides. Shielding her. Protective.

Her eyes widened and she pressed back in her seat as they drove through the gates of the formidable James couple's opulent home. It was a two-storey, luxurious mansion, like something out of a magazine, set in flawless landscaped gardens. The back area was as impressive as the front.

They pulled up. Reluctant to leave the security of the vehicle, she sat, vaguely aware of him moving around the front of the vehicle, opening her door and hunkering down beside her. Gentle fingers stroked her arm. Empathetic eyes met hers when she looked up.

'Remember, this is all for show. The house. The decor. Their attitude. Real life is you, me and our baby.'

His hand splayed protectively over her stomach, radiating warmth with his touch, diminishing her fears. A little.

'You won't be left alone with either of them. They can insinuate all they like; they'll only learn what we choose to tell them.'

Unbuckling her seatbelt, he helped her out. She gripped his hand, felt his flesh dent under her nails. 'I'm worried I'll let you down.'

He shook his head. 'Impossible. You're the bravest woman I've ever met. Our marriage, our lives, are exactly that. *Ours.* Don't forget, it's they who are on notice.'

Giving her that special Ethan smile, he raised her hand and pressed his lips to her palm. Electrifying quivers sped along her veins, through her, settling in her stomach. A lovely, if slightly scary feeling. She smiled back and he led her round to the front steps. She was thankful her flowing dress hid her condition, grateful for the strength of his fingers entwined with hers.

CHAPTER THIRTEEN

ETHAN RANG THE DOORBELL, wishing they were home... alone. Alina's trembling vibrated through his palm and his heart twisted. Taking her into his arms, he kissed her for comfort, keeping it tender. Until he heard her contented sigh. Until she softened into him.

'Try to contain yourself, Ethan. There's no excuse for a public exhibition.'

Alina flinched. Ethan barely stirred at the caustic remark from behind him, though his gut tightened with irritation. Then he reluctantly lifted his head, scanning the large empty garden before grinning wryly.

'Hardly public, Father.'

His chest expanded as he smiled down at Alina, seeing her sweet blush and the glow in her eyes. *He'd* done that—taken her from apprehension to desire. With a kiss that contained a promise for later.

'Alina, this is my father—Martin James. Father, I'd like you to meet Alina Fletcher.'

His father inclined his head towards her. 'Please come in, Ms Fletcher.'

Embarrassment flooded Ethan at the stilted remark. He stiffened, quite prepared to walk away. Alina forestalled him, moving forward, hand extended. Leaving his father no choice but to accept her greeting.

'Thank you, Mr James. It's very kind of you and your wife to invite me.' Deliciously tongue in cheek.

The air whooshed from his lungs. He stared in admiration at this poised woman whom he'd sensed had been ready to bolt a few minutes ago. She'd been surprising him from the moment they met. Anticipation of the months ahead zipped along his veins.

They entered together, Alina's hand in his once more. Was she comparing the cold, immaculate decor to the welcoming, comfy atmosphere of Louise's courtyard home in Barcelona? He did—every time he came here.

A sharp intake of breath at his side made him aware he was crushing her fingers. He loosened his grip, gave her an apologetic glance—and was completely thrown when she winked her left eye at him. A simple act that triggered a fuzzy memory of something shared. Of concealed laughter.

Alina noticed his startled expression, but had no time to jog his memory. Sophia James was waiting for them. She lifted her chin, quite prepared to confront the woman who would one day take great pleasure in telling her son, *I told you so.*

He knew it, accepted it, and would handle it with his natural diplomacy. At least he'd have the consolation of his son or daughter.

Why the sudden depression? She'd asked for her freedom—had to have it. Had to keep moving. No ties. No commitments. Keep the memories blocked out. She feared there was now going to be so much more she'd have to not remember.

Sophia was standing regally, ready to be greeted. She reminded Alina of the titled women of history—so proud, so extremely conscious of their presumed status in life. With another quick squeeze of her hand Ethan led her forward, not letting go as he greeted his mother with a light kiss on her proffered cheek.

'Mother, you've already met Alina—though I understand it was a brief encounter.'

Alina hoped she was the only one who heard the nuances in his introduction. Felt a flush of warmth at his championship.

'Yes, it was quite a surprise. Welcome, Alina.' Sophia gave her an obligatory social air-kiss on both cheeks. 'Shall we all sit for drinks?' She raised a perfectly trimmed eyebrow at Alina. 'Do you have a favourite cocktail, my dear?

'Iced water, thank you. I don't drink.'

Spoken so woodenly she didn't recognise her voice. She cringed inside at the pointed look exchanged between the older couple. This wasn't a family dinner; it was a formal… She didn't know what it was.

She *did* know she had the support of the man whose firm hand now guided her to the deep-cushioned sofa. For as long as she stayed in Australia—maybe even longer. His innate integrity ensured that he'd never betray or disown her. Life would have been so much better if only this staid, society-obsessed couple had appreciated the genuine affable qualities of their children.

Ethan kept his arm around her, even after a pointed scowl from his father when he gave them their drinks. He now fully comprehended the primitive male urge to protect a mate. It reinforced his determination to have everyone believe that he had married for love.

'How is the Gold Coast hotel coming along, Ethan? Is the projected opening still viable?'

'Yes, Father, but I'd rather not talk business. This is family time. Mother, I hear the charity night at the opera house you helped organise was a great success?'

'Thank you, Ethan. I'd hoped to see you there.'

'Not my scene. To support your cause I did buy three double tickets, as a bonus for ardent followers at work.'

'Opera's an acquired taste. You never gave it a chance,' his father stated.

'Simone attended with her parents,' his mother chimed in. 'She was very gracious with her condolences, and apologised for missing Louise's funeral due to a modelling assignment in New York.'

Her voice slowed as Ethan's head jerked up. His brow furrowed as a powerful surge of emotion ripped through him. *Louise. The wink.*

He flicked a quick glance at Alina, whose gaze was focused on his mother.

His sister's favourite ploy as a child—and sometimes in adulthood—had been winking, always with the left eye, to defuse a tense situation. It was one that had so often had them squirming in their seats, trying not to laugh. Alina had deliberately given him a reminder of happy times.

'Simone is the daughter of friends, Alina. She and Ethan have been close for *years*. Now, tell us about yourself. Do you have a profession?' Sophia's words were syrup-sweet, politely phrased with a definite hint of disdain.

Alina met her condescending brown eyes full-on, thought of how Louise had suffered because of this woman's attitude, and remembered her happiness when the procedure had worked. In less than a heartbeat all her apprehension evaporated.

'No. I've never needed one. I speak three languages fluently; get by in a few others. Travelling through Europe has taught me more than I'd have learnt at any university. Hands-on life is a great teacher.'

'Oh, so how do you make a living?' Slightly more acidic.

'By accepting honest casual work in a variety of places and industries.'

She felt disapproval radiate through the room. Should she continue? She hated deceit, even when it was warranted or unavoidable. This wasn't.

'Barcelona was my base. That's where I became friends with Leon and Louise.'

'So that's where you two met? Ethan…' Sophia stopped talking, flashed a wary look at her son.

'Please continue, Mother.' Ethan's arm tightened around

her shoulders. His flat, calm tone should have served as a warning. His mother missed it.

'I realise dealing with everything was paramount, but you never mentioned meeting anyone there. It hasn't even been two months since the accident, and she's...'

Another hesitation. Alina guessed it was very unusual for this very outspoken woman.

'She's what?' Harsher. A definite signal to back off.

'Oh, come on, Ethan. What do you expect?' Martin James obviously couldn't contain himself. 'You chose not to tell us about her, when you met or how. She's obviously led a nomadic life, with no ties or responsibilities. Now she's moved in with you. I assume she's not working?'

Alina's heart pounded; her stomach heaved. She heard the words, understood the implications but not the undertones. They seemed to be talking of someone or something else, using her as the target. She'd been prepared for personal questions or subtle jibes—not this blatant hostility.

No one had ever treated her this way—as if she weren't good enough to be in their company. Swinging her head from wife to husband, she saw only harsh dissatisfaction. She wanted out. She turned to Ethan—and froze.

Cold chills swept over her as she recalled his pained features after he'd read the surrogacy documents, his fury when she'd suggested his family might not want the baby. Right now he was rigidly controlled, icy. Much more intimidating.

Ethan had never been angrier. Not when a trusted friend had betrayed his loyalty. Not when a long-time girlfriend had cheated on him. Not even when a stupid, avoidable thing like a faulty brake had taken his sister and his best friend from him.

The rage building inside him was a culmination of years of their haranguing him to conform to their views, virulent criticism of his own choices. Their deplorable treatment of Leon and Louise. Plus a deep conviction that defending Alina was paramount—above anything he had ever done. Or ever would.

He rose to his feet, taking her with him, acutely aware that his teeth had ground together and his free hand had balled into a fist. One glance at Alina's face and his only thought was to get out of there, so he could beg her forgiveness for subjecting her to this poisonous atmosphere.

'This charade is over.'

'Ethan, we—'

He flicked his hand, silencing his mother, dismissing both parents. Tenderly brushing a curl from Alina's brow, he kissed her forehead. 'Let's go home, darling.'

He turned his head as they reached the door, subliminally noting their gobsmacked expressions.

'Stay away from our home. Any calls will not be answered or returned.'

The son who'd always been the mediator had finally rebelled.

Ethan refrained from gunning his car as they left the property. The fierce urge to put distance between him and his parents was tempered by the knowledge that he had the most precious cargo.

He had no doubt they'd blame Alina, having always previously claimed to their friends that it was business commitments that had caused his withdrawal from their social world. *Damn. Idiot.* He ought to have insisted their first meeting be held in a restaurant, where they'd have had no choice but to be socially polite.

Probably wouldn't have changed the end result.

He glanced across, met wounded eyes in an ash-white face and hit the brake, swinging into the kerb. He flung off his seatbelt, hauling Alina into his arms as he fumbled for her clasp. Holding her against his heart, breathing in her subtle aroma, was so liberating after the overpowering room they'd left behind, his anger began to dissipate.

'I needed this. Needed your sweetness.' He stroked her back, brushed her hair with his lips. 'I'm sorry, Alina— forgive me for taking you there. You've done nothing to deserve the way they treated you. Nothing.'

She gave a muted sound suspiciously like a sob into his chest. He threaded his fingers thorough her hair and tilted her head up. Wanted to wipe the deep sorrow in her eyes away for ever. Hated that he didn't know how. Her trembling lips broke his heart.

'Why are they like that? No one's ever treated me as if I'm nothing, not good enough to be polite to. *No one*—in all the places I've been.'

'And they'll never get another chance.'

'No.' She pushed away, shaking her head. 'They're your parents, Ethan, your family. Don't lock the door. Life can change in a split second and then it's too late to go back. We both know that.'

He threw his head back against his seat, closed his eyes. He did know, and it hurt like hell. Her self-deprecating laugh penetrated the anguish.

'I think, somewhere deep in my head, I expected them to accept me the way Colin's parents did.'

His eyes flew open at the mention of her husband. She sat, half turned towards him, hands in her lap, eyes downcast. He held his breath, didn't dare move a muscle.

'We met when he was twenty, still at uni. I was only seventeen, and a major distraction to his studies, yet his parents welcomed me, treating me like a loved daughter. They were so thrilled when...'

Lord, it was so hard not to reach for her as she painfully struggled for the next word.

'When M... M... Michael was born. We were a real family.'

She went silent. Seemed immobile. Waiting was excruciating, but he sensed there was more she wanted to say. For her own sake.

'They're all gone. I'm not.' Her head came up, eyes big and dark with despair. 'Why just me?' She began to tremble violently.

Now he moved, spurred by the stabbing pain that raked him. He enfolded her into his warmth. Desperate to comfort her, desperate for comfort himself. She'd been the only survivor. She might have died too.

Headlights lit up the windscreen. Alina pulled back, blinking, trying to regain composure. She hadn't spoken about the accident since it had happened. Why now? Why to Ethan?

'Take me home. Please.'

He didn't move, kept a loose hold on her, his features grey and heartrending, his eyes dark and tortured.

'Ethan?'

His shoulders shook as he shuddered. His eyes refocused.

'Home. Yes, let's go home.'

When they arrived at the apartment Alina stayed Ethan's hand when he reached for the light switch.

'Leave them off.'

The lights from the city gave the room a soft glow, a more confiding atmosphere. He'd defended her against his parents' insinuations; he deserved to know more than the half-reveal she'd given him. At least the meagre details she hadn't been able to avoid learning.

She poured herself a glass of water, and took her defensive place on the settee. Ethan followed with a cold beer—the drink he usually favoured in afternoons. When he saw the way she was huddled in the corner his brow furrowed, but he chose the other end, folding one leg up, his body towards her.

She drank half the glass to clear her throat, then fixed her gaze on the window. There was no emotion in her flat, detached voice.

'We'd been on a week's holiday, touring places near the New South Wales and Victoria border. The plan was to stop for the night, then drive home. Colin and his dad were both careful drivers, changing over whenever we stopped. It was getting dark, and I heard them talk of the next town being about thirty minutes away before I fell asleep.'

Ethan gripped the cold metal can so hard it began to buckle. His throat was so tight he could hardly breathe. He knew what was coming, didn't want to hear it. Couldn't avoid it. Couldn't take his eyes from her pale, impassive face and blank, unseeing eyes. He watched her drain her glass, swallow with difficulty, and shiver as she drew in breath.

'Everything's a blur after that. Screams, thuds, screeching metal. Voices and sirens. That hospital smell. I don't remember who told me. Someone in the corridor mentioned a kangaroo and a semitrailer. I didn't want to know—never want to know.' Her voice broke. 'I had concussion from a head wound, lots of cuts and bruises. And they all died.'

Her empty glass fell into her lap. She hunched over, covering her face with her hands.

Ethan's hand shook as he put down his drink and automatically moved her glass to the table. Her words had torn an agonising path into the depths of his soul. A tiny twist of fate and he'd never have known her.

Would she push him away if he reached for her? His confidence faltered.

'Alina?' Desperate. Begging to help her. 'I'm here. Whenever you want or need me.'

She lifted tortured eyes that stared at him as if she wondered who he was, why he was there. Then her face cleared and she flung herself into his arms.

'Ethan. Hold me.'

He cradled her as close as humanly possible, needing to reassure her. Needing reassurance himself. *She was meant to live. Meant to have this baby with him. Meant to love again one day.*

'Hold me tight, Ethan. Hold me. Please don't let me be alone.'

He held her. For as long as she'd let him, he'd hold her.

'You're not alone any more, darling. I'm not going anywhere. Not without you. I'll be here to hold you, comfort and care for you. You, my beautiful, courageous Alina.'

He caressed her back, murmured words from his heart, knowing she might not understand. Knowing only that he needed to voice how much she'd come to mean to him. The baby she carried was an added joy.

He kept talking, even after her body softened in sleep against him. He had no idea when she'd be ready to hear his admission in the cold light of day.

A long-forgotten sensation infiltrated Alina's brain, enticing her to wake; less pleasant ones held her in limbo. A familiar earthy aroma surrounded her. A light breeze stirred her hair. She moved, yet the warm wall at her side stayed. Warmth spread from the weight on her stomach.

Her senses kicked in. Her eyes fluttered, flew open. She was lying on her back, early-morning light allowing her to see an unknown painting on the wrong wall. A white-sleeve-covered arm stretched out from under her neck. She was in Ethan's arms. In his bed. Still wearing her dress.

Her last recollection was of Ethan twisting them both so they lay prone on the settee, of his hands soothing her to sleep. He'd done as she'd pleaded, had cradled her. Hadn't left her on her own.

She turned her head. He lay on his side, his chest moving in steady rhythm. Hassle-free in sleep, his features were softer, the tiny lines at the corners of his eyes less obvious. His stubbled jaw was strangely appealing. He slept so peacefully for a man whose world had been blown apart. By her.

She arched her neck. To wake the sleeping Prince with a kiss? Crazy notion. She rolled towards the edge of the bed.

'Alina?' Slumber-rough and drowsy.

His hand caught her arm, slipped off, and she slid onto the floor.

'It's late. I have things to do.'

Like run from an awkward situation.

CHAPTER FOURTEEN

ETHAN HAD THE table set when Alina arrived in the dining area, calm and guarded. She quickly sat down without speaking, not giving him the chance to be polite. He understood her reticence, hoped she'd still feel able to talk about her family.

She flicked a glance at him as he put a mug of peach tea in front of her. A delicate rosy hue coloured her skin. Where was the feistiness she'd shown in the past?

He felt her gaze follow him as he took his seat, grabbed his favourite cereal and filled his bowl.

'That was cowardly of me.'

Subdued tone. Why was she so nervous? Waiting for her to elucidate, he prayed her confession hadn't caused a regression in their growing relationship.

'When I woke up in your bed I bolted like a naive teenager.'

He nodded. 'A natural reaction after your revelations, Alina.'

She filled her bowl with fruity nut muesli, kept her head down while she ate, as if mulling over an important issue.

'Was there a woman in your life when I came?'

He spluttered on his coffee. Hell, she kept finding new ways to surprise him.

'There hasn't been anyone for a long time. I swear there will be no one as long as you are with me.'

Her nod was barely perceptible. She swallowed as she averted her gaze, reinforcing her apprehension. Hidden under the table, her left hand would be performing its ritual dance.

'Do… Do you expect… Want me to move into your room after the wedding?'

She completely took his breath away with that one. His jaw dropped; adrenaline zapped through his veins. He'd been trying to work out how to introduce the topic gently; she'd come right out with it. He leant back, studying her, wondering if she realised how courageous and strong she was.

'Alina Fletcher, you are amazing. I've bulldozed you into agreements you'd rather run a mile from. My actions have rekindled harrowing memories you'd prefer were left buried. Yet you offer compromises which will reinforce our child's parentage.'

Her eyes widened as he spoke. The soft blush he'd begun to anticipate and adore tinged her cheeks. Across the table was too far a distance. Pushing his chair away, he walked around it, took her hand and lifted her to her feet. Cupped her cheek.

'Having you in my arms as I fell asleep felt better than anything I can remember. As if protecting you and our baby gives my life true meaning for the first time. I'd like to feel that way every night, but the choice is yours, Alina. Now, after we're married or never. I want you there only if it's where *you* want to be.'

She placed her hand over his heart, her lips curling into a sweet smile and a warm glow flickering in her eyes.

'It felt nice.' She glanced away, breathed in, then met his eyes again. 'Can we talk about Colin's aunt and uncle? Jean and Ray?'

Any subject was fine by him. Every conversation revealed a little more of who they were and brought them closer. He settled her back into her seat.

Alina gathered the thoughts that had tumbled through her mind as she'd showered and dressed. Looking into Ethan's sympathetic eyes, she suddenly found it easy.

'They were the ones who held it all together for me after… Well, you know. They and the solicitor arranged everything—cleared the house and sold it, put everything in storage.'

She stopped, turned her head to stare at the floor. Looked at him again.

'They took me in and cared for me, even though they were grieving too. I owed them so much and I ran. Fled the country. I phoned or wrote occasionally, and sent postcards of the places I visited. Yesterday she was so welcoming… refused to let me feel guilty.'

'Because she understands. You needed time and distance to heal. I'd like to meet them. And I think you'd like them to be at our wedding.'

'Yes, very much.'

'After we've eaten, ring and see if they're home today.'

Unlucky to see the bride before the wedding? *Yeah, right— that had really worked for her before.*

Sophia James had probably insisted that Louise follow tradition. And Alina hadn't been able to deny Jean's request after she'd been so supportive, even promising to keep the wedding a secret.

Ethan had won Jean and Ray over with his charm and sincerity, convincing them that Alina was the only woman he'd ever wanted to marry. Jean truly believed he loved her. Only Alina knew he wanted to ensure the baby's right to his name.

After a teasing protest he had agreed to let Alina and Jean spend two nights in the hotel suite in order to shop and prepare. His compromise had been being allowed to have a short time alone with Alina the night before the ceremony.

He'd sat beside her in the lounge, took her hand and pressed his lips to her knuckles.

'Everything had to be arranged so quickly we didn't follow many of the usual traditions. This one I can make right.'

Before she could speak he stunned her by dropping to one knee without relinquishing his hold.

'Alina Fletcher, will you marry me tomorrow? Be my wife for as long as you feel you can?'

Her heart lurched at the hitch in his voice on the second question. Her eyes misted; her throat choked up. She looked into sincere cobalt eyes and her answer came easily.

'Yes, I'll marry you, Ethan.' She refused to think about the time limit right now.

He pulled a flat black box engraved with a familiar jeweller's name from his jacket. The exquisite amethyst pendant was a flawless match for her engagement ring. Another thoughtful gift she wasn't sure she deserved.

She stared wide-eyed at this man who'd so drastically changed her life, pushed and cajoled her in matters he deemed important, eased off and given her freedom in others. Like where she slept. Knowing she was attracted to him, yet still unsure of herself, she hadn't slept with him again. As promised, he hadn't mentioned it.

Over the last two weeks they'd slipped into an easy friendship she wanted to maintain though it was inexplicably frustrating sometimes. Hormones again?

'It's lovely, Ethan. Why…?'

'Because I wanted to.'

His lips covered hers in a long tender kiss. She slid the box onto the couch, leant in and wound her arms around his neck. Somehow she ended up in his lap on the floor, wishing he could stay.

When he left his whispered, 'I'll miss you…' was as tender as his kiss.

The wedding party was waiting for them in the roof garden. She had no reason to stall. Her hair shone with new highlights, its longer length framing her face and curling on her neck. The make-up applied by a beautician was light and perfect. Her long chiffon dress, shimmering with shades of lilac and silver, fell softly over her burgeoning bump. Her new necklace completed the illusion.

This wasn't the shy girl in a white princess gown who had trembled with eager anticipation eleven years ago. The woman staring at her today was a mature stranger, fulfilling a vow to friends. No wildly beating heart. No dreams of eternal love. Strip off the trappings and tonight's ceremony was just a formal recognition of the decision Ethan had made to remedy a family dilemma.

Everything changed the moment she stepped out of the elevator. He was watching for her, impeccably dressed in a dark suit, white shirt and dark blue tie, his brilliant cobalt gaze immediately zoning in on hers. A dashing knight waiting for his princess.

Her feet refused to move forward. Sensations cascaded through her brain, impossible to separate. Except for the one certainty she'd clung to since consenting to his scheme—her trust in this man, and her absolute belief that he'd never hurt or betray her.

Her palms began to sweat as they gripped her orchid and fern bouquet. Her insides melted in a rush of heat while her heartbeat crashed into a rock 'n' roll drum rhythm.

A gentle nudge came from behind her. 'He's waiting for you, Alina.'

Not any more. He strode forward, eyes gleaming, his radiant smile just for her. Taking her hands, he drew her to him, the rough timbre of his voice revealing his emotion. 'Exquisite. Unforgettable.'

Through misty eyes she was vaguely aware of Jean moving past her to join the others, glimpsed a photographer beside the celebrant. The city noises faded until there was only Ethan holding her, surrounded by a neon-enhanced darkening blue sky.

His lips touched hers lightly, reverently. In an instant her mind cleared. Her reservations dissipated. She kissed him back, standing on tiptoe for deeper contact. The tremor that shook his body echoed in hers. They walked together to the flower festooned arch where she relinquished her bouquet, allowing them to join hands as they stood face to face.

At this service the male response was calmer, clearer than the one so long ago. It ought to be impassive. Yet there was something in the resonance of his voice, in the pressure of his grasp and in the depths of his eyes that chipped at the barricades guarding her heart. She replied with the vows that would bind her to him in kind, without qualms or hesitation.

'I pronounce you husband and wife.'

Not waiting for permission, Ethan kissed her with all the fervour of a loving groom. Hugs and kisses were exchanged, and after the certificates were signed they all moved to a small lamplit marquee.

The first toast was to the bride and groom, wishing them a long and happy life together. As they clinked glasses Ethan's piercing eyes sent a message for her alone. His distinct, 'To us!' triggered a pleasurable shiver.

The celebrant left and then their entrées were served. The wine waiter refilled their glasses and moved discreetly away.

Ethan spoke next. 'To those who will always be remembered, living on in our hearts.' He held out his glass to Alina, dropped his gaze to her stomach and mouthed *Louise and Leon*. She reciprocated, touching her glass to his.

Then *her husband*—a phrase she'd believed she'd never think or say again—surprised her even more. His fingertips gently lifted her chin and his eyes darkened with intensity as he repeated the salute. Her eyes misted as she understood his generous gesture. For Colin, his parents and Michael.

The sweet liquid caught in her throat as she suddenly realised there'd been only a numbing sorrow as she'd thought their names. Had she come through the darkness, as Jean had suggested this morning? Not really. Ethan found it so easy to believe in *our* baby. Her maternal feelings had died on a dusky country road.

She was definitely appreciative of the delicious specially prepared courses, making a mental note to send a written thank-you to the chef and his staff. Everyone in the know had been loyal and discreet—a tribute to the man by her side.

Ethan fiddled with his new gold ring. The sun had set. Hot drinks and handmade chocolates had been served. He was married—something he hadn't envisaged in his foreseeable future. If he ever had, he would have imagined his choice would be one of his peers—a successful woman with interests they'd share, who had no desire to procreate.

Circumstances and his code of honour had dictated otherwise. Yet to his amazement he felt satisfied, content, as if he'd found a unique treasure he hadn't realised he'd been searching for. The vows he'd made to her were real. Her vows had been defined and strong.

As if sensing his attention, Alina turned to meet his gaze. When she smiled shyly contentment morphed into something earthier, lustier. He'd never had the urge to swing any other woman round and then drag her into a mind-blowing kiss. Never had an impulse to sneak away at a family function for a kiss and a cuddle—maybe more. Now he stared into enticing violet eyes and imagined it all happening.

Tonight there were no shutters; her wide-eyed open expression raised the hairs on his nape. Tingled his spine.

Flipped his heart. *Alina James*. The name rolled sweetly off his tongue.

'Well, Alina James, do I call for the car or do you want more dessert?'

'I'm full. It was all so delicious.'

The tip of her tongue licked her lip, as if searching for a final taste, sending a fiery jolt to his groin.

They were alone apart from the limousine driver. Ethan wrapped his arms around his bride and kissed her, slow and deep. His body responded with a sharp tug, low in his gut. She tasted sweet—pavlova-sweet. He craved more. He craved pure Alina taste.

His wife. They were legally one. She…

He was doused in a cold shower of reality. He could do nothing that might remind Alina of her first wedding night. Nothing she might regret in the morning.

He settled back holding her close, murmured, 'We'll soon be home, Mrs James,' into her ear.

Home. The word echoed in Alina's head. Her home—for as long as she chose to stay. Ethan had given the impression he meant every word of his vows. Only she knew he didn't.

'Tired, sweetheart?' The tenderness in his eyes melted her misgivings.

'Just thinking. Thank you for making tonight so wonderful, even if it's n—'

His mouth cut off the rest. Powerful and firm. Punishing. 'It's as real as any other,' he grated, tilting her face, his flashing dark eyes boring into hers. 'Don't ever forget that.'

Her body chilled, as if she'd dived into icy water. She'd offended him—the last thing she'd intended. Tears prickled in her eyes as she struggled for words to put it right.

Suddenly she was crushed against him and kissed, with a thoroughness that left her body alive and burning.

He looked dazed when he broke away, bemused and

aroused. She knew he'd see the same in her. Complete obliviousness to their surroundings.

Ethan's fingers shook as they cradled her cheek. 'Alina, darling...' He trembled as he drank her in. His reaction when she'd denied their marriage was real had astounded him. He'd endeavoured to show her how valid it was to him. Succeeded spectacularly. With a kiss like none he'd ever known.

He struggled to draw air into empty lungs, fought to clear his brain. He'd been lost in a fantasy world where the only reality was the taste of Alina on his tongue and the softness of her in his arms. Heaven.

Her stunning eyes were dark and bewildered. His stomach twisted. Bewitched by her beauty, and by her response to his kisses, he'd allowed his own ardour to override the need for restraint. Only noisy revelry out on the street as the vehicle stopped had thrown him back to reality.

He leant his forehead on hers and sucked in air scented with spring and his wife. 'I'm the one who's apologising now. Not for the kiss. Never for the kiss as long as I live. Not for anything we've shared—especially tonight. I have no right to be angry when you've complied so willingly with everything I've asked of you.'

He helped her from the car, thanked the driver and hugged her to his side as they walked to the elevator, squeezed tighter as they flew upward. When the ping announced the opening of the doors he scooped her into his arms—ignoring her protests—and stepped out.

'This is for me, sweetheart.'

Her pupils dilated, making her eyes even more alluring.

'This will be my once in a lifetime.'

He jiggled her body onto his chest as he used his key card, pushed open the door, and covered her lips with his as he carried her over the threshold. She slid her arm around his neck, her fingertips curling into his hair.

After kicking the door shut he continued the kiss, slowly letting her slide down until her feet were on the floor. Clasping her hands, he stepped back, imprinting her into his memory.

'Tonight was special in so many ways, but this is the memory I'll keep for ever. You—so incredibly beautiful, so enticingly sweet.'

Alina watched his Adam's apple bounce as he swallowed his emotion. She'd been right in thinking their relationship might change—wrong to believe that it was a bad thing. Hormones or not, she couldn't deny she cared about Ethan James.

'You made it special, Ethan. I was… Oh, I don't know how to explain. Then you were there, and everything was right.'

'And now I have to let you go to bed.'

She heard the desire in his voice, saw it in his eyes. For a second she wondered why she wasn't pulling away and running. Then she gave her answer without any qualms.

'I'm your wife.'

She felt his tension flow out, even though their hands were their only contact. Heat flared in his eyes, quickly softening to concern.

'And much more than I deserve, Alina James. Turn around.'

He unclasped her necklace and trailed light kisses across her neck. Slipped his arms around her and drew her close, his breath teasing her earlobe.

'Go to bed, darling. While I can still let you leave. Tonight I want no regrets.'

Her cheeks burned. She'd refused to think of *that other* first night, and yet he'd understood how it might come flooding back. She'd blatantly offered herself, denying the possible—probable—consequences.

Twisting to face him, she touched her fingertips to his

lips. 'I'm sorry, Ethan, I'm being selfish. I thought if you held me it wouldn't—'

'It still might. But I'll hold you in whichever bed you choose. Tonight we'll sleep. Tomorrow we'll start our honeymoon.'

She raised up onto her toes and pressed her lips to his, kept it brief.

'Thank you, Ethan.'

Her final thought as sleep overtook her was I'm Mrs Alina Paulette James…

CHAPTER FIFTEEN

ETHAN STOOD BY the lounge window, swirling his brandy in its glass, oblivious to one of Australia's most iconic views. He was reliving the emotional rollercoaster he'd ridden since the elevator doors had opened to reveal his exquisite bride.

The moment she'd seen him her stunning eyes had seemed to fill her face. She'd stopped, giving him the chance to take in every gorgeous centimetre of her. His heart had hammered; his stomach had clenched. His brain had ceased to function logically.

Her tongue-tip had flicked nervously over her tempting lips. With her bouquet held defensively over her baby bump, she'd been like a frightened animal, captured in a hunter's spotlight, unable to move. So adorable. So courageous.

He'd made no conscious decision; his movement towards her had been instinctive, as natural as breathing. Drawing her close and kissing her had eased the unaccustomed ache from being apart from her. The brightness in her eyes as they'd stood face to face, hands joined for the ceremony, had given him cause to hope.

Yet as she'd sworn, ''Till death do us part…'' her fingers had lain cool in his, her voice had been calm and steady, making him wonder if she still had no intention of honouring that vow. Then she'd returned his kiss with a fervour that had made his head spin.

His cognac was failing to have its usual satisfying effect. His complete focus was on Alina.

He rinsed the glass and went to find her. She lay on her side, in *his* bed, one hand tucked under her cheek. His wife—for as long as he could persuade her to stay.

Sliding in beside her, he cradled her into his body and splayed his hand on her belly. *Alina James. Baby James.* His family. Here in his arms where he could protect them. All was right with his world.

With a deep sigh of contentment, he fell asleep.

Inching carefully out of Ethan's arms, Alina sat up, curbing the impulse to stroke his stubbled jaw. With his long dark lashes and tanned muscular body, plus a secret smile as if he were dreaming of hidden delights, he created a magazine picture that would have women lining up to buy it.

His brand-new gold ring caught her eye. She glanced down at hers, bright and shiny, a symbol of hope. She was *married.* Tendrils of the past crept into her head, were dismissed immediately. The future was unknown, not to be thought about. The now…

Her skin tingled. Lifting her head, she met Ethan's wide-awake gaze and sensual smile.

'I was looking forward to waking you with a kiss, Mrs James.' Husky. Thick.

'From your expression, whatever you were dreaming must have been better,' she teased.

A second later, she was flat on her back, drowning in dark cobalt contemplation.

'Nothing could be better than kissing my wife good morning.'

Appropriate action swiftly followed his declaration. She closed her mind, and surrendered to the ardour of his skilful lips. Everything was changing. Every day the fine line between role-playing and reality became more blurred. No longer a solitary entity, she was once again joined with someone.

'I meant to wake earlier. We have a full day in front of us, Alina.'

His rough inflections as he gulped air while trying to talk amused and thrilled her.

'Then you'd better let me go.' Teasing, half hoping he wouldn't.

He braced himself on his arms, blue eyes gleaming with suppressed delight. 'Ultrasound, then lunch. Okay?'

She nodded, not quite sure where he was going with this.

'After that my visit to tell my parents we are married will take a couple of hours. Which gives you plenty of time to pack. I've booked a holiday house in the Blue Mountains until Sunday.' He grinned like a magician who'd pulled off an amazing trick.

If an open mouth and wide eyes was the reaction he'd hoped for, he got it. Alina's heart pounded as she realised that their recent discussion on Australian tourist spots had been him info-gathering. He'd taken note of the places she'd never been to, ensuring his plans didn't clash with her memories. Another chink in her armour widened.

'Just the two of us, alone in the Blue Mountains. Time to get to know each other better without any distractions.'

'What about work?' He'd be getting calls all day.

'All fixed. Emergencies only.'

The pavements were crowded. Alina stared through the tinted glass at people living normal lives, fiddled with her two rings. It wasn't nerves. Heck, she'd been through this procedure three times. Truth was, she was scared she might begin to care for the life inside her once she'd seen an active image on the screen. Feared she wouldn't. She wasn't sure which would be worse.

'Try to relax, Alina.' Ethan covered her restless hands with his. 'With new technology the imagery will be enhanced.'

So they'd see everything more clearly. She'd prefer vague and fuzzy.

'This was meant to be a happy time…the three of us were supposed to be together at every stage.' Her voice cracked. She bit her lip, refusing to cry.

'Now you only have me,' he remarked wryly. 'A poor substitute, but I'll do my best.'

Hearing the sorrow in his voice, she felt contrite. They were both in need of comfort.

'I wish I could talk about them without being torn apart. About the way Leon's face lit up when he saw the blue lines, their laughter when he picked Louise up and spun her round… It hurts that their happiness only lasted a few weeks.'

'Happiness *you* gave them. For that alone I'll always be in your debt.'

He let go of her hands, hugged her so close she felt his ragged breath rumble up his chest. She thanked her lucky stars—not that there'd been much evidence that she had any—that she'd made the decision to come to him earlier rather than wait until after the birth.

A short time later Alina lay on the examination table, gripping Ethan's hand, staring at the blank monitor. He brushed his lips across her cheek.

'Our baby, Alina. An individual person.' His compelling dark eyes held her spellbound. 'Created by Leon, Louise and you. Unique in its own right.'

The technician breezed in, all smiles and goodwill. Showing soon-to-be parents images of their babies must be one of the best jobs ever.

'Hi. Alina and Ethan James, right? I'm Gary.' He grinned as he sat on the stool, checking her chart. 'Ready for some hi-tech wonder. Tuck your top up and brace yourself. Maybe one day they'll develop a lotion we can apply warm.'

He squeezed the cold gel onto her abdomen, causing her to wince and screw up her nose. Making Ethan laugh.

'Same reaction from all the dads,' Gary mused. 'Funnily enough they always refuse the offer to try it. Now, do you want to know the sex?'

'No!'

Two voices in unison. Their eyes met: hers grateful, his in accord.

'Thanks for asking,' Ethan added, his thumb moving reassuringly over her knuckles. 'We'd like to be surprised in October.'

'Lots of people still would, myself included.' He noted their refusal.

Alina watched avidly as images formed on the screen. Goosebumps peaked on her skin as she made out a moving shadowy form floating on a black background. From the dark recesses of her mind voices begged her to shut her eyes. She didn't.

The picture became clearer, the image bigger, as Gary manipulated the mouse, mouthing quiet satisfactory grunts as he worked.

'Okay, we have two arms, two legs, good proportion of head to body. Right size for fourteen weeks…' He jiggled something, the clarity increased, and then the cursor pointed to a tiny pulsating blob. 'There—can you see?— your baby's good, strong heartbeat.'

Her breath caught in her throat. Tears for her friends who would never experience this wonder filled her eyes.

A strangled gasp resonated at her side.

She swung her head and her own heartbeat stilled. Ethan's lips were parted, his eyes big and glowing with amazement. His body leant forward as far as the table permitted. His rapt expression rebooted her heartbeat into aching double time. A lifetime ago she'd seen the same wonder on another face.

She watched his Adam's apple bounce as he tried to

swallow, heard his deep indrawn breath and emotional gruff tone.

'Our baby. Gives a whole new meaning to the word "daddy", doesn't it?'

'This is the moment it all becomes real,' replied the technician.

'Oh, yeah.' Ethan's smile could have lit up the city and then some. 'Thank you, Alina.'

His misty eyes chipped at her defences. His next words, whispered by her ear, tugged at her heart.

'Thank you for allowing me to be part of this incredible experience.'

She wiped a tear from his cheek and let her fingers rest on his skin. 'It's amazing, isn't it? I know the baby's there. I can see it moving. Yet I can't feel anything.'

Her brain wouldn't be forced into accepting 'our' or 'my'. That was the plan. No caring. No bonding. The right to return to her solitary life with no past, only an uncertain future. The day she'd flown to Australia she'd had no doubts it was the best possible outcome.

Since meeting Ethan certainties were becoming cloudy and convictions ambiguous. Somewhere in the clump of wool that masqueraded as her decisive mind was the niggling certainty that this was being caused more by the man who was regarding her now as if she was all the treasures he'd ever dreamed of rolled into one than by her condition.

Ethan's gaze swung from the monitor to Alina and back. He didn't know whether to holler out loud or cry. That indistinct wriggling blur was his niece or nephew—living proof that he hadn't totally lost the two people he loved most. Five weeks ago unpredictable and unbelievable. Now an almost touchable actuality.

In less than one of those rapid heartbeats he lost his heart. Utterly. Irrevocably. For ever. *Our baby*. Now he truly believed what he'd originally claimed for appearances' sake. At that instant he became a father, silently vowing to become the kind of daddy his friend would have been.

His interest in the technology vanished. He was filled with reverent awe, seeing life as it began. In six months this tiny creature would emerge as a living, breathing person. *His* child, *his* responsibility for life. He wondered how he'd ever believed he was as unemotional as his parents. His heart had swelled fit to burst.

Alina brushed away tears he hadn't realised he'd shed. Touched his cheek. A new softness shone in her beautiful eyes, curved in her smile. However deep she'd buried her maternal instincts, it wasn't enough. The natural mother he suspected her to be was going to surface, no matter how hard she fought it.

His mouth felt dry, his chest tight. His heartbeat powered up. Whether because of their baby or her it didn't matter. From this moment they really were a family. The voice in his head was telling him to somehow keep it that way.

'Okay, Mum and Dad, I've got the information I need.'

Ethan blinked as the monitor clicked off. Over already? He wanted to watch longer, see more.

'Check with the receptionist for your photos and DVD.' The technician handed Alina a box of tissues. 'Good luck. I might see you when you come in again.'

Ethan took the tissues and began to wipe off the gel, desperate to be physically involved, not wanting to come down from his euphoria. He concentrated on her stomach, absurdly self-conscious after revealing a side of him few people had ever seen.

Coward. He'd said thank you—a pathetic reward for the miracle she'd brought to him.

Throwing the tissues in the bin, he turned to meet compassionate violet eyes. A deep yearning, alien to his normal awareness, flowed through him. Along with the desire to cherish and protect as long as he lived. He shook with its intensity.

'Ethan, are you all right?'

Her fingers rested on his arm. For her a friendly gesture. For him, much more.

'Better than I've ever been.'

He smoothed her top down and helped her from the bench. Kissed her tenderly until he ran out of breath, needing her gentleness, her sweetness. *Her.*

'Let's go home, darling.'

After an early lunch Ethan drove to his parents' home alone, psyching himself up for the confrontation. He'd always been the mediator, acting as a buffer for others. Not any more. Today he was the activist.

His parents' judgemental nature along with their unachievably high standards had caused so many problems. He was convinced their agreement to Louise's marriage had been motivated only by the idea of hosting a flash high society event. It was their interference that had motivated the newlyweds to move to Barcelona. Now they'd gone he had no one else to champion. Except the quiet beauty he'd left alone in their apartment, and the grandchild he *might* inform his parents was on the way.

He walked round the house, growling in frustration. It was ridiculous that their offspring had to use the front door like guests once they'd left home, that he had to ring the bell even though they must know he'd arrived. His greeting to his father was polite, yet clipped, the reply mundane.

'This must be important, for you to take time off from work. Is it something to do with the estate?'

As expected, no welcome.

'No.'

He walked straight to the lounge. His mother sat in her chair, perfectly groomed. Just once he'd like to see her in casual clothes, with mussed-up hair. His thoughts flew to the heart-warming image of his wife in the blue chainstore outfit she'd worn at their first meeting.

'Good afternoon, Mother. I won't be stopping. I have an appointment.'

To take my bride on a honeymoon I hope will bring us even closer than we've become.

She frowned at his lack of physical greeting. He compared her barely touching air-kiss for Alina with the loving embrace he'd received from Jean when they'd met. Didn't feel the slightest guilt.

'Good afternoon, Ethan. Is there something wrong?

His father was now seated in an armchair. There was no mention of that disastrous visit, nor the fact that there'd been no further contact until yesterday morning, when he'd phoned them. They'd never deign to make a conciliatory move, and he was only here for Alina's sake.

He took the settee, placing a long envelope on the coffee table.

'I have something to tell you prior to an official announcement. If you don't approve, that's hard luck. It's a done deed.'

They both stiffened. He paused. This was for his sister, his friend. *Their baby.*

'Alina and I were married yesterday evening.'

'What?' His father sprang up.

'Sit down, Martin.'

Sophia's curt tone had its effect. He obeyed, glaring at his son. She continued, her censure radiating through the air.

'Is this some sort of warped joke because you took umbrage at our concerns over her background? I know application forms need to be lodged a month before, so…'

'It was done. We had a quiet wedding, with friends as witnesses.'

His mother went rigid, unusually lost for words. It was his father who spoke.

'Really, Ethan. We coped with immature dramas from your sister. Never expected any from *you*. You've always been practical and reasonable—'

'Maybe too much so,' Ethan cut in brusquely. 'I lost precious time with Louise and Leon because you would not accept they were meant for each other. Time I'll never get back now they're gone.'

Dismissing the protests that erupted from both of them, he leant forward, balanced his elbows on his knees and clenched his hands together.

'I love Alina.' Not a lie. It wasn't the same as being *in* love. How could he not love someone who'd given him the most priceless gift he'd ever have? 'And anyone who upsets or disrespects her will be out of my life. I don't give a damn what people think or say. Accept it or not—she's my wife, my priority.'

He waited, quite prepared to walk out. The looks they exchanged didn't faze him. He didn't care what explanation they gave their social acquaintances for his hurried secret wedding. Their society image mattered only to *them*. Tragedy had taught him that there were far more important things in life.

His mother finally found her voice. 'How are we supposed to explain this rushed event to our friends?'

All they cared about was how it would affect their image. He almost laughed out loud—couldn't remember when he'd last heard genuine amusement from either of them. Alina had a quiet sense of humour, enjoyed quirky comedies, and encouraged him to see the fun in them too.

'That's not my concern.' He flicked the envelope with his finger. 'This is a copy of the notice that will be placed in the paper on Saturday, plus a list of friends and relatives whom I will inform later this week. I would prefer you to wait until then to tell anyone else. We'll be away on our honeymoon until Sunday, so I'll only be answering urgent calls.'

'What about the Starburst chain?' His father sounded shell shocked.

'Under control.'

'I see. As usual, you've covered everything.'

He wasn't fooled by his mother's resigned tone.

'Will we see you when you return?'

He hesitated. Dared he trust them around Alina, especially as her pregnancy would soon be apparent?

'That depends on your attitude. Our baby's due in October.'

Ignoring their gasps and aggrieved expressions, he stood up.

'I'm happier right now than I have ever been in my life, and thrilled that my wife is carrying my baby. Anyone who isn't can just stay away.'

He said goodbye soon after, breathing a sigh of relief as he went through the gates. He ought to feel guilty for the subterfuge. Instead his head was filled with Alina—her beguiling smile, the way her violet eyes revealed her emotions. Her extraordinary courage.

My wife. The simple yet profound phrase kept repeating in his brain. As he drove, singing along off-key with the radio, he felt giddy and irrationally happy. He was going home to claim another long kiss, as sweet as the one they'd shared before he left.

once we work out their feeding schedule. My "all hours" policy allows clients time until dusk. So I'll only be away for a couple of hours at the latest during the week. We'll talk about the different times. How about about now, shortly?'

CHAPTER SIXTEEN

'TURN RIGHT IN four hundred metres. Clifftop Lane.'

Ethan obeyed the GPS instruction, grateful for the hassle-free drive. He pulled up in front of a white weatherboard house, switched off the engine and checked the time.

'Twelve minutes short of the two-hour estimate. You feeling okay, darling?'

'Apart from needing to stretch. This car rides much smoother than most of the vehicles I've travelled in.' She opened her door.

He was there to help before her foot touched the ground. Arching his back, he drew in a deep breath. 'Ahh…'

Alina followed suit. 'Eucalyptus. Invigorating! True Australian aroma.'

His heart sang. Could she look any more beautiful, any happier? 'Shall we take a look inside?' He jingled the keys he'd picked up on the way through Katoomba.

'Can we go for a walk first? I'd like to see the sun set on the mountains.'

They walked along the path behind the house. Through the trees they saw glimpses of brown, green and gold against a darkening blue sky, dotted with pink-tinged clouds.

'Picture-perfect.' Alina sighed, stopping to implant it into her memory.

'I agree,' Ethan replied, ignoring the scenery and embracing her from behind. He trailed soft kisses over her neck, revelling in the way she quivered with each one. Trembled himself when she twisted round, wrapped her arms around his neck and pressed her lips to his.

He inhaled the spring essence that was Alina. Fought

the craving to show her how much he wanted her. His heart pounded into his ribs. And darn near exploded when her lips parted, inviting more intimate contact.

Without hesitation he accepted, loving her with his tongue, aligning their bodies with pleasurable strokes of his hands, letting her know how blatantly he was aroused. His world shrank to the two of them. It was all he needed, all he desired.

Alina arched into him, letting his heat simmer through her, returning his kiss with a passion that shook her. Her anticipation had been building since they'd arrived, diminished by the expectation of guilt. When it hadn't come, she'd pushed the boundary by kissing him.

Danger signals abated to an almost inaudible buzz. Painful consequences were a long way in the future. For the moment she was caught in the *now*. Yearning overrode everything, holding the darkness at bay.

Necessity for air broke them apart. The transparent desire in Alina's eyes told Ethan all he wanted to know.

He swung her up, cradling her close to his chest. 'Mine.' Hoarse with emotion.

'Yours…' Hot. Breathless. Murmured into the skin above his polo shirt.

He strode back to the house, king of his universe.

The sun's rays teased Alina's eyelids open. She blinked, snuggled further under the cover, trying to recapture the magic of her dream. Reached out for…

Her eyes flew open.

She was cradled by a solid wall of naked muscle, moving to a gentle rhythm. Warm breath tickled her earlobe. Firm fingers lay on her hip. A delicious glow spread from her core to every extremity at the memory of Ethan's ardent lovemaking. She turned over to look at him.

Ethan. Her husband. Her lover. Her lips curled as she recalled the tension in his muscles as he'd held his own need in check, caressing and soothing her until her barriers had finally exploded in a fiery burst of passion.

A wave of shyness engulfed her. He was a mature man who'd made love to many women. She'd only known the gentleness of first love before. Ethan had awakened the woman in her, freed her heart. But did he want it? Swearing to care for her and protect her was an abyss away from loving her.

He made a low contented sound in his throat, rolled onto his back and arched. Lazy cobalt eyes opened, widened. His lips curled in a slow, satisfied smile that held such tenderness it tugged at her heart.

'This is the perfect way to wake in the morning.'

He reached out for her, covering her mouth with his, his tongue tempting her lips to open for him. How could they not when she'd hardly recovered from the dizzy heights he'd taken her to during the night? In this big bed that she'd never forget.

'Ethan, I…' Where were coherent words when she needed them? 'Last night I…'

'Last night was more than I'd dreamt it would be…so much more than I'd fantasised.' He stroked her tousled hair, tangled his fingers through her curls. 'Promise me you won't regret what we shared. I sure as hell won't. Never. Not for a second as long as I live.'

Alina yearned to drown in the dark blue pools of his eyes, longed to share it all again now. Couldn't say the words.

Ethan ached to make love to her again, but saw the confusion in her bemused violet eyes. Knew he'd have to wait. Knew he'd have to find the right moment to tell her he wanted to make this marriage real in every way. Wanted her to always be his wife.

'Go shower.' Sometime soon he'd share one with her. 'I'll get breakfast, then we'll go sightseeing.'

She nodded, shuffled to the edge of the bed and hesitated. He smiled, loving her shyness even though she'd been married before. Was married *now*. He couldn't contain his chuckle as she shot from the bed. Paid for it as his body reacted to the sight of her running naked to the en suite. Pulling on his boxers, he headed for the kitchen, planning their day, their evening. Their night.

'Ethan!'

The panic in her voice froze his blood, sending him racing for the bathroom, his heart pumping. A heart that screeched to a halt at the sight of her huge frightened violet eyes. He dropped to his knees in front of her, hunched forward on the toilet lid, wrapped in a white towel, her arms clasping her stomach. Dragged her to his chest, fighting his own gut-wrenching fear.

'Alina, darling—tell me. What's wrong?'

She shuddered. A pain-filled cry jarred against his bare skin. 'It h-h-hurts. In my stomach—'

Her stuttering stopped with a sharp sound that cut through him.

For a second his mind went blank, refusing to process the horror her words evoked. Then it cleared. Alina needed a practical, take-action man. Lifting her as if she were delicate china, he carried her to the bed, brushing his lips across her forehead. Telling her everything would be all right. Silently cursing the fates for putting her through more torment.

Grabbing his mobile, he opened Alina's unpacked suitcase, rummaging for underwear and a dress with one hand, thumbing his phone with the other. He wrestled into the jeans and polo top he'd worn on the trip and slid on his sneakers one-handed, holding the phone to his ear with the other.

His answers to the operator's questions were clear and precise. Details could wait. Alina was frightened. His heart wrenched every time she shuddered and cried out. Their tiny baby might be in danger. He didn't dare think beyond getting them to the hospital—thankfully not too far away.

With a plan in action, he helped Alina into her clothes. He murmured reassuring phrases he'd never be able to recall, trying to ignore the resurging irrational fear gnawing at his insides. He told them both how cherished they were. He couldn't, *wouldn't* lose either of them. They were so close to becoming a family, and he'd fight like hell to keep that prospect attainable.

True to the operator's word, a medical team and trolley were waiting at the emergency entrance of the hospital. They whisked her away, leaving him to find a place to park.

Walking through the front doors, he was confronted with corridors, signs, and not a trace of Alina. Now she and their baby were in good care his composure crashed. His life, his future, was somewhere in this building and he wanted to be close to them.

He needed them. They needed him.

There'd be a path from his prowling back and forth worn into the waiting area if they didn't come for him soon. How far away was she? Had she asked for him?

He repeatedly checked his watch, matched it with the clock on the wall, tensed when anyone in hospital garb walked in.

The guilt gnawing at him now was worse than he'd felt after Louise and Leon had died. This time he'd been actively to blame. Last night when Alina had welcomed him with kisses and caresses he'd loved her with a passion that had shaken him to his core. Emotions he'd have claimed not to be any part of him had surfaced, taking them both soaring to the edge of ecstasy and tipping them over.

This was *his* fault. That book said sex was safe after the first trimester as long as there were no problems. He hadn't considered that there might be. He slammed a fist into his other palm. Prayed to all the gods that anyone believed in not to let Alina suffer another loss.

'Mr James?'

He swung round and locked eyes with a man who hardly looked old enough to be an intern.

'I'm sending your wife for an ultrasound and she's asked for you to be with her. This way.'

They fell into step and he continued. 'The physical examination shows nothing wrong. There's no bleeding, and your child's vital signs are strong.'

Ethan's brain filtered out whatever came next. Tension whooshed out of him, leaving him loose and vulnerable. *Nothing wrong. Strong vital signs.* Their baby was a fighter. It didn't lessen his culpability.

'Doctor, last night we made love. Could that have been the cause?'

'Alina told me. It might have some bearing, maybe not. Even if the ultrasound shows all's well I'd like to keep her in at least overnight, so we can monitor them both.'

'Do whatever's necessary to keep them both safe.'

Ethan sank into a chair in the private room, his eyes glued to the monitor recording their baby's heartbeat. He tried to swallow the lump in his throat as he watched that life-affirming pulse—faster than his, normal for an unborn child.

He hadn't let go of Alina's hand the whole time, needing the contact more than he needed air to breathe. His fingers caressed her knuckles. His free hand brushed strands of hair from her forehead. It tore him apart to see her so pale, so still, with a drip inserted in her wrist. He didn't know what it was—didn't care as long as it helped. Her breathing was steady; his was as erratic as leaves in a windstorm.

'If you'd like a break I can sit with her while you go for coffee.' A nurse laid a comforting hand on his shoulder.

'No, I have to be here. I have to be with them.' He wasn't going anywhere.

Ethan wasn't going anywhere. He'd even walked alongside the trolley, his hand wrapped around hers, but for the first time his warmth hadn't been able dispel Alina's icy chills. Everything had been a blur since he'd carried her from the en suite, his soft words unintelligible through the fog in her mind.

Her barricades had crashed back up with the first stab of pain, sucking her into the dark void of bereavement and despair. Resisting the impulse to cling to him, she'd lain passive in his arms as he'd carried her to the bed and the car, desperately trying to close down her nightmare.

During the ultrasound she kept her eyes closed, blanked out the technician's voice and Ethan's replies. Didn't comprehend what he said to her, only realised by the squeeze of her fingers and his kiss on her forehead that the baby was okay. For now.

Then something deep inside her shifted, shimmied through her, releasing a long-denied emotion. She gasped at the overwhelming surge of love for the tiny child fighting for survival inside her.

'Alina, does it hurt?'

The anguish in his voice focused her thoughts. She looked up, saw the furrows in his brow, the clench of his jaw, and stared into anguished eyes. Cobalt blue eyes in a captivating face that, without her realising, had become as dear to her as Colin's. She loved him—loved him *and* the baby.

No! To love was to risk everything. Mind-numbing. Terrifying. She'd fought her way back once. If she lost again she'd *never* recover.

Scrunching her eyes shut, she forced her mind to think of the remote places she'd escaped to before. Anything but him, his eyes, his touch, the way he'd loved her last night. She forced herself back to the emotionless detachment that had kept her heart safe for seven years.

Two days later Ethan took her back to the holiday house.

The next morning they returned to Sydney.

She'd done it again. Slipped away while he still slept. In the four weeks since her stay in hospital Alina had drifted into an abstract world Ethan wasn't privy to. She lay apathetic in his arms at night, rarely initiated conversation and almost never smiled. He'd built an empire with persuasion and action—now nothing he said or did helped.

He'd ensured she had time with Jean and with Dr Conlan, hoping she'd open up to one of them, or both. Giving her time and space, he hadn't pressed her, had kept their daily life as normal as possible while letting her know he'd change his schedule any time she needed him. He'd encouraged her to use her computer, knew she didn't, tried to be reassuring without crowding her.

At night he cradled her and caressed her until she fell asleep in his arms. Every day he let her know how precious she was to him in words and actions. He was determined that she'd understand how much he cared for and wanted her, even though he made no attempt to make love to her. For her sake and their baby's.

More than anything he ached for what might have become a special part of his day: waking with Alina nestled against him, her hand over his heart, her breath soft on his chest. He longed to start each morning by kissing her awake, his heart soaring as she reacted sleepily, returning his ardour as her senses awoke.

This morning he found her in the kitchen, making herbal tea. His pulse raced even as his heart twisted at the sight of her slumped posture. He lifted her chin, dipped his head, watching for a flicker in her sorrowful eyes. The same flicker that had raised his hopes time after time, only to dash them as it quickly died.

He stepped away, ran agitated fingers through his hair. He'd been patient, willing to try anything to reach her, knowing she wasn't to blame. Today he'd run out of ideas.

'Alina, talk to me. We can work through this together, but I need to know how you feel, what you're thinking.'

She backed away, fuelling his frustration. 'I don't feel anything. Nothing.'

'Try, darling. For me. For our baby.'

She shook her head, squared her shoulders in defiance. Raised her voice. 'I can't. *I can't.*'

He bunched his fingers to prevent himself from hauling her close and kissing her hot and hard in an attempt to melt the ice that held her prisoner. Knew he was close to doing just that.

'Forget breakfast. I need space to think.' He strode to the door, grabbing his keys on the way.

His stormy departure stunned Alina, leaving her breathless, mouth gaping, fingers curled tight. She sank to the floor, leaning against the cupboard. That was the same expression she'd seen once before, when he'd walked out of their first meeting, angry, shattered.

Then she'd been unsure if she'd see him again. Now the same feeling washed over her, so much stronger. She felt desolated. Abandoned. Alone.

Wrapping her arms around her swelling stomach, she hugged herself and rocked, chest tight and body trembling. Suddenly she stilled. She wasn't alone. Her hands were cradling their baby. *Their baby.* Ethan was right: it was easy to say it once you believed.

She also believed he'd never desert Louise's child. It was his prime consideration.

He'd given his word to take care of them both. Since her stay in hospital he'd been gentle, compassionate, treating her as if she were fragile. He cuddled her close at night, whispered comforting words she hardly heard, and never attempted to make love to her.

Because he was protecting her and their baby? Because Dr Conlan had advised him not to?

She'd driven him away—maybe lost him. One night of loving might be all she'd have to remember...a magical night that...

He'd said it had been more than he'd dreamt, more than he'd fantasised. She closed her eyes and pictured his face when he kissed her, always with open eyes.

Now she recognised the love that shone in that darkening blue. Every act, every caress had been for love. For her. For their baby.

A wave of serenity washed over her. She went to the window, seeing only his smile, his quirky eyebrow rising. His cobalt blue eyes, so suspicious at first. So frustratingly angry when he'd left today because of her withdrawal, her stupidity in not sharing her fears and giving him the chance to help her.

Could he ever forgive her?

Please let him come home soon so she could tell him how much she loved him *and* their baby. She'd try to explain the mind-numbing grief, beg for his understanding and help. If he still wanted her she longed to stay, to be his wife and this baby's mother. The three of them could become a real family...

CHAPTER SEVENTEEN

TURNING LEFT AT ground level, Ethan walked aimlessly without stopping, crossing streets or turning corners depending on the traffic lights. His brain spun; his gut churned. He was the mediator, the one who found solutions. Why not for Alina? He'd broken her barriers down before—now he seemed to be the reason they'd been rebuilt.

He sidestepped a toddler, squirming in his mother's grip, quirked a smile at them both. Hopefully that was his future—an active, adventurous child with Louise and Leon's DNA. Their love of life, their loyalty, their... His throat tightened. Would there be anything of Alina? How could there not be when she'd nourished and cocooned their baby for nine months?

A red light. He swung left. Ahead lay Circular Quay and the Manly Ferry.

Alina's eyes had sparkled that day; her smile had enthralled him. He'd loved her sweet response to his kiss. Loved her... *Loved her.*

He stopped short, barely registering the stroller slamming into the back of his leg or the young father's apology.

'Not your fault, mate. I stopped.'

And he'd stopped being an idiot. He moved over to the building, his body trembling as he acknowledged how much of one he'd been. That original tightening in his gut, his complete trust in her from the start and the primal urge to protect her... His desire to know her would have been as strong whenever, *however* he'd met her.

Alina had captured his heart from the moment he'd stood in that doorway. He hadn't realised it because he hadn't believed he was capable of the feeling. For weeks he'd been following a nightly ritual in secret, not comprehending he'd truly meant it for both of them. If he'd let himself believe he might have prevented the rebuilding of her barricades.

He began to run—back to the apartment, back to claim her for his own. Back to offer her his love and life.

Opening and then closing the door silently, he moved forward, muscles tense, pulse racing. Heart praying.

Alina stood by the window, staring out. It was an echo of their first meeting, only this time he rejoiced in the gloriously familiar gut-clench.

Alina stroked her stomach, whispered words of encouragement, letting their baby know everything was going to be all right.

'Your daddy's temper flares quickly…cools almost as fast. He'll ponder the problem, think out a solution. Come home to take action.'

The back of her neck tingled.

'Alina?'

She turned, her heart flipping at his voice. Cobalt blue eyes set in impassive features scanned hers with the deep intensity she knew so well. His muscles were taut, as if prepared to ward off a devastating blow. His lips twitched.

Her mouth dried. Chills ran down her spine. She couldn't move.

He came towards her. His arms swung out, fingers spread. 'I can't go on like this.'

She froze. He couldn't mean it. He couldn't leave her. Or send her away. Her legs felt like jelly and yet they refused to buckle.

Her brain screamed. *Tell him you want to stay. Tell him you love him.*

The words wouldn't come.

One more step brought him close enough to caress her baby bump. He didn't.

'Can you imagine what it's like, waiting for you to fall asleep every night before I can tell you how much I love you?'

Grated out as if in protest.

Heat raced through her veins. Her legs crumpled. Ethan caught her, crushing her to his chest.

'You *do* that?'

He'd been saying he loved her. *He did love her.* Her arms wrapped around his neck, holding fast.

'Every night for weeks. I believed I was incapable of loving the way Leon and Louise did, so I told myself it was for our baby. Persuaded myself the physical attraction was because you were so beautiful, so sweet and courageous.'

His eyes sparkled. His hands soothed her. His brilliant smile was for her alone.

'I love you, Alina James. Probably from the moment I saw you. Recognising it took my head longer than my heart. Stay with us. I swear—'

'I love *you*, Ethan James. There's nowhere else I want to be.'

Ethan's lips sought hers tenderly, lovingly, savouring the taste of her, becoming more fervent as she responded in kind. He heard a low groan of desire, wished it were hers. Knew it came from him.

Breaking the kiss, he scooped her up, settling on the settee with her in his lap, her head on his shoulder, his hand splayed over her growing baby bump.

'I'm sorry for not trusting you to help me, Ethan. I've been so scared of losing you, losing you both. So fearful of getting trapped in the darkness again, being alone with no way out this time. You saved me and I pushed you away.'

'We're together now, and nothing's—'

His heart lurched as she suddenly sat up, eyes vivid and wide, a delighted smile lighting up her face.

'Our baby *moved*! Like a tiny ripple. Ethan, our baby's letting us know we're not alone.'

He kissed her softly, reverently. 'I promise you'll never be alone again, my love.'

September thirtieth.
Baby active.
Kept Alina up most of the night.

Ethan closed the diary and stretched. Alina was resting in the lounge, at his insistence, after rising early, claiming she couldn't get comfortable in bed.

He was just about to check if she wanted anything, tell her he'd work from home today, when she waddled in.

Her concerned expression had him on his feet in an instant.

'Do you need something, darling?'

'I didn't tell you earlier—thought it might be a false alarm.'

His body hit full alert in a heartbeat. He crossed the room, clasped her arms and pinned her with a warning glare.

'The contractions started before dawn. I've been timing them and—'

'Don't say it.' If it was voiced out loud it might happen. 'We've got three weeks to go. Must be a Braxton-Thick false alarm thing.'

Please let it be.

She gave him an indulgent smile. 'Braxton-*Hicks*—and that's why I waited until I was sure. I finished packing the bag, in case, then phoned Dr Conlan. She said she'll meet us at the hospital and to drive carefully.'

'No ambulance? No paramedics, trained in case the baby comes en route?'

'We have plenty of time, Ethan. I promise. The hire car's on its way.'

He strode from the room. Came back frowning.

'We need to…um…*hell*!' His mind was a fuzzball.

The hospital bag. He walked to the door, pivoted at the musical sound he normally loved to hear. His gorgeous wife was laughing at his indecision—a moment after telling him she was in premature labour.

He did the only thing a man could do in the circumstances: pulled her close to stop her mirth with his mouth. A breathless eternity later he lifted his head. It was time to man up. Or daddy up. He knelt to kiss her stomach, then splayed both hands there.

'Okay, bub, your timing's out, but you're in charge. Unless you want to reconsider and stay where you are, nice and cosy for another three or four weeks.'

His response was a firm kick. With a wry grin he straightened up.

'I guess we're gonna have a baby, Mrs James. You keep timing the contractions. I'll get the bag.'

'You'll have to call your mother on the way.'

His features hardened. 'Why the hell would I do that?'

In five months he'd only occasionally seen them socially, phoned them when necessary. Refused to give them any chance of upsetting Alina.

'Jean and I bumped into her at a baby shop last week. We talked for a few minutes, then arranged to have lunch today. I was going to tell you how it went tonight.'

'My mother was in a *baby shop*?' An unbelievable event. She ordered gifts online from exclusive stores.

His features softened and he drew Alina as close as their baby allowed.

'You agreed to meet her after the way they treated you? You are a very special lady, Alina James, and I'm a very lucky man.'

* * *

Dr Conlan was waiting for them. As Alina was wheeled away Ethan caught her arm.

'It's too soon. You said late October.'

She patted his hand and smiled. 'Babies don't always follow our planning chart, Ethan. This one's decided today's its birthday, whether we're ready or not.'

He wasn't. This was his woman. Their baby. He desperately wanted to take her home, where he could keep them both safe until the due date.

'Can't you delay it? At least until our baby's bigger?'

'Too late for that. Looks like your child's made an executive decision. Welcome to fatherhood, with all its unpredictability.'

It was happening. Louise's baby. Louise who'd hated being late for anything, who had always been early, eager to savour the first moment, the overture. His little miracle was about to be born.

Adrenaline pumped through his veins. It was like that exultant moment in a business deal when he knew he was on the cusp of victory. Only a thousand times better.

It wasn't the exclusive birthing suite he'd booked. Didn't matter. They were in the safest place possible. Dr Conlan was there, there were paediatric specialists within call. He could see the special incubator, positioned discreetly by the wall.

He rubbed Alina's back and encouraged her to puff and blow. Wiped the sweat from her brow, kissed her and repeatedly told her how much he loved her. He wished he could take the pain for her, and didn't flinch when her nails dug into his hand.

'Okay, Daddy, let me take over here.'

The nurse was there, nudging him aside. He growled. 'No.'

This was *his* place. *His* prerogative.

'Go help deliver your baby.'

Deliver? Him? He looked at Alina, who nodded.

'Go.'

Her reassuring smile filled his heart to bursting point.

An urgent, 'Come on, Ethan!' had him scrambling to the doctor's side.

He obeyed instructions, his eyes totally focused on the thick thatch of damp dark hair emerging. A whoosh of movement and suddenly his arms were full of a squirming, slippery, wrinkled creature. He intuitively hugged the red-faced newborn to his pounding heart, fascinated by the petite button nose and bow lips.

When a delightful squeak became a distinctive howl of objection he blinked away his tears of joy. They had a daughter. He was a fair dinkum father.

'Hi, bub. We've been waiting for you.'

To his amazement, as if soothed by his voice, her crying was tempered to a whimper and the cutest hiccup. He gazed into unfocused cobalt blue eyes, a reminder of Louise, then looked at Alina, who lay with her head back, face pale and eyes closed. And loved her even more.

He watched impatiently as this miniature of his sister was weighed and checked, exulted when her fingers wrapped around the one he used to touch her palm lightly. Scowled when she gave a tiny mew as they took a blood sample from her heel.

With the doctor's all-clear he carried their baby to the woman he adored beyond reason. His hopes soared as her eyes opened to reveal misty love-filled violet. As he gently lowered their little girl into her arms he held his breath, praying this little angel would finally erase the last vestige of her grief.

'We have a little girl, my darling. A beautiful daughter.' He said it proudly, aloud for the world to hear. His next whispered words were for her alone. 'As beautiful as her mothers. *Both* of them.'

Still cradling his daughter's head, he wrapped his arm around his wife. He believed his emotions had peaked until her finger softly caressed the tiny cheek, and they zoomed even higher. His heart threatened to burst through his chest as she pressed her lips to the ruddy pink forehead. She gazed down in wonder, her lips curled into the most beautiful smile he'd ever seen.

When she looked at him, her eyes shone like diamonds. 'We have a daughter, Ethan. I love you both so much,' she said huskily.

Her words thrilled him. Her kiss echoed her spoken words.

Alina had welcomed his tender caresses, his declarations of affection as he'd tried to ease her pain. Had seen his disconcertion at the nurse's attempt to take over. She'd always treasure the memory of his startled expression when their baby had slid into his hands, quickly replaced by one of wondrous awe as he tenderly gathered the precious bundle to his chest. She saw a tiny fist waving in protest and felt her breasts respond to the plaintive cry.

Her heart had blipped when he'd nestled the baby into her arms. Blipped and then beaten steady and strong as she saw dark hair, cobalt blue eyes, bow lips and long fingers: the perfect blend of her natural parents. As she'd touched the soft rosy cheek the last trace of anguish had faded, leaving only the gentler sorrow for what might have been.

She choked up at the sight of Ethan's hand cradling their daughter's head—protective, loving. The way he'd cradled *her* from the start. With tenderness and patience he'd demolished her defences, allowing her to recall the good memories without pain, allowing her to love again.

She kissed their daughter's brow and guided her searching mouth to her breast. Rejoiced at the ecstasy of this unique moment of bonding. *Their daughter.* How wonderful it sounded now.

Gazing at her husband she wondered if a heart could burst with joy. She stretched her neck to kiss him, luxuriating in the knowledge that he was hers. Basking in the glow from his darkening cobalt eyes.

'Louisa.' He stroked their daughter's hair. 'A priceless gift. Very much wanted and loved.'

'Louisa Leona James,' she countered. 'A mother has naming rights too.'

* * * * *

"I'd like to get to know you again."

His eyes turned serious when he added, "How about if we start fresh, pretend we just met? Could we do that tonight?"

She tried to speak but could get nothing past her throat, not even breath.

You can't pretend that, her conscience protested. *Tell him about his son. He needs to know.*

"Nate," she finally managed. "I think it would be best if—"

He touched her lips. "Think less. This one time."

He pulled her chair closer, close enough for him to cup the back of her head. "On second thought, you should know my intentions before we set our plans in stone." His voice was so soft.

Her heart beat so hard she could barely draw the breath to speak. "What are your intentions?"

Tenderly his lips settled on hers, soft as down. How could she have forgotten the feel of them, the scent of his skin? It was a homecoming.

She kissed him back with yearning and passion and a hunger she couldn't satisfy on a neighborhood porch.

This is wrong, her conscience cried out.

If it was, it was an exquisite, magnificent mistake.

* * *

The Men of Thunder Ridge:
Once you meet the men of this Oregon town,
you may never want to leave!

HIS SURPRISE SON

BY
WENDY WARREN

MILLS & BOON

First Published in Great Britain 2016
By Mills & Boon, an imprint of HarperCollins*Publishers*
1 London Bridge Street, London, SE1 9GF

© 2016 Wendy Warren

ISBN: 978-0-263-92001-7

23-0716

Our policy is to use papers that are natural, renewable and recyclable products and made from wood grown in sustainable forests. The logging and manufacturing processes conform to the legal environmental regulations of the country of origin.

Printed and bound in Spain
by CPI, Barcelona

Wendy Warren loves to write about ordinary people who find extraordinary love. Laughter, family and close-knit communities figure prominently, too. Her books have won two Romance Writers of America RITA® Awards and have been nominated for numerous others. She lives in the Pacific Northwest with human and non-human critters who don't read nearly as much as she'd like, but they sure do make her laugh and feel loved.

For my daughters, Liberty and Elliana, beautiful through and through. Thank you for being my teachers, my miracles, and for having the best laughs in the world. I love you.

Chapter One

Thunder Ridge, Oregon

Izzy Lambert considered herself an honest person, and she'd bet her last dollar that most people who knew her would agree. In her whole life, she'd told only two whoppers. And if you wanted to get technical about it, the first was really more a lie of omission than an outright fib.

She'd spent a whole lot of time afraid her secrets would be discovered and nearly a decade and a half on the lookout for the man from whom she'd withheld the truth. Sometimes she'd think she was seeing him…

…at the Thunderbird Market, reaching for a quart of creamer in the dairy aisle…

…in line at the bank…

…in the car behind hers at the Macho Taco drive-through in Bend…

And once she'd nearly choked on a Mickey Mouse

pancake at Disneyland, because she thought he was there, pushing a double stroller.

In reality, it never had been him—*thank you, God*— but each time Izzy thought she saw Nate Thayer, her heart began to pound, her pulse would race, she'd feel hot and dizzy, and flop sweat drenched her in seconds.

Kinda like right now.

"Join us for lunch at The Pickle Jar. A joke and a pickle for only a nickel," she said distractedly as she handed a flyer to a group of tourists. Her eyes darted from their sunburned faces to the tall, dark-haired man at the far end of the opposite side of the block.

One of the women waggled the flyer. "Is this a genuine New York deli?"

"It's a genuine Oregon deli," Izzy murmured, squinting into the distance. She remembered a headful of thick black hair just like on the man down the block. And broad, proud shoulders like his.

"Where is it?" one of the other women asked.

"About a hundred feet that way." Taking several mincing steps, Izzy made a half turn and pointed. As she turned back, a tour bus pulled up, blocking the man from her view. *Dang it!*

"Is that why you're dressed like a pickle?" asked an elderly gentleman who was perspiring in the sun almost as much as she was.

Admonishing herself to concentrate on the prospective customers, she forced a smile. "I'm not just any pickle— I'm a kosher dill."

Yeah, she was dressed in a foam rubber pickle suit, the latest in her series of desperate attempts to scare up some new customers for the aged deli. "The Pickle Jar has quarter-done, half-done and full dill pickles, all homemade from a secret family recipe. You can take some home in a collector jar, too."

According to her online class, Branding is Your Business, having a mascot emphasized the idea behind the product, built connections with customers and humanized the company. Although one could argue that a pickle was not human.

It wasn't as if she *enjoyed* dressing as a giant briny cucumber. Once upon a time Izzy had imagined herself in college, studying business, then having an office of her own and wearing beautiful professional attire. Of course, once upon a time she'd imagined a lot of things that had turned out to be nothing more than fantasies. She'd learned several years back that you couldn't move forward unless you were first willing to accept reality. So with The Pickle Jar losing potential customers every day to the newer, hipper eateries in town, Izzy had succumbed to desperate measures, even going online to purchase this warty green pickle suit, only "slightly" used.

It was swelteringly hot and dark inside the costume, and the cylindrical interior could use a good steam cleaning. None of the other deli employees would even consider putting it on. But she did, because the costume was a marketing tool and allowing the business to close was not an option.

The tourist to whom she'd been speaking, dressed in the same Keep Portland Weird T-shirt as his wife, crossed his arms. "Can we really get a joke and a pickle for just a nickel?"

"Absolutely."

She spared one last glance across the street, but the tour bus was still in the way. With perspiration trickling below the wimple-style head of the pickle suit, she swiped her brow. The man she'd thought she recognized was probably gone, anyway. Believing she saw Nate Thayer was nothing more than a weird function of her overanxious mind. For some reason, it was almost always in times of personal

stress that she would imagine she saw him. Probably because she could think of few things *more* stressful than
having to confront him again.

Focus on business, she counseled herself. *Business is
real.*

The Pickle Jar wasn't only her place of employment; it
was her home. It was where she'd discovered family for
the first time in her life. She was the manager of a failing
restaurant, but she could fix it. She *would* fix it.

Forgetting about everything else, Izzy returned her
focus to the tourists and gave them her most gracious
smile. "I've got a million jokes, but the pickles are even
better. Follow me to the best little deli west of the Hudson."

So far, Nate Thayer's trip down memory lane was prov-
ing bumpier than anticipated. Seated across from Jackson
Fleming, who'd quarterbacked for Ridge High back in the
day, Nate listened with half an ear as his former teammate
complained about…ah, pretty much everything, from the
boredom of driving a milk truck for a living to the pressures
of raising four kids who sucked up every penny he made,
to the slowness of the service at The Pickle Jar, where, in
fact, they hadn't been seated for more than a couple of minutes and were currently perusing the plastic-coated menus.

In Thunder Ridge on business, this was Nate's first trip
home in fifteen years. It had been his suggestion to have
lunch here, and while Jack griped about life post high
school, Nate allowed his attention to wander around the
deli. On the surface, not much had changed. He remembered sitting at that chipped Formica counter, studying for
his final high school exams, nursing a drink and eating his
fill of mouth-puckering pickles until Sam Bernstein started
sending over free corned beef on rye. "Eat," the older man,
short of stature but huge of heart, had insisted when Nate
refused the gratis meals at first. "I see you in here all the

time, studying hard." Sam had nodded his approval. "The brain needs food. I'm making a contribution to your college education. You'll thank me by having a good career."

He did have a good career, a great career actually, as a commercial architect based in Chicago. Over the years, when he'd thought of Thunder Ridge, he'd found himself hoping the Bernstein brothers would approve. Today Nate didn't see either of the two old men who owned the deli. The force of his desire to find them alive and well surprised him. He had written once or twice after he'd left for college, but there'd been a lot of water under the bridge, too many complicated feelings for the communication not to feel awkward; soon it had fallen away altogether. Nate wouldn't be in town long, but it would feel good to mend that particular fence.

His relationship with the brothers was not the only casualty from his past, of course, but the other issue was unlikely to ever be repaired. Isabelle Lambert had left town shortly after he had. In high school, he and Izzy had been in different grades and had run with different crowds; he hadn't so much as heard her name in a decade and a half. More than once he'd thought about looking her up but had always talked himself out of it.

Nevertheless, it was impossible to return to Central Oregon and not think about the girl with the caramel hair, skin soft as a pillow and lake-colored eyes so big and deep Nate had wanted to dive into them.

When he noticed his fingers clutching the menu too tightly, he forced himself to relax. After fifteen years, his feelings still had jagged, unfinished edges where Izzy was concerned.

"Are you ready to order?"

Distracted by his thoughts, Nate hadn't noticed the waitress's arrival. She filled their water glasses, then set the plastic pitcher on the table and stood looking down at them.

Her name tag read Willa, a good name for the petite, fair beauty whose long auburn waves and serene appearance made her look as if she'd emerged from another era.

Jack grinned at the waitress. "What's special today? Besides you?" Despite being married and having a houseful of children, he was obviously smitten.

Nate winced, but the woman remained unfazed, her cool expression revealing nothing as she responded. "We're serving a hot brisket sandwich on a kaiser roll. It comes with a side salad. The soup today is chicken in the pot."

Quickly Nate ordered the sandwich, hoping his friend would do the same without further embarrassing himself, but Jack had other plans. "I'll take the sandwich, and bring me a cold drink, too, gorgeous. 'Cause the more I look at you, the hotter I get."

"Jack," Nate began in a warning undertone, but the former Thunder Ridge Huskies football hero—emphasis on *former*—clearly thought he still had the goods.

Jack grinned at Nate. "You're in town awhile, right? Maybe Willa's got a friend, and we can double-date."

Willa picked up the pitcher of water, murmuring, "I'll get your sandwiches," but Jack, who had clearly lost his mind, patted the woman's butt, then reached for her wrist. The redhead tried to jerk away. Jack held on.

What came next happened so quickly Nate wasn't sure exactly what had occurred. He was aware of a voice hollering, "Hey!" and the next thing he knew, a large green… cucumber?…appeared at the table concurrent with a tidal wave of ice-cold water washing over him and Jack. Mostly Jack.

Jack yelled, the cucumber yelled back, and then it slipped in the puddle of water, falling in a heap of flailing green arms and legs.

"Pickle down!" a busboy shouted.

Ah, it was a pickle.

Nate rose to help.

"You threw that water on purpose," Jack accused.

"Shut up," Nate suggested as he knelt next to what appeared to be a life-size vegetable mascot. "Don't move," he said, unsure of where to check first for injuries. At least there was an abundance of padding. "Let's make sure you're not hurt before you try to get up."

Ignoring him, the irate dill pointed toward Jack. "You need to leave this restaurant. Now." Then it turned back to Nate. "And you. You—"

She stopped—it was definitely a she.

Half a lifetime fell away.

"Izzy?" Her name escaped on a rush of breath.

It took her longer to say his name, and when she did, her voice crackled. "Nate."

"You know her?" Jack glared. "She got water on my Wallabees." He raised a leg, pointing to his boot. "These are suede, man, and I haven't Scotchgarded them yet. I want to see the manager."

Because he found it impossible to break eye contact with Izzy, Nate felt rather than saw the small crowd that was gathering around them. He heard someone say, "She *is* the manager," and then people started talking over one another, their voices seeming distant and irrelevant.

Izzy.

That's what was relevant. The fact that Izzy Lambert was here, right where he'd left her—despite her avowal that she would leave this town someday and head for a big city with opportunities that were bigger and better than anything she'd known in Oregon.

"What happened?" he murmured.

"I slipped on the water."

He shook his head. Not what he'd meant. But he hadn't intended to speak his thought out loud, anyway.

He'd been told she left town and recalled his tangled

emotions at the time. It had taken some work, but he'd finally made peace with the fact that they'd been kids when they'd dated, that their relationship had been meant to last a summer not a lifetime and that, thankfully, the only people they'd truly hurt were themselves. Still, Izzy Lambert remained the big unanswered question of his life.

"Coming through. What happened here?"

Khaki-colored trousers appeared in Nate's peripheral vision. He glanced up to see a sheriff, who stood with his hands on his hips, looking amusedly down at Izzy.

"Izz. You hurt?"

"No."

"Okay. Up you go, then." The lawman, a big, good-looking guy, extended a hand.

"Wait a minute." Rising, Nate faced the sheriff. Now that he was standing, he realized the man was about his height…*maybe* a half inch taller…and roughly the same weight. Nate didn't like the slight smile around the other man's lips. "She shouldn't get up until we know for sure she hasn't broken something."

To the casual observer, the sheriff's smile appeared friendly, but there was a distinct challenge in the dark gaze that connected with Nate's.

"Sheriff Derek Neel." He introduced himself with a nod. No handshake. "And you are?"

Nate glanced at Izzy. Her eyes looked huge. "An old friend," he responded, not above a twinge of satisfaction when the sheriff's brow lowered a bit.

"Must be really old," Sheriff Neel surmised. "I've known Izz twelve years. I can't recall ever seeing you around."

It was Nate's turn to frown, and it felt more like a scowl. "Izz" must not have left Thunder Ridge for very long. She'd gone without getting in touch with him, without leaving a forwarding address. And back then she hadn't had email or a cell phone. Nate had already moved to Chicago to attend college, was already deeply immersed in that life. Other than phoning Henry to ask if he knew where Izzy was—and Henry had claimed he had no information about Izzy—there had been no way, really, to track her down.

Out of nowhere, the feelings he'd had half a lifetime ago came rushing back, brief but surprisingly powerful. The tight throat, the sick gut, the confusion, even the desire to punch something when he'd heard Izzy was gone—all those sensations were there again, despite the years and the experiences between then and now.

Izzy seemed frozen in place, but his glance unlocked her, and she struggled to sit up. The bulky costume impeded her efforts.

The sheriff grabbed her beneath the left elbow the same moment that Nate's fingers closed around her right arm. She looked at him, not at the other man, her eyes alarmed. Her soft, perfectly formed lips parted…and damned if he didn't feel it again—the old desire, the possessiveness he'd never felt about anyone or anything except Izzy Lambert.

She seemed to be primed to say "thank you," but no sound emerged. Instead, she stared back at him, breathing through her open mouth, silky brows arched, and he recalled the way she *used* to look at him, as if she'd been hungry for the very sight of him.

His glance dropped to her torso. Couldn't help it. Though he couldn't see it, he knew that beneath the bulky costume was the body he had gotten to know well. Too well, let's face it. He had seen it in sunlight, moonlight and the stark light of a doctor's office. He remembered it all.

Did she?

He shouldn't feel a damned thing for Izzy Lambert after all these years. Their relationship was a cold case. It had begun as a summer love and ended the way most everyone had predicted it would—with Nate leaving for college in another state and Izzy...

Well, he wasn't certain exactly what had happened to Izzy. All he knew for sure was that between the beginning and the end of their relationship, they had lived a lifetime, bonded in ways some couples never did. In one summer they had been forced to grow up, whatever innocence they'd once enjoyed gone for good. Maybe that was why the feelings weren't completely dead, at least not for him. In all the years since, he hadn't lived with that much intensity. Or passion.

With his blood feeling too hot for his veins, Nate wondered if he should have stayed away despite the passage of time. Then, just as suddenly, as if someone had turned on the air-conditioning, the heat of resentment cooled.

She'd planned to make a mark on the world, yet here she was: *a pickle.*

An angry pickle, coming to the defense of her coworker. Suddenly, he couldn't prevent the quirk of his lips. *Izzy, Izzy...* Somehow, the ridiculous situation suited her. She'd always been unpredictable, always surprising.

Nate glanced again at the sheriff. Who was he? Friend? Lover? Something more? Maybe. *But if she is, I wouldn't want to be in your boots, pal.* Izzy was still looking at him, not at the lawman.

Nate's relationship with Isabelle Lambert might be fifteen years dead and buried, but he could feel the current running between them right now, and suddenly Nate knew in his gut: returning to Thunder Ridge was either a mistake or the best decision he'd made in a long, long time.

Gridlock. That was the state of Izzy's brain.

Nate's fingers were wrapped around her upper arm as he and Derek lifted her to her feet. It might have taken

one second or ten minutes. All she could feel was Nate...
and fear.

His touch ignited a flash fire of memory. The years
disappeared and once more she was standing between his
arms, her back against his truck, feeling his heartbeat and
his heat, inhaling the amazing, perfect scent of his skin as
he pressed against her, his whisper warm in her ear: *"Do
you know what the feel of you does to me?"* He'd been the
only person who'd ever made her feel truly special. More
than a decade later, parts of her body that had been in hi-
bernation a long, long time suddenly woke up. That was
not good.

To regain her composure, she tore her gaze from his.
She needed time to think. Even after all the years of looking for him, of fearing she might run into him somewhere,
he'd still managed to catch her completely off guard now
that it had actually happened.

And then, the worst...

Big Ken, the affectionately named clock tower in front
of City Hall, struck two. *Boom...boom...*

Oh, dear Lord. She didn't have much time at all. Seven
minutes if she was lucky.

Her heart galloped as one thought rose above all others: *Get rid of him!*

"Nice to see you, Nate. I have to get back to work.
Meal's on the house."

Izzy considered that a nice touch...friendly, but Nate's
blue eyes narrowed. "We haven't eaten yet."

"Oh. Not a problem. We'll get you a sandwich to go."

Nate's frown deepened.

"You know what *I'd* like?" Jack, the jerk Izzy had seen
groping Willa, stepped forward. "An apology for ruining
my boots. Maybe even a reimbursement."

Izzy stared at the man. She'd caught him *fondling* her

employee, a woman so buttoned-up and proper that Izzy never told a blue joke in front of her.

Nate's friend was a big hulk of a guy. Izzy didn't recognize him, but she knew his type. Her mother had dated men like him: big, arrogant and dumb as rocks. Convinced you were as impressed with them as they were with themselves. *Forget the jerk. Get rid of Nate*, her brain counseled wisely. Her temper, however, which tended to get the best of her under stress, kindled.

"A reimbursement. Sure." She nodded. "Check's in the mail."

"All right. That's more like it."

"I was being facetious." Forgetting that from the neck down she was still dressed as a dill, she waddled up to the man to take him down a peg. "You know what *I* think? I think you need to apologize to Willa."

"To Willa?" Derek was beside her in a flash. "What happened?"

"Nothing!" Twisting a ring on her right hand, Willa shook her head. "It was all just a misunderstanding. It won't happen again."

"What won't happen again?" Derek squared off, ready for a showdown, which made Izzy realize instantly she should have kept her big mouth shut. Derek's history was dotted with confrontation, and he tended to be even more mulish than she.

"The lady said it was a misunderstanding." Nate stepped in. Unintimidated by Derek's badge, his stature or his expression, Nate spoke in a tone at once mildly appeasing and strongly cautionary. "Let's take her word for it. Jack, apologize to Willa."

Jack spoke up from safely behind his friend. "Why should *I* apologize?"

"To save your life." Nate tossed the wry reply over his

shoulder while maintaining eye contact with Derek, who now directed his glower toward Nate.

"Who are you again?" Derek demanded, his hands on his hips. "And how do you know Izzy?"

Izzy's heart began to pound. She and Nate had kept their personal business private. Because of her home life, Izzy had not socialized much, and because she and Nate had both had jobs, they'd reserved their limited time together strictly for each other. With the exception of Henry and Sam, who owned the deli and knew almost everything about her, most people had assumed she and Nate were just a fleeting high school crush. Here today, gone tomorrow. Which was exactly what she wanted them to assume.

I should use Gorilla Glue instead of lip gloss. If she'd kept her mouth shut, Nate and his friend might be out of here by now.

His gaze fell on her as he answered Derek. "Izzy and I are…old friends."

Was it her imagination, or had Nate hesitated a hair too long before he said "old friends"? In addition to Derek, half her crew had rushed over to help when she fell. She did not want to court their curiosity.

Addressing herself to Jack, she said, "Never mind. You know what? Check *is* in the mail."

"No, it's not." Nate turned toward her, his expression uncompromising. "He owes Willa—and you—an apology." The steadiness of his gaze made her skin prickle inside the hot costume.

"Whose side are you on?" Jack complained. "She got water on you, too, man."

Nate didn't glance his friend's way. His attention and low, intense words were all for Izzy. "Stand your ground, Isabelle. Don't let some jackass push you around."

"Hey!" Jack protested behind them.

Locked in a battle of gazes with Nate, anger blazed through Izzy like a brush fire.

Fifteen years ago, she would have given almost anything to have Nate Thayer on her side. To hear him stand up for her, stand up for *them*. But his supportive words were a decade and a half too late.

"You're giving me advice, Nate? No, thank you. What I want is for you to take your friend and go." She wasn't a weak, starry-eyed girl any longer. "I want you to go *right now*." The last words were so choked, so intense, Nate may have been the only one to hear them.

The surprise on Nate's face offered a modicum of satisfaction. He seemed to be on the brink of saying something more before his expression shuttered, concealing his thoughts.

Slowly, he turned to his loudmouthed friend. "Apologize, and let's go."

"Apologize? For being friendly?"

"Do it," Nate said. "I'm sure the sheriff would like to kick your ass, Jack, and if he doesn't, I might. Stop arguing and start apologizing."

"Fine. Who do I have to apologize to? The cucumber or the waitress?"

Hands resting just above his gun belt, Derek got in Jack's face. "She's a pickle."

Nate shook his head. "Apologize to both of them," he ordered.

Face reddening, Jack turned first to Willa. "Okay. Sorry. I didn't mean anything by it." He raised his hand to show off the gold band. "I'm married." A resounding "ugh" circled through the small group of onlookers. Redder still, he looked at Izzy. "I apologize for making a big deal about the Wallabees. But they are new, and—"

Nate's hand clamped down firmly on Jake's shoulder.

"I think you can stop there." His gaze returned boldly to Izzy. He nodded. "Good to see you, Isabelle."

With her heart pounding against the foam costume, she gave a jerky nod.

He seemed to hesitate a moment longer, which made her nerves flare, then apparently deciding there was nothing else to say, he turned and walked toward the deli's glass door.

"Time to get back to work," she muttered, feeling slightly out of breath.

Her busboy Leon, and Oliver, the cook, returned to their jobs. Willa hurried after them.

Derek watched the petite redhead for several seconds, then looked at Izzy. His eyes narrowed. "Explanation, please. Who was that guy? 'Cause your face is as green as that ridiculous costume."

Chapter Two

"Shh." Izzy waved her hand, indicating that Derek should lower his booming voice. "I'll tell you later, I promise, but—" She stopped, her breath catching painfully in her throat.

As Nate and his friend reached the deli's entrance, a teenage boy pulled open the door.

Izzy's heart took off like a startled colt. For perhaps the second time in her life, she understood the term "blind panic." A cold sweat covered her body.

She wanted to run to the door, but her bones felt weak and rubbery, and she wouldn't know what to do once she got there. She watched helplessly as the boy held the door. Nate must have thanked him, because the teen smiled and nodded.

As Nate walked down the street, he glanced back through the broad window fronting the deli. Could he see far enough into the restaurant to note that she was still watching him? It seemed that he looked right at her before his friend drew his attention and they disappeared down the block.

"You look like you're going to be sick." Derek's voice boomed beside her. "What the hell is going on here today?"

"Not now." Her mouth was so dry, she could barely speak. "I'll tell you later, but—"

"Mom!"

Eli, her beautiful son, nearly as tall as she was now, with the same fair skin and straight brown hair as hers, loped toward them. The sight of his gangly body and broad smile never failed to make her feel as if she'd taken a hit of pure oxygen. Today the sight of him filled her with anxiety, too.

"Hey, Uncle Derek." Eli's speech was somewhat marred by the hearing impairment he had suffered as a baby.

"Hey, buddy."

"I'm staying," Eli announced, then used his expressive hands to sign the question *What's for dessert today?*

Instead of asking him whether he'd eaten lunch, Izzy both spoke and signed back, "There's strawberry cheesecake in the walk-in fridge. Help yourself."

Eli's eyes, hazel-green, like his mother's, widened in surprise. "Cool." She never offered him dessert before a healthful meal or, at the very least, a snack. Eli taught swim classes at the local parks and rec. She was always harping on him about healthful refueling. Now he trotted toward the kitchen, stopped and looked at her. *I had a sub sandwich with lettuce, tomato, spinach and pickles,* he signed. *In case you were wondering.* With a grin, Eli said hello to a waitress, dodged around her, then rounded the counter and disappeared into the kitchen calling, "Yo, O!" to Oliver, the lead cook, who had once bought Eli a set of childsized saucepans and played "chef" with him for hours.

Oh, God, how she loved her little family. Nate's presence here could threaten everything she'd defied the odds to build.

"I'm on duty tonight," Derek said, keeping his voice low, "but I'll see you tomorrow. I expect a full debriefing."

He had never asked about Eli's father. Derek had too many of his own ghosts to request that Izzy dredge up hers, but once, during a vulnerable moment, she had told him a little bit about the summer she was seventeen.

"Tomorrow?" Derek had been a good friend for years, but would she be ready to tell him—or anyone—the truth by tomorrow night? Not likely. She needed time, time to find out how long Nate was going to be in town…time to figure out how to protect her son, because this wasn't just about her. "I'm…not sure I'm free tomorrow."

"What's the problem?" Derek asked. "You close at sundown on Friday nights."

"Yes, but I'm… I've got to… There's a very important—"

"Cut it out, Izz. You're a crap liar."

That's what you think. She chewed the inside of her lip.

Derek crossed his arms. "You're making me so curious I might stop by tonight on my shift."

"No." Eli would be home tonight. "Tomorrow," she relented.

Reappearing, Eli carried a plate of the deli's mile-high cheesecake. "This is the bomb," he said, pointing to it with his fork. Setting the plate aside so he had both hands free, he asked, *Mom, is it okay if I sleep at Trey's tonight? His dad said he'd drive us to Portland in the morning.*

Eli and his friend Trey were attending the same summer camp in Portland. After tonight, she wouldn't see him for two whole weeks.

"I can drive you." Glad to think of something other than Nate, she focused on the plans she'd already made. "I took the morning off. I thought we'd stop at Voodoo Doughnuts for maple-bacon bars." She smiled, for the moment just another mom trying to tempt her teenager into spending a little more time with her.

A flash of guilt crossed her son's features. Typically more comfortable with signing than oral speech when he had more than a few words to say, he used a combination of ASL and finger spelling to explain, *Trey's dad was a counselor for Inner City Project when he was our age. He's going to introduce us around.*

"Ah." For the past several summers, Eli had attended a camp for deaf kids. This summer, he'd insisted on "regular camp." The fourteen-year-old was the one thing in Izzy's life that had turned out absolutely, perfectly right. Refraining, with difficulty, from telling him he was already way, way better than "regular," Izzy had spent more money than she should have to register Eli for the camp with Trey.

"Traveling with Trey and Mr. Richards sounds like a great idea," she said. "You have a good time. In fact, I'll take off early and help you pack."

I'm already packed. I can sleep at Trey's so we can get an early start tomorrow. His mom invited me to dinner.

"Oh. Well…great. Great, because I wasn't even sure what to make tonight." His favorite monster burritos, actually. *Have a fabulous time, First Mate*, she signed without speaking.

Aye, aye, Skipper, he signed back, playing along with the endearments they'd been using since he was in third grade and they'd eaten their dinners at the coffee table, watching reruns of *Gilligan's Island*. She probably ought to stop calling him cutesy names that would make a less patient kid gag.

I'll see you in a couple of weeks, Mom. He looked at Derek. *Take care of her for me, Uncle Derek.*

Derek both signed and spoke back, "I'll do that, buddy."

Eli made a move toward his mother, then looked uncertain. *I'm not sure how to hug you when you're a pickle.*

Solving the problem, she tossed her arms around her

son, gave him a warm squeeze, then began to run through the list of safety precautions he needed to take at camp.

Eli nodded for a while before interrupting, *Mom, I got the memo. Literally.* He looked at Derek and splayed his fingers. "She wrote five pages."

Izzy blushed. "It's easy to forget things when you're away."

Mom, I'll be safe, respectful and aware of my surroundings. I won't lose my hearing aid, 'cause it's really *expensive, and I'll be back in two weeks with all my body parts.* And then, just so she would have a memory to reduce her to tears every day that he was away, Eli kissed her on the cheek and said with his most careful enunciation, "See you, Skipper."

She refused to cry. Until he was out the door.

After exchanging a manly hug with Derek, Eli jogged out of the deli. Izzy didn't start sniffling audibly until the glass door closed behind her only child, leaving her with her worries and a sense of loneliness that made her feel hollow as an empty tomb.

"Aw, come on, Pickle. He'll be home soon." Derek's arm went round her in what turned out to be a kind of stranglehold. "Do you know pickles have no visible shoulders? Makes it hard to be friendly." He adjusted his arm a bit more companionably. "If I wasn't on duty tonight, I'd keep you company. I'll bring pizza tomorrow. The works?"

"Sure."

Willa walked by carrying a lox platter, and Derek's attention instantly swerved to the petite redhead. "For pity's sake, ask her out already," Izzy whispered. "You stare at her every time you come in."

"She doesn't stare back."

Izzy shook her head, content to focus on someone else's fears instead of her own for a while. "Sheriff Neel, are you telling me a big, strapping lawman like you is afraid of a tiny, little woman who hasn't uttered an unkind word since she's been here?"

Derek grunted.

"When was the last time you went on a date?" she needled. "You can't be a sheriff 24/7, buddy. You need a reason to wear street clothes once in a while."

One of Derek's brows arched. "Look who's talking. You're a pickle. How's your date card these days, Isabelle? Do I need to find someone else to watch *Shark Tank* with?"

The last time Izzy had felt motivated to take a good hard look at her love life, she'd wound up alone in the back office, eating a quart of matzo ball soup and putting a sizable dent in a chocolate chip babka. "Fine. Never mind," she muttered. "I was trying to be helpful." She and Derek lapsed into grumpy silence for several seconds, disgusted far more with themselves than with each other.

Finally, Derek spoke. "If you need something before tomorrow, call me. I mean, with the kid leaving."

She nodded. "Thanks. I better get back to work,"

"Me, too. Lives to protect and all that."

"Yeah. Pickles to serve."

With one last, not-very-subtle glance at Willa, he headed toward the coatrack at the front of the deli, where he'd hung his hat.

Izzy sighed. All right, so they were both terminally pathetic when it came to romance. At least Derek had a town to watch over, and she—

I have a restaurant and a family to save. Here in this dying deli were people she loved who loved her back. That was something. More, in fact, than she'd ever thought she would have. She intended to protect what was hers, no matter what.

First, though, she had to get out of this pickle suit, which felt like a personal sauna, and go somewhere alone so she could think clearly.

Waddling to the counter, she told Audra, who had worked at the deli longer than she had, "I'm leaving for a couple of hours. If you can hold down the fort, I'll be back in plenty of time for the dinner shift." Without Eli at home, she'd be better off working instead of worrying. Maybe if she took a break, she could figure out what to do about Nate Thayer and the child they'd made together.

"We can do this, no problem," Izzy grunted, standing on the pedals of her bike. "Going uphill is good…for…us." Her teeth ground together. Every downstroke was harder to come by than the one before as she pumped determinedly up Vista Road. "We're going to start…doing this…every…day," she panted to her beloved dog, Latke, a Shar-Pei rescue whose ambivalence toward physical activity gave credence to the distinction *nonsporting breed.*

Her heart and head both thudded painfully, but even that was better than the avalanche of questions that buzzed in her brain on the heels of Nate Thayer's return. So far, she had not a single answer, not even a clue as to what was going to happen if and when her son discovered that his father was in Thunder Ridge…or vice versa.

Nausea and dizziness the likes of which she hadn't experienced since she was pregnant overwhelmed her. Eli had questioned her about his father a few times, mostly during the tween years when his own identity was in minute-by-minute flux. The answers she'd provided hadn't been satisfying, but at least they had cooled Eli's incessant wondering about the man whose life goals had not included a pregnant teenage girlfriend.

"'Kay, I think I'm going to puke now."

She had to stop pedaling, hop off the seat and close her eyes. Latke accepted the rest stop as an opportunity to prostrate herself in the bike lane.

Izzy leaned over the handlebars. "We'll get going in a sec, baby, just as soon as Mama's heart attack is done."

"Would rehydrating help?"

On a fresh surge of adrenaline, Izzy's eyes popped open. A clear plastic water bottle, icy cold with condensation dripping down the sides, dangled in front of her.

"Bike much?" Nate Thayer arched a brow, lips twisting sardonically.

Silently cursing fate, Izzy stared at him. She had deliberately ridden away from town and in the opposite direction from the dairy farm where Nate had grown up. "What are you doing out here?" The question sounded like an accusation.

"Tsk, tsk, tsk." He shook his head. "We need to polish our welcome committee skills. This is the second time in one day that you haven't greeted me on my return home."

"Home?" Izzy felt as if a giant fist were squeezing her stomach. "You're here to stay?" Her distaste for that possibility was clear as a bell and drew a deep frown from Nate.

Unscrewing the top of the water bottle, he held it out again. "Take it. You're about to keel over."

"No, I'm not."

A smile tugged his lips. "Take it anyway."

Willing her fingers to stop shaking, Izzy plucked the bottle from his hand, careful not to touch him. Lowering the kickstand, she stepped away from her bike with Nate observing her every move. Even when she stopped looking at him, she could feel his eyes on her, the way she used to sense him watching her in the deli fifteen years ago. Back then her skin would tingle with excitement, even as she'd pretended not to notice. Today, anxiety made her skin prickle like needle pokes.

She bent toward her dog. "Here, sweetie." Tilting Nate's offering, she let Latke drink. The Shar-Pei's heavy jowls flapped as she slurped with the grace of a hippo sipping from a martini glass.

During the summer that she and Nate had been a couple, Izzy had never truly confronted him. How could she? She had been so besotted, so damn *grateful* that the high school heartthrob had chosen her, a girl with an embarrassing family and no prospects for a decent future. Now, when her dog was finished drinking, she stood and met Nate's gaze with challenge in her own. "Latke says thanks."

He addressed her dog. "You're welcome."

Wearing the same clothes he'd had on in the deli—J.Crew jeans and a sea-blue V-necked T-shirt that matched his eyes almost identically (yeah, she'd noticed), his hair still ridiculously thick and shiny—he shrugged. "I only brought the one bottle. Come back to my room. There's more water in the minibar."

Izzy glanced in the direction from which Nate had come. The heavily shingled roof of the Eagle's Crest Inn peeked through a grove of pine trees. "How did you even see me from the inn? " she asked.

"My room faces the street. And my desk faces the window. When I saw you crawl by, I thought, 'Well, what do you know? Fate must want us to have a reunion, even if Izzy doesn't.'" His gaze narrowed. "It's been a long time. You must have a few minutes to spare for an old friend."

There it was, the liquid velvet voice that used to make her feel as if she were wrapped in the most comfortable blanket ever created.

"I haven't, actually. I'm due back at the deli." Shoving the empty bottle into the saddlebag on her bike, she climbed back on and tried to tug sixty pounds of wrinkled canine to a standing position. "Let's go, girl." No movement.

"I think she needs a nap."

What her pet needed was a couple thousand volts. "She's

fine. She loves to run. Let's go, Latke." Izzy put her right foot on the bike pedal, intending to pull the dog into a standing position if she had to. She jerked with surprise when Nate clamped his fingers around the handlebars.

He leaned forward, his shadow looming over her. Humor fled his expression, replaced by curiosity and displeasure. "If I didn't know better, Isabelle, I'd say you plan to avoid me until I leave town. Why?"

"That's not my intention at all. I'm just very busy right now. I'm sure we'll find time before you go. When did you say you're leaving?"

"I didn't say."

"Well, I'm sure we'll run into each other again. And now I know where you're staying, so…" She tried to back the bike up, but he was still holding her handlebars.

"So you'll get in touch?" His voice grew quiet, penetrating. "I should expect a call? Like last time?"

"Last time." Izzy's stomach began to twist so hard she wanted to double over. "What do you mean?"

"When I went to Chicago, you and I agreed to talk once a week. Then suddenly you were gone, no forwarding address, no warning."

Threads of anger wove through Izzy's fear. "No warning? Yeah, I suppose you're right. I should have told you all about my plans. Ten minutes once a week wasn't a lot of time, though. I'd have to talk really fast."

"I'm not following you."

"You're not? Every Sunday afternoon," she reminded him, "from five to five ten Pacific Time? Nate Thayer's obligatory check-in to the girl he'd knocked up back in Oregon. Very thoughtful, those calls, but you have to admit they didn't leave a lot of time to talk about anything in depth." Which, she had thought at the time, must have been the point.

Surprise hijacked Nate's features, and Izzy took the

opportunity to wrest the handlebars from his grip. He moved in front of the bike immediately. "That's what you thought I was doing? Just fulfilling an obligation?"

"That *is* what you were doing. Look, Nate," Izzy chided, "it's ancient history, but let's not rewrite it. When I got pregnant, you saw your college dreams flushing down the toilet. So, you and your parents came up with a solution—put the baby up for adoption and check in with the pregnant teenager once a week to make sure she's still on board. Perfectly logical. Frankly, if I'd had a scholarship to a big university and parents who'd already picked out the frame for my diploma, I might have felt the same way."

"You agreed that adoption seemed like the best solution."

"I was seventeen, pregnant and dead broke. I wasn't in a great position to argue."

Nate's brows swooped low. A muscle tensed in his jaw. "Are you saying you didn't want to put the baby up for adoption?"

Her mind began to race like a machine that was out of control—couldn't slow down, couldn't stop.

"You agreed we were both too young to be good parents," he said, glancing at a car that whizzed by. "I don't want to discuss this on the street. Why don't you come up—"

"I don't want to discuss this at all." She made a show of looking at her watch. "I have to go." When she tried to push the bike forward, however, Nate held on.

A sharp burning sensation rose behind Izzy's eyes. *Don't cry. Don't you dare cry, not after all this time.* But she remembered one occasion—just the one—when Nate had stopped being logical and reasonable about how they were too young and too uneducated and not financially able to raise a baby properly. On that single occasion, before he'd left for college, his brow had hitched in the middle like it was right now, worry muddying the usually clear and confident expression in his eyes, and he'd said, "Do you think it'll be a boy or a girl?"

In that one moment, they had felt like parents, not two kids who had made a colossal mistake.

She swallowed hard.

"You know what I remember, Nate? I remember what your mother and father said—that our relationship was 'a lapse in good judgment.' And that we'd be crazy to throw our futures away." They had meant their son's future, of course. There hadn't been many people around at that time who'd held out much hope for her future. "We shouldn't blame each other for anything. It might have been different if we'd loved each other, right? But we were just kids." Her sad smile was the genuine article. "You're lucky you had parents who were looking out for you."

"Izzy—"

"I really do have to go now."

Using the heel of her running shoe to flip the kickstand, Izzy climbed aboard her bike and pushed forward toward Latke, urging her to fall into step. Nate watched her every move but didn't try to stop her this time as she checked for traffic and made a U-turn on Vista Road.

Traveling downhill, Izzy went as fast as she dared push her trotting dog, desperate to outrun worry and the tears that, finally, would not be denied. She swiped the back of her hand across her nose and used her palm to wipe her eyes. Determined to keep the details of her home life private when she was younger, she'd kept to herself in middle and high school, flying as far under the radar as possible and even earning the nickname "Loner Chick." After a while, she'd been largely ignored, which had been fine by her. She'd never traded one word with Nate Thayer until the summer after he'd graduated.

What a tangled web she had woven when she, a girl from as far over the wrong side of the tracks as you could get, fell in love with the golden boy of Thunder Ridge. And got pregnant.

That hadn't been her biggest sin, though. No, not by a long shot. Her biggest sin had been believing Nate loved her back, that he would change his mind about the baby and that they would live happily ever after. Her biggest sin had been telling herself the lie that when you loved hard enough, all your dreams would come true.

Chapter Three

For Izzy, "home" was the one-word description of the blood, sweat and tears she had put into constructing not just a building but a family. The deli had been her first real home, and she had happily painted its aged walls, twisted new washers onto leaking faucets and waxed its linoleum tiles until the memory of their former luster glinted through the wear and tear.

It was the same with the cottage in which she and Eli made their home. When she'd first laid eyes on the 860-square-foot space, her heart had sunk. The tiny house was all she'd been able to afford and even then she'd had to borrow the down payment (paid back in full) from her boss Henry, who by that time had become more of a surrogate father to her.

The prospect of owning her own home, a place she and her son could call theirs forever, had pushed her to overlook the dark wood walls, the ugly threadbare carpets and the cracked enamel in the ancient claw-foot tub, not to mention the spaces in the roof shingles through which she could actually see the sky. Izzy and Eli, who by then had turned seven, dubbed the little house Lambert Cottage, and she'd learned all she could about repairs and improvements.

Today their home was a sunny, whitewashed space with a scrubbed pine floor she'd discovered beneath the carpets, and pale pear-green furniture she'd reupholstered on her own. She made Thanksgiving dinners in her tiny kitchen and hosted birthday parties in a garden filled with azalea, honeysuckle and lydia broom. It was no longer possible to see sky through the roof, but there were times late at night as Izzy lay in bed saying her prayers that she gazed into the darkness above her head and was sure she could see heaven. Coming home never, ever failed to soothe and reassure her.

Except this afternoon.

Unleashing Latke, she set out a bowl of fresh water, chugged a tumbler of iced tea, rinsed her glass and set it upside down on the wooden drain rack, just as she would have done on any normal day. The difference was that today her hands shook the entire time, and she thought she might throw up.

Since she'd pedaled away from Nate, memories had been buffeting her so hard she felt like a tiny dinghy on a storm-ridden sea. Some of the memories were good. So good that yearning squeezed her heart like a sponge. Others were more bittersweet. But there was one memory that rose above the others, whipping up a giant wall of emotion that threatened to capsize her: the recollection of the day she'd accepted that the boy she loved was never going to love her back, not the same way, and that she'd rather be alone the rest of her life than beg for a love that wasn't going to come…

Fifteen years earlier...

Nate ran his fingers through his hair—that famously thick black hair—then remained head down, elbows on knees, hands cradling his forehead. "Damn it."

Izzy winced at the frustration in his tone, wondering if he was directing it at her, at the news she'd just given him or at both. Probably both. What hurt the most, she thought, was that the best summer of her life was now quite clearly the worst of his. "I'm sorry."

What a stupid thing to say! Plus, she'd whispered the words, which made the fact that she'd apologized even worse.

She was no wimp. But sitting next to Nate on a bench in Portland's Washington Park, exhausted and freaking terrified, she figured that if *I'm sorry* was the best she could do, then so be it. Seventeen had felt so much older and more mature just a week ago. Tonight she felt like a little girl afraid of the dark and of the unknown.

"You're positive?" Nate demanded. His voice, which had always made her think of soft, dark velvet, tonight sounded more like a rusty rake scraping cement.

Izzy nodded. She was "positive," all right. She'd bought four early-pregnancy tests, which had sucked up three hours' worth of income from her job waiting tables at The Pickle Jar deli. Every single test had turned up a thin pink line. She'd never liked pink.

"I'm pregnant," she confirmed. *May as well get used to saying it out loud.*

"How?" Raising his head, Nate looked at the evening skyline beyond the Rose Test Garden, where they sat, rather than at her.

How? *How* was obvious, right? They'd been having sex since May. Nearly four full months of his waiting for her when she got off work at the restaurant and then whisking her away in his old Toyota pickup. It could have been a limousine or a horse-drawn carriage—that was how lucky Izzy had felt to be driving into the night with Nate Thayer.

"I mean, we used protection," Nate said now, trying to reason out her news. "Every time."

Hardly the words of comfort—and solidarity—she'd been hoping for.

Suck it up, Izz. He's shocked.

A year older and already graduated from high school, Nate had plans for his life…so did she…plans that did not include becoming a teenage parent.

"Not every time," she countered.

"What?"

"Protection. We didn't use it *every* time. Not on the Fourth of July."

"The Fourth? Yes, we—" He stopped. And swore again.

Her heart, which for the past few months had felt as if it were unfolding like one of the roses in Washington Park, suddenly shriveled around the edges.

They'd made love in the bed of his truck nearly two months ago on Independence Day, atop a thick pile of sleeping bags. With most of the people in their hometown watching the fireworks down at the river, she and Nate had agreed to keep their romance as private as possible. Izzy hadn't wanted to invite prying eyes or unwelcome comments. So on that Fourth of July, they'd driven to the resort where he'd worked over the summer. Parked near a small lake, with Santana cranked up on the radio, Nate had gazed down at her. The lights in the distance had illuminated his face—so beautiful, so serious. Wondering at his expression, she'd touched his cheek, and he'd whispered, almost as if he was surprised, "I feel better with you than I do anyplace else."

Her love had exploded like the fireworks.

"Are you sure it's mine?"

Sudden and sharp, the question plunged into Izzy's chest with the force of a dagger. Her gaze fused with his and she saw the truth in his eyes, so obvious that she couldn't catch her breath: he hoped another boy could be the baby's father.

Suddenly, the scent of spent blooms from the end-of-summer roses became overwhelming. Running for the cover of the bushes, Izzy retched into the ground.

While her stomach surrendered its contents, her mother's words from earlier this summer tumbled through her brain.

"Running off with that hottie? If you're smart, you'll get knocked up. Then maybe you can get him to take care of you." Felicia had punctuated her advice by raising her beer can in a mock toast. *"It never lasts, but it's better than nothing."*

On her way out the door—yes, she had *been going to meet Nate*—Izzy had turned to give the woman who'd only sort of raised her a withering glare. *"I would never do that. I'm not like you."*

Genuine laughter had erupted around the cigarette Felicia had put between her lips. *"Oh, sweetie, you are exactly like me. The only difference is you think it's classier to give it away for free."* As Izzy slammed the screen door, Felicia's words tagged after her. *"You're going to wind up like me, too. Count on it."*

It took Izzy a while to realize that Nate was beside her, one hand smoothing her light brown curls from her face, the other supporting her shoulders as she bent over the ground.

"I don't want your help." With her forearm, she knocked his hand away. Nate reared back in surprise.

Of course he was surprised. Up to now, she'd never been anything but sweet and agreeable. She'd been so happy, so grateful to be with him.

"Hey!" He grabbed her arm when she attempted to rise

on her own. "Stop. You're going to make yourself sick again. Just relax a minute."

"Relax?" Was he serious? "Good idea. Maybe I'll sign up for prenatal yoga. I'm pretty sure Ridge High offers that senior year."

Nate rubbed both hands down his face. "Okay, look, I was being an ass when I asked if it was mine. I'm sorry. I don't… I don't know how to do this, Izzy. No one has ever told me she was pregnant before."

"Well, that makes two of us, because I've never said it before."

He nodded. Then, ignoring her protest, he put his arm firmly around her waist and led her back to the bench. Finding a napkin in the picnic basket she'd packed for them, he wiped her brow. His touch and the fact that he insisted on helping her was sweet torture. She'd spent her whole life relying on herself, no longer daring to hope for one person she could lean into until she'd met Nate. When he collapsed against the bench, not making physical contact with her, she had to fight the urge to scoot closer.

He stretched his neck up, as if searching for an answer in the dark sky. "I'm supposed to leave for college in two weeks," he said.

"I know." He had told her from the beginning, and lately she'd hoped… Never mind what she'd hoped.

Don't panic. Panicking won't help.

"I've got to tell my parents." He sounded as if he was about to tell them he'd found out he was dying.

"Maybe they'll be supportive."

Nate's laugh told her otherwise. "Izzy, my father works twelve-hour days on a dairy farm and moonlights as a handyman so I can have a college fund. My mom taught piano and cleaned hotel rooms to pay for my after-school sports fees, because she thought it would help me get a scholarship. You think they're going to enjoy hearing this?"

"Don't yell at me, I didn't get pregnant alone!"

"I know that!" His energy felt explosive as he rose from the bench. "I'm just saying this changes everything. Not only for us. For other people."

"I can get a full-time job," she said, hearing the desperation in her voice. "I can work while you go to school, so—"

"You can't support three people."

"You said you were going to work while you're in college."

He nodded. "I've got to help with tuition and books." He shoved his fingers through his hair. "If I'm lucky, I'll have enough left over for living expenses."

"I can pay my own way. I have for years. I don't expect you to—"

"Izzy! Who's going to take care of the baby while you and I are in school and at work and studying? I'm going to college in Chicago. We'd be two thousand miles away from anyone we know. No," he said when she opened her mouth to protest. On a giant exhalation, he plowed both hands through his hair, then moved as if he were slogging through thigh-deep sand to sit beside her.

An anchor of fear pulled at Izzy's heart. Looking at the Portland skyline, she blinked as the city lights blurred. *No tears. Absolutely no tears.*

They didn't live in this sprawling city. Both she and Nate were from a Ridge community three and a half hours away. They'd come to Portland to soak up a view that was a taste of the bigger life awaiting them.

He was going to build skyscrapers.

She had planned to be the first person in her family to earn a high school diploma and go on to college.

Suddenly, Izzy felt as if nothing was holding her upright, as if she might slide off the bench. Stiffening her spine, she sat side by side with him—silently and with space between their bodies, which had not been their way this summer. The August evening felt hot and oppressive.

At the point where the silence was about to become unbearable, Nate spoke again. This time he sounded like someone who'd been running in the desert. "We'll figure it out. I'll talk to my parents. There's got to be something… We'll figure it out together." Nate's large palm and beautiful long fingers curved around the hands she clutched on her lap. Chancing a look at him, Izzy saw that he was staring at the ground.

The warmth that usually flooded her body when he touched her did not come.

Not once in four months had Nate actually said the words *I love you.* Izzy had counseled herself to be patient. Told herself she didn't have to hear the words to believe he felt them.

She shook her head. *Stupid…stupid!* How could a girl like her possibly know what love looked like?

With the rose-colored glasses off, the truth became painfully clear. Now, even though she was right next to Nate, even though he'd said they would find a solution together, she felt the heart that had warmed and softened this summer turn as cold and hard as stone.

"So the waitress says to the man at the counter, 'We have two soups today, sir, chicken with noodles and split pea—both delicious. Which would you like?' And the customer says, 'I'll take the chicken.' But, after the waitress calls in the order, the man changes his mind. 'Miss,' he asks, 'is it too late to switch? I think I'd prefer the split pea.' 'Not at all,' the waitress replies, and she turns around and hollers to the cook, 'Hold the chicken, make it pee!'"

Henry Bernstein leaned back in the guest chair in The Pickle Jar's tiny office and smiled the sweet, mischievous smile that usually warmed Izzy down to her toes. Henry had told her at least one new joke every week for the past seventeen years. At seventy-six years young, he liked to claim he knew more jokes than a professional comic.

"Where'd you hear that one?" Izzy tried to smile, but she wasn't up to her usual hearty laughter.

"I spent a week with two hundred senior citizens." Henry shrugged. "It's a laugh a minute in those retirement homes. Lots of company, three meals a day and all the Bengay you want. Not a bad life."

Henry and his younger brother, Sam, had just returned from visiting their friend Joe Rose, who lived at Twelve Oaks, a senior residence along the Willamette River. "I'm glad you enjoyed it, but I'm even gladder you're back," Izzy told him sincerely. "It's never the same around here without you. And I hope you're ready to get back to work, because I've been putting together some marketing ideas. I think I know how we can pump up business."

Raising the elegant, elderly hands that had scooped pickles out of an oak barrel back in the day, Henry said, "In a minute, in a minute. First, tell me what's so awful that you haven't been sleeping."

"Who says I haven't been sleeping?"

"Your eyes tell me. Is it business that's keeping you awake, Izzy girl? Remember—" He raised a finger. "'Tension is who you think you should be—relaxation is who you are.'"

Now she did laugh. "You heard that from someone at the retirement home. Only someone retired would say it."

"It's an ancient Chinese proverb."

"Written by a *retired* ancient Chinese prophet."

Henry grinned.

"Business isn't all that's keeping me up at night," she admitted. In her life, she'd had only one person to whom she could turn with any problem, and that was the thin, wise, gray-haired man in front of her.

"Nate Thayer," Izzy said, speaking the name aloud for the first time since yesterday afternoon. She'd avoided it, as if not saying his name might make his presence less real. "He's here, in Thunder Ridge. He came to the deli yesterday. He saw Eli."

Henry was rarely given to quick or exaggerated expressions, but now his brows arched above the line of his glasses. "He knows?"

"No. He didn't recognize Eli. And Eli had no idea, of course. He held the door open for Nate. They smiled at each other."

"But you and Nate spoke?"

"Yeah. I was wearing the pickle costume, and I fell on the floor, and— Never mind." Shaking her head, she pressed her fingers to her temples. "It was awkward."

Henry folded his hands above his belt line and nodded. "I thought he would come back someday."

Too agitated to sit still, Izzy rose, wrapping her arms around her middle as if it was nineteen degrees outside instead of close to ninety. "He took his time. Not that I'm complaining. I wish he'd never come back. I wish I didn't have to think about Nate Thayer again until Eli is an adult."

"Did he come here looking for information?"

"I don't know. He hasn't asked anything yet. But he's not entitled to information." Henry gazed at her. "He's *not*," she insisted before Henry could share some ancient wisdom about fathers' rights—fathers who hadn't wanted to raise their children to begin with.

"Nate and his parents wanted me to put our baby up for adoption. He was willing to wait until Eli was eighteen before he ever saw him. So let him wait a little longer."

"You're worried," Henry said, nodding. "It's understandable. But you're speaking out of fear."

"You're darn right I am." The tiny office didn't leave much room for pacing, but Izzy made use of the space that was available. "You remember how Eli was a few years ago. His self-esteem was terrible. He hated everything about himself, including the fact that he had a father who didn't want him." She had never told Eli that, of course, never even hinted, but short of lying and saying that the man who had fathered him died or was living in Tunisia, what else could a father's absence in his son's life imply? She had told him only that his father was a boy she had known. A boy who hadn't been ready to be a father and who had moved far away. Eli had never asked for a name, an act of self-control that seemed to give him a sense of power. He had referred to the man who'd fathered him once as "the guy with the Y chromosome." Then he'd stopped talking about it all together.

"He's on the right track now," she said emphatically. "He's a good student. Responsible and productive. He's happy. I intend to keep him feeling good about himself. I won't allow Nate to waltz in here and mess up my son's life."

Behind wire-rimmed glasses, Henry's brown eyes watched her closely. "Eli *is* on the right track. And circumstances are very different now. Eli was also upset about being deaf in a hearing world. The cochlear implant made a great difference."

"Yes. Because being able to hear took his mind off what he doesn't have. He never talks about not having a father anymore. It doesn't make him unhappy now. He has you, and Sam and Derek. He knows you love him."

"And always will. That doesn't mean he's stopped wondering, dear heart."

"Of course not. That's not what I mean. I've never underestimated how much Eli would want a father. You know that," she insisted. "But he's finally focusing on what he does have, not on what he doesn't." She looked at Henry hopefully, seeking his consensus.

Sun-weathered brow puckering, Henry removed his

bifocals and began to clean them with his shirttail. Izzy opened a desk drawer, withdrew a tiny spray bottle and cloth she kept just for Henry and Sam, then wiped the lenses until they were clear before returning them to him. "As far as Nate and his parents know," she said quietly, "I went through with the adoption plan. Nate's never gotten in touch to ask for information before. In all likelihood, he's come back to town for a reason that has absolutely nothing to do with us. If he does find out about Eli, and still has no interest in contact or in being a father..." She shuddered, the possibility too awful to contemplate.

Growing up unwanted left scars you could hide but not heal. Izzy knew that from experience and would do anything to protect her son from the miserable feeling that he wasn't good enough to be loved. It was far, far better to accept reality than to hope for a love that would never come.

"I still remember the day you told me you wanted to leave Thunder Ridge so you could have the baby somewhere else," Henry said. "I didn't want you to go. The thought of you being alone in a strange city..." He shook his head. "You were so young."

"Well, I wasn't alone. Joanne was wonderful."

Henry and his late wife had had a friend named Joanne, who'd been recently widowed, and Henry had offered to contact the woman about Izzy. Joanne had been happy to have the company of a quiet, studious seventeen-year-old... even a quiet, studious, four-months-pregnant seventeen-year-old. Izzy had been able to leave Thunder Ridge with most people, including her own mother, unaware that she was even pregnant.

Joanne and Izzy had gotten along so well that Joanne had invited her to stay on in Portland after the baby was born. She'd watched Eli while Izzy had attended community college and worked. She'd taught a teenager how to care for a baby.

A little more than three years later, Izzy had returned with an associate degree, a baby and no one any the wiser that Nate was the father. People had seemed to accept her story that the baby's father was someone she'd met in Portland.

"I'm still grateful that you introduced me to Joanne. She's wonderful," Izzy told Henry. She and the older woman were still in touch, and Izzy visited with Eli when she could.

"She's grateful, too." Henry nodded, but his brow furrowed, making Izzy wonder what was coming next. "Nate *did* call after you left for Portland," he reminded her. "He sounded worried. He wanted very much to talk to you. In the back of my mind, I've always wondered what would have happened if I'd told him you changed your mind and were keeping the baby."

"Nothing!" Izzy answered swiftly, her pulse speeding. "Nothing good would have happened. He'd already made his decision. If you had told him I was keeping the baby, he'd have sicced his parents on me again, so they could make me change my mind, and I was stressed enough without that."

Insisting that adoption was the only sensible solution to the "problem" of Izzy's pregnancy, Nate's parents had argued their point of view convincingly. The Thayers were blue-collar folks who had worked day and night, literally, to ensure that their son's life would be easier than their own. Wasn't Izzy also eager for a better life? Didn't she, too, want to attend college? And if she truly cared about Nate, how would she feel watching the plans for his future slip away? Those were some of the arguments they had used to convince her everyone's life would be ruined unless she put the baby up for adoption.

At first Izzy had allowed them to persuade her, and Nate had gone to college believing Izzy agreed with the adoption plans and assured by his parents that they would "watch over" Izzy during her pregnancy. And they had.

Mrs. Thayer had accompanied her to an ob-gyn in Bend, far enough away that no one in Thunder Ridge would know what was going on. Then his mother had made an appointment with an adoption lawyer, too, and had sat beside Izzy, holding her hand, throughout the first visit. No "mother" had held her hand before.

And so Izzy had done what she had sworn to herself she absolutely would not do again: she had hoped. She had begun to believe the Thayers liked her, that the baby was becoming real to them, as it was to her. Surely this caring—this is what family did for one another.

And Nate's weekly check-in calls…

At first, she had excused the fact their duration was brief and the content superficial. After all, the first weeks of college were busy and stressful. He would tell her a bit about his life when she asked him specific questions and he would ask her how she was feeling—whether she was eating right, if she was able to keep up with senior year homework. That, along with his parents' interest, had been enough for her to begin dreaming again…

Maybe Nate would miss her and ask her to come to Chicago…

His parents would realize they couldn't give up their first grandbaby…

She would prove that she could become a mother and support Nate's studies and eventually his career, and someday the Thayers—and Nate—would look back and thank God that Izzy and her child were part of the family.

Welcome to fantasyland, Izzy thought now, *where we pay no attention to pesky details like* reality.

She had Mrs. Thayer to thank for setting her straight. With crystal clarity, she'd shown Izzy that Nate did not want her or her baby.

So in her fourth month of pregnancy, Izzy had left town, telling the Thayers she preferred to handle the adoption on her own, without their help, and that they could pass that information along to Nate, since she had no desire to see him again.

"I gave Nate's parents exactly the out they were hoping for," she said to Henry. "It was better for everyone's sake to let them think they were getting what they wanted. The truth wouldn't have changed the outcome anyway. It just would have created more tension and fighting."

For a moment, Henry looked as if he wanted to argue, but how could he? They both remembered exactly how Nate's family had felt about her. She had reminded them of everything they had worked so hard to rise above.

"Eli will be at camp for two weeks," she reminded Henry. "I'm not sure how long Nate plans to be in town, but he is not entitled to any information that could hurt Eli in the long run." As she spoke, she began to feel stronger. "Our policy has got to be don't ask, don't tell. Eli has me. He has you and Sam and Derek and everyone else at the deli. He knows you all love him and accept him exactly as he is. If he wants to look for his father when he's eighteen, that's his prerogative. Until then, it's my job to protect him." That had been her purpose all these years. "The Thayers wanted perfection—a son with a degree, six figures a year and a perfect family. Eli and I will never fit that mold."

Henry shook his head. "You talk about what his parents wanted, but what did Nate want, dear heart?"

She smiled at the endearment. *Dear heart.* God had been good to her: despite her false starts, she'd been given a family. She answered Henry's question honestly. "Nate wanted the life he planned before he met me." She shrugged, way past the grief that had once consumed her. "We really were too young. If nothing else, the Thayers were right about that. Nate was a college-bound jock looking for a light-hearted summer romance, and I was a desperate, love-hungry teen."

"You're too hard on yourself."

Izzy shrugged, unconcerned. "Maybe."

Taking her seat, she fired up the computer. She had fought for the life she now lived, and it was a good one, built on hard work and a stern levelheadedness. She didn't try to fool herself anymore.

Did she ever want more than she already had? Yes, sure. Sometimes. It was only natural that deep in the night, she would occasionally wish for a hand she could curl her fingers around, a bare foot to bump into, someone to hold her and make her feel warm again when life's relentless everyday worries left her cold. But in those hungry, vulnerable moments, she would picture Eli as an adult—tall and strong, confident and self-accepting, pursuing a career he was passionate about and maybe starting a family of his own—and that would keep her on her path.

Right now, she needed to get back to business. Business was always a safe harbor.

She knew Henry would be pleased with some of the ideas she'd had while he was on vacation. Tapping on her keyboard, she said, "I've got some interesting advertising options to show you."

In minutes they were talking about social media and mail outs and not mentioning Nate Thayer at all. Deep, deep in her gut, though, she wondered how long she could keep it that way.

Chapter Four

Nate hadn't experienced small-town life for a long time, and while some things had definitely changed, others remained memorably the same. The Thunder Ridge Public Library was a perfect example.

Still a two-story structure with a basement and ground-level square footage, the seventy-year-old building had the same heavy wooden tables and chairs and ancient shelving Nate remembered. Still smelled the same, too—a little bit like old books and a little bit like the dogs that had always been allowed to accompany their owners indoors. The major difference as far as he could tell was the current librarian, Holliday Bailey.

Ms. Bailey looked and smelled nothing like old Mrs. Rhiner, who, as Nate recalled, had resembled George Patton and smelled faintly of cooked broccoli.

"I can place a hold on some of the books you're looking for and have them sent here through our interlibrary loan system. The problem is you're not a local, Mr. Thayer. How am I going to get you a library card?"

Holliday tapped shiny cherry fingernails on her mouse, her matching red lips pursed as she looked from the computer screen to Nate. "And you said you're staying at the inn? All by your lonesome?"

"That's right."

"Have you any friends in town, Mr. Thayer? Of the very close variety?"

"None with library cards they want to loan me, if that's what you're getting at, Ms. Bailey."

"That's exactly what I was getting at." When she shook her head, silky dark brown hair that looked like a shampoo ad brushed her shoulders. "We need to connect you with someone in a position of power…so you can get the books you need."

Nate grinned. Holliday Bailey was one of the most physically stunning women he had ever met. Long neck, perfect bone structure and slender as a willow with spitting-intelligent eyes, she would require a man who could keep up with her. While Nate was pretty sure he could, he knew instantly that the woman was harmless, far more interested in playing with his mind than with any other part of his anatomy.

"Thanks for your help."

"You're more than welcome."

Shaking his head in admiration, Nate walked away, heading for the nonfiction section and trying to remember if he'd ever dated anyone like her. His tastes had always run to women whose beauty was subtler, their attractiveness unfolding the more he got to know them.

That thought led inevitably to the woman who was trying so hard to ignore him.

When he'd first met Isabelle Lambert, he hadn't intended to be anything other than polite. She'd been a high school student, one year behind him in school, and a waitress, and he'd respected that. In his senior year of high school, Nate had taken to spending part of every day at The Pickle Jar, where he could order a drink and, when he had the extra cash, a sandwich and study for a couple of hours without being interrupted, since his friends rarely if ever showed up at the deli. Izzy had waited on him a number of times.

She seemed to be there, working or studying at the counter, anytime he came in. Hazel-green eyes and sandy-brown hair she scraped back in a nondescript ponytail wouldn't have drawn his notice necessarily, but her manner did. Calm, serious and almost deferentially polite, she was so different from the other teenage girls Nate knew that she became a puzzle to him, and he loved a good puzzle.

"You're very welcome to stay and study as long as you like," she'd told him when he'd asked if they needed the table during one lunch hour. Her eyes, free of makeup, had held his gaze steadily and all of a sudden he'd realized they were large and changed color—sometimes the color of an aspen tree's leaves, other times the color of its bark.

"I see you studying at the counter," he'd said in his first real attempt at conversation with her. "Whose classes are you in?"

He'd noticed her mouth then—pink, unglossed and bowed at the top as it formed a surprised O, as if she hadn't expected him to ask her anything not related to his lunch.

"I have Billings for history and Lankford for Literature. I'm working on an essay about *The Grapes of Wrath* and how a current depression would manifest differently from the Dust Bowl Migration of the 1930s. Especially on a local level."

He'd whistled. "Who assigned that as a topic?"

She'd hesitated a second. "No one. *The Grapes of Wrath* was assigned reading, but I chose the topic. It's interesting."

Her intelligent eyes had lowered as if she'd thought

she'd said something she shouldn't have, and he'd noticed a pulse beating rapidly at the base of her slender neck. In that moment she'd reminded him of a cross between a falcon and a hummingbird. And he'd had a surprising revelation as an eighteen-year-old, realizing that around most girls, his smiles started on the outside and sometimes worked their way in; with Isabelle Lambert, his smiles started deep inside.

He never did get around to flirting with Izzy. One day he'd found an eagle's nest while on a hike and asked if she'd like to see it. She'd said yes, and…that had been their first date, which was weird, because he hadn't planned to date anyone at all. He'd dated plenty in high school, and he hadn't wanted the distraction or the drama so close to graduation.

Because he'd known he was leaving for Chicago at the end of summer, he and Izzy had agreed to keep things light. They had broken that agreement in a dozen different ways.

"Yum! It *so* pays to have friends in the right places." Holliday's naturally sultry voice carried clearly through the library. "Mmm, lunch. And at exactly the right time. I'm wasting away."

On the heels of her exclamation came the aroma of food and a voice that responded, "I wanted to check on the availability of the Black Butte room for a class on ASL in the Workplace next week. I forgot to reserve the room, so I thought I'd bring a little lunch to butter you up."

Nate heard the crinkling of a paper bag. "Pastrami, Swiss and coleslaw on rye?" Holliday sounded reverential. "I will give you anything your heart desires."

"You're so easy."

"Is that rumor still circulating?"

Peering around the row of books, Nate let his eyes

confirm what his ears and nose already told him: Holliday's visitor was Izzy, bearing food from The Pickle Jar.

Shaking her head, Izzy admonished around a smile, "Holly, lower your voice. Don't give the gossips anything else to complain about. Last week, Evelyn Cipes was in the deli grousing that we're the only town between here and Portland with a librarian who wears stilettos to work."

"Goody! I loathe stereotypes. Want to join me in my office while I do justice to this delicious meal? I'll get Maggie to cover the front."

"Sure."

Nate sprang into action before he had time to think. "Talk about ironic." He addressed himself to the librarian as his stride carried him toward her desk. "Isabelle keeps telling me she doesn't have time to talk to me, and yet everywhere I go, there she is." He leaned forward to speak confidentially. "I think she's following me." He raised a brow, hoping the unique Ms. Bailey would play along. "Do *you* think she's following me?"

The brunette looked delighted. "I don't know," she whispered loudly. "Let's find out." She looked at her friend. "Izzy, have you been stalking this big, good-looking man?"

Izzy looked horrified. Nate would have laughed if not for the fact that he didn't feel like letting her off the hook so easily. Why the devil was she treating him like a stranger—and a very unwelcome one?

"Of course I'm not stalking. I don't stalk." Trying hard not to glance at him, she told Holliday, "I better get back to work."

"I thought you were going to have lunch with me," her friend protested.

"I know. I forgot that I need to get back. There's a big party coming in for…brisket."

"Yeah, I heard brisket is trending today." Nate leaned

casually against the desk, still addressing himself to Holliday. "I don't believe her. Do you?"

The brunette's forehead creased. In lieu of answering, she asked, "How do you know Izzy?"

One glance at Izzy's face told him she did not want him to answer.

"We knew each other in high school," he said, watching her closely.

"No kidding." Holliday looked at Izzy, whose expression gave her the appearance of someone standing in line to get a root canal. "Were you...good friends?"

Fifteen years after he'd first noticed her, Izzy still had skin like a porcelain doll. He could see the red flush beneath the creamy fairness and wondered why seeing him again was so hard for her. He hadn't returned to Thunder Ridge expecting to see her but considered their reunion a bonus. They may have been kids when they were together, but they'd shared adult experiences he still hadn't shared with anyone else. And there were questions, unanswered for fifteen years now.

"I thought we were good friends," he answered Holliday's question. "Certainly enough to merit a few minutes' worth of catching up. That's what old friends do when they meet again. Right?"

"I know *I* would." Holliday's red lips curled with humor, her heavily lashed eyes darting with rabid curiosity between Nate and Izzy, who frowned mightily at her friend.

Suddenly, the sheriff from yesterday flashed in Nate's mind. Was he the stumbling block to their spending a little time together? Nate may not have expected to see Izzy on this trip, but now that they were together, he'd like some closure. Not that he was channeling Dr. Phil, but he had questions that were fifteen years old. Didn't she? If nothing else, he'd like to know why she'd refused to be in touch with him after she'd miscarried their baby.

"Five minutes," he said to Holliday. "That's reasonable, don't you think?"

"Take ten," she suggested, ignoring Izzy's expression.

"You're right. Ten. Can we use the meeting room?" When Holliday nodded, he turned to Izzy. "One-sixth of an hour, Isabelle. My watch has a timer. I'll even let you hold it, so you'll know I'm not cheating."

Maybe he didn't know Izzy well anymore—maybe he never had—but he could see the wheels spinning in her head. She was trying to think of a way to reject his overture, again. And then—

"Ten minutes," she said decisively. "And then I have to go."

If Nate could feel the waves of curiosity rolling off Holliday, he was sure Izzy felt them, too, but she strode ahead of them toward the Black Butte room without a backward glance.

At the door to the meeting room, Izzy stopped, allowing Holliday to pass ahead of her. The librarian reached into her bra, of all places, to extract a set of small keys, one of which she used to unlock the heavy oak door. She flipped the light switch and stepped back, only slightly less provocative when she asked, "Do you need a chaperone?"

Izzy looked as if she was about to say yes.

"We'll manage," he replied. "Maybe another time." Taking Izzy's arm, he led her into the room. Holliday closed the door behind them, gently albeit reluctantly.

A rectangular table and a dozen or so chairs filled the center of the room. Framed posters of foreign countries graced the plain ivory walls.

Izzy pulled out of Nate's grasp without waiting another second. Yanking out a chair, she sat and glanced at her watch. "Ten minutes, and your time starts…now."

Exasperation poured into him. "Fine." Pulling out the chair right next to hers, he sat facing her. "Where did you go after you left town? Did you ever get that business degree you wanted so badly? What brought you back to Thunder Ridge, because from what I recall, you hated it here? And why the hell are you so angry after all these years?" Glancing at his own watch, he set the timer and said, "Okay…go."

The eyes he remembered as tender and affectionate and innocent clouded with surprise and confusion, and he wasn't above a moment of pure satisfaction as he realized he'd thrown her off guard.

Seconds ticked by without a verbal response. The expression in her eyes morphed from confusion to pain, and that was when regret slammed into him like a sledgehammer. He knew that expression—it was the one she'd worn the night she'd told him she was pregnant and again on the day he'd left for college. It mirrored the pain he had felt the day his mother had phoned from Oregon to tell him Izzy had left town with strict instructions—instructions he hadn't followed—for Nate not to get in touch with her again. She wanted, Lynette Thayer had said, "to start over…move past her mistakes…forget everything that had happened."

Was that what this was about? She'd "forgotten" everything between them, and he was bringing it up again? Maybe what happened between them was a secret she kept from the important people currently in her life. The sheriff flashed to mind again, and Nate sighed. What right did he have to make her dredge it all up if she didn't want to? None, probably. But he had something he needed to say, just to her.

"As hard as things got, I have good memories of that summer, Izzy, good feelings about the months before we became two high school kids who had to deal with some very adult decisions. I worried about you when you left without telling me." He hesitated, then figured, what the hell? He'd probably never get this chance again. "It made sense that you'd want to move on with your life. You certainly had that right. I get that. But it would have been nice to know you were okay after the miscarriage. One final check-in call." He wiped a hand down his face. "I suppose I still don't understand why we never said goodbye. So, how about we begin with my last question and work our way back? Why do you still want to avoid me?"

Miscarriage.

Izzy heard nothing after that word. *He thinks I miscarried our baby?*

Was it really possible that Nate believed there was no baby, no toddler, no child or teenager to wonder about? That he believed she'd moved on from their relationship more or less as he had—older, wiser…and childless?

Her breath came fast and shallow as the truth became clear. One thing about Nate: he didn't lie, not even when it would be more convenient. He hadn't said "I love you" to get her into bed, and he hadn't said their baby wasn't his when it would, after all, have been the word of the high school valedictorian against the girl everyone had assumed would follow in her mother's footsteps.

No, he didn't lie. But he had been lied to.

Izzy's palms grew damp as nausea filled her stomach.

"We have a time constraint here, Izzy." Irony shaded Nate's voice. "Not that *I* have anywhere pressing to be today."

He tilted his head in question. *Will you change your mind and talk awhile?* Nate was in his early thirties, like she was, but in this moment, even beneath the fluorescent glare, he looked eighteen again, sweet and teasing and persuasive.

She wanted so badly to get out of here so she could think. For the entire length of her son's life, she'd told herself that Nate knew he'd fathered a child and simply didn't care. She'd thought he'd been content to assume his child had been adopted and that he was completely off the paternal hook.

His lips curved as he gazed at her, and an electric feeling zinged through her veins. The first time she'd noticed him watching her, she'd been waiting tables at the deli, joining sweet, elderly Mr. Wittenberg in a quavering rendition of "Happy Birthday" while Mrs. Wittenberg giggled at the giant slice of New York cheesecake Izzy had set in front of her. The dessert was topped with so many candles Mrs. Wittenberg's face had glowed like a girl's in its light.

The Wittenbergs had been married as long as Izzy or anyone else could remember. They'd been old that long, too, and tended to look after each other like a parent hovering over a newborn—with a tenderness and tolerance that was both enviable and, for Izzy, as out of reach as the burning sun.

After Mrs. W had blown out her candles, with help, Izzy had headed toward the kitchen, passing the booth where Nate had been nursing an iced tea and studying. That was when she'd noticed him watching her. Holding her gaze steadily, he'd said, "That's exactly how I want to spend my birthday when I'm their age."

She'd started loving him a little bit right then. By the time she'd realized she was pregnant, Izzy had loved Nate Thayer with every fiber of her teenage heart. When it had appeared he didn't love her at all, she had taken cold comfort in believing he was just one more irresponsible, self-centered teenage boy who'd had his fun and wanted to get on with a life that did not include a girl he didn't love and a baby he hadn't intended to make. Keeping that thought always in the forefront of her mind had gone a long way toward helping her let go of Nate. It had helped her let go of romantic fantasies altogether.

But now...

Dizziness and nausea rolled through her again. "Did

your mother tell you about the miscarriage?" Was that her voice? She sounded calm.

Nate nodded.

Raw, burning anger filled Izzy's body. She started to shake.

"I know it must have been painful. Terrible," he said. "But I could never figure out why you didn't tell me yourself. You were a gutsy girl."

Gutsy. Is that what he thought? "I was never gutsy. I was always terrified." She regretted the words the moment they left her mouth.

No hint of a smile remained around his lips. "That would have been more reason to phone, wouldn't it?"

There was no miscarriage to phone about! She wanted to scream it. Shriek it. She wanted to find his parents and throttle them, and she was not a violent person.

Was she "gutsy" enough to tell him the truth now?

Would the truth have made a difference back then?

No. Nate went to college and moved on with his life. She was just the girl who was going to ruin everything for him. Her baby was such a "mistake" that Nate's parents chose to pretend he'd died rather than be part of his life.

Revulsion filled Izzy until she honestly thought she was going to throw up.

My son is not a mistake, and nobody—nobody—is going to make him feel that way. The Thayers had thrown away the chance to get to know Eli, to be part of his life, to influence him in a positive way. The Thayers—Nate included—had never done a thing to deserve Eli Lambert.

"You were involved with college, Nate."

"So?"

"You'd moved on with your life."

"I was in Chicago, not the antipodes. I cared about what was happening back here."

Which is why you found another girl right away. "You were busy all the time—"

"Not too busy to talk to you, damn it!" Obviously frustrated by her responses, Nate slammed his hand on the heavy oak table in the meeting room.

"We cannot do this here," she hissed, rising from her chair and glancing at the door as she slung her purse over her shoulder. She shook her head. "I don't want to do this at all."

"Too bad." Nate blew the air forcefully from his lungs as he, too, rose. The conference room felt claustrophobic as he advanced on her. "Look, I didn't come to town intending to stir up the past. I didn't even know you'd be in Thunder Ridge."

Izzy's teeth clenched. Was that supposed to make her feel better?

"But we're both here, for the first time since we were kids." His demeanor softened. "That's got to mean something."

Oh, no, she refused to get sentimental. Maybe he had nothing to lose by rehashing the past, but she did. Eli did.

"It means you have business in town, and I liked Thunder Ridge enough to make my home here. That's *all* it means."

"You sure?" He regarded her steadily, and her skin began to prickle with awareness. "I have time tonight. We can have dinner."

"No." Absolutely no. Scraping back her chair, she rose so quickly she got dizzy.

With one hand on the table, he leaned into her. "You're going to keep avoiding me, aren't you?" His eyes and his voice were velvet—soft, smooth, strong.

She remembered that voice in the dark, remembered the way his whisper had seemed to penetrate her very pores and how she'd often thought she could feel his words vibrate inside her.

"Meet me tonight," he stated again.

"I have a previous engagement."

"Break it."

"I can't do that." She had to go somewhere and think. Right now. Making a show of looking at her watch, she announced, "I have to go. I'm late for work."

"Fine." He straightened. She felt a momentary relief until he said, "Call me later today when you know your schedule, and we can set up a time to talk more."

Without answering, she headed toward the door.

"Don't wait too long, Izzy."

Reflexively, she turned. His blue eyes were narrowed and considering, trying to decide, she knew, if he could trust her to call him. Black hair, as thick and shiny as it ever was, fell across his tanned forehead.

Her reluctance to see him was only whetting his curiosity.

Swallowing hard, she shot out the door, realizing he'd followed right behind her when she heard someone say, "Nate Thayer, is that you?"

The voice belonged to an older man. She didn't recognize it right off and refrained from turning around. Even though she was a fixture in town today, back in high school she'd primarily hung around the deli or by herself at the library. Or in the broken-down trailer she shared with Felicia. It was Nate who'd been something of a local hero. Varsity football quarterback who'd led the Thunder Ridge Huskies to their first state finals. Valedictorian. Polite and well raised. Never made a misstep until he'd met her.

Izzy walked quickly toward the front of the library. Holliday was still at her desk, apparently postponing her lunch hour. Her customary provocative smile was in place as she looked at Izzy, but it dropped the second she noted her friend's expression.

"Do you want to talk?" she offered, half rising from her chair.

Izzy had always been a private person—more so, she had been told, than most. For once, though, she knew she needed her best friends.

"Derek's bringing pizza tonight," she managed to choke out as tears clogged her throat.

"I'll bring a salad and drinks and see you around six thirty."

The tears reached her eyes. "Thanks." Quickly scrounging in her purse, she found her sunglasses, slipped them on and gave one wave to Holliday before leaving the library.

The sun was directly above her, the clouds picture-perfect in the late-June sky as Izzy stepped onto the street. After two slogging steps toward the deli, she changed her mind and headed for home. She'd been at work since five that morning; no one would complain if she took a break, and she didn't want to see anyone now, not even Henry or Sam. For the first time in memory, she was actually glad Eli wouldn't be home when she got there.

She couldn't remember a time when she'd felt more confused. If Nate thought she'd had a miscarriage, then he wasn't the total bad guy she had believed him to be all these years. On the other hand, he'd wanted her to put their child up for adoption and left her in the dubious care of his parents while he pursued a solo life in Chicago. So, he wasn't the man she'd once hoped he was, either. Did she owe him the truth today?

Arms swinging, feet pounding the hot pavement, she wished she could outrun her thoughts.

What she needed tonight was a little pizza, a little wine, a whole lot of ice cream and her friends to remind her of who *she* was: a woman tasked with the job of protecting her son from heartache and confusion. A single mother by circumstance and by choice, committed to raising a secure, confident human being who knew he was the pride and joy of the people who loved him. The biggest threat to her success would be falling, once again, for a man who didn't want to be a husband to her or a father to their son.

Her heart couldn't handle making that mistake twice.

Chapter Five

"Wow."

Izzy smiled weakly at Derek's stunned expression. She'd felt far too nervous to take more than an obligatory bite of the pizza he had brought over, but he and Holliday had done justice to the extra-large "kitchen sink" pie while Izzy pieced together the story of her high school romance. When she got to the part where she'd told Nate she was pregnant and his parents had convinced them that having the baby would ruin their lives and their child's, Derek stopped chewing, leaned his elbows on his knees and listened intently. His brows lowered more with each word, and Holliday traded her dinner plate for a wineglass, her green eyes filling with concern.

"Were his parents pissed off?" she asked.

"They didn't show it. Not in the beginning," Izzy answered honestly. "They were certainly disappointed. I think they'd started Nate's college fund the day he was born. He was voted Most Likely to Succeed *and* prom king in his senior year of high school. All set to take the world by storm."

"Were they compassionate?"

"At first." As her mind traveled back to the memories, Izzy felt the surge of emotions she usually resisted. "The Thayers made their points kindly. That was the problem. If they'd been furious right off the bat, maybe I would have kept my perspective. And before Nate left for school, he was…"

She closed her eyes against stinging tears.

"Before he left for school, Nate was what?" Holliday urged.

"Protective. He seemed to care…about me *and* the baby. He told his parents he was worried about how I would manage if there were problems with the pregnancy and he wasn't here. He knew my mother wasn't going to be any help. Plus, choosing the adoptive parents, dealing with the lawyer—he said it would be too much for me alone." His beautiful eyes had been awash with concern. No one had ever—ever—looked at her that way before.

He'd even kissed her as he'd left for the airport. They hadn't been romantic since she'd given him the news. Pregnancy had hijacked their relationship. The goodbye kiss had been just a sweet, soft touch of his lips to her cheek, but he'd done it right in front of his parents.

"I didn't know anything about family back then. It was easy to convince myself that what Nate and the Thayers were offering was as good as it ever gets. I even began to pretend Mrs. Thayer was my mother-in-law."

"What happened when you realized you couldn't go through with the adoption?" Shifting on Izzy's sofa so that she was more comfortable, Holliday nursed her wine while she waited for more of the story.

"I worked up the courage to tell the Thayers I wanted to keep the baby and give them the gift of a wonderful grandchild. I'd honestly convinced myself they'd be happy. I said I was sure Nate would fall in love with the baby the minute he saw it."

Derek swiped a hand down his face. He knew what was coming. By her expression, so did Holliday.

"Yeah—" Izzy nodded "—that spooked them. I was an obstacle to everything they'd worked so hard for. Suddenly, they weren't as nice anymore, and I was such an idiot, I was actually surprised."

Derek swore, colorfully. "You weren't an idiot. You trusted them, and they were—"

"Frightened," she said before he could use a much less kind word. "They were really frightened. Mrs. Thayer even told me that Mr. Thayer hated being a 'glorified janitor,' but he'd had to take any job he could to support a family. She implied their marriage wasn't all that happy and asked if that was what I wanted. She said Nate had dreamed of being an architect since he was ten years old and wouldn't it hurt me to see his resentment if he stayed in Thunder Ridge and wound up like his dad."

"Powerful stuff," Holliday said quietly.

"Yes, but I didn't let that stop me. I told her I was strong and a good worker, and I would never let Nate quit college. I said I'd work as hard as I had to for as long as I had to. She looked at me for a long time, and I thought I'd actually convinced her. But then she brought out the cannon."

Derek frowned. "What do you mean?"

"She showed me a photo Nate had mailed his parents. He had his arm around a girl. They were at a party, and they were grinning at each other. She was really beautiful… stunning…wearing an evening gown, and he was in a tuxedo. They looked just the way I'd imagined us looking if we'd gone to the prom together. And Mrs. Thayer said, 'I'm sorry, Isabelle, I really am. But Nate has plans, too. Does he look like a boy who's thinking about becoming a father with the girl he dated *one summer* after high school?'" Izzy shrugged sadly. "It was the truth."

"What did you do?" Holliday set her glass on the table, tucked her legs to her chest and rested her chin on her knees as she watched Izzy.

"I told Henry and Sam I was pregnant, and they helped me move to Portland to live with a friend of theirs. My mom had done one of her disappearing acts, so no one thought it was strange that I left."

"And he just carried on with his life?" Derek looked and sounded disgusted.

"That's what I thought." She explained the rest of the story as she knew it—how she had impulsively told Mrs. Thayer she didn't want to speak to Nate ever again, and how today she'd discovered that Nate thought she'd had a miscarriage.

Holliday put both hands to her mouth.

"He should have looked for you!" Far from behaving like the levelheaded sheriff the townspeople had come to trust, Derek stormed around the room. "You were a kid, and you were alone. Now he thinks he can come back here like the prodigal son. I've seen him all over town, shaking hands like he's running for mayor. I don't know how long he plans to stay, but we are not going to make it easy for him."

Holliday lowered her hands. "Now you're talking, Wild Bill," she said. "Let's take him out to the stockade."

Derek glared. "I don't endorse a mob mentality, which you would know if you ever bothered to come to a town meeting. I'm talking about loyalty and invoking a sense of community on Izzy's behalf."

"Or we could babble him to death."

"Now look—"

"I love you two." Watching her bickering friends, Izzy felt a burst of thankfulness for them both. "But I don't want you to do anything. Maybe Nate didn't love me the way I loved him, but he was a good person at heart."

"Except when he cheated on you the first chance he got," Derek reminded her furiously. "While you were pregnant."

Yeah, except for that, which was so out of character. Izzy frowned.

"Izzy," Holliday interjected quietly, "what do *you* want?"

Nate's face, the way it had looked today in the library, lodged in Izzy's mind. He had been intense, earnest... interested? Yes, he'd looked interested in her, in the way that had always made a flight of butterflies rise and swirl inside her.

What did she want? What she had always wanted, she supposed. A white picket fence. A husband, a few kids and a dog. A yard filled with laughter, a house filled with love. And a future that seemed predictable even if it wasn't, really. She wanted all the things she'd thought would never be hers until she'd met Nate Thayer and started to believe that a future was possible.

"Come on, jump in. What are you waiting for?" Grinning, water glistening on his shoulders and dripping from his hair, Nate bobbed in the swimming pool at The Summit Lodge and challenged Izzy. "I'll race you. Winner gets a neck rub in the hot tub."

Izzy stood at the edge of the pool in the perfect light of an early summer evening and shivered. She wasn't cold—she was nervous.

Nate's father was the head of housekeeping and janitorial services at The Summit, a seventy-five-year-old lodge built of giant beams and rough stones, hundreds of which formed a fireplace and chimney so wide and deep that Santa, his sleigh and eight reindeer could have fit into it all at once. Constructed during the pre-WWII years, The

Summit nestled at the base of Thunder Ridge and had been the site of numerous movies and, in its day, celebrity weddings. Now it was a tourist destination, hosting skiers all year round. Izzy had never been here before.

Working for his father in the summers throughout high school, Nate cleaned the pool area and mopped the lobby floor at four in the morning. He was perfectly comfortable in the lodge and absolutely at home in a pool.

"Nate, I don't… I'm not really…" *Oh, just say it.* "I'm a terrible swimmer. I never learned, not really, and I…I'm kind of afraid of the water." In fact, she felt a little sick just standing at the edge of the deep end of the pool.

Surprise altered his features. Diving beneath the surface, he swam to where she stood, then emerged, looking like a merman, somehow otherworldly and more perfect than real life. Pushing himself out of the water, he stood before her.

"You sure look good in that bikini."

Izzy shivered again as his gaze embraced every bit of her body not covered by the purple triangles.

"Trust me?" he asked, and she nodded yes. Because she did. Over the past several weeks she had begun to trust Nate Thayer more than she'd ever trusted anyone.

Taking her hand, Nate walked with her to the shallow side. There was no one in the pool, save for the two of them. With snow clinging tenaciously to the side of the Ridge, most of the lodge guests were still skiing. The magic of swimming while the late-afternoon sun glistened on the water and on the snow just above the pool area was not lost on her.

"We'll take it as slow as you want." His voice was coaxing as he led her into the water, the shock of cold offset by the warmth of his hand and his eyes.

First, he held her around the waist while he taught her to trust her body to float. The delicious sensation of water slipping between their skin distracted her from fear, and eventually she didn't know what was more buoyant, her mood or her body, as she realized the water was supporting her. Their legs tangled happily as he moved them into the deeper area and taught her to tread water.

He helped her to float on her back and to feel comfortable submerging her head, every word, every gesture, gentle and encouraging. Then, when she was so relaxed she thought she could stay in the pool forever, Nate made magic. Having her hold his shoulders, her body resting on his back, he plunged them both beneath the surface, giving her the experience of swimming underwater. She felt like a mermaid! Never before had she realized that trust could feel so exhilarating or that safety in another person's care was such a gift.

When they resurfaced, she was laughing, and so was he. "You did it," he said. "You're a water baby."

"'Baby' is right." She giggled, pleased and embarrassed by his obvious pride in her. "I only did what most five-year-olds can do."

"I don't know too many five-year-olds who can swim *and* rock a bikini," he pointed out, fire in his eyes and an intoxicating huskiness in his voice. "And you are definitely, definitely doing both."

Delight filled every nook and cranny of Izzy's body.

Holding on to the side of the pool, she and Nate grinned at each other. One of his arms curved around her, his hand on her back. And then, as if the lapping water were nudging them, they moved closer until her legs rested on his hips and both his arms were around her. They weren't two bodies anymore. The water and the wonder created the illusion that they were one. Or maybe, Izzy imagined dreamily, less than one; it was as if they moved inside a single cell.

As their lips met and their chests touched, she felt Nate's heart beat with hers. *For* hers. Suddenly, she couldn't think anymore and, for once in her life, felt no need to. With every word, every action, he made her feel important, special exactly as she was.

Lingeringly, as if they had all the time in the world, they spoke by touch and in kisses—soft and sweet, warm and deep, a language that, tonight, was all theirs and theirs alone. Izzy knew that loving Nate had changed her. She would never, ever be the same again.

She would never, ever want to be.

Anticipating getting Izzy's voice mail after several rings, Nate was vacillating between leaving a message and hanging up when finally the ringing stopped, and a tired voice answered, "Hello."

Concerned momentarily that he'd woken Izzy up, he checked the digital clock by his bed in his room at the inn: eight thirty. "It's Nate. Did I wake you up?"

There was a pause. "No."

"Are you home?"

Another pause. "Yes."

"You busy?"

He thought he heard a soft sigh. "No."

He stared at the mug of coffee on his end table. Fourth cup of caffeine since he'd left her today. He was never going to sleep tonight, but he craved the taste of coffee when his mind wouldn't settle, and at the moment every one of his thoughts felt like a speeding train.

Izzy had already told him to get lost, hadn't she? *Get lost* was closure.

Problem was, he seemed not to want to let it go, and the dog-with-a-bone feeling persisted. It didn't feel half-bad. For the past couple of years, he hadn't cared enough about anything to fight his way upstream.

When Julianne, his now ex-wife, had suggested they separate, she'd said, "We have a pleasant relationship, Nate. A nice life. But there's not much passion, is there?" She'd said it gently, clearly not looking to blame, and in the end he'd had to agree. There hadn't been much passion—in or out of bed. There should have been: they were both good-looking, smart, and worked in similar fields. Somehow, though, they'd been like two matches without the friction necessary to strike a spark. He wouldn't have ended the marriage over that, however. Commitment, responsibility—those were the principles on which he based his adult life. When Julianne left, he'd tried to carry on with business as usual, but he kept getting stuck in memories. Memories of a time before his marriage, before he was truly an adult. Memories of a time when passion had been the rule rather than the exception. And not only passion in bed.

With an elbow on his knee and one hand palming his forehead, he held the phone in his other hand. "We're not finished, Izzy. You know we're not. There are things left to say."

Her response was so quiet he had to strain to hear it. "I know."

Surprise made him straighten. "You'll meet me again?"

"Do you remember Hooligan's restaurant in Trillium Springs?"

"Sure."

"I'll be there in one hour."

"All right," he agreed, and then impulsively, before he could think better of it, he asked, "Izzy, are you in a relationship with the sheriff?"

Her hesitation lasted longer than before. "No."

Good. He thought it, decided not to say it. "See you in an hour."

As he ended the call and stood, he felt a rush of anticipation in his body, the kind he hadn't felt in a long time. The kind he used to feel just before he'd leave his house and head to the diner, knowing she would be there.

Chapter Six

Hooligan's was about thirty minutes away from her home in Thunder Ridge, but after hanging up with Nate, she'd changed clothes and left her house immediately, because she'd wanted to arrive first, get a table and look as if she was calm and in charge of the situation.

She sat facing the door, an iced tea she wasn't sure she could swallow on the table in front of her.

Holliday and Derek had left before Nate phoned, and she hadn't told either of them she was meeting him. Derek would have said she was nuts; Holly would have commended her for her courage, but courage had nothing to do with why she sat at the heavily laminated wood table way in the back of the restaurant. When he'd said they weren't finished, everything inside her agreed. She wanted to see him again.

When Nate walked in, she thought she was ready, but the first sight of him made her pulse increase unsteadily and perspiration rise to the surface of her skin. His physical appearance was still powerful. A black T-shirt hugged his broad shoulders, skimmed across his still-flat belly and disappeared into pale blue denims that perfectly outlined the glorious V of a *very* fit body. He wouldn't be solid muscle unless he worked out, a fact that made her squirm a bit in her aqua sundress. Lately, other than the occasional myocardial-infarction-inducing bike ride, she'd talked herself into believing that work, housekeeping and climbing the bleachers to watch Eli's track meets provided all the exercise she needed.

As he gazed around, clearly expecting her to be seated toward the front of the restaurant, she took a more objective look at him than she'd gotten the past couple of times they'd seen each other. The impossible thickness of his black hair had been one of the first things she'd noticed when he'd started coming to the deli during his senior year of high school. Her own hair was a nondescript brown, straight and fine. Unfortunately, Eli took after her in that department. And Nate's face—it was worthy of a sculpture, with angles and lines that seemed to be a deliberate attempt on the part of Mother Nature to create something flawless. The decade and a half since his teenage years had been good to him. Or maybe he lived an easy life unlikely to leave its imprint in signs of fatigue or stress.

A passing waitress stopped to talk to him. Nate's answering smile transported Izzy to the past, when the kindness and concentration he'd shown her had made her feel special.

"Man, I was a cheap date," she said beneath her breath, in no hurry for him to notice her this evening. If she could have, she'd have sat there indefinitely, observing the man who, when still a boy, had changed her life so profoundly.

When finally he spotted her, his attention became laser sharp, and the waitress's smile fell.

Nate headed in her direction. Izzy knew she'd be lying

to herself to say she wasn't excited by his single-minded focus. The anxiety roiling in her stomach turned into a frisson of...*just admit it, Izzy*...pleasure. *Drat!*

Yeah, that's how you reacted fifteen years ago, too, and we know how that turned out.

She'd taken psychology and early-childhood development courses in community college; she knew that neglect in childhood led to a desperate search for love wherever and however one could find it. She was over that, thank you very much.

Straightening her back, she reached for her iced tea, intending to take a nonchalant sip, but got no further than her fingertips touching the moist, icy glass. Nate's expression— so focused, so intense—made her breath come shallow and fast, no matter what her brain told her.

He slipped into the booth across from her, never breaking eye contact. "Thank you."

She didn't have to ask, *For what?* His wry smile said he knew she hadn't wanted to meet him.

After an answering nod, silence stretched until the waitress arrived with a menu.

"Are you eating?" he asked Izzy.

"I already had dinner."

"So did I," he told the waitress, then deferred again to Izzy. "Dessert?"

She shook her head. "No, thank you."

He considered her, then looked at the waitress, taking note of her name tag. "Kimmy," he said. The younger woman's instantaneous smile conveyed that she thought Nate was yummier than anything on the menu, making Izzy glad she had changed out of jeans and a T-shirt, at least, for this meeting. These days her confidence came from the inside out, but she nonetheless found her toes curling self-consciously inside the flat, comfy sandals she wore. Did she even own a pair of heels anymore?

"Do you have hot-fudge sundaes?" Nate asked Kimmy.

"I make a great hot-fudge sundae," she replied, her smile promising that she did other things really well, too.

"I'm sure you do, but here's what I'd like," Nate said. "Three dishes. One with ice cream, one with hot fudge and one filled with whipped cream. Can you do that?"

Kimmy shrugged. "If you want. We put crushed toffee and a cherry on top, too. Do you want those in a bowl?"

His eyes held Izzy's as his lips curved. "Not neces-sary." He passed the menu to Kimmy. "And I'll take a coffee, please."

As Kimmy left to fill the order, Izzy felt heat rising to her cheeks. *He remembered.*

"It took a full month of ice-cream sundaes for me to find out that all you really wanted was the hot fudge and whipped cream." Amusement sparked in the silver-blue eyes.

Izzy's fingers played with the damp napkin beneath her iced tea. "Back in the day when I could eat anything I wanted, yeah. I'm more careful now." *More careful about everything.*

"From where I'm sitting, it looks like you could eat a bathtub full of hot fudge and whipped cream, and your figure would be just fine. You always were too hard on yourself."

His voice still sounded like silk slipping over skin.

"So. You look good," she said. "Happy. How's your life been? Did you get everything you wanted?"

His brows rose slightly. Her tone had been clipped, oddly businesslike; she could hear it and wished she didn't sound so cold, but her voice did that when she was nervous. The time was rapidly approaching when she would need to decide one way or the other whether to tell him about Eli. She needed to find out some things first.

Nate leaned forward, resting his forearms on the table,

fingers loosely linked. "Good question. In fact, I've been thinking about that a lot lately. Did I get everything I wanted when I was eighteen?" He pondered. "It's taken a while to realize that what I wanted before I met you turned out to be different from what I needed."

She looked at him quizzically.

Kimmy returned with Nate's coffee. She set down a little dish of nondairy creamers, and Izzy knew what was coming next.

Grimacing, Nate apologized. "Sorry, I should have told you before so you wouldn't have to make two trips. I like cream," he clarified. "Or milk. Whatever you've got. No rush, though. I can wait until you bring the dessert. Oh, and two spoons. Did I say that before?"

"No, but I guessed." She glanced at Izzy, the envy plain on her face.

You're too young for him, Izzy thought. *You're too young, period. Go to college, have a career and then figure out your love life.* It was the advice she gave Eli, sprinkling it on him like salt on popcorn, hoping to coat every little kernel in his brain. Kimmy walked away, dejected, but perked up when a group of twentysomething young men came in looking for a table.

Nate followed Izzy's gaze. "You think she's older than we were when we met?"

Surprised that he'd had a similar train of thought, she answered, "Yes. I hope so, anyway. She's probably closer to twenty, don't you think?"

"Hard to tell these days. Seems like people mature earlier all the time."

Finally, she felt like smiling. "Hate to break it to you, but that answer makes you sound old enough to be her father." She inwardly cursed herself for her careless verbal slip.

An answering curve quirked his lips. "Sometimes I feel old enough."

Izzy continued to fiddle with her napkin. She wanted to ask whether he had kids, but that would invite the same question in return, and she needed a lot more information before she decided what to divulge. Carefully, she responded, "So you think kids grow up too quickly these days, hmm? Have you had some experience with that?"

"Last summer, I coached a football league for a group of ten- to twelve-year-old boys who were considered 'at risk' in their schools. We spent as much time talking as scrimmaging. Most of the boys wanted girlfriends or claimed to already have one. They weren't even teenagers. I don't remember reaching that stage until high school."

"Interested in sex for the sake of sex?"

Nate's eyes narrowed. "No. Restless, confused about the future. Hungry for a connection they don't even know how to define." He nodded toward her hands. "That napkin's a goner."

Izzy looked down. The damp napkin beneath her iced tea glass had all but disintegrated beneath her nervous fingers.

Lifting her glass, Nate placed his dinner napkin beneath it. "Better?"

"Thank you." Clasping her hands, Izzy set them in her lap. If anxiety could be measured on a Richter scale, she'd be at a ten-plus by now.

"What makes you think I was interested in sex for the sake of sex when we were together?"

Uh...you never said I love you. *You didn't want me to come with you when you left. You didn't want our baby. You started dating another girl two months after you got to Chicago. Take your pick.*

"Nate, it was all so long ago. I don't know what you wanted," she said. "I was just referring to teenage boys and what they're like. Boys fall in lust, girls fall in love." Quickly she added, "Or we *think* we're in love. After a while, you realize you were looking for a feeling. Young romance—it makes you feel like you've conquered the world and all its dragons." She shook her head. "Adolescence is such a confusing time, isn't it? Hormones are raging. We're vulnerable. And we dive into something that seems wonderful and powerful and crucial to our happiness, and it isn't until later that we realize the relationship we thought was so important wasn't even real."

"You think our relationship wasn't real?" The friendliness had gone out of his eyes. "I don't want to make you relive a difficult time in your life, Isabelle, but if you think I was interested in sex only for the sake of sex when we were together, you're dead wrong."

"It was a long time ago, Nate. It doesn't matter anymore—"

"Would you stop saying that?" Catching his raised voice, he leaned forward and spoke more quietly. "It matters."

She wanted to believe him. She wanted it way too much. "I'm not saying you were insincere." She tried to make her shrug easy-breezy. "I prefer to be realistic these days, that's all." She leaned forward, too, hands flat on the table instead of fiddling nervously. "Being pregnant at seventeen was tough. But the hardest part was you and I being on such different pages when it came to what to do about it. I kept hoping for a different outcome than the one that was obvious from the start. I was living in fantasyland."

"How so?"

"It was my personal Cinderella story. In my version, the girl in rags gets pregnant, goes to the ball anyway in a gorgeous maternity gown, and her feet aren't too swollen to fit into the glass slipper. She marries the prince, they raise the baby in the castle and the kingdom is at peace. The end." She infused her smile with as much irony as she could. "Fantasyland. A nice place to visit, but you'd have to be delusional to think you could live there."

Nate's expression didn't change much, but when he spoke, his voice was so deep, so intimate that it felt briefly as if they were alone. "I should have been more careful with you. Right from the start."

"What does that mean?" she asked when he simply watched her instead of continuing.

"I wasn't interested in sex for the sake of sex, but I did want to make love to you. You were beautiful and sexy and smart and funny. Still are." He cocked his head. "Except for the 'funny' part. You seem more…staid now."

"Staid!"

"I said 'seem.' I haven't decided for sure."

She felt an angry flush creep beneath the neckline of her sleeveless dress. That hardly sounded like a compliment.

Nate grinned. "Settle down, because I have more to say. You can swear at me later." Making sure she held his gaze before he continued, he said, "I knew before we met that I was leaving for college. I wish I'd gotten to know you without having sex. I wish I'd protected you in that way, because you were different from everyone else. Inexperienced—in a good way. The world had already hurt you, and you were willing to give it another chance…with me. I don't think I ever told you how honored I was that you trusted me. I wish I'd taken better care of that trust."

Izzy's lips parted. Shock widened her eyes.

"When you realized you were pregnant, the guilt kicked me in the gut. But the fact is I was a lot guiltier about what I'd just done to our futures and to my parents' trust than about what I'd just done to you. I was young, and I was an idiot—that's my only excuse. You already know that. What you don't know is how much I regret leaving you with my parents. They're good people, and they cared about you, but I should have been here. Before they told me about the miscarriage, I'd already decided to come back and see things through with you. It doesn't change anything now, and maybe you won't believe that, but I want you to know. For whatever it's worth at this late date, I want you to know I'm sorry. And that I'd planned to come home."

Nate watched a fine sheen of perspiration cover Izzy's silky skin. Her chest rose and fell with each breath. He waited. He'd said it, finally unloaded as much of the truth as he had a right to give her. He wasn't sure what he expected as the outcome. Relief for her, perhaps, if there was any lingering resentment. Closure for himself, because now he'd seen her, spoken his piece, and it was over.

At seventeen, Izzy had been one of the least cynical people he'd ever met. And that in itself had been a miracle. Nate could still recall several details about the one time he'd met her mother, Felicia. Usually after a date Izzy would insist that he drop her off at the mouth of the dirt road leading to her home. One late night, however, he'd ignored her protests, driving instead to the front door.

Sitting in the dark, on the tiny porch of a trailer that rested on crunchy brown grass and gravel, had been Izzy's mother. As they'd pulled up, Felicia, with a beer can in hand, had stumbled down the steps and into the beam of Nate's headlights. A barely there nightgown had revealed more of her too-thin body than Nate had ever needed to see. In a haze of cigarette smoke so acrid it smelled as if she'd gone through the entire pack that night, she'd drunkenly dismissed her daughter and started flirting with Nate before he'd cut the engine. Izzy had been mortified. Nate had helped her get Felicia into the house and intended to stay to make sure Izzy would be okay, but she had begged him to leave so she could settle Felicia down and pour her into bed.

Nate knew that if he lived to a hundred, he would never forget the expression of pure shame on Izzy's face. She hadn't wanted to see him again after that, either, but he hadn't listened. Knowing where she came from had made him admire her all the more. Nate's parents had given him everything, including a generous dose of self-esteem. How did a girl with Izzy's background become a diligent student and reliable worker before the age of seventeen? How did she overcome her natural guardedness to look at someone with an innocence and a trust that was breathtaking?

Before he could say anything further, Kimmy arrived with a huge goblet of vanilla bean ice cream and two smaller bowls, one filled with hot fudge and the other with pillows of whipped cream. She set the dessert plus the milk for Nate's coffee in the middle of the table, then held up a handful of spoons. "So do you want one spoon for each bowl, or just one spoon for each of you?"

"One spoon for each of us." When the girl left, Nate looked across the table. "Tell me the truth—do you still love chocolate and whipped cream together?"

Izzy's breath was coming in rapid puffs; her cheeks were still pink as a cherry on top of a sundae. "Izzy, are you all right?" he asked.

"Everyone…" Her voice sounded strained. "Everyone likes chocolate and whipped cream."

"Not as much as you."

He held out a spoon, and after a brief hesitation, she took it, though she didn't dip into the dessert.

He used to think Izzy was as soft and sweet as the whipped cream that used to make her hum with pleasure when she ate it. But, inside, the vulnerability that had once defined her had grown teeth. He'd noticed the change almost instantly. Only now, sitting in the booth opposite him, did she seem vulnerable, almost fragile, again. The urge to touch her fell on him like a ton of bricks.

Before he could make a move, she set the spoon on the table with a clatter and pushed out of the booth. "I need to use the restroom."

He began to rise, too. "Izzy, is there something—"

"You stay." She held out a hand. "I'll be… I'll be back."

Grabbing her purse, she sped toward the ladies' room.

Nate heaved a giant sigh and sat. He looked at the dishes of ice cream and whipped cream and realized they were going to melt right where they sat. He and Izzy were not going to slide back into easy companionship. The comfort and rightness he'd felt that summer were not going to be recaptured. Maybe that feeling had not been anything more than youthfulness.

Pouring milk into his coffee, Nate stared grimly at the spreading clouds and muttered to himself. "That went well."

Chapter Seven

Fifteen splashes of cold water cooled Izzy's face, but not her brain, which felt as if it was on fire. Looking into the scratched mirror above the sink, she used one of the rest-room's rough paper towels to wipe at the mascara running beneath her eyes.

In all the most complicated moments of her life, she'd taken one step at a time, just the next single, obvious step. But no step seemed obvious now, and she couldn't calm down long enough to think.

Nate had planned to come home. To her. To the baby.

Don't get carried away. He didn't say that...exactly. He just said he was coming home.

That was right. That could have meant coming home to help her through the adoption process and then leaving again.

Or it *could* have meant he'd been coming home to be a family with her and the baby. It *could* have meant he'd changed his mind.

Listen to you! He didn't say "love." He didn't say he was coming home to get married, raise a family and build a picket fence.

Maybe she should ask?

Stop!

Izzy looked in the mirror. Did she look crazy? She felt crazy. Reaching into her purse, she pulled out her cell, thinking she would call Holliday, but she got no further than staring at the face of the phone. Holliday wouldn't have the answers to her problems—the answer was in the mirror.

Raising her face to the wood-framed glass above the sink, Izzy breathed deeply to calm her racing mind.

I loved him. I loved him so damn much.

He was the first good and decent person she had ever cared about who'd cared about her, too. When the dream of being with him forever had died, the part of her that was willing to allow another person to break her heart had died, too. Now that hard, protective shell began to crack.

The important thing was Eli. She had to push aside her feelings, to get back out to the table where Nate sat, and become a detective. Would he welcome the news that he had a son? Was there anyone in his life unlikely to treat Eli with love and acceptance? How would his parents react?

Consciously, she steeled her nerves, made her muscles move. She was going to go back out there and be strong for her son. Just like before, she would get behind the wheel and start driving. She would not allow herself to fall apart until…well, she simply wouldn't fall apart.

Izzy did not walk, she *marched* back to the dining room, spine straight, shoulders squared, ready to set aside emotion in favor of intellect, discernment, common damn sense—

Oh, crikey.

Her feet faltered. Knees turned to jelly—warm, sloppy, melting to liquid jelly.

Nate was looking right at her, waiting for her, with a charming half grin pushing his lips.

When she reached the table, he stood. "No windows in the bathroom?"

"What?"

"When you left, the look on your face suggested you weren't coming back. I thought you might be planning to sneak through a window or out the back door."

"No." She slid into the booth and met his blue eyes. Those winking midnight eyes. "I don't run away." *Anymore.*

"Good to know. Have some dessert." Dipping the spoon into the chocolate sauce, he coated the bowl of the utensil, front and back, allowing the excess to drip back into the cup. Then he scooped a king-size pillow of whipped cream.

That's exactly how I used to do it.

Handing her the spoon, he sat back. Déjà vu smacked her upside the head, and nerves fluttered in her belly. Her fingers felt so shaky and clammy, she nearly dropped the spoon. "It's not polite to stare."

His smile deepened. "Never used to bother you."

Oh, it had bothered her, all right—hot and bothered her. He used to watch her eat the first bite. Every time they ordered a hot-fudge sundae at Hooligan's, he'd leaned back in the booth, his eyes at half-mast, a smile playing about the corners of his mouth, and she would blush—all over—as she tasted her concoction, exquisitely aware of him.

If she tried to eat now, she'd choke. *How high can a person's blood pressure rise anyway, before she has a stroke?*

When Izzy's phone chimed inside her purse, she grabbed it, letting her spoon clatter onto the saucer that held the cup of whipped cream. Holliday's face appeared on her cell phone screen.

Thank you. "Excuse me," she mumbled. "Hello!"

"Hi. Just wanted to see how you're doing. You looked

so vulnerable when Derek and I left." Holliday's voice was gentle with concern.

"Thanks. Wow. I completely forgot about the July Fourth band shell committee meeting."

"What?"

"Yeah. Are you sure you need me tonight?"

"Where are you?"

"I'm at Hooligan's with an old friend from high school."

"You're with Nate?" Holly's voice rose.

"That's right."

"Holy kamoly. And you want to leave?"

"Right, right. Well, I suppose I can still make it if you absolutely have to have details about the food booth tonight."

"Oh, yes. I *must* have details tonight," Holliday confirmed. "Not about the food, though."

"Obviously. Okay, I'll leave here in a few minutes."

"Call me when you get home."

"Will do. Bye." Izzy ended the call and arranged her features in what she hoped was an apologetic grimace. "Sorry. I've got to go. Committee meeting. I completely forgot." Oh, man. Her relationship with Nate was turning her into the town Pinocchio.

Nate's head tilted speculatively, his smile gone. "No problem."

His lips barely moved, and guilt stabbed her. She needed to see him again, to ask important questions before she decided if, when and how to tell him about Eli. But first she needed to regroup. *Right. I am not running away. I am regrouping.*

"Well, thanks," she said, already sliding across the booth. Talking to Holliday would help. Holliday, after all, had a *lot* more experience with men, even if she'd never been in exactly Izzy's situation. "Thanks for dessert and… everything."

Nate gave her a brief nod, that was all, but he rose politely. After an awkward moment—Handshake? Hug?—Izzy stupidly patted his arm and started walking. She felt his eyes on her back until Hooligan's heavy oak door closed behind her.

She didn't wait to get home to phone Holliday. Switching to her headset, she made the call and pointed her car toward home. Holly answered instantly.

"Nate was coming back. Before his parents told him I'd miscarried, he'd planned to come home from college." The words spilled out like the tears suddenly running down Izzy's cheeks. Her friend inhaled sharply. "And that's not all. He bought me ice cream tonight, and I got déjà vu, and I don't think—" She gulped. "I don't know if I ever really stopped l-l-lov—" The tears began to pour in earnest.

"It's okay," Holliday soothed quietly as Izzy became unable to speak. "I get it. I get it."

When Izzy left Hooligan's, it had not occurred to Nate that they would be together the next afternoon, watching a placid stretch of Long River, tracking the progress of kayakers and tourists on bikes as they navigated the trail along the water.

"I was surprised when you phoned," Nate said, trying not to stare at Izzy, who had donned pale blue shorts, a deeper blue tank top and a sheer, patterned overshirt for this, their second deliberate get-together. She looked utterly casual and sexy as hell. Her hair was loose, falling below her shoulders in the straight, silky curtain he remembered. "When you left the way you did last night, I wondered if I would see you again at all."

"Sorry." She glanced at him, seeming shy and…something else. "I was caught off guard last night," she admitted. "Especially when you said you'd decided to come back home. It was a surprise."

He nodded. "It was frustrating not to know where you went or how to get in touch with you. I'm not blaming," he hastened to add. "Just saying."

Izzy began to fidget, ducking her head and fingering the ends of her silky hair. She'd always been a fidgeter.

In flat sandals with multicolored straps, she looked seventeen again. "You haven't changed."

She snorted. "I've changed a lot. Anyway, that's not really a compliment unless a woman is over thirty-five. Before then, we want to change, and we want it to show."

"Interesting. I'll try to remember that." A breeze swept the warmth of the sun off their faces as they walked. "You do look the same, though. Except for your eyes. They were always intense, but back then they were unsophisticated, too—in a good way."

Today, the giant hazel eyes he'd always loved were hidden by sunglasses as her head snapped to him. "Seriously? You think you can tell a woman she's unsophisticated in a *good* way?"

"Yes, I do. You were innocent. Trusting. And with everything you'd been through..." Nate looked at her, stating the truth. "I was impressed by that."

The lower part of her face was a mask of neutrality.

"How are your parents, Nate?" she asked, changing the subject.

"I don't know if you remember that my parents had me when they were older—in their forties. By the time I was in high school, Dad had diabetes and high blood pressure. He had a heart attack in the middle of my freshman year at UI Chicago. He never completely recovered and needed a lot of help. My mom was really protective of him, but it was more than she could handle, particularly since they lived pretty far from town. I didn't think she could take care of him on her own and work, too, so I convinced them to move out. We muddled through together until I began my career and could contribute more financially."

"How is your dad now?"

"He passed a couple of years ago."

"I'm sorry. I had no idea."

"Why would you?" Putting his hands in his pockets, he mused, "Dad loved Illinois, said it felt like home. I'm glad of that."

Izzy nodded but seemed distracted. They walked in silence for a time, listening to the sound of oars lapping the water and a family's laughter.

"And your mother?" she asked finally. "Is she well?"

"Pretty much, yeah. After Dad died, she moved to a senior cooperative housing project. Keeps busy volunteering now, but I see her aging." His lips quirked. "She laments the fact that I haven't had kids."

His offhand comment seemed to snap Izzy to full attention. "Is that so."

"In fact, she's the one who convinced me to take the job that's brought me back to Thunder Ridge."

Izzy stopped walking. "What do you mean?"

He looked at the girl he'd never been able to forget, soaked in the furrow of her brow and the way wisps of her hair were carried by the breeze. "Sometimes you have to take a big step back in order to move forward," he commented quietly. "That's what she told me. She said she had a sixth sense that I needed to 'go home.' I thought it was strange, because she's not usually philosophical, and in all the years we'd been away, she'd never once referred to Thunder Ridge as home." He hoped Izzy believed him when he said, "I'm glad she pushed me to take the job. Glad I'm here again." He refrained from adding *because of you*, but that was the truth. What he knew about her life today wouldn't fit inside a thimble, but something inside him was hoping there was room for him.

Lowering her head, Izzy moved to the railing that lined their path and stared out at the water. "Did either of your parents ever come back to Thunder Ridge? For a visit, or…anything?"

Joining her, resting his elbows on the top wooden rail, he shook his head. "Uh-uh. When we were here, we lived on the farm Dad managed on top of his job at the lodge. The housing was free, and some of the furniture belonged to the landlord. There wasn't much to take with them, and my parents were both east coasters to begin with. No family to come back to in Oregon."

"I remember the farm," she said. "In fact, I remember that your father took the job there, because with no rent or mortgage your parents were able to put more money toward your college fund."

"Which they'd started the day I built an apartment building out of blocks in kindergarten." His lips twisted wryly.

"And you cried, because the teacher wouldn't let you glue it together so that it wouldn't fall down in the event of an earthquake or some other natural disaster in the classroom."

Nate slid his sunglasses down the bridge of his nose. "I told you that? Doesn't seem like a great date topic."

"I probably would have been impressed, but no, you didn't mention it. Your parents told me." Her attention shifted to the river again, where a young girl was learning to paddleboard. "I think they were reminding me that your future was planned—and invested in—a long time before you and I met. So it wasn't fair to expect you to drop all that when I got 'in trouble.'"

The beautiful day grew shadows. Anecdotes about his childhood interests and his parents' single-minded commitment suddenly seemed indulgent.

Reaching for her arm, he turned her to face him. "You

didn't get pregnant alone." He still remembered when she'd told him that. "You were right the day you said that. You shouldn't have been the only one whose plans changed. I should have stayed with you to face high school, work, the adoption lawyer, all of it. My parents should have expected that of me. I would, if I had a kid in the same situation. I understand what they were thinking at the time, what they were afraid of, but they were wrong."

She looked at him, her deeper thoughts still hidden by the dark glasses. Izzy's lips formed a perfect bow, but they looked tense.

With calls of "On your left!" a group of cyclists clattered over the wooden footbridge on which they stood. Butterflies swooped and floated in the wildflowers that lined the path. Izzy pulled away from him and started walking again. A couple with a dog crossed in front of them, and Nate dodged around, catching up with Izzy at an overlook, where a few people stood with fishing poles.

"You were seven when you read *Famous Buildings of Frank Lloyd Wright*," she said without looking at him. "At eight, you requested *The Future Architect's Handbook* for Christmas. You loved sports, but you never let your grades fall because of them, and you were one of the few teens who truly seemed to enjoy giving volunteer hours to the community."

He shook his head in disgust. "That sounds like a perfect person. And I was not."

"No. But in your parents' eyes, you were as close as you could possibly get." Her tone was tolerant, not judgmental. "Everyone deserves someone who sees him that way."

"Or who sees him realistically, recognizes his screwups and calls him on them. Izzy, don't whitewash what you went through because of us."

She did look at him then and, even with her sunglasses in place, he could see a steely strength she had not possessed at seventeen. "I'm not whitewashing anything, believe me. But if my child had a great future and I thought someone or something might take that away, I would protect him, too. A bulldozer would have to go through me to get to him. I might even make big mistakes, costly mistakes, while I tried to figure out what to do."

The vague feeling that had dogged Nate forever began to take a shape. Izzy understood passion. Despite a background that had given her no experience with loyalty, she spoke of being protective with a fierceness that humbled him to the point of discomfort.

He knew the answer to his next question but asked it anyway. Almost as if he were punishing himself. "You needed support when you had the miscarriage. I'm guessing Felicia was unavailable?"

"Felicia was never available." Izzy started walking. "When was the last time you went kayaking?" she asked, abruptly changing the subject.

"Are you and the sheriff seeing each other?"

Her head whipped toward him. "What?"

"The summer you and I dated. That's the last time I went kayaking."

"Oh." They walked a bit more. "We're friends," she muttered.

"You and the sheriff?"

Izzy nodded.

"Is there anyone else who might get his nose out of joint if he saw you in a kayak with me?"

She tilted her head, and he liked the way her hair swung in a shiny curtain around her shoulders. "Are you talking about going kayaking today?"

"That's the idea. Are you married? Engaged? Dating?"

"No, but—"

"Good. Let's go." He headed toward the rental dock.

"Wait." When he turned back, she was shaking her head. "I don't want to."

Nate sighed heavily. "Oh, that's right. You need a lot of lead-in time."

"Pardon me?"

"You weren't spontaneous. I forgot about that."

Openmouthed, she stomped toward him. "Is that a joke? If anything, I was too spontaneous with you."

Pretending to mull that over, Nate returned to the railing overlooking the river. The memory of being on the river with Izzy became vivid. When was the last time he'd felt that free, content to do nothing more than float and think about the girl in front of him? The strange, restless yearning that had prompted him to accept the job in Oregon rose inside him again.

"Sure do miss the river," he mused.

"You live in Chicago. What's that thing called that runs through your city? Oh, yeah, the Chicago *River*."

"True, we have a river. It's not the same, though. There's nothing like a hometown tributary." The grin he shot her was laced with humor. He shrugged. "Anyway, I work a lot. It's hard to relax. A vacation seems like the perfect time to get back to kayaking."

"I thought you were in Thunder Ridge on business."

He looked at her steadily. "So did I. But that was before I knew *you* lived in Thunder Ridge again."

Her lips parted ever so slightly in surprise, and he caught the swift intake of breath before she looked away from him. He had to rein in his impatience while he waited for her to say something. When she relented, her voice was low, almost flat. "Are *you* married? Or engaged?"

"No." He turned and began to walk slowly toward the rental dock. When she followed—also slowly—the intensity of his relief and pleasure came as a surprise. They were halfway there, a stack of kayaks in sight, when he added, "Not dating anyone, either. In case you were wondering."

"I wasn't."

Her expression told him she was lying. Nate turned away as a grin spread across his face.

Chapter Eight

Liar.

Heck yes, she wondered if he was dating someone.

But only because of Eli.

Mostly because of Eli.

In large measure because of Eli. She had to make sure no one was going to cause friction and unhappiness in her son's life if she told Nate the truth.

When she told Nate the truth. She was certain now that it was the right thing to do. Maybe she wasn't positive she could trust everyone in Nate's life with Eli's well-being, but she was sure she could trust Nate. And that was saying something.

As Izzy buckled the straps of the life preserver the kayak rental guy had handed her, she thought, *I'm not going to tell Nate right this second, so why am I doing this? I should be at work, coating my ulcer with a cheese Danish.*

She already had the salient information she'd hoped to attain today.

She was sorry about Nate's father and shocked that his mother had told him to come home to Thunder Ridge, knowing Izzy might be here. She didn't know about Eli, but perhaps the woman regretted her lie about the miscarriage? Izzy had never borne the Thayers any ill will, and now she believed she could forgive them altogether. That alone was a giant relief. After all, when it came to fudging on big truths, who was she to call the kettle black? Still, Izzy was just as bearish about Eli's well-being as they had been about Nate's. If Mrs. Thayer wanted to be a grandparent to Eli, she was darn well going to have to be grateful for him. Just as he was. And with Izzy as his mother.

"You doing okay over there, Gilligan?"

Nate's question made Izzy jump so hard she nearly fell into the river.

Gilligan. Oh, my Lord. She'd forgotten. She'd totally forgotten. Another feeling of déjà vu washed over her, so powerful she felt like passing out.

"Fine. I'm fine!" she lied.

Back in her kayaking days with Nate, they'd gotten caught in a sudden storm after paddling far from the more populated stretches of quiet water. Spying a finger of land, they'd pulled their tandem kayak up onto the bank, found a copse of trees to huddle beneath while they waited out the weather and sang the theme song from *Gilligan's Island*, a show they had both watched in reruns as children. On that day, during the storm, for every bar of the song they'd remembered, they'd kissed…

"Ready to get in?"

"Um…sure."

She must have had the subconscious Freudian brain fart of the century when she'd started using the nicknames Skipper and First Mate with Eli. She'd bought all the DVDs of *Gilligan's Island* to watch with him, because it had been one of the few really lighthearted memories of her childhood.

While the rental dude stood by, holding their oars, Nate stepped over to her and reached for her hand to help her in. He'd requested a tandem kayak, just like the one they'd used years before.

As soon as his hand closed around hers, a jolt of primal awareness vibrated inside her, starting low in her belly and racing down her legs.

Getting into the kayak, she held on to the dock, helping to steady the boat while Nate got in behind her. They took their oars and pushed off.

"You feeling energetic?" Nate's resonant voice made the hair on the back of her neck prickle.

She nodded.

They dipped their oars into the river and paddled in unison, finding their rhythm with unconscious ease.

The first time she'd taken Eli kayaking, he'd fallen in love with it. Even though she didn't find the time to get on the river much lately, her son was a river rat.

She and Holliday had decided that info about Nate's parents and his significant-other status was all she reasonably needed to know before she told Nate he was a father. There was nothing to stop her now.

Nothing except terror. Once she told him, everything would change.

Her relationship with Eli would change.

She dug her oar into the water. What if Eli was furious with her for not telling him about Nate sooner? Much sooner. Some kids never forgave their parents for keeping secrets. And Nate must earn more money in an hour than she earned in a day. In two days. With the deli in the red, she knew Henry and Sam were overpaying her as it was, and she was tightening her purse strings so she could take a voluntary cut in pay until business improved. *Which it would.* But until then, she and Eli were on a necessities-only budget. Nate, on the other hand, could afford the kinds of things a teenage boy coveted. What if Eli decided he wanted to live with his father in Chicago? What if Nate turned into an overindulgent parent who spoiled Eli rotten and turned her beautiful son into a shallow money-and-status-driven—

"It's not a race, Gilligan!" Nate called up to her, humor edging his voice. "Take it easy."

She didn't want to take it easy. Paddling with all her might had kept her moving forward up to this point in her life. If she slowed down, fear would capsize her.

Digging her oar into the green Long River, she couldn't paddle fast enough to outrun her imagination. How would Nate handle Eli's hearing impairment? Often, people who didn't know Eli well had trouble understanding him.

Her chest squeezed so hard she couldn't take a breath. She wanted to turn this rig around and hide under her duvet until Nate left Thunder Ridge, as ignorant of Eli's existence as when he'd arrived.

Becoming a mother had brought out all the courage in her. And all the fear, too.

Perspiration trickled down from Izzy's forehead, mingling with tears that stung her eyes, and she was glad for the physical release of paddling, as well as for the relative silence. With her emotions in her throat, she didn't want to talk.

They paddled until the picnickers and sunbathers along the river's edge faded into the background behind them and the water narrowed to a snaking channel with reeds and tree-lined banks.

As it became harder to paddle, Izzy noticed the kayak pulling toward the marshy area near the shore. She waited for Nate to lean the kayak, but it continued to drift starboard.

"Nate, we're going the wrong way. We're going to get stuck!" She paddled harder, to no avail. "Why can't we move this thing? Why—" She turned to look at him. "What...what are you doing?"

Nate's arms were crossed behind his head, his oar resting uselessly in front of him. Face turned toward the sun and glinting off his aviator glasses, he wore the satisfied smile of someone utterly at peace. Didn't he realize—

"We're going to run aground! What's the matter with you? Paddle, damn it, paddle!"

His grin reminded her of a slow dance—nice and easy. "You're still a type A rower." He clucked his tongue. "Relax, Izzy. Trust the river. The current will take you where you want to go."

Was he crazy? Cattails and saw grass clogged the river closer to the bank. "Kayaks wouldn't come with oars if we weren't supposed to paddle," she pointed out.

White teeth flashed as his laughter rang across the river. Now she remembered. This was how it used to be: Nate would be relaxed and calm. He'd be enjoying life while she worried enough for ten people. He'd make decisions and move forward while she fretted and stewed and redecided. How could she trust Eli's well-being to a man who thought so differently than she? She'd be on a Xanax drip while he took the path of least resistance. He was so...so... He was...

He was so right.

Correcting course on its own, the kayak began to float back toward the middle of the river.

Still leaning back, Nate said, "You know, I don't think you ever stopped paddling before. Good for you."

Izzy whipped around to face front again. A soothing breeze fanned her skin and ruffled the tree leaves—the only sound to interrupt the gorgeous quiet. Despite her surroundings, she felt hot and agitated.

Play it cool today. You're on a fact-finding mission, that's all. No drama. No recriminations and no big revelations. Don't show your emotions at all. Holliday had coached her before she'd left for this meeting with Nate.

But, really, who did he think he was, telling her to follow the river. To "trust the current"? All her life she'd felt like a salmon swimming upstream and never more so than when she'd realized the boy she'd thought she'd loved with all her heart did not love her. Never had she felt less capable of trusting life than when she'd been a pregnant high school senior, desperate to keep her baby *and* get an education, and give both herself and her child a decent life.

Think like Holliday. Holliday would be sarcastic or crack a joke. Holliday would tell him to *piss off.*

"You okay up there, Gilligan?"

"Piss off!" Instantly, tears sprang to Izzy's eyes and—*drat it!*—a sob caught in her throat. She had never, ever said that to anyone before. Not even in sign language.

"What's the matter?"

She paddled harder. If she couldn't stem her tears, she could pass them off as sweat.

"Whoa, Izzy, you're going to give yourself a heart attack. Slow down."

Nate increased his efforts also, which consequently reduced hers, and Izzy realized how tired she was.

"See that inlet about thirty feet up ahead? Head there, and we'll rest on land."

His tone told her not to argue, but ultimately it was her own fatigue—emotional and physical—that persuaded her. She couldn't fight it as he paddled backward directing them toward the shore. The second they reached the riverbank, however, she struggled out of the kayak, wordlessly helping to drag the boat to higher ground, then stalking toward the woods.

"Izzy, wait!" Catching up, he grabbed her arm. "Would you tell me what's wrong?"

"Just drop it."

"Not a chance. Talk to me." His eyes looked fierce.

"Okay, you want to know what's wrong? You. You're what's wrong!" Breathing heavily, she felt years' worth of fear and exhaustion and hurt boil over. "You think you can come back and tell me you're sorry you left town and, golly, you sure meant to come back, so that means you and I are at ground zero again. Well, it doesn't work that way."

"I never said that. I—"

"You don't have to *say* it, Nate. You've always gotten what you want. Good-looking, good grades, good family. Well, good for you. 'Just trust the current, Izzy.'" She threw his words back at him. "Maybe the current takes you where you want to go, but in my life, I have to row."

They stared at each other, and the awareness in his eyes told her that, for the first time, he realized how deep her resentment went. She hadn't even realized it herself until this moment.

"When did I become your enemy?" he asked.

He seemed to genuinely want to know.

Don't say anything, don't say anything...do not say anything. Remember what Holliday told you—now is not the time to get emotional.

"Never mind." She shook her head. "Forget it. Let's go back." She turned.

Nate grabbed her arm. "No. Izzy, I'm not just here because of work or for a vacation. I came back because nothing in my life, *nothing*, has ever felt as right as that summer we were together. It was special. *You* were special."

Tears leaked out the corner of her eyes, and her nose began to run. Hastily, she wiped her face, glancing toward the forest to gauge whether she could make a run for it. Nate had always been the one person who could break her heart wide-open and then make it knit shut again, tighter and harder to crack than before.

"I was 'special'? Nothing felt as 'right' as that summer?" She nodded broadly. "Wow, that is a happy surprise. There's just one thing I don't understand." *Don't do it, Izzy, don't. Holly was right—don't get emotional.* "How were you able to date another girl so soon after you left town? I don't think I could have done it if I'd been in your shoes. I wouldn't have forgotten someone so special that my entire summer felt 'right' just because we were together, and then be able to go off and date somebody else. Then again—" *No, seriously, stop yourself.* "It's also hard to understand why—if I really was that special—you never wanted to introduce me to your cool high school crowd or to your parents. At least not until I got pregnant, and you panicked and told them about me so they could convince me not to keep the baby!" Her whole body felt like a volcano ready to erupt. She marched so close she could see the dark blue rim of his eyes. "You didn't fight for *us*, you fought for your future. You knew I didn't fit into that future. And I knew it, too, I really did, but I was willing to pretend, because I—" *No. No-no-no-no-no.* "I…I—" *I forbid you to say it! If you say it, you will never be able to take it back.*

"Izzy—" he began when she halted. "Back up. What do you mean, I got another girlfriend after I left?" He scowled. "Dating was the last thing on my mind when I left town."

"I don't care if you dated." *Not much.* The photo of him and the beautiful, sophisticated blonde had been a knife in her heart. "I'm sure there were plenty of appropriate girls in Chicago."

"Appropriate?"

"Women who would have made your parents comfortable."

"Izzy, my parents were middle class with middle-class values they embraced."

"They didn't want *you* to embrace them, though."

Sighing, he rubbed his eyes. "Maybe not. But after what happened with us, I needed a break to figure things out. Post-traumatic relationship disorder." His smile was sad and ironic. "That's what a friend of mine called it."

"You're saying you had post-traumatic relationship disorder? *You* did." She looked at him in disbelief.

"Yes," he confirmed. "Hell, Izzy, do you think I didn't care that I got you pregnant? That it wasn't eating away at me that I made your life harder when it was already tough enough? Is that why you left without even calling me?" His eyes narrowed. "The baby you miscarried was mine, too."

There was no miscarriage! She nearly screamed it, but another thought intervened. "A baby you didn't want to raise in the first place? You must have been at least a little relieved to hear there was no baby."

The storm that crossed his face seemed to turn the entire afternoon dark and dangerous. "If that's what you believe, then you don't know me. You don't know me at all. Even worse, I apparently didn't know you."

He waited, staring, glaring at her, but she remained stubbornly mute. Her mind, however, was busy.

Was it possible that Nate was telling the truth about not dating and that his mother had misrepresented the situation to her, just as she'd skewed the facts when relaying them to Nate? All Izzy knew for sure from that photo was that Nate had attended some kind of formal event and posed for a snapshot with a pretty girl. If he hadn't been dating anyone else—

It doesn't matter. He didn't want to raise a baby. He didn't want a family. And you did. There was no future. Now, ironically, they had come full circle: intuitively she knew that when she told him about Eli, their complicated relationship would have to be put aside to address their son's needs.

While her brain spun a tangled web, Nate, it appeared, had had enough.

"Fine," he said between gritted teeth. Stalking around her, he headed for the kayak. "Let's get back."

Chapter Nine

"George Eliot's *The Mill on the Floss*, 1860 first edition. Oh. My. Gosh. Your wife had fabulous taste in books, Henry." Reverently, Holliday stroked the brown cloth cover of the small volume she had plucked from the cramped bookshelves in Henry Bernstein's living room. "*Northanger Abbey*, circa 1930," she murmured, reading more of the titles. "*Buddenbrooks*—another first edition. Be still, my heart." She turned toward the man seated on the couch. "Are you sure you want to donate these to the library? You have some really coveted editions here, and they're all in good condition. You could get a pretty penny."

Seated on the carpeted floor as she rummaged through a box of china she'd brought up from the basement, Izzy watched Henry nod and wasn't surprised when he said, "Elaine loved the library. She was one of its best customers. With her books displayed in a case, a little part of her will always be there, watching over everything."

Though she'd never met Elaine, Izzy had heard enough

about her through the years to feel as if she'd known Henry's wife. It was obvious that her passing had not ended their relationship.

Holliday shook her head slowly, hugging *The Mill on the Floss* to her chest. "That's lovely. Whenever you've talked about Elaine, it's obvious how much you two loved each other."

Izzy's head popped up. The indulgent, wishful tone sounded nothing like her friend. Holliday was perhaps the least romantic person Izzy knew. That was one of the things Izzy liked best about her. Holliday had lived exclusively in large cities and had traveled the world before settling in Thunder Ridge. She said she took Mae West and Diane Keaton as her role models.

Henry's hands were folded over his little tummy. His soft brown eyes smiled. "It was a good marriage. Forty years. I was a child groom, of course." He winked.

Holliday laughed, then said, "Tell us your secret for staying in love."

Izzy nearly dropped the antique chocolate pot she was unwrapping. She wasn't sure she wanted to hear this conversation today.

Swimming in a sea of uncomfortable emotions since their silent paddle back to the kayak rental place, she'd been popping antacids since last night. Last month, Henry and Sam had announced they wanted to participate in the annual Thunder Ridge yard sale. Izzy had tapped Holliday and planned to spend several hours this weekend sorting and pricing the belongings with which they were ready to part. After a sleepless night, she'd hoped that helping the brothers would distract her, but so far, no such luck.

"Lemonade and cinnamon *mandelbrodt*," Sam announced, entering the room before Henry could respond. He balanced a tray laden with four glasses of iced lemonade and a plate of the wedge-shaped cookies he baked once a week.

Jumping up, Izzy took the tray, setting it on the coffee table while Sam lowered himself to the couch beside his brother. "What were you talking about?" he asked.

"Who wants a lemonade?" she countered, hoping to derail the topic. No such luck.

"Did I hear someone say 'love'?" Sam looked as eager as a puppy with a rawhide.

It was no secret that keeping track of romances both local and global was Sam's favorite pastime. At age seventy-five, he had never married, but he had fallen madly in love at age nineteen with a girl he'd met while serving a stint in the navy. The relationship hadn't worked out, but Sam had never forgotten her and remained convinced that she was his soul mate. Every time he brought up the fact that he had lost his one true love—and he brought it up fairly often—Izzy got an uncomfortable squeeze in her stomach.

"I was asking Henry to tell us how he managed to stay in a relationship for forty years," Holliday said, accepting the glass of lemonade Izzy handed her but missing—or ignoring—Izzy's pleading stare.

She'd told Holliday all about her meeting with Nate. Confusion, anger, guilt and a pervasive sadness she could identify only as grief had dogged her since yesterday afternoon. So much so that she felt as if she had an emotional hangover today.

"True love," Sam said in answer to Holliday's query. "That's how you stay together. You find your one true love, and you never leave and you never give up." Sam considered himself an expert about relationships. "Isn't that right, Hank?" he deferred to his brother.

"That's a good start, Sammy, a good start. But, no, I don't think that's what sustains you for forty years. The question was wrong."

"What do you mean? My question was wrong?" Holliday asked.

Henry nodded. "I'm afraid so. You're assuming Elaine and I stayed in love for forty years."

Holliday, Izzy and even Sam stared at Henry in surprise.

"What are you talking about?" Sam looked horrified. "You and Elaine were *bashert*."

"What?" Still holding Elaine's book, Holliday walked over and sat in one of the chairs opposite the couch. "What does that word mean? Besh…what?"

"Bashert," Izzy murmured. She'd heard the Yiddish word often enough since coming to work for the brothers. "It means 'meant to be.'"

Sam nodded. "And you only get one. One *bashert* per customer."

"So you think we're fated to meet that one right person, or not?" Holliday seemed truly interested. That same question had plagued Izzy for years until she'd decided that true love was either a myth or something that struck rarely, like lightning.

Sam, however, nodded decisively. "That's exactly what it is. Destiny."

Reaching across the sofa cushions, Henry patted his brother's knobby hand, a gesture so sweet that Izzy felt her eyes sting. "Maybe not exactly," Henry said, a gentle curve to his lips. "The way you put it, Holliday—to meet one right person or not—implies a certain fatalism. The meeting will or will not happen despite anything we do. And if we meet our fated one, we will be together and stay together, also despite anything we do or do not do. But to be a *bashert* is not so easy, I'm afraid."

Leaning forward, he picked up a glass of lemonade and a *mandelbrodt* and took a bite of the cookie. Nodding as he chewed, he winked at his brother. "Your best batch yet." Henry issued the same compliment every time and seemed to mean it.

"So, a *bashert*," he continued, "depends on the philosophy that before our lives begin, we are given certain abilities and a mission that only we can fulfill in this world. As a gift, we are given a special person, a partnership to help us become the best 'us' we can be. But it's difficult, this business of being someone's *bashert*, because as another gift, we're given free will." With the hand holding the lemonade glass, he gestured. "Izzy knows this."

Izzy's heart began to thump hard and fast. Surely, he wasn't talking about—

"I'm quite certain she considers that Eli was meant to be her son. That she and only she was meant to be his mother."

Her heart calmed down.

"But it was her choice to have this *bashert* son of hers," Henry said. "And it is a choice to raise him, to love him through good times and less good ones. To believe so much in this special partnership that she keeps going… kept going even when he was twelve and—" he bobbed his head from side to side "—maybe not so lovable all the time. But Izzy made a choice, an agreement to stay in the mother-son relationship, because she believes in it. Being someone's meant-to-be takes great patience and perseverance. To be a witness for another's life is a sacred trust. It's easier, I assume, to maintain this commitment with one's child than with a spouse."

"But you did it?" Holliday's expression and the hesitancy in her voice mirrored Izzy's reaction. Was Henry saying that he and Elaine were not the love affair everyone had assumed? "You maintained the commitment?"

"Elaine was my witness for as long as she was alive. I was hers. Sometimes we loved what we saw, sometimes—" he shook his head "—no. But it didn't matter. We made an agreement. We kept going."

"Sounds like a lot of work," Holliday muttered.

"Finding your *bashert* doesn't necessarily make life easier," Henry agreed. "It makes it better. The next question I see in your eyes, dear Holliday, is whether we kept loving each other, and the answer to that is yes. When we looked for the love, we found it. Over and over. In forty years, we lost it many times and found it again." His eyes filled with a wistful expression that made him appear years younger. "Always better than it was before. One day of marriage to Elaine was better than a lifetime of looking for happiness someplace else."

The room went so silent Izzy could hear the others breathing. Henry and Sam were each immersed in their own memories, and Holliday quietly rose to resume her study of the bookshelves.

Izzy reached into the box of china again, but her hands shook. The newspaper-wrapped cups and saucers actually seemed to be moving, swirling together as if they were being tumbled in a dryer. She was so, so dizzy. Her heart beat so hard and so quickly, she began to fear she was having a heart attack.

I have to go. I have to go.

"Where?"

Holliday's question made Izzy realize she'd spoken out loud. Holly's eyes were huge as she stared at Izzy in concern.

"What's wrong? Do you feel sick? You look gray."

What *was* wrong with her? She felt as if she needed to run—right now and very fast. One word thrummed through her mind: *escape.*

"I need to get some air. I just… I'll be right back." Pushing to her feet, she moved as steadily as she could toward the door.

The night Nate had insisted on driving Izzy right up to her door was the night she had known they would never last.

Now, standing in front of the decrepit trailer she had

called home until she was seventeen, Izzy took several deep breaths. It had finally occurred to her that she'd been having a panic attack at Henry and Sam's earlier in the day.

For the past several years, she'd addressed fear by reminding herself how far she had come in her life. Nowhere was that more clear than amid the morass of dry weeds, rusted metal and dark memories that comprised her childhood home.

She'd once believed she was no better than where she'd come from.

The day after he'd met her mother for the first time and had witnessed the way Izzy lived, Nate had come to the deli to see her. Certain he was going to break up with her, she had prepared a goodbye speech of her own, thinking that if she beat him to the punch, there would be less chance of breaking down completely.

When Nate heard her stilted goodbye monologue, delivered in the alley behind the restaurant, he hadn't exhibited a bit of surprise. He'd simply listened, then told her he'd arranged with Henry and Sam for her to take off early. Despite her insistence that they were officially broken up, he'd persuaded her to get in his truck and had taken her to Trillium Lake, where he'd already set up a cloth-covered folding table and chairs, candles and actual china, which, it had turned out, he'd borrowed from his mother's wedding set without asking. He'd set up a CD player, tucked flowers into the needles of a pine tree and made the whole scene look magical.

"Why did you do this?" she'd asked.

He'd held her face in his hands and had said, "Because you shouldn't have to ask why when someone does something special for you." His voice had dropped to a whisper, his face moving so close to hers she could no longer see his lips. "You should understand—" he'd kissed her, and her bones had begun to melt "—that it's because *you're* special."

A decade and a half later, Izzy forced herself to walk to the front door of the broken trailer she used to call home. "Come on, Latke."

Looking like linen that refused to iron out, the Shar-Pei hauled herself up from where she'd plopped down the moment they'd arrived and followed her mommy to the cock-eyed aluminum steps. Izzy stopped there. Close enough.

Felicia had not lived there—as far as Izzy knew, no-body had—for years and years. Izzy had been in Portland, having her baby, when her mother had met yet another man and, this time, had followed him to God only knew where. She hadn't left a forwarding address; nor had she ever tried to get in touch with her daughter again. When Izzy had returned to Thunder Ridge, she'd contacted their old landlord, who had been one of Felicia's drinking bud-dies. He hadn't had a clue as to Felicia's whereabouts but had told Izzy she could do whatever she wanted with the trailer; for years he'd been meaning to sell it for scrap but hadn't gotten around to it.

"We don't have to go in this time, Latke."

Sometimes, like when she'd been getting her business degree online and had felt too tired to study for finals, she would go inside just to remind herself why she worked so hard. She was building a future for her son that would be the polar opposite of her own past. She was strong, she had values, she was not a quitter…

Today she had come simply because the pull to do so had been overwhelming. As gloomy as her memories of the years in this trailer could be, they often illuminated her present.

Crouching beside her dog, she cuddled Latke's comfort-ing heavy folds. "You should have seen the flowers Nate put in the trees. Peonies and pink roses. It looked like a scene from *A Midsummer Night's Dream*." Latke turned her head to swipe her broad tongue across Izzy's chin.

"I love you so much, too," Izzy murmured. She rubbed Latke's ears in the way that made the dog stretch her neck forward in ecstasy. "I know why I had the panic attack at Henry and Sam's," she told her loyal companion. "It's because that night on the lake with Nate, I understood what *bashert* felt like. For the first time in my life. It was like finding out you can fly without wings."

When she was very young, she'd tried so hard to gain every ounce of affection that she could, to find someone to belong to. Before she'd had Eli, the best Thanksgiving she could remember was the one year Felicia had a boyfriend named Rick, who drove a Schwan food truck. He was a nice man, one of the few who had hung around awhile, and he'd brought over a complete Thanksgiving meal for the three of them to share, with pumpkin ice cream he'd said was especially for Izzy. The food had been completely prepared and only needed to be reheated, but Felicia had complained that staying home was "a drag" and had begun to drink. She'd managed to burn the stuffing and potatoes while Izzy and Rick had played checkers. In the end, Felicia had threatened to go out and "have some adult fun *on my own*" if Rick didn't join her. So Izzy had stayed home alone, cleaned up the mess and scooped pumpkin ice cream straight from the container while watching TV. She'd made turkey sandwiches with cranberry sauce and mayonnaise to share with her mother when she returned, but Felicia hadn't come home until two days later, and she'd scoffed at the plastic-wrapped sandwiches Izzy had pulled from the fridge. "Throw that garbage out. I broke up with Rick. What a loser."

Izzy had been entertaining fantasies that Rick was going to be her father, but no way had she been about to say that and incur Felicia's ridicule. So she'd taken the

sandwiches outside, walked far away from the trailer and
set the food out for any animals who might not mind Rick's
offering. Then she'd sobbed until she'd thought she was
going to throw up. She'd been twelve at the time.

By fifteen, she'd decided she was done with feeling so
much. A coldness had seeped into her bones, and she'd
welcomed it. After a while, it had seemed nothing could
touch her. A perfect sunrise, a thoughtful gesture, Felicia's
cruelty—it had all become the same to her. And then…

"I realized I was dying of thirst in the desert, and Nate
became my rain." She gave the top of Latke's head a gentle kiss, more soothing to her than to the dog. "Yesterday,
on the river, I felt that way again. With everything I have
now, everyone I love, there was still a moment when I remembered what it used to be like, and…" Giving Latke
a tight hug, she admitted, "I wanted Nate as badly as I
wanted him before."

She looked again at the trailer. Broken, corroded.

It was hard to be courageous when you were contin-
uously trying to fix the broken parts of you. With that
thought, an odd, blanketing peace settled around her.
Maybe she didn't have to do that anymore. Maybe she
was already as fixed as she was going to get, and the broken bits that were left were there simply to remind her
she was human.

Suddenly, she knew what she had to do.

"Come on, pancake baby. "It's time to go back to the
present."

Chapter Ten

Izzy sneaked up the staff-only staircase of the Eagle's Crest Inn so that no one she knew would see her going inside Nate's room. She knew now that they would never be more than friends. She planned to tell him tonight that he had a son, and there was no way she was going to carry on an affair or a fling or even a flirtation with her teenage son's father, to whom she had been neither married nor engaged. This was not *The Gilmore Girls*. She needed to let go of the resentment, the hope, the longing, and start sort-of-over again with Nate. They needed to be teammates, players on Team Eli.

She didn't have much time, either, to make progress: Eli would be home from camp in a few days.

Screwing up her courage, she raised her fist and knocked on the door. Three rapid taps with her knuckles. Then she waited. Nothing. It was after nine in the evening. There was precious little to do at this hour in Thunder Ridge unless Nate was frequenting bars these days, or perhaps the twenty-four-hour Laundromat.

She had raised her hand to knock again just as the floor creaked. She glanced to her right.

Nate was walking down the carpeted hallway, looking right at her. He did not appear friendly.

"Hi," she said, hand lowering to her side.

He said nothing, just kept walking until he was in front of her, and she had to hop out of the way while he tucked a book under his left arm and opened his door with a card. The door remained open after he entered his bedroom suite, and Izzy had a pretty clear view of what appeared to be a studio-style apartment, with a queen-size bed, a kitchenette to the left with a small table with two chairs. A desk was placed beneath the window that overlooked the street.

Tossing his book onto the table, Nate went to the refrigerator and pulled out a bottle of water, which he opened and chugged, still with his back to her. "I assume you're here to see me," he said, replacing the bottle and shutting the refrigerator door.

Uh-oh. No more Mr. Nice Nate.

"Yes. I thought if you had time to talk, I'd like to. Talk." His demeanor was no help to her nerves, and she felt the urge to hyper-babble. Resisting the urge to speak, she waited through the difficult silence.

Opening a cabinet in the surprisingly spacious kitchen, Nate pulled out a plate, then grabbed a bag from the top of the fridge and withdrew four large cookies. Setting the dish in the center of the table, he lowered himself to a chair, nodding to the one opposite his. "Have a seat."

"All right, if you're sure."

"I'm not. But you're here."

Wow. This was a different Nate altogether than she had ever seen before. He looked the same, dressed in black denims and a sky blue polo shirt that enhanced his eyes and clung handsomely to his shoulders, chest and muscular arms. But his features looked as if they'd been carved from granite.

Izzy approached the table, pulled out the chair he'd indicated and sat. She'd dressed in a flowy, rose-colored skirt and lace-edged white tank top, thinking the ensemble made her seem approachable. The fashion equivalent of a white flag.

"You're probably wondering why I'm here."

"I'm wondering how I didn't see you in the lobby."

"Oh. There's a back staircase for the staff."

"You work here?"

"No. The Pickle Jar delivers take-out meals when someone phones from the inn. We leave our menus in the rooms, and—"

"I saw. Were you delivering a meal this evening?"

"No."

"You didn't want to be seen visiting me?"

"No," she said honestly, "I didn't want to be seen visiting you. Back when we were dating, I didn't know that many people, and they didn't know me. Now I'm kind of a fixture around town. I manage a local business, and—"

Oh, crap, she'd almost said, *I'm on the PTA.* That revelation had to wait a bit longer. "I'm pretty active in community work."

"And being seen with me would affect you…how?"

"I love Thunder Ridge."

His eyebrows rose. He remembered how desperate she'd once been to leave.

"I do love it here," she insisted. "It took leaving and coming back for me to appreciate that I can have all I want right here. I look at Thunder Ridge as my permanent home."

"No plans to leave again?"

"Nope."

He nudged the plate of chocolate chip cookies closer to her. "Help yourself."

She reached for one to give her hands something to do. "Thanks."

"I'd have gotten peanut butter if I'd known you were coming over."

He remembered that, too. "This is great. Fine. I like these."

"So, go on," he said. "You were telling me why you don't want anyone to see you with me."

"It's not that. I just don't see the point in encouraging gossip. This town has changed over the years, but in some ways it's as small as it ever was. And…" She fumbled a bit. "I'm hoping we can get to know each other again without prying eyes."

Perspiration broke out in a fine sheen on her face, which she was sure was turning bright red. After their fight at the river, he could reject her utterly. Leaning back in his chair, legs outstretched, he watched. And waited.

"I want to apologize to you for the judgments I made when we were younger. And for the judgments I made more recently, because, let's face it, it's not as if I ever stopped judging you."

His left eyebrow rose.

"Except now," she hastened to add. "I'm stopping now. You're right that we were both kids making adult decisions. It was an incredibly difficult time, and we ended badly." Izzy took a steadying breath. So far, she felt hot and prickly instead of relieved, but she was determined to finish. "I hope we can end that chapter in our lives and begin a new chapter as…as friends."

Nate was still frowning.

"Maybe," she amended, "*friends* isn't quite the right word. *Acquaintances*. We can be good acquaintances."

His eyes narrowed. "Or...people," she tried again. "Good people who...know each other."

Note to self: Should your current job end, do not consider a career in communications. Of any kind.

Nate took a bite of his cookie, considering her while he chewed. After a pregnant pause, the awkwardness of which was rivaled only by her entire three years of high school, he said, "You don't like chocolate chip cookies."

"Pardon?"

He gestured to the one untasted in her hand. "You never did like them. If we're going to be 'good acquaintances,' you need to tell me what you're really thinking."

Izzy searched for a spark of humor in his flinty eyes. "All right."

"If we move from acquaintanceship to actually being friends, I'll buy peanut butter cookies."

"Really?"

"Yes. I would do that for a friend."

"That's nice of you. Would that be the sandwich kind? With the peanut buttery filling?"

"Those are gross."

"It's what I like."

"All right, then." He licked a few crumbs from his fingers, then noted, "You never used to tell me what you wanted."

"I didn't?"

"No. You ate dozens of my famous home-baked chocolate chip cookies before you ever hinted that you preferred peanut butter."

"Well, who doesn't like famous home-baked chocolate chip cookies?"

"You. You like peanut butter with gross peanut buttery filling, so that's what you should have."

"Doesn't happiness come from being content with what

you have rather than believing you should have everything you want?"

"Of course. But the key word is *everything*. No one gets everything he wants, but you've got to believe you're worth at least some of what you want."

"Is there anything you've wanted that you haven't gotten?"

He looked at her quizzically. "Are you serious?"

"Yes. You wanted to be an architect, and you are. You wanted to live in a big, exciting city, and you do. What didn't you get?"

"I was married for five years. As hard as we tried, we couldn't make it work." He didn't have to say he considered that a failure—she could read it in his eyes.

"What happened?" Though she wasn't entirely certain she wanted to know, Izzy couldn't keep the question from popping out.

"Julianne is a great woman. An interior decorator with a successful career of her own. She's smart, beautiful, giving to her friends. And to me."

I am so sorry I asked.

"I like to think I was a good husband, too. That made it all the more confusing when we both realized we weren't happy. On paper, our marriage should have worked. Our *lives* should have worked." He shook his head. "It's true that no one has it all, but when you realize you don't feel… whole…then you know you have to make a change."

"Are you the one who wanted the divorce?"

"She asked, but I knew I shouldn't fight it. Julianne was looking for what she called 'a more authentic life.'"

"What does that mean?"

"I think it means she wanted to feel that she was where she was supposed to be. After our divorce was final, she compared her life to a three-course meal and said she was still waiting for the entrée. Obviously, she didn't think it was ever going to arrive if she stayed with me.'"

Ouch. Izzy winced on his behalf. "But how do you *know* you couldn't have made it happen, made that feeling come, if you'd stayed together? How does she even know that what she wants actually exists?"

Nate smiled. "When you walked in tonight, I had no idea we'd be having this kind of conversation. Did you?"

"No." A smile played around Izzy's lips, also. "Am I being too personal?"

"Nope." He leaned forward, forearms resting on his knees. There seemed to be an invisible beam connecting their gazes. "I can't speak for Julianne, but I think we got married in the first place hoping the feeling of emptiness would go away. This didn't go over so well the last time I told you, but I felt whole for the first time that summer before college. There was nothing I wanted, nothing I needed that I didn't already have. There was nobody I had to become."

"Don't you think that was because you'd already gotten into college? All your wheels were on the right track."

Nate shook his head. "It had nothing to do with that. I'd spent four years of high school 'on track' and never feeling like I could stop moving or striving toward something. It took me a long time to realize—longer than it should have—that I felt whole for the first time in my life that summer. Because of you."

Wow. That's almost as good as "you complete me."

Nate was going to make it hard to keep her wits about her if he said things like that.

"That was really only true over the summer, though. Don't you think?" she asked, determined to keep their relationship in perspective. "After I found out I was pregnant, I *did* hope that you would change. I wanted you to say you were ready to become a father." *And a husband.*

"You wanted to keep the baby."

Getting warmer. "Yes. I said I agreed to the adoption plan, but it wasn't what I wanted. It made sense. Of course it did. We were so young and had no way to support ourselves and a child, like you said. But I'd never had a family, not really. I didn't know what a mother's love felt like. I couldn't imagine not taking care of my baby. I wanted someone I could love completely. Someone who needed me. It was selfish of me, I know."

Nate's frown deepened. Darkening to ocean blue, his eyes seemed to hide a tempest of thoughts. "It wasn't selfish." There were more words inside, wanting to emerge, but he lowered his head, his forehead on the heels of his palms. When he looked up again, the frown was gone, but his eyes looked older, tired. "You said you'd wished I'd changed. I wish I had, too."

Whoa. He wished…that he'd been ready to be a father?

Pure longing rushed like white water through Izzy's body, over the stone around her heart, wearing it away, smoothing the rough edges.

The room pulsed with intimacy. It seemed smaller—much—than when she'd first walked in. Nate reached toward her, something she realized only when she felt him taking her hands in his and holding them. Gentle, warm, secure—his touch was all the things it used to be. Including electrifying. It was impossible not to remember in that moment that she was in his hotel room. With a bed that was bigger than anything else in the room.

They'd had sex too soon, and at first, to Izzy, it had felt like falling down a waterfall—exhilarating but frightening, with no idea at all of whether she was going to land safely or not. Once she'd given him the last bit of her heart, their lovemaking had changed to something that felt more like standing beneath the waterfall with every pore in her body dying of thirst.

And every time, he had stared at her afterward as if what they'd just shared was something rare and important. In later years, she'd wondered what it would have felt like if she'd known he loved her, too. What if every kiss, every touch, had been a promise sealing their forevers?

Nate brought his chair closer to hers. Their knees were almost touching. "I really want to kiss you." His whisper touched every cell in her body.

Dear God, help me remember why it's wrong...even though it sounds so, so right.

Eli. Eli. This is going to be hard on him...complicated... Don't make it worse.

Nate moved closer. It took every ounce of strength she possessed to squeeze the big, strong hands that held hers. She squeezed tightly. *You have no idea what's coming. You don't need more complications, either.*

"I have to go now." The soft words echoed in the silent room. "But we need to see each other again. Get to know each other better. Very soon, please."

His disappointment was palpable, the tension in his body traveling through his fingers. Raising her hands, he pressed his lips to the back of her knuckles—obviously the only kiss he figured she'd allow—and agreed, "Very soon."

Chapter Eleven

"'**D**ouble support' means both of your feet have to be touching the pavement at the same time," Derek insisted as he, Holliday and Izzy slogged back into town after an hour and a half of training for the Ridge-to-the-Coast Relay. They were participating as Team Pickle Jar, and Izzy had made T-shirts—gray with the words "Got Pickles?" underneath a smiling green dill that had arms and legs and running shoes. So far, no one but she was willing to wear the shirt.

"I didn't see both your feet on the ground at the same time once today," Derek harassed Holliday, who had been rolling her eyes more than her feet while Derek coached them.

"On the day of the race, I will be wearing my Daisy Dukes and a Got Pickles? T-shirt that I have preshrunk and cut to midriff length. No one—except you—will be looking at my feet. Guaranteed."

"You're really going to wear your Got Pickles? tee?"

Izzy exclaimed, feeling her energy return. Holliday smiled beatifically. "Thanks!" Every bit of advertising was going to help.

"You think sex is going to sell pickles?" Derek scoffed. Both women looked at him.

"Jeepers, I'm not sure, Sheriff." Holliday mock frowned. "It's hard to tell what'll sell here in Mayberry. Hey, I know," she said, and her expression cleared. "Let's ask Opie!"

Derek's scowl intensified. He hated Holliday's periodic references to the old *Andy Griffith Show*. She'd accused him more than once of trying to keep Thunder Ridge in the dark ages with his old-fashioned values. The town-hall lecture he had given the previous month on the perils of littering, jaywalking and other misdemeanors—complete with a pie chart he'd labeled Small Crimes, Big Fines— hadn't helped matters.

"The Pickle Jar is a family restaurant," he said. "That's what I'm saying. Izzy doesn't want to confuse the customers. Do you, Izz?"

"Oh. Uh, well…no," she agreed at Derek's thunderous expression, "of course not. Although, you know, it might not *confuse* them exactly. And Holly is the local librarian. There's an implied wholesomeness right there."

"Wholesome?" both Holliday and Derek protested, but then Holly turned to the sheriff and growled, "Watch it, pal. I'm a county employee, too."

Izzy shook her head and moved on as the bickering continued. Who cared if Holly wore cutoffs and showed her midriff? It was hard to confuse customers who didn't exist.

As they walked past Burger-ology, one of Thunder Ridge's newer venues, Izzy's mood dropped a bit. Okay, a ton. Burger-ology, which was decorated in fire-engine red, cloud white and sleek chrome, appeared to be doing a bang-up lunch business. When she'd phoned The Pickle Jar at the end of their walk, Willa had answered and admitted that lunch had been slow.

"I'm thirsty after all that walking," she said, changing the channel in her mind. There would be time to obsess about work after she showered and returned to the deli. "Anybody feel like getting an ice-cream soda?"

Thankfully, both of her friends agreed, and they all headed to The General Store. A couple of blocks away from the small market and soda fountain, they could see a large crowd gathered outside. The sound of raised voices made Derek pick up the pace while Izzy and Holliday jogged behind.

"Raybald, you nutcase! Come down from there, you hear me?" Jax Stewart, owner of The General Store, stood at the front of the crowd, shading his eyes as he looked up. "This is my building. And I do not want you hanging off the second story."

"I rent this second story, and I know my rights. This barber pole is *my* property. I can be out here if I want to be! I can sing 'America the Beautiful' if I want to. In fact, I think I will. 'Oh, beautiful for spacious skies—'"

Ron Raybald had, from what Izzy could see, tied himself to the striped pole outside the window of his second-floor barbershop.

"What the devil—" Pushing through the crowd, Derek shouted above the chatter, "Ron! What the heck are you doing?" Ron continued to sing. Derek turned to Jax. "What's he doing?"

"Sealing his fate. He's going to wind up in a loony bin for the rest of his sorry life!" The latter part of Jax's statement was yelled at Ron, who responded by singing louder.

Pinching the bridge of his nose, Derek lowered his head. "Can anybody here tell me what is going on? Where's Russell?"

Russell was one of Derrick's deputies.

"He went up the Ridge," Jonas Bates, owner of the hardware store, called out in the creaky voice that reminded Izzy of the rusty nails Jonas always advocated replacing. "Two summer skiers got into a tussle on the chairlift, so Russ went to sort them out. But I can tell you what's going on." He pointed to Jax. "Jax gave Ron a notice saying he's planning to remodel the building, and Ron thinks that's going to hurt business."

In the middle of a rousing "and crown thy good," Ron abruptly stopped singing and said, "I was not worried about business! I'm not thinking about myself. It's my civic duty to protest the destruction of culturally relevant structures. I am a member of the Thunder Ridge Historical Society."

"Hysterical Society is more like it," Jax sniped. "And I am not destroying the building, you rabble-rouser, I'm improving it."

"Words, words, words," Ron sang. "That's all I hear is meaningless words."

"Come on down, I'll give you something meaningful," Jax shouted.

"That's enough, both of you!" While Derek attempted to calm the storm, Izzy motioned to Holliday that she was heading home. When Eli wasn't around, she rarely stayed away from the restaurant.

"What's going on?"

Izzy looked up. Nate greeted her, his expression open and relaxed, a contrast from when she last saw him. In perfectly cut jeans and a crisp white T-shirt that highlighted the classic V of his torso, he emitted the same golden-boy aura she'd sensed the first time she'd ever laid eyes on him.

He'd certainly changed, though. If people were cars, Nate would have been a Mustang in high school—sporty, fast, cool. As an adult, he was a Jaguar—powerful yet smooth, confident but not pretentious, great looking with substance.

"Sidewalk sale?" he inquired humorously as they met at the curb.

"No, just a difference of opinion between Jax Stewart and Ron Raybald."

"Jax?" One of Nate's ridiculously well-shaped black brows arched. "That's who I'm coming to see. What's happening between him and Ron?"

Briefly, Izzy described the conflict. "Jax and Ron are reflecting what's going on all over town. Half the people are screaming for progress—a new cell tower, more modern shops, a fast-food restaurant—and the other half want everything to stay the way it is, because they're afraid to lose the sweetness of the town."

Nate nodded slowly, thoughtfully. "It *is* a sweet place. More run-down than I remembered it, though. Is it realistic to keep it the way it is?"

"It's always been run-down. You're probably noticing it more because you've been away."

"Which side of the divide do you stand on? Are you a fan of progress or preservation?"

"Both, I suppose. I see the value of remodeling the older buildings, but people like Ron can't afford to close down during construction. And Jax can. He's inherited quite a few properties around town. Ron thinks Jax would be happy to close him down so he can have the whole building, because when Jax's grandfather owned the building, he gave Ron a ninety-nine-year lease. Now that Jax has inherited the business and the property, some people think Jax would like to force Ron and a few other tenants out."

"That doesn't sound like Jax. He's a good man."

A kernel of memory popped in Izzy's brain. Nate and Jax had played football together. Like Nate, Jax had moved away after high school, but he'd returned a few years ago with a business degree.

"In addition to inheriting, Jax has been buying properties all over Thunder Ridge, from what I understand. A lot of business people are renting from him now. It's understandable that they're fidgety, wondering what he has in mind. He's not endearing himself to people by dissing the local Historical Society."

Nate pulled out his phone and started texting, then slipped it into his back pocket and smiled at Izzy. "Want to get something to drink?"

"I thought you were here to see Jax."

"I just told him we can reschedule. Sounds like he's busy." Nate's gaze skimmed Izzy. "You still look good in shorts."

Instantly, she felt self-conscious. Her hand rose to her hair, which was damp with perspiration. "I'm a sweaty mess."

Nate shook his head. "Women never understand what turns a man on."

"Sweat?"

He took a step closer as Jax and Ron's audience started to disperse. "Passion. Drive. You look like you were very driven today. Plus, you're wearing a Got Pickles? T-shirt."

"And that's hot?"

"Oh, yeah."

Awareness sizzled inside Izzy. The anticipation of what they would say next tasted like champagne. She jumped as a hand patted her back.

"Hi, there," Holliday said. She draped herself over Izzy's shoulder. "Derek went up to the barbershop to unhook Ron from the pole. Ron can't get the knots out of the rope he used. Jax is getting a pair of gardening shears. There's just never a dull moment around here." She sent a dazzling smile from Nate to Izzy and back again.

"Nate Thayer, I heard you were back!" An older gentleman Izzy did not recognize pumped Nate's hand while clapping him on the upper arm.

While the two men started chatting, Holliday whispered to Izzy, "He's been ogling your legs."

"No, he hasn't. Really?"

"Yes, indeed. Are you two getting together right now?"

"No, I was going to go home."

"Alone?"

Her tone was so insinuating Izzy felt a chuckle in her chest. "Yes, you scary sex addict, alone. I have something serious to discuss with him, remember?"

"You're allowed to talk during sex."

"Didn't you recommend remaining calm, cool and collected during my encounters with Nate? 'Keep a cool head. Keep your emotions under control'—that's what you said."

"I'm always calm, cool and collected during sex. Besides, I told you all that before I saw the way Tall, Dark and *Deee*licious looks at you. Now I think you should have sex *and* tell him he's the father of your child."

"Shh," Izzy pleaded, even though Holly's voice was already a murmur. "I'm not that girl anymore. No sex until—"

"The afterlife?"

"Hilarious. No. No sex until Eli is out of the house, and I find someone to share the rest of my life with."

"With the magic Mr. Right? What if you never find him? Birds do it, bees do it, even girls in pickle tees can do it."

"Very funny."

"And it rhymes."

"Shh, here he is again."

Nate's conversation wrapped up, and he returned to the women, but as he opened his mouth to speak, an elderly female voice exclaimed, "Izzy, darling, my lawn looks like an Old English sheepdog. Is Eli available to mow?"

Holliday's arm tightened around Izzy's shoulders even as Izzy tightened up all over.

"Hi, Evelyn!" she said to the eightysomething redhead, who approached with single-minded determination. *I can't think of anything else to say*, Izzy thought in blind panic. She looked at Holliday, who also appeared stumped.

Wearing a lightweight pale pink jogging suit, Evelyn stopped directly in front of them. "Darling, I know it's summer, but I'm still watering my lawn, and it's growing like wildfire. When can Eli come over?"

Oh, dear lord. This was not how she wanted Nate to find out he had a son. "Right. Well, Evelyn, I think, um… Didn't he tell you? He went out of town. I think he'll be available again next week. I'll have to check my calendar. My yard's a mess, too!" Good! She'd made him sound like a gardener. Holliday gave her an approving squeeze.

Evelyn, however, gave her a strange look. "You think he'll be available? Don't you know? I don't approve of all this not-knowing what goes on these days. Honey, Eli is still only—"

"He is still the only person I'd trust with my lawn," Holliday interrupted, releasing Izzy and flinging her arm around Evelyn instead, "if I had one." She began leading the woman away. "Evelyn, did I tell you the books you put on hold are in? There are three other holds, though, on *Hip Hop for Dummies*, so we should pick that up for you right away."

"Ooh. All right, I don't want to lose that one. But you'll call me?" she asked Izzy anxiously over her shoulder.

"Yes. Very soon."

Faintly bemused, Nate commented. "Sounds like Thunder Ridge could use a few good landscapers."

"Yeah." Emitting a high, ridiculous-sounding laugh,

Izzy grabbed Nate's elbow and propelled him across the street. *I have got to tell him before he finds out from somebody else.* As they stepped up on the opposite curb, in front of the park, she announced, "I don't have to work tonight. I was thinking about driving into Portland to…" *It was summer—what was going on in Portland?* "To… go to…the…summer concert series! At the zoo. Remember those?"

"Yeah, of course. I saw Earth, Wind and Fire there."

"Wow. Well, tonight is—" *Oh, crumbs.* She had no idea who was playing at the zoo tonight. *Don't get specific. Keep it general.* "Who knows who's playing? So, would you like to? Go with me? To the concert?"

If a bobblehead doll could speak, it would sound exactly like me. She wasn't entirely surprised when Nate studied her dubiously a moment, then said, "I'll walk you home."

So, that would be a no?

Great. Now she was going to have to figure out another time to tell him, and she preferred to be away from Thunder Ridge when she did it.

Taking the lead, she walked beside him, silent as the sun warming their skin. Nate looked enviably cool, but Izzy could smell his skin. Perhaps it was more memory than reality, but he had that yummy Nate's-skin scent that used to make her want to snuggle into him and stay there indefinitely.

Nate seemed as content to walk without speaking, beyond the streets that formed the center of town, and into the residential area where she shared the little cottage with—

Oh, fudgeknuckles. She couldn't invite Nate in—there were photos of Eli everywhere. Three houses away from her own place, Izzy slowed down, trying to remember if any of her son's things—bike helmet, basketball, mud-caked size-nine hiking boots—were on the front porch.

Well, it would be a conversation starter, she reasoned,

but, oh, my goodness, her head and heart were pounding in unison.

At the border of her yard, which Eli had mowed and edged before he'd left for camp, she saw that the porch was clear of everything except two deck chairs, a single low table and an umbrella stand.

"This is me." She gestured to the house, abruptly aware of how proud she was of her little place.

Her cottage might be tiny by most standards, but it was a cheerful butter yellow. The creamy white trim had been repainted just last summer, and oversize wood-and-chrome wind chimes flanked a huge hanging basket of bright pink fuchsias. *Happy people live here.* That was what the front of her house said.

Briefly, Izzy closed her eyes. *Please let happy people continue to live here.*

Nate studied the building, his gaze roving up, down, left and right. She wondered if he was looking at it as an architect. If so, he could no doubt catalog a host of changes he would make. Izzy's stomach dropped as once again she realized Nate would be able to give Eli so many more of the things that mattered to a teenage boy, including, she was sure, swanky digs and his own state-of-the-art gadget-filled bedroom.

She was just about to picture the moment that Eli was going to tell her he wanted to move to Chicago when Nate commented, "Great place. It suits you."

"I bought it myself," she said, allowing pride to infuse her voice. "Well, not entirely. Henry and Sam helped with the down payment, but I finished paying them back last year."

Surprise and respect infused his expression. "That's quite an accomplishment."

Pleasure began to fill her until she remembered that it had taken the entire past decade to repay the ten thousand dollars. She shook her head, appreciative but realistic.

"You're being nice. You know darn well the down payment for this house is probably what you spend on a summer vacation. Come on, let's sit on the porch."

He grabbed her hand, pulling her back until he was looking directly in her eyes. "Buying your own home—any home—is a tremendous achievement. And your house is lovely." Her hand was still clasped in his, the pressure of his fingers firm and steady and warm. "You should be proud as hell of what you've accomplished."

Without waiting for a response, he headed for the porch, releasing her only as they took their seats. Escaping the direct sunshine was a relief as it was still blisteringly hot with no breeze, and Izzy knew she ought to offer Nate a drink.

I wonder if he'd mind sipping from the garden hose.

"Have you made good memories here?"

She cleared her throat. "I have, yes. Very good." She drew a shallow breath. Should she tell him now?

A butterfly flitted around the flowers she'd planted in front of the porch railing. Izzy was strongly tempted to pretend it was a normal afternoon. If they'd never broken up...

I'd take his hand again.

And tell him how nervous I feel about Eli going to college in a few years with a hearing loss.

He'd tell me not to worry, that our son can handle it and we'll both be there to help him when he needs it. He'd say we can get through anything as long as we're together.

And I would believe him.

Izzy chewed her bottom lip. Dandy. Just dandy. Apparently, it didn't matter how smart she got or how strictly the school of life educated her, she was always going to be that girl who wanted a hero to come along—even though she was a single mother, and it was far, far too late for fairy tales.

"I'd like to go to the concert with you tonight."

There was a "but" in Nate's voice that made Izzy's head swivel in his direction.

"First, you should know why I want to go."

Sounded ominous. "Because you like outdoor concerts?" she tried, hoping to keep the mood light for a while longer, at least.

Humor tugged at his lips. Briefly. Then he looked serious again. "I like you. I'd like to get to know you again."

She tried to swallow. A heart couldn't literally jump into a person's throat, could it?

"How about if we start fresh, pretend we just met?" he asked. His voice dropped to a hum as soothing as the rustle of the breeze through the maple leaves. "Do you think we could do that tonight?"

Mesmerized, feeling reality begin to fade away, she nodded.

No, don't nod. You can't pretend that.

But he had her at "I like you."

Her conscience protested. *Tell him. He needs to know. Get it over with. Tell him now.*

"Nate," she began, "maybe it would be best if…"

He wagged his head, touching two fingers lightly to her lips. "Think less." It was a request. A favor. "This one time."

No. Way.

"Okay," she breathed. "Okay, let's just go to the concert."

Augggghhh!

He reached out, grasping the arms of the wicker chair in which she was seated. With little effort, he scooted it toward him, turning his own chair at the same time until they were close enough for Nate to reach behind her with his free hand and cup the back of her head. She could see tiny flecks of brown in the sea of his blue irises and the infinitesimal scar high on his right cheek from the case of chicken pox he'd had when he was five.

"On second thought, you really should know my intentions before we set the plans for tonight in stone." His voice was so soft.

Her heart beat so hard she could barely draw the breath to speak. "What are your intentions?"

She saw him moving ever closer to her lips but didn't think he was actually going to kiss her, or she'd have moved. Of course.

Or…not.

Oh. My. Goodness. How could she have forgotten this, as if her bones were melting like butter? The touch of his lips, the scent of his skin…

It was a homecoming.

Tenderly, his lips settled on hers, soft as down. She raised her hands to touch his neck, first just with her fingertips, but as the kiss deepened, her hands delved into his hair, and she was kissing him back with yearning and passion and a hunger she couldn't satisfy on a neighborhood porch.

It will never be enough. Oh, this was an exquisite, magnificent mistake.

Nate had his hands around her waist and was pulling her toward him so that she sat on the edge of her chair, their knees tangling. His kiss grew more insistent before he drew away, lowering his chin until their foreheads touched.

He swallowed. "So, do you want to?"

Izzy licked her lips. Her eyes remained closed. "Do I want to…?"

"Set our date in stone?"

Date. They shouldn't call it a date—

Shut up.

"Stone is good."

Chapter Twelve

If Izzy worried about awkward silences on the hour-long ride to Portland, she needn't have. Nate kept the mood light with anecdotes about his recent attempts to join a recreational football league.

"Some of the guys were straight out of college or still in, but they had injuries and couldn't play competitively anymore."

With one hand on the steering wheel and his right resting on the stick shift, he was the picture of relaxation. He'd insisted on driving and had picked her up in a rental car that cost several times the price of her very well-used four-wheel-drive wagon, which was practical as all get-out but did nothing to enhance her sex appeal. Nate, on the other hand, looked like an ad for *Motor Trend* Sports Car of the Year.

"So, I figured I could play ball with these guys, flash some moves, but the very first scrimmage, I fall and realize I've messed up my wrist. I am the oldest guy there, and no way am I going to admit that I sprained my wrist and don't want to play anymore."

"What did you do?"

"Acted like a macho jerk until the pain was so bad, I started to cry."

"You cried?"

"In front of several very large football players who probably dislocated their shoulders on a regular basis and never noticed it. They thought I was a wuss."

His grin practically tugged her to him. Izzy wanted to smooth her fingers over his forehead. Instead, she kept her hands on her denim capris. "You're not a wuss."

Nate laughed. "You're too kind."

"What happened next?"

"I limped to my car, got an X-ray and a very tall beer and went back to the gym from then on instead of to the football field."

"You quit your team?"

"Oh, yeah."

"Did they try to talk you out of it?"

"Oh, no."

A fizzy warmth tickled her chest. Seeing the vulnerable, imperfect side of Nate was a new experience. In high school, his success at sports, at academics and in the social realm had seemed effortless.

Izzy hadn't told anyone that Nate had kissed her today. Hadn't stopped thinking about it, either.

When she lapsed into a fantasy that included her, Nate and Eli together, she would forcefully wipe it from her mind. She was getting so good, she could complete the "wonder, drop it, wonder some more" cycle in about three minutes, then start up again with barely a break.

Instead of taking Highway 26 to their destination, Nate asked Izzy if she would mind his taking Burnside through downtown and up to Washington Park, where the Oregon

Zoo sat like a hilltop village. Along the way, he asked her about all the places that had been remodeled or built during his absence, and she understood that he was viewing downtown Portland with the eye of a commercial architect. At eighteen, when they'd ventured into the city, he had dreamed aloud of someday constructing skyscrapers.

"You made it come true," she said, letting the awe truly sink in. She'd spent so much time resenting him she hadn't really considered his achievements. "You build skyscrapers."

"Yes, I do."

His tone was hard to read, so she probed, "You must feel crazy proud when you drive by one of your buildings."

His fingers curled around the wheel. "I thought I would." A muscle worked in his jaw before he spoke again. "In school, I wanted to focus on sustainable design for large commercial projects. But when my parents moved to Chicago after my father's heart attack, it hit home that they were getting older and needed more help, so I started taking jobs. Anything I could get in a field related to architecture. One of the companies I worked for hired me right out of school, and I never looked back." He shook his head. "I never looked around, either."

"That seems reasonable. Under the circumstances."

"Yeah." He shrugged. "Dreams and circumstance make interesting dance partners. I haven't found the rhythm."

Izzy stared at him, stunned. "Are you saying you're not happy with your career?"

They were just passing Powell's City of Books, and he glanced at the multilevel store as he answered. "I have no right not to be happy. I've had plenty of opportunities that others haven't." He gave her a sidelong look from behind his Ray-Bans. "I do realize that. But if I'm being a hundred percent honest, I feel disappointed a lot of the time." His lips twisted. "Don't say it."

"What?"

"'You're a spoiled brat, Thayer.'"

Was she thinking that? She certainly *had* thought it, once upon a time. "I've never called you 'Thayer.'"

He laughed, appreciating the irony. Then he remembered. "Yeah, you did call me 'Thayer' once. Remember the day we had a picnic at Trillium Lake, and you bet me the last five potato chips that you could spell more nine-letter words beginning with *S* than I could?"

She frowned. "Vaguely."

"And, because I knew how much you loved barbecue potato chips, I magnanimously allowed you to win, after which you said, 'Hand me the bag, Thayer.'"

"You remember that?"

"I remember because you didn't even want to share."

"Well, you eat more potato chips than I do. And you did not magnanimously let me win."

"Did, too."

"You did not."

"I thought you said you only vaguely remember this."

"It's coming back to me. I won with *salacious*. I earned those chips."

He shrugged. "Guess we'll never know. Unless you want a rematch. You still love barbecue chips?"

"As long as they're ripple."

"Thought so. I brought a bag."

Just as with the cookies, she was absurdly touched that he remembered little details about her.

"And gummy worms mixed with popcorn." Grimacing, he shook his head. "Do you still eat that?"

"Only when I go to the movies. Or watch one at home. Or think about watching a movie either in the theater or at home."

"Even though I worry about the sanity of anyone who would eat that—"

Our son loves it.

"—I brought you some nonetheless. So, rematch while we wait for the concert to start?"

"Okay."

As they left the city proper and headed into the wooded majesty of Washington Park, she recalled the other times they'd made this drive, in his battered pickup. The last time had been the evening she'd told him she was pregnant. "Why does your life disappoint you?" she asked. "What are you disappointed in, exactly?"

Navigating the turns in the road up to the zoo, Nate seemed to think carefully about his reply. "Some of it is obvious, I suppose. I want to design commercial buildings that are environmentally sound. And I want their exterior design to be harmonious with the surroundings rather than overpowering. But I have a secure job, and I have financial responsibilities, even though I'm not always on the same page as the people who commission building plans." He flicked his gaze at her. "That sounds like a cop-out, even to me."

She offered a small smile. "Not necessarily. I know about making choices based on responsibilities. Is there anything besides career that disappoints you?"

He hesitated only a moment. "When you get up each morning, do you have a sense of purpose, Izzy?"

Whoa. "Yes." *I have your son.* "I feel responsible to Henry and Sam, all the employees at The Pickle Jar. I suppose the fact that the restaurant is always struggling gives me a sense of purpose." She wrinkled her nose. "I never thought about that before. It's kind of a paradox, isn't it? Maybe if we were a great success, I wouldn't feel so driven. Do you think that's your problem? You're too successful?"

Nate didn't smile. "Maybe."

He turned the car into the entrance of Washington Park, where dense foliage in a dozen shades of green gave it a magical, almost otherworldly feel, protected and safe from the slings and arrows of the city below. That was how she had felt with Nate. "I loved that summer with you," she said quietly. "It didn't seem to have anything to do with the rest of my life. I guess that's what you've been saying, too. So maybe that's what we were?" She shrugged, still trying to figure it out after all these years. "Each other's escape?"

He frowned mightily. "Maybe." The word sounded heavy, reluctant.

"The problem was that real life intruded, and the bubble burst."

On their right was a small parking lot in front of a clearing used for archery practice. Nate pulled the car into a space, unclicked his seat belt and turned to her. "You think it's that straightforward?"

She nodded. "Yes. We were kids. What did we know?" She tried to laugh. "What do kids ever know about romance? We barely know ourselves at that age."

"Maybe we knew more then than we do now," he suggested, leaning forward.

Just like this afternoon, his eyes and the expression in them mesmerized her, but she was determined to keep her wits about her. She shook her head. "It's a fact that the human mind isn't fully formed until a person reaches his twenties, you know. There's a lot of research on this. Until then, people don't have the, um…"

Was he moving closer?

"…the capacity to, uh…the capability to think clearly and be logical and…"

He *was* moving closer.

"…not impulsive, so they shouldn't be having relationships."

"I don't think it's that simple."

"Yes." She nodded emphatically. "Yes, it is. What's simple is abstention. We should abstain from relationships. Focus on school."

"Tall order." His voice dropped to that low hum that made her stomach buzz. "What if you meet the right person early in your life?"

"Well, then you…wait. You wait."

Nate reached for her, his warm, warm hand on the back of her neck, making every hair on her nape tingle and stand on end. For years, she'd been using her mind to override her emotions. She knew how to take control of her body and, except when it came to Eli, of her heart, as well. But now Nate kissed her, and it left her brain spinning.

She kissed him back. Her palms rested on his chest. When she found the strong thud of his heartbeat, her body trembled, years of yearning pushing against the dam she'd built to hold back her desire. It was easy not to respond to other men. Not so with Nate.

Just a little more, her body begged. *We'll stop in a second. Honest.*

It took several seconds, however, and Nate was the one who pulled back. Not, she noticed, without effort.

"It is not," he repeated his earlier words, "that simple."

This time, she agreed.

If viewed aerially, the concert lawn at the Oregon Zoo would doubtlessly resemble an undulating sea of people, all milling about as they searched for seats, got in line for shave ice or ordered bento boxes, or bratwurst and beer from one of the tents set up around the venue. Nate held Izzy's hand as they wove through the bodies preparing to listen to Chicago perform their greatest hits. The atmosphere was as festive as a Fourth of July, but no matter how many other people were present, Izzy's attention remained solely on Nate. Or, more specifically, on his hand. Because just holding hands with him was more exciting than anything she'd experienced in years, and she was kind of curious about the delicious sensation, since a hand was a hand was a hand.

Except that Nate's hand—the feel of his palm and his fingers—made her feel 100 percent safe and warm and loved. And for once, she wasn't even worried about that.

I should be completely freaked out.

But she understood that this perfect sensation was temporary. Maybe that was what made the feeling okay. This time, she wasn't going to be surprised when it ended.

Just a little bit longer, and then I'll find the right moment to tell him about Eli, and after that...

Disappointment, sharp and sudden, tugged her heart down like an anchor. Once she told Nate about Eli, they would have to stop thinking about themselves, pull up their big-parent panties and pour all their energies into learning how to co-parent a teenage son.

Co-parent. Such a grown-up, modern word.

Tiny needles of dread pricked her skin from the inside out.

"You okay?" Nate turned his head in question as they cut through a line of people at one of the beer tents.

Sick to her stomach, she nodded. *What if he wants Eli to move to Chicago? What if Eli wants to go? What if his mother still doesn't accept Eli, or if she can't accept his hearing loss? What if Eli feels terrible about himself after meeting his father? What if he feels terrible about me? What if—*

"You're cutting my circulation off, Izzy." When they reached a bit of a clearing, he faced her, holding up their hands. "My fingers are blue. What's up?"

"Fear of crowds."

"Really? Is that something new?"

"I guess." He surveyed the scene around them. "Did you see the sold-out sign when we came in? There are probably more people here than usual. Do you want to leave? Walk around the park instead?"

"No." The music would start soon, and it would be too difficult to talk, and that would buy her time to calm down.

Coward, her conscience chided.

Bite me.

"Would you like to get something to eat?" They'd been forced to leave their snacks in the car when they'd realized no outside food or drinks were allowed during the concert. "Or some wine before we sit down?"

Izzy's stomach recoiled at the thought of food, and while a small wine buzz sounded tempting, she knew better than to dull her wits when she needed them more than ever. Frantic for something to do, however, she blurted, "Shave ice. I'd love a shave ice."

Nate led her to the long line in front of the tent where multihued ridges of ice were served with fat straws to sip sweet, frosty liquid that came in myriad flavor combinations. She and Nate stood side by side, their hands still clasped. There was no chance they were going to lose each other standing in line, and Izzy grew self-conscious. Should she let go first? Their hands were just hanging there, together, as if they were dating.

"Bet I know what you're going to order." He grinned.

Izzy glanced at the board with flavors scrawled over it. "How do you know what I'm going to order? I don't even know." Coconut, mango, chocolate, leche, Thai tea, banana, Northwest Marionberry—the list of flavor options went on and on.

"I know you won't be able to make up your mind. So you'll order what they're having." He nodded to a group of teenagers leaving the tent with their mountainous treats painted a rainbow of flavors. The colors bled together, one skinny stripe huddled so closely next to its neighbor that not a single flavor would be discernible.

Ha! He didn't know her as well as he thought. Years ago, she might have hungrily tried everything, like the teens, but these days, she knew that insisting on having all she wanted could end in a terrible gut ache.

"Actually, I think I'd rather have just one or two flavors." She pointed as a cup mounded with a creamy-looking, two-colored treat topped with toasted coconut passed by. "Like that one—" *Oh.*

Oh, no.

No, no, no. It couldn't be.

Squinting after the T-shirted young man who was walking away from her, Izzy sent up a quick prayer that her eyes were, in fact, deceiving her. That kid looked just like Gabe Pentzel, one of Eli's classmates, which wouldn't be so horrible, except that Gabe was a junior counselor this summer at the same inner-city camp as Eli.

Izzy's eyes darted throughout the tent. Up ahead in line, she spotted a group of younger kids dressed similarly to the boy she'd thought was Gabe, in shorts and red tees with white lettering. She squinted but couldn't make out the words on their shirts.

"Thanks for inviting me tonight," Nate said, squeezing her hand briefly. "This was a good idea. The venue's a lot more elaborate than I remember."

"Yeah, it is." Distracted, she watched another couple of red T-shirters leave the tent with their shave ices. They were younger than Eli; Izzy didn't recognize them. She strained to read their shirts. *Camp...*

She couldn't see clearly, but unless the circle of white lettering said Crimp Innards Critter, it was a darn good bet she was looking at the Camp Inner City kids. And that meant...

Her heart skittered like a pack of marbles rolling down stairs.

"You know," she turned to Nate, "I think this was *not* such a good idea, after all. It's so crowded."

Concern filled Nate's expression.

"Why don't we walk around the park like you suggested?" She would take him to the International Rose Test Garden. That was where she'd told him about Eli the first time. There was a kind of poetic full circle-ness to the idea of going back to the same bench to tell him again that he was a father. She should have thought of that before.

"Let's go." This time, she pulled Nate as she wove them through the crowds. Each time she saw a cluster of red shirts, she switched direction. "Excuse me…pardon us…" The flow of traffic was against them, the crowds growing ever thicker as showtime neared.

Her forehead perspired as they reached the edge of the concert lawn. The Africafe, a large concrete hut that served sandwiches and fries, was ahead of them, and there were fewer people congregated there. They could follow the concrete walkway that circled the building and then head to the parking lot.

Izzy wondered if Nate felt the slickness of her palm. Yuck. Her mind lurched ahead to what would happen when they got to the Rose Garden. She had pictures of Eli on her phone, of course. She would show them to Nate. Text him a few, if he wanted. Would he want that? And she would have to explain about the hearing impairment and decide how to tell Eli his father was here in town and that she'd never actually told him she was keeping their child…

There was a tug on her hand. Nate had stopped moving. She turned to see him looking at her in deep concern. Letting go of her sweaty hand, he stepped forward until he was standing over her, a half foot taller than she, holding her shoulders.

"Breathe, sweetheart. You're okay, crowd or no crowd." He inhaled deeply, urging her to do the same. "Just breathe."

Filled with compassion, his eyes reminded her of Henry's words: *Finding your* bashert *doesn't necessarily make life easier, it makes it better.*

Except that regarding her and Nate, the situation between them was the cause of her current distress, and she was about to complicate his life exponentially.

"Nate. I have something I want to say. There's something you should—"

"Hey, Mrs. L!"

Beside her, a young boy almost as tall as Nate appeared. His smile revealed braces that could not detract from his good looks. He wore the red Camp Inner City T-shirt and baggy basketball shorts with Thunder Ridge High colors.

Trey.

Their son's best friend was standing before them.

Chapter Thirteen

Suddenly, Izzy's tongue felt too large for her mouth. She'd known Trey Richards since he'd been a scrawny seven-year-old with a perpetual grin and infectious laugh.

"Are you here for the concert?" Trey asked. "Did Eli know you were coming? He didn't say anything. He's inside, getting a burger with the some of the team—that's what we call the kids in our group. The rest of the team's over there." He gestured with his chin to a group of young people sitting in the bleachers, reaching into bags of fries. "They're with the captain—that's what we call the senior counselors." Genuine and unaffected, Trey had always talked a blue streak. After the cochlear implant that allowed him to hear, Eli had joked that it had been easier to be friends with Trey when he was deaf, but the boys had been inseparable since second grade. "Yeah, so you want me to go inside and tell Eli you're out here? We're not supposed to call parents unless there's an emergency, but this is probably an exception, right?"

The prospect of her son meeting Nate like this, with no warning at all, helped Izzy find her voice. "No, Trey, don't bother. I had no idea you'd all be here tonight." Abruptly, she realized Nate's hands had dropped away from her shoulders. "We're just leaving, in fact."

"Oh."

Izzy saw him give Nate a good look for the first time. Eli's friends never saw her with a man other than Derek, or Henry and Sam.

"Hi." Shifting his bag of food, Trey stuck his right hand out to Nate. "I'm Trey."

Izzy held her breath as the two hands clasped, and her "date" responded, "Nate. Good to meet you."

"Sorry," she murmured, for failing to introduce them. Was it her imagination or did Nate's voice sound tight? "Enjoy the concert," she told Trey, beginning to walk away from the venue. "See you soon."

"Okay. Thanks."

Trey was still standing there watching her and Nate quizzically when she turned away and headed for the exit as fast as her legs and the crowd would allow. As Nate fell into step beside her, she dared a glance from beneath her lashes. His jaw looked like granite. Gazing straight ahead, he appeared to be deep in thought. They made it all the way to the car without speaking.

He opened her door, she slid in, and he walked around to the driver's side, still stone-faced and silent as she tried to figure out how to open the conversation once they reached the International Rose Test Garden. But he didn't start the car.

"You have a child," he said, part statement and part question.

"Yes."

"A son?"

She nodded, looking at him, though he was staring out the windshield. "Eli."

Nate's Adam's apple dipped. "And he's a teenager. Like Trey."

Thud...thud...thud. Her heart knocked against her chest. Apparently, they were going to have this conversation here. And even though she'd had days to think about what she was going to say, she had no idea how to make this news less...shocking.

"Eli is—" she swallowed hard "—fourteen."

There was stone-cold quiet until Nate slammed his palm on the steering wheel so hard the car shook. "Damn it! Don't make me ask all the questions. Just tell me."

With the windows rolled up and the temperature reaching eighty in the shade, the car was stifling. A deep breath was impossible, but Izzy managed a shallow one and plunged ahead.

"I didn't have a miscarriage. The last time I saw your parents, I told them I didn't want to give up my baby. I thought we...you and I...might be able to make it work. They were scared. I can see that now, especially with Eli not so far away from the age I was when I got pregnant." She wiped the perspiration from her face. "Can we roll down a window?"

He obliged. "Go on."

"Your parents reminded me of all the reasons I shouldn't be thinking about keeping the baby, and, of course, they were right. But I wasn't going to change my mind."

"You didn't tell me."

He pushed the words through gritted teeth, reminding her of a volcano preparing to erupt.

"No. I saw a photo of you at a party. It looked like a wedding or something formal, and you were grinning at the camera with your arm around a beautiful blonde girl. The previous few weeks, you hadn't had time to talk to me. It looked like…it *felt* like…you'd moved on with your life. I didn't belong in your new world, and you didn't belong back in Thunder Ridge." She tried not to allow the past hurt to infiltrate her tone, but she wasn't sure she was successful. That memory had always been painful.

Nate shook his head, his expression equal parts bafflement and ferocity. "I don't know what photo you're talking about. Or what party, but the situation wasn't about just you and me and who belonged in what world. It stopped being about you and me the instant you decided to raise a baby that was mine."

"Right. It became about *the baby*. I wasn't going to involve a birth father who didn't want him and grandparents who thought he was ruining their son's future."

"You never gave me a choice!"

There was no doubt about it; she had become the enemy. Pain welled up. She tried to stay calm. "You had a choice. For months you had a choice. I may not have done everything perfectly, but don't rewrite history, Nate. You didn't want a baby."

"And at the time, you said you agreed we weren't ready."

"We weren't! No one's ready for a baby at that age. But we were having one anyway." Pressing her fingers to her temples, she shook her head. "I told you, I never wanted to make an adoption plan. I went along with it hoping everyone would change their minds."

"When it looked like that wasn't going to happen, was that when you said you'd had a miscarriage?"

Heavy censure stained his voice. Once, she might have reveled in correcting him, happily placing the blame for the lie about the miscarriage squarely at the feet of his mother.

Now, though, she, too, was the mother of a teenager with a future more promising than her own, and she understood the desire to protect her son. *I hope I'd go about it differently.*

"Communication between your mother and me wasn't the best," she said carefully. "I think she misunderstood what I was telling her."

"Which was?"

"That I was going to keep the baby and raise him myself." She met his eyes to deliver the final truth. "And that I didn't want anything more to do with you or your family."

Nate's fingers curled tightly around the steering wheel. "And you came to that decision because I didn't have time to talk as you would have liked?" Resentment dripped from his tone. Put that way, she seemed immature and petty.

"It was partly that, yes." Only scrupulous honesty would suffice at this point. "When I saw the photo, I was sure you didn't want to be with me, with us."

"Where did you see this mystery photo?"

"Your mother showed it to me."

"A picture of me at a party." He lifted a hand. "I don't even remember going to any—" Abruptly, he snapped his mouth shut. Thumb and forefinger came up to press against his eyelids. "I went to a wedding in Michigan," he pushed through gritted teeth. "For a cousin. That's the picture you saw. I have no idea who the girl was. Probably a distant relative."

He faced front again.

The next time Izzy tried to swallow, she felt as if she were swallowing glass. What had his mother said when brandishing that photo? *"Does he look like a boy who's thinking about becoming a father with the girl he dated one summer after high school?"* She didn't clearly state that he had a new girlfriend, but that had been the implication. Hadn't it? Izzy closed her eyes and shook her head. It was all so long ago now.

She reopened her eyes when the ignition roared to life again. Glancing at Nate, she saw his profile, looking as if it had been carved on the side of a ridge, rock hard and unyielding.

The only sound on the hour-long ride home was the rumble of the BMW's motor and the roar of the tension between its passengers.

I have a son. A teenager.

Fists buried in the pockets of a lightweight hoodie he didn't really need, Nate strode through the streets of Thunder Ridge at two in the morning, his head covered and his eyes downcast, as if he were a teen himself.

He couldn't sleep. Hadn't even tried, actually. *I have a son I've never seen. Never even knew about.*

Eli.

The entire ride home, he had wondered whether Izzy would have told him about Eli at all if they hadn't run into the other boy. Nate couldn't remember the kid's name now, probably wouldn't recognize him if he was standing right before him. Once he'd realized Izzy had a son, *his* son, everything else had gone blurry.

Just before he'd dropped her at her house, Izzy had asked him whether he wanted her to tell him about Eli. He'd said, "Not now." He wouldn't have heard anything— there were too many thoughts, too many questions and accusations running through his brain. Now he felt guilty. Being a father—wasn't that about being present all the time, even when you didn't think you could be?

Being a father.

What did he know about that? Nothing.

Fury and resentment swelled inside him again. He couldn't deny Izzy's claim that he hadn't wanted to be a father at eighteen. But he'd actually thought about coming home, being responsible, until he'd heard about the miscarriage.

His fists balled tighter.

He couldn't even wrap his brain around being misinformed that Izzy had had a miscarriage. He'd wanted to phone his mother immediately last night, but in that moment he was too angry, his thoughts too accusatory to be of any service. There would be time enough to ask her why she'd shown the photo of the wedding to Izzy. He remembered now that he'd mailed it to his parents, since they hadn't been able to be there.

His shoes ate up the pavement, pace increasing with the rise of his anger. He walked until he reached town, and when the moonlight filtering through the trees turned to the light of streetlamps and twinkle lights that were never doused, the reality of his situation hit harder than ever before.

There's The General Store. Eli and Izzy have gone there for ice cream. When Jax's dad owned the place, he gave a free birthday scoop. *I don't know what flavor my son would choose.* Taking his hands from his pockets, he smacked a fist into the opposite palm.

Nate passed the bank. When he was a kid, they had "squirrel" accounts for elementary school students. Had Izzy walked Eli into the bank hand in hand to open his first account? Had Eli felt grown-up and important?

Lightning Hardware. First tool belt. Did Eli know the proper way to hammer a nail?

I've missed everything. Damn her. Damn them all.

Nate felt powerless in a way he'd never felt before in his life. The desire to smash the hardware store window and watch his reflection shatter into tiny, murderous shards was almost overpowering.

And then he saw another reflection, a patrol car pulling slowly along the curb. When Izzy's sheriff friend emerged from the car and sauntered over like Wild Bill Hickok on a posse hunt, Nate pivoted, spoiling for a fight.

"I've known Izz twelve years."

That was what the sonovabitch had boasted. Twelve years with Izzy and with *Nate's son*.

"It's a little late to go window-shopping," the sheriff drawled as he stepped onto the curb.

"I don't recall Thunder Ridge having a curfew." Nate heard the belligerence in his own tone. *Did you help my kid build his first birdhouse? Did you dress up like Santa Claus when he was five?*

"Well, you've been gone a long time. There's probably a lot of things you don't remember. Like the fact that we don't keep big-city hours."

"How do you know how long I've been gone?" *Did you toss him his first football?* "Is business so slow that you have time to check up on everyone who rolls into town?"

There was a sneer embedded in the question. The sheriff bristled.

"I forgot your name," Nate said, "and Izzy hasn't mentioned it in all the times we've been together. What is it?" *Yeah, take that, you rat bastard.*

"Sheriff Neel," came the deliberate reply.

"Sheriff Neel. So, what's that? Your first name? Like 'Hey, kids, Sheriff Neel is here to teach us about bike safety.' Or 'Look, folks, Sheriff Neel brought his ferret to show everyone how friendly the law is in Thunder Ridge.'"

At that moment, the law looked anything but friendly. "I'd like you to walk a straight line for me. Step over here." He pointed toward the edge of the curb.

Nate took a step, but forward, toward the sheriff, not toward where he pointed. "Haven't had a drop of alcohol in days."

"I didn't ask you that." Snapping his words into precise pieces, the sheriff ordered again, "Step over there."

Again Nate stepped forward. "No."

That did it. The sheriff began to take this more personally, as Nate intended. His anger roared to life, like turning on a gas fireplace. "Listen real careful, golden boy. You may have been used to getting whatever you wanted last time you were in Thunder Ridge, but it isn't going to work that way this go around. You screw with me or upset Izzy in any way, and I'll throw your self-important ass in a jail cell and forget where I put the key."

Sheriff Neel made every point by stabbing his finger in the direction of Nate's chest.

"Or," Nate said, baring his teeth, "you get it through your head that I'm not going anywhere. And when it comes to Izzy and *my son*—" Nate shoved a finger at the sheriff, making contact with the man's shoulder "—mind your own damn business."

Jaw clenched, Neel growled through his teeth, "Step back and keep your hands to yourself."

Like an eight-year-old goading a sibling on a car ride that had lasted too long, Nate stayed right where he was, keeping his finger aimed at the other man. "Maybe that's what you should have done. Kept your hands to yourself. Get your own family instead of pretending with somebody else's."

Self-control whooshed from the sheriff like air from a blown-out tire. "You dumbass," he said. "*I'm* pretending? Where the hell have you been? What family did you create? Obviously, you know about Eli, so the only words that ought to be coming out of your mouth are *thank you for stepping in when I was too selfish or indifferent to give a crap that I got a girl pregnant and—*"

The remainder of his dressing-down was lost as Nate's fist connected with Sheriff Neel's mouth. It didn't take but a second for the larger man to strike back with a punishing sock to the gut and then an attempt—but only an attempt, Nate was later proud to remember—to pull Nate's arms behind his back.

The next minute was filled with the men circling each

other, getting in as many shots as they could, spitting both blood and accusations and generally behaving in a fashion that would later make them supremely grateful they were having this fight at two in the morning on a deserted street.

Rocky road brownies, banana cream pie, four-cheese lasagna, Texas chili and corn bread, meat loaf... Biting her thumbnail, Izzy surveyed the buffet spread across her kitchen counter or bubbling on the stove and wondered what else she could make.

"Lemon-blueberry mousse." She headed to the pantry. Eli loved her lemon mousse. Light, fluffy and sweet-tart with tiny local blueberries, it would be just the thing to welcome him home from camp the day after tomorrow. Along, of course, with all the other Eli favorites she'd been making almost since she walked in the door last night.

She wasn't kidding herself. She knew teenage boys were different from PMS-ing women, who could be distracted by clever culinary maneuvers. Cooking gave her something to do with her nerves.

Exhausted, she piled ingredients onto the tiny slivers of counter space that remained. Even Latke, who typically stood by to gobble any morsel that fell to the floor when Izzy was cooking, had trudged off to her dog bed hours ago. The kitchen was a shambles, and so were Izzy's emotions.

Where did she stand with Nate? She had no idea. All she knew was that at two, no—she glanced at the kitchen clock—two *forty* in the morning, fear seemed more real than comfort.

Nate hadn't wanted to talk, hadn't wanted to listen, either. All she could do was wait for his next move. Clearly, they were not going to be bosom buddies, conferring lovingly on all things Eli. Not yet, at any rate.

"I'm going to go to bed. I am," she muttered to herself.

She already had enough food for Eli and Trey and a bunch of their friends. And other than identifying fear, she couldn't make heads or tails of how she was feeling.

Guilty? *Yes, darn it.*

Angry? *Well, yeah, sort of.* She hadn't cornered the market on bad decisions in this scenario, after all. Nate and his parents had a few bozo moves on their balance sheet, too. She swiped at a dusting of flour on the sink tiles.

Put the food away and go to bed, even if you don't sleep. Her nighttime thoughts were rarely clear and even more rarely helpful.

When the doorbell rang, she nearly dropped several pounds of lasagna.

Abandoning the glass pan in the kitchen, she hustled to the living room, her imagination already conjuring disastrous news about Henry or Sam or—

When she looked through the peephole and saw Derek, her heart turned over. *Eli.*

Flicking on the porch light and yanking open the door, she began to pepper him with questions. "What happened? Why were you called? Where is— Oh, my God." She peered closely at Derek's face, then exclaimed, "What happened to you? Your eye is—"

"Not as bad as his." Derek jerked his thumb toward the right. Nate stood on the porch, too, one eye almost completely shut, a cut on his cheek and several buttons ripped off his shirt. And he was handcuffed.

Izzy's jaw fell at the sight. She looked at Derek. "Why is he—"

"May we come in?" Derek's tone dripped sarcasm.

She backed up. Derek entered, followed by Nate, who looked angry enough to kill something once the handcuffs were removed.

Derek sniffed the air. "You baking?"

She nodded.

"So we didn't wake you up."

"No."

"Good." He jerked his head toward Nate. "Your friend has a bad temper."

Nate's injured eye started to pop open. He winced. "*I* have a bad temper? Look who's talking."

"Unless you want me to take you to a cell, shut it."

"Sure, take me to jail. It'll give me a chance to work on the police brutality charge I'm planning to file."

"Listen, you jackass—"

"Stop!" Izzy insisted, her nerves already raw. "You both have cuts that ought to be looked at." All she had on hand was antiseptic and a selection of drugstore bandages. No gauze or tape or anything. "I think you might need stitches," she told Nate.

"No, I don't," came the instantaneous, belligerent reply.

He lurched forward, shoved from behind. "Be polite," Derek growled.

"Derek," Izzy protested. Nate objected more colorfully to the push. "Will someone tell me what is going on here, please?"

"I found him loitering in front of the hardware store."

"Loitering," Nate scoffed, shaking his head.

"I said, shut it," Derek ordered.

"Up yours."

"Oh, for heaven's sake." Izzy went to get bandages while the men argued in her living room. She had never known Nate to get into a fight; nor had she ever heard him speak so rudely.

As for Derek, he had a distant history of getting into trouble but had been a veritable Boy Scout for nearly two decades. He even corrected Eli if her son used the word *stupid*.

Returning to the living room with bandages and disinfectant, she found Nate and Derek seated on her sofa, surly expressions on each of their bruised faces. Nate sat with his cuffed hands folded tensely on his lap.

"Derek, take the handcuffs off," Izzy requested.

"When I'm assured *your friend* can keep his hands to himself and after I've decided whether he needs to visit the jail for a spell or can be released on his own recognizance."

Nate rolled his eyes. "As if you know what *recognizance* means."

"And away we go," Derek said, reaching for Nate's arm.

"All right, obviously we are all in the midst of a tense situation," Izzy interjected.

Derek snorted. "Tense?"

"Can you define *tense* for him, too?" Nate suggested.

Derek growled, "How about we define *contempt for the law*, you arrogant—"

"That's enough, both of you!" Izzy set the first-aid items down *hard* on the coffee table. It was difficult to believe these were the rational men she'd loved.

"Derek," she said, "Nate just found out that Eli is his son. Obviously, he's feeling conflicted, at odds—"

"I know what *conflicted* means," Derek bit off.

"I know you do. And I'm sure you're feeling—" she almost said *vulnerable*, but neither of them was going to cop to that right now "—a lot of things, as well. You're involved in Eli's life—this affects you."

It was impossible to miss the resentment that filled Nate's expression.

"It's not going to be easy for any of us to figure out the new normal," she said, "but we have to, for Eli's sake. Whatever happened before now, whatever any one of us is feeling, Eli's needs have to come first. Can we agree on that?" When neither man spoke immediately, she put her hands on her hips. "Because if we can't, you are both welcome to leave. I mean it. History or no history. Future or no future."

The reprimand silenced them both. She pointed to Nate's hands. "Uncuff him." Derek released Nate and Nate rubbed his wrists. The requested silence reigned, highlighting the intense awkwardness of the situation. Whom, Izzy wondered, should she give first aid to first?

"Coffee? Tea? Lasagna?" she asked. Nobody answered and nobody smiled.

Derek stood. "I'm on duty."

Okay, Derek first. "I'll look at that cut on your face before you go."

"I'm fine." He headed to the door.

Oh, man, how long before they would be normal with each other again? Izzy followed him. "Derek," she said softly as he stepped onto the porch, "nothing will change between you and Eli, or you and me."

His mouth worked as if he wanted to say something, but in the end, his lips pressed into a thin smile. "Night, Izzy."

She remained on the porch until the squad car's headlights came on and Derek pulled away from the curb. Sad and confused about how to handle any of this, Izzy went back inside and shut the door.

Alone again with Nate.

Chapter Fourteen

Sitting on the couch, in Derek's vacated spot, Izzy soaked a cotton ball in antiseptic and touched it to Nate's forehead, slapping his hand when he tried to push the cotton away.

"If you're man enough to fight, you're man enough to suffer the consequences." When he looked at her, surprised by her matter-of-fact attitude to his injuries, she added quietly, "That's what I would tell Eli."

Nate was quiet for a moment. "Has he ever gotten into a fight?"

"Once." She continued to work on him as she shared the first of many stories she would likely tell him about his son. "He was eight, just finishing the second grade. He's always loved school, but that year was particularly hard for him because Reid Stoltz, who'd been his best friend since preschool, decided he couldn't play with Eli anymore. And he was very clear about why."

Nate's right brow rose above his swollen eye. "Why?"

This, Izzy realized, was one of the things she'd felt so

much trepidation about telling him. Shaking her head at her own faintheartedness, she forged ahead. "By third grade, the kids in Eli's class were starting to notice and care about who was 'different' and who was 'normal.' Reid decided he wanted a normal friend."

She reached up to put a bandage on the cut above Nate's eyebrow, but he stopped her.

"Explain that." He was watching her intently.

Izzy looked Nate straight in the eye. "Eli is deaf. He has assistive technology that helps him perceive some sounds, and an interpreter to help him in school, and he does really well. A's and B's in all his subjects. But in the schools he's gone to, he's always been the only kid with a serious hearing impairment. He stands out. That was especially tough when he was younger."

If Izzy was honest with herself, she'd been wondering for years how Nate would react to the news that his child was deaf. She noticed everything now—the lowering of his brow, the clouding over of his expression as questions raced through his mind. She saw him swallow. And then the question she realized she'd been dreading for over a decade:

"Was he born deaf?"

Izzy had worked through the guilt and the if-only's a long time ago. Such thoughts were useless in helping Eli move forward, so she'd relegated them to the late-night hours. She'd known, though, perhaps instinctively, that if Nate ever asked that question, the shadowy feelings would return.

"No. His hearing was normal." Rising from the sofa, she crossed to a bookcase, where several large photo albums nestled side by side. Pulling one off the shelf, she resumed her seat and opened it on her lap.

"This is Eli at a year and a half. He'd been toddling around for a few months already. He went on his first pony ride and loved it. And this—" she pointed to another photo "—is when we went berry picking on Sauvie Island. He ate so many blueberries his tongue was purple for hours."

Nate looked hungrier for the sight of his son than Eli had been for the berries. The certain knowledge that he had no intention of walking away without meeting Eli settled on her. And if he met Eli, he would want to remain part of his life; she knew it. The awareness was a relief and a worry.

"We lived in Portland his first couple of years. I got my GED, then worked as a waitress and took classes at Portland Community College."

Nate lifted his eyes from the photos to her. "And took care of a baby. That was a helluva lot on your shoulders."

She smiled. "Apparently, shoulders have a lot of muscle. The more you use them, the stronger they get."

Nate did not smile. "It was hard going."

"Some times were harder than others. I moved to Portland while I was pregnant. I lived with a friend of Henry's, who got me a job at a preschool that was in the office building where she worked. It was a perfect job, except I seemed to catch every bug the kids brought in. When Eli got sick the fall after we picked the berries, the diagnosis was congenital CMV. It's a virus I caught at the preschool and probably passed on to him while I was pregnant. No one knows exactly what happened, but the speculation is that his immune system fought it until he was twenty months. Then the virus began to manifest, and over a few months' time, he stopped talking, stopped responding the way he had been. He used to react to everything. There was nothing anyone could do. When he was two, he had almost total hearing loss."

Pain tightened Nate's features. "That must have scared the crap out of you."

She nodded. "Yes. Yes, it did." At one point, she had barely slept for two weeks. There was no point, however, in telling him that. She'd have given anything to have a hand to hold at night, someone who grieved as much as she that Eli could no longer hear a blue jay announce the dawn. There were people who had cared, but no one who'd shared the parenting moments with her.

"For a long time," she confessed, "I blamed myself. I even wondered if other people would blame me." She flapped a hand. "You know—idiotic teenage mother didn't know how to keep her baby safe. And if I messed up so early in his life, how on earth was I going to get through the rest of his childhood? There was one particularly bleak night when I even told myself I should have gone through with the adoption plans, because then I wouldn't have worked at the preschool and maybe he'd never have gotten sick."

He took her hand and squeezed hard. "You know that's not true."

She nodded. "Yes, I do know." But it was good…it was very, very good…to have Nate tell her, his eyes intent and sincere, his hand warm and strong around hers. If they had stayed together, if he had wanted to become a parent with her, those shoulders would have carried half the worries. "I don't know why I'm telling you this," she murmured, "except that I've never said it out loud before."

The photo album was lying across both their laps now, half on her left thigh and half on his right. Their clasped hands rested on top of a photo of Eli sitting on the back of a giant stuffed lion she'd found at a yard sale.

"How did you make your way back to Thunder Ridge?" Nate asked.

"I was still living with Joanne, Henry's friend, but she was getting ready to retire and planned to move in with her sister in Idaho. I was too busy and too stressed to make plans to find my own place. Henry and Sam cleaned out a room in their house and gave me my old job back with an offer to make me the manager as soon as I felt I could take on the extra responsibilities. So I came back and got a job and a place to live and babysitters. Lots of babysitters. All their support freed me up to advocate for Eli in every way I could."

The hand holding hers tightened again. "You were a rock star." His voice was rough, ragged. He meant it.

"How do you know?" she asked softly.

He raised their hands. His lips touched her knuckles. "I know, because I know you. I know—" He swallowed heavily. "I know you said yes when I said no. Thank you for doing that. Thank you for raising our son."

She nodded *you're welcome*. Hope kindled, hope that he was not going to view Eli as damaged, but simply unique.

The moment of connection between them was profound and bittersweet. It was the moment they might have shared in the hospital as they marveled at the brand-new life they'd taken part in creating. Over the top of their baby's head, they would have held gazes as they were doing now. And they would have kissed.

Their faces were so close it wouldn't have taken more than an accident for their lips to touch. Someone must have moved back, though—Izzy wasn't sure whether it was she or Nate—because the moment of soul-aching intimacy ended with a spurt, not a spark.

Gently Nate released Izzy's hand so that it rested again on the scrapbook. Then he ran his free hand through his hair and asked, "How does Eli communicate? How will I talk to him?"

How will I, not *if I.* And so they moved into a new phase of their relationship: an informed truce.

She explained about the cochlear implant Eli had at age eleven and about how frightening the change had been, even though they had welcomed it.

"I want to get to know him before he finds out I'm his

father." Nate appeared to be deep in thought as he said this. "I want to be able to ask him questions, get the answers without filters."

"Okay. I understand wanting to get to know him without the pressure of trying hard to make it work. But I don't think we should wait too long. Teenagers really don't like secrets, unless they're the ones keeping them."

Nate nodded. "A couple of meetings. Can you help me learn to sign language?" He looked at her with such open need, like a brand-new father asking how to hold the baby.

Working as a team, they strategized how to introduce Eli to Nate, and Izzy taught Nate a couple of super simple signs and the finger alphabet. As they pored over the scrapbook together, she signed as well as spoke her descriptions of the photos.

"It's beautiful," he said, sitting back at one point and simply staring at her.

She'd just signed and said, "I love Eli's face in this photo."

Nodding at his compliment, she murmured, "I know. He has a perfect nose, doesn't he?"

"I meant the signing," Nate said, sipping the coffee she'd made. "The way your hands move—it's beautiful. I like watching you."

She blushed, but happily. "You don't *have* to use ASL, you know. He can hear decently now, and when he can't understand something, he reads lips. It's still hard for people who don't know him well to understand his speech, and I think it's easier for him to sign certain things. Plus, signing is his first language, really. That's a hard thing to give up."

"I'll learn it. I want to."

Izzy stared. Finally, she whispered, "I was scared." It was a discovery as much as an admission, which Nate seemed to understand, because he waited while she gathered her thoughts. "There have been times…like when he went into surgery for the implant…that I wanted to phone you. I wanted to tell you about Eli so badly, even if you decided not to pursue a relationship with him. But I was too scared."

He nodded, looking down at his clasped hands. "Okay. I'm trying to understand that. You didn't know how I'd react, I could have walked away again… I'm trying to understand all that, but it's hard, damn it. It's hard to accept your reasons—anyone's reasons—for not telling me."

She nodded, knowing she couldn't change how he felt, that it wasn't even her right. But truth was important, so she continued, "That's not the only thing I was afraid of. With Eli, I had a family for the first time. Real family. I didn't want to lose it."

He looked surprised.

"I was selfish," she admitted. "What if you or your parents did change your minds and wanted Eli in your lives?" She stopped short of adding *and you didn't want me*. She didn't have to say it. "I didn't want to share. I didn't want to lose him." Her voice cracked, even though she was less afraid now, because she trusted that Nate wasn't going to take Eli away. She was still afraid, however, of the changes in store. "It was wrong of me. I should have told you I kept him. I *am* sorry."

Lowering his head, Nate covered his face with his hands, then pushed them through his hair. "Me, too. You're not the only one who was scared. I couldn't imagine any future but the one I already had planned. I'm sorry I walked away and sorry my parents lied. You deserved better. You deserved a hell of a lot better."

"Well, that future of yours looked pretty darn good, even from the cheap seats." She gave him a smile tinged with self-deprecating humor. "I don't like that your parents lied, but if Eli became a father at eighteen…" She took a deep breath, blowing it out hard. "I'd probably think I knew what was best. Maybe I'd even let the end justify the means."

She closed the scrapbook they'd been looking at and set it atop the two others on the coffee table. "I've certainly been playing God with Eli's life and yours and mine." Her smile turned weary. "I'm willing to stop."

"What do you mean?"

What *did* she mean?

Looking at Nate the man was superior, she realized, to looking at Nate the boy. Sheer physical beauty had turned into something more complex, as if he'd been broken and put back together again even better. A little rougher around the edges, a little battered in spots that had once been perfect. But through those worn bits, she could see his soul, and it looked good.

"I mean I trust the right thing to happen if I let go. And by letting go," she hastened to add, "I do not mean you can take him to Chicago with you tomorrow. I'm just saying it's time to be honest and to see where it takes us. See where it takes you and Eli. And me."

Nate leaned toward her, his eyes at once sober with gratitude and shining with anticipation. "If he's anything like you, I'm a lucky man."

Izzy tried to ignore the knocking of her heart and the way her gaze seemed to want to fasten on his lips. She cleared her throat. "Eli will be home the day after tomorrow. Come to dinner on Friday?"

"Absolutely."

Chapter Fifteen

"Who's this guy?"

Since he'd returned from camp, Eli had been using his voice more than his hands to speak. Izzy thought her son had grown an inch also, but that could have been her imagination. Eli seemed to have matured in the two weeks he'd been away. Now, as they stood in the kitchen, assembling ingredients for the "monster burritos" that were her son's favorite meal, Izzy's stomach buzzed with nerves.

"I told you, honey, he's an old friend, and he'd like to meet you."

"He's the dude Trey saw you with at the zoo?"

"Yes."

Pausing in his cheese grating, Eli popped a hunk of the cheddar into his mouth. "Mom. You're dating."

"No! I'm not." Pushing her loose hair behind her ear, she chopped an onion, taking care to look up so Eli could assist his own hearing by reading her lips while she spoke. "Eli, don't try to read anything into this, okay? Just enjoy getting to know him. I think you'll like Nate."

"Do *you* like Nate?"

Affecting an innocent look, the fourteen-year-old continued to eat rather than grate cheese. He wasn't used to her spending time with unfamiliar men, Izzy reminded herself, and that was why he was probing. She hadn't dated anyone in a hundred years. Slicing the onion with perhaps a little more vigor than necessary, she responded as if it should be obvious, "Why would I introduce you to someone I *don't* like? Can you please grate at least the same amount of cheese you're scarfing?"

Eli grinned. And shoved several tortilla chips into his mouth at once before resuming his duties.

The soothing sounds of chopping and grating lulled Izzy for the moment while she pondered again the wisdom of having Eli meet Nate before explaining who Nate was. They really didn't look that much alike. Eli wasn't going to guess, at least not tonight. And Nate had confirmed earlier today that he wanted time to "get Eli to like me" before they told him the truth. Nate still seemed so nervous about it that Izzy had agreed. But she was worried. There had already been too many secrets.

It'll be okay. It will, she reassured herself. Nate was likable and very cool. At least, he seemed like the type of person a teenage boy would find cool. She was making far too big an issue of *when* they told him; really, they should probably focus on *how*. And if she thought she was nervous tonight, she could only imagine how Nate was feeling—

"So, Mom, do you *like* him like him?"

"Oh, my gosh, Eli!" Izzy nearly sliced her finger off with the knife. The question sent her heart rate into orbit. "Can we just please— Let's concentrate on making dinner, 'cause we're running late. What kind of olives do you want for the burritos? Black or the green kind with pimentos?"

Wiping his hands, Eli pulled his phone from his back pocket and began thumb-typing.

Izzy swatted him with a dish towel so he'd look at her. "What are you doing?"

"Texting Trey to tell him he's right." Eli laughed, thoroughly enjoying himself, and Izzy realized with no small amount of surprise that her son was truly fine with the idea that his mother might want to date.

The sound of the doorbell, along with the flashing chime they'd had since before Eli's cochlear implant, precluded further conversation.

Izzy raced to the sink to wash her hands.

"I'll get it," Eli announced, still laughing as he sped from the kitchen with the clear intention of beating her to the door. Izzy had to stop herself from turning off the water with soap still on her hands. She'd already promised herself several times that she would let this meeting and all subsequent meetings between father and son unfold without her interference. Man, it was hard. Bracing her hands on the edge of the sink, she counted her breaths. *Let them do this on their own. Trust.*

On the other hand, there would never be another first meeting between father and son. She should get a picture. *Or, at the very least, watch it so I can describe it back to them at a later date.*

To get to the living room, she had to hurdle over Latke, who was taking a rest stop in the hallway. Izzy skidded to a stop as Eli swung the door wide and said in his nasal monotone, "Hi. I'm Eli. Are you Nate? My mom is in the kitchen. Come on in."

Nate seemed to be frozen on the threshold. Izzy held her breath.

Hungry eyed, Nate stared at her son…his son…their son…with an expression approaching awe. She could see him absorbing every detail—fair skin tanned a light gold, hair the color of an oak leaf in autumn, his mother's eyes, all ten fingers, the legs of a colt, feet encased in a serious pair of sneakers.

Nate stuck out his hand. Izzy understood instantly that the gesture was not about good manners. *He wants to touch.*

She was gratified that her lessons on etiquette had not gone completely unheeded. Grasping Nate's hand, Eli pumped it heartily.

Nate, clearly, could have continued standing there, shaking hands indefinitely. It was Eli who eventually dropped the hold and said, just in case Nate hadn't heard the first time, "You can come in."

"Hi!" she called brightly, acting as if she'd just come around the corner. "Glad you could make it, Nate. Come into the kitchen. We're just putting the finishing touches on dinner. We're having monster burritos, Eli's favorite. You can help me grate some cheese. Eli keeps eating it all. Eli—" she backhanded Eli lightly on the arm as they passed "—pour Nate an iced tea, would you, please? We'll sit down to eat in a little while."

Okay, so much for allowing the evening to unfold without her interference. But the evening did improve from there.

As they sat down at the table to eat, Nate asked Eli what his favorite subject was in school.

"We're learning about the Renaissance," Eli answered. "My class is making models of the Capitoline Museums."

Nate's eyes lit up like sparklers. "Italy is on my bucket list."

Eli nodded. "Mine, too."

Izzy hadn't even known her son had a bucket list! "What are the Capitoline Museums?" she asked.

Both Eli and Nate looked at her, their expressions so alike that her breath caught at the similarity.

"Mom, seriously? You went to high school, right?"

"Yes, smart aleck, and I'm quite sure the Capitoline Museums were not mentioned."

Eli looked at Nate. "Where did you go to high school?"

As their son worked on a too-big bite of burrito, Nate and Izzy shared a sharp glance. "Right here," Nate answered. "Same high school you're at."

"Is that where you met my mom?"

Izzy's appetite vanished. Was this where the whole truth would emerge or more lies would be told?

"Yes." Wiping his mouth with one of the cloth napkins Izzy had laid out, Nate sat back. "Your mother was a grade behind me."

Eli looked between them, a broad grin taking over his face. "What was she like?" Izzy opened her mouth to redirect the conversation, but Eli held out a hand. "You don't get to answer this, Mom."

Izzy's heart gave her ribs a pounding as Nate considered his response.

"She was...very much the way she is now. Sincere. A hard worker. Serious."

"Kinda boring, Mom," Eli teased.

Nate smiled. "She was also loyal and giving. And brave." He looked directly at Izzy. "One of the bravest people I know." He returned his gaze to Eli. "She'd walk through fire for you."

Though he kept his tone light, he left no doubt that he meant every word. Izzy's heart settled into a sweet, soft thud.

"So, Italy is on your bucket list, hmm?" she said to Eli, heaping tortilla chips onto his plate. "First I've heard of it."

"I want to do a year of college there. I thought I'd wait to break the news to you." He glanced at Nate. "She gets kinda emotional and writes a lot of lists when I leave Thunder Ridge. Not really looking forward to the scene when I leave the country."

"I am very supportive of your independence," Izzy protested, tearing up at the mere thought of her son, her baby, living an ocean away.

With the conversation safely deflected from questions about her and Nate, Izzy settled back and watched the two men she'd loved the most in her life. They discussed architecture and the Trail Blazers, the merits of kayaking versus paddleboarding (kayaking won by a mile), and why they loved the TV show *Grimm*. Izzy shuddered.

When Eli switched from spoken language to ASL, which he did unconsciously sometimes when addressing her, Nate simply looked to Izzy for translation.

Shooing them back to their seats as they rose to help her ferry the dinner plates to the kitchen, she met Nate's eyes above Eli's head. *Thank you*, he mouthed.

And when she returned a few minutes later with pound cake and fresh peach ice cream, Nate looked up again as Eli was teaching him how to play Geometry Dash on his phone and this time mouthed, *He's fantastic.*

Altogether, Nate stayed three and a half hours. Eli said he was still recovering from two weeks with younger kids and that he was ready for bed, so Izzy walked Nate to his car.

It occurred to her as she closed the front door and stepped into the evening that for the first time in Eli's fourteen years, she could discuss her boy with the only other person likely to be as proud of his every burp as she'd always been.

Nate had eaten at Michelin star restaurants, conversed with CEOs and foreign investors over Kobe-steak crostini and bottles of wine worth four hundred dollars. But he knew he would forever think of this as the best night of his life.

Beneath a lavender sky that was deepening rapidly now

to purple, Izzy walked beside him, dressed in another of her simple sundresses, with skinny straps and a formfitting top that showed her figure hadn't changed much since she was seventeen. It was easy to imagine, just for a moment, that they'd stayed together, that his life was right here where stars, not streetlamps or skyscrapers, lit the night, and where "Good night, son" and "I love you, Isabelle" could have been the last words he said every night.

Common sense tried to tell him he was reacting to the big emotions of the night, nothing more. He glanced down at Izzy, her silky hair brushing her bare shoulders, her feet small and pretty in simple sandals, and he thought, *How could I not love her for what she's given me?* The delicate-looking woman beside him had more strength in her pinkie than he had in his entire body. Real strength. The kind that mattered. He owed her more than he could ever repay.

Turning toward her as they reached his rental car, she said, "It was a good night. A great start, I thought. Eli really likes you."

Hope and pleasure swelled inside him. "Think so?"

"Oh, yeah. You had him at Trail Blazers." Her impish smile shot straight to his heart.

"He's the luckiest kid in the world to have you for a mother."

She blinked, temporarily lost for words. "I've stumbled a lot," she said at last, shrugging. "I just keep loving him."

He nodded. "Like I said, lucky kid. I wouldn't have been half the parent you've been."

"That's not true."

"It is. You knew yourself, Izzy. Even at seventeen."

"Me?" She shook her head. "No. Being Eli's parent has taught me all sorts of things I didn't know I needed to learn. That will happen to you, too."

His throat felt thick. She was speaking as if she accepted

that he would be an ongoing presence in Eli's life. "I meant it when I said you were brave."

She nodded. "I know you meant it. Thank you."

Pressing his thumb and forefinger to the inner corner of his welling eyes, he admitted, "I was pretty damn scared Eli wasn't going to like me at all."

Compassion transformed her face. "Well. What's not to like?" A moment passed, and she said quietly, "Good night, Nate."

He didn't want to end this night, not by a long shot, but it was getting late, and she probably had to get up early the next day. As for himself, he wasn't going to sleep a wink.

Afraid to touch her, knowing that if he did, he wouldn't be able to let her go, Nate settled for drinking in one long last moment with the mother of his son, before he said, "Good night, Isabelle."

Izzy turned from Nate with conflict pulsing through her veins. She couldn't wait to get back to the house, to talk to Eli if he was still up and to debrief with herself, too. On the other hand, leaving Nate tonight felt as hard as it had been when she was seventeen and leaving him meant returning to a lonely, miserable trailer.

She'd seen new expressions on his face tonight, expressions she was willing to bet that no one but she had ever witnessed. Enjoying their child together had been holy. Magical. And then there had been the moment by the car when she'd thought…sensed, really…was almost *certain*, in fact…that he was going to kiss her again.

But he didn't.

And, let's face it, almost kissing someone didn't count for much of anything. It wasn't worth thinking about. Anyway, she knew she couldn't kiss him anymore. That would be insanity. The very definition of *irresponsible*. Utter emotional suicide, and he surely realized that, too.

All these thoughts Izzy managed to pack into the two steps she took away from Nate.

Before the third step, she felt his fingers clamp around her left wrist. Taking her by surprise, he turned her around and pulled her back to him, and before she could even wonder what to expect, his lips were on hers.

Warm. Firm. Hungry but gentle…exploring more than her mouth, exploring her feelings, too. A good kiss was more than foreplay; it was a conversation, and, oh wow, she could talk to Nate all night long.

His hands held her face, then moved into her hair. Her fingers curled into his chest, then slid up to his shoulders to delve into the hair at his nape. By the time he raised his head, Izzy was panting. Either she was seriously out of shape, or this kiss was aerobic.

She lowered her forehead to his chest, and Nate placed a lingering kiss on the top of her head, which was almost sweeter than his kissing her lips. Well, *as* sweet, anyway.

She shook her head. "Complications," she murmured.

Tucking a finger beneath her chin, he raised her face so he could see her. "What?"

"We shouldn't add complications to our situation."

He dropped a quick, soft peck beside her mouth. Teasing, she thought, and very erotic.

Endeavoring to keep her wits about her, she placed her palms on his chest to create a little space between them. "Every kid with estranged or missing-in-action parents has the same fantasy."

Breaching her space-creating efforts, he dropped another kiss, this time on her jaw. "Yeah?"

He wasn't listening. The barely there shadow of his stubble rubbed her chin. He felt so good. Smelled so good. "Yes," she murmured, closing her eyes, fingers gathering a fistful of his shirt. He felt so good. Smelled so good. "Every kid wants his estranged parents to get together again. But mostly that happens in the movies. In real life, it's so much more complicated, and when it doesn't work out, everyone is disappointed, and…" One of his hands was massaging the back of her head.

Letting go of his shirt, she thumped a fist against his pecs—excellent, rock-solid pecs. "Eli comes first," she said with more force as he nuzzled her ear, which sent goose bumps shivering up and down her arms *and* legs, then nipped her lobe with his teeth, a tiny, playful nibble. "If anything else we do could hurt him—"

She didn't have to finish that sentence.

Inhaling deeply, Nate pulled back, though he kept her in the circle of his arms.

"All right, I hear you. We should put first things first."

She nodded.

"We didn't do that last time," he acknowledged.

"No." She shook her head, feeling sad suddenly. "Cart before the horse, and all that."

"Yeah." His hands moved to the less intimate area of her upper arms. Lightly, he rubbed up and down, then gave her a squeeze and let go. The letting-go part was filled with palpable reluctance. "Okay," he said in a rough, trying-to-control-himself voice that was very flattering. "Job one—getting to know my son."

"Yes."

In the darkening night, he searched her face. "What happens in the movies…when the parents get back together?"

"They usually don't show anything beyond the reunion. Maybe it works for a while and then the couple part again and break their children's hearts."

"Cheery. Or they pull each other up every one of life's mountains and enjoy the view together for the rest of their lives."

Izzy wanted that so much it scared the stuffing out of her. "In a Disney movie. But who lives in a Disney movie?"

"No one," he agreed. "But almost every story is rooted in at least some truth." He reached out to tuck strands of her hair behind her ears, then brushed his knuckles down the side of her cheek. "So, I was a big Lewis Carroll fan as a kid. *Alice in Wonderland*. Go figure. You know what Alice says?"

She shook her head.

Nate's lips curved. "Something to the effect that she believes in up to six impossible things. Usually before breakfast."

Chapter Sixteen

Nate flew to Chicago for four days the following week for business and personal reasons. He took care of the business, then went to see his mother.

Lynette Thayer's Lincolnshire, Illinois, condominium was a world away from Nate's childhood home in Thunder Ridge. Back then, the Thayers had been strictly working-class, and their personal belongings had reflected that fact. Now a hutch filled with bone china and fine crystal graced one wall in the dining area, where Nate and his mother sat, awkwardly pushing Caesar salads around their plates.

"You knew," Nate said, his voice the only sound in the apartment, "you knew about Eli, didn't you?"

With her eyes on her lettuce, Lynette nodded slowly. Behind the designer glasses she favored these days, her small eyes blinked several times. "I've known for quite a few months now. I didn't know how to tell you. When your friend Jax called you about his project…"

Setting her fork on the edge of her plate, Lynette sighed.

Her hands, thin and heavily veined, folded resignedly in her lap. She spoke so softly Nate had to strain to catch the next words.

"I was frightened, but glad you were going back. I wanted to tell you years ago that we lied about Isabelle and the baby. But your father had his first heart attack, and then you met Julianne, and—" She sighed again. "Everything seemed so perfect between you two. We assumed Isabelle would put the baby up for adoption when she left town. I told myself it couldn't be good for anyone to dredge up the past."

Lynette looked at her son, and for once her carefully applied makeup was incapable of masking her age. She looked older than he'd ever seen her. "It's impossible to deceive another person unless we deceive ourselves first," she murmured. "I learned that lesson the hard way."

When her lower lip began to tremble, Nate could see his mother reach deep inside for the steely strength that was more typical of her.

"When I told you Isabelle miscarried the baby, I first had to convince myself that I was protecting your future rather than my desires for your future. I told myself that my life experience gave me the privilege to decide what was best. I robbed you of the only child you might ever have. And I let that girl…that young girl…deal with pregnancy and childbirth on her own."

Nate had expected a difficult conversation today. He had cautioned himself not to accuse or blame even though he'd wanted to shout and point fingers and demand an explanation he could accept. Now he knew there would be none of the above. No shouting, no chastising, no pound of flesh and no explanation that would ever make up for the years he'd missed with his son. The years they had all missed.

"Izzy managed well." He said it as matter-of-factly as he could. "Her bosses at the deli helped. She's a great mother."

Lynette nodded. "I hired a private detective to find the child after you and Julianne broke up. It didn't take him any time at all to locate Isabelle and…your son. He sent me photos." She looked at Nate, and this time she was incapable of stemming the tears that flowed down her cheeks. "I had no idea how to tell you. I'm proud of nothing I've done. But I hope now you'll be able to have some kind of relationship. Some sort of…"

Lynette hid her face behind her hands as sobs shook her body.

Nate didn't have to think or weigh his options. He moved to his mother's side and put his arms around her. In the past couple of months, he'd learned enough about human frailty and family to know they sometimes walked hand in hand.

"I think we all have enough regrets to fill an ocean," he said and felt her nod against his cheek. "I'm done with that. We start from here."

"Have you seen him, Nate? Does he know?"

"I've seen him. He's terrific. He doesn't know who I am yet."

"Oh, dear—"

"That'll come. I have pictures on my phone. You want to see?"

Sniffling into her napkin, Lynette looked at him with watery appreciation. "May I?"

While Nate was in Chicago, Izzy reflected that having him back in her life made it harder than ever to be away from him. Thankfully, approximately thirty hours after he left Thunder Ridge, he phoned, saying he missed her and Eli. Izzy felt happy, champagne-like bubbles popping in her chest. Then he said he was wrapping up some business and added, "I went to see my mother."

Instantly, trepidation turned the champagne bubbles into fizzing anxiety.

"She hired a private investigator and found out you and Eli were in Thunder Ridge. She's felt guilt ridden for years, but for a long time couldn't face admitting what she'd done and then didn't know how to tell me once she found you. When the job opportunity with Jax came up, she waited, hoping I'd discover everything for myself—admittedly not the best way to handle it, but I think it's accurate to say she was terrified."

Izzy put a hand to her temple. "This is hard to take in all at once. Did you tell her you met Eli?"

"I did. She cried. We don't have to decide anything now, you know, about visits or anything. She'd like to write to you, though, if you're okay with that, and apologize."

Izzy wasn't sure what she was okay with in this moment, but she agreed, nervous yet finally trusting that Nate would always protect their son's feelings. And hers.

Even though Nate had planned to be away four days, he didn't last that long. On day three, he returned. "Indefinitely," he responded when she asked how long he could stay.

She invited him to join her and Eli on a bike ride to Trillium Lake for a picnic. After they ate, Eli grinned knowingly, gave her broad winks and a thumbs-up behind Nate's back, then took off when he met two of his friends.

Nate was obviously disappointed he wasn't going to spend more time with his son. He glanced around at the families, tourists mostly, camping in the park and rowing or swimming or sunbathing on the lake. He seemed particularly interested in a young couple with a toddler. It was easy to follow the train of his thoughts, and Izzy experienced a stab of guilt that Nate and Eli had not been able to share a first swim and first canoe ride like the little family he was watching.

Feeling her guard lowering more and more where he was concerned, she told him how she felt.

"Let's take guilt off the table, okay?" he suggested. "I've had several big helpings already, and all I have to show for it is indigestion." Lying on his side on the blanket she'd brought, he squinted up at her. "It's probably too public here to kiss you, hmm?"

Pleasure colored her cheeks. "Probably."

"Yeah, and we have that agreement about not putting the cart before the horse."

"We do."

"I bought a canoe," he announced. "Big enough for three. Would you and Eli like to join me for a float on the lake tomorrow?"

Oh, boy, would she. But she donned her mother hat. "I have to work tomorrow. You should take Eli. Just the two of you." Nate looked excited and adorably nervous. She placed a hand on his arm, enjoying the role of reassuring him instead of the other way around. "He'll love it."

After half a day on the lake with his son—his *son*!— Nate was sure he'd found the missing link in his life. He couldn't get enough of looking at Eli, studying the boy the way one would study a painting by a master.

Nate was remembering, too, to look directly at Eli when speaking, and Eli's speech was becoming more accessible to him all the time. As they finished their lunches on the shore while their canoe bobbed in the water, Eli talked about his basketball coach's obvious hairpiece and about how one year, the team glued a toupee onto a basketball and some kid named Lyle dribbled the thing all the way up the court before the coach noticed.

Nate laughed, enjoying his son's delight in the retelling as much as he enjoyed the story.

"Do you want to take one more spin around the lake?"

he asked as he wrapped up the remains of the lunch Izzy had packed for them.

Izzy. Standing at her front door in jeans and a Pickle Jar T-shirt, with her hair in a simple ponytail and her face free from makeup, she'd looked utterly beautiful this morning. Standing with her and Eli on the front porch, Nate finally had the feeling for which he'd been searching nearly two decades: wholeness. He felt whole.

He had a surprise for Izzy, one he hoped would make his intentions for their combined futures very clear. But there were details to be hammered out, and he couldn't tell her for a couple of weeks.

"Yeah, let's go again," Eli agreed. "Straight across. We can beat our last time."

"Not much for relaxing paddles around the lake, are you?" Nate mock complained, but, really, he felt invigorated by his son's boundless energy.

Grinning, Eli jumped up to help pack the remains of the picnic so they could get into the water. As he began to fold the blanket they'd been sitting on, he asked, "So, you like my mom?"

The question was so unexpected Nate dropped a thermos of lemonade. He looked at his son, wondering how to play this. Sincere? Casual? Should he affect misunderstanding?

But Eli wasn't judging and didn't seem unhappy about the prospect. Nate answered honestly but carefully. "Yes, I like your mom. I like being around her. I like being around you, too."

Instantly, he regretted saying that to a teenage boy, but Eli didn't seem awkward or embarrassed.

"Okay." Nodding with more sophistication than he probably had, Eli advised, "You should keep seeing her, then. I think she likes you, too."

Nate would have loved to pursue that, but today was about Eli. He shoved the picnic items in a cooler, stowed everything under the bushes where they'd docked, and tossed out a challenge. "*Twice* across the lake. First time with only you rowing, and second with only me. We time it, and the winner buys root beer floats."

Eli's smile seemed to spread all the way across his face. "Triple-scoop waffle cones."

"Done."

They got in the canoe, and Eli worked tirelessly, muscles pumping while Nate timed him. He crowed with victory as they reached the bank.

"Not so fast," Nate said darkly, but he enjoyed his son's competitiveness. "My turn."

The sun was hot and high. Peeling his T-shirt over his head, Nate got down to business, grabbing the oars. Eli heckled him good-naturedly. Nate was grinning before he was halfway across the lake. By the time he'd reached the far bank, he was crowing victory, just to see Eli's reaction. It didn't occur to him until the race was over that Eli was no longer laughing. No longer even talking. Or smiling.

He didn't even want to argue over who'd won. "It doesn't matter," Eli mumbled, sullen. "It's late. I have to go."

No conversation was desired. Nate didn't have enough experience to know how to address the sudden mood shift. He tried joking. "If you demand a rematch, I guarantee I don't have enough energy to win."

"I don't want a rematch. I need to go."

The silence extended uncomfortably. "Eli, if I did something…or said something that bothered you…" Nate stopped, having no idea how to continue. "Do you want to talk about something?"

But Eli wasn't even looking at him. He was pretending, Nate was sure, that he didn't hear what was being said.

Fear, frustration and guilt—he wasn't sure over what— began to gnaw at Nate. By the time they got back to town, he was as grouchy as Eli.

Carrying the picnic gear to the house, he thought he might drop everything and run so he could return to the hotel and try to figure out what the hell he'd done wrong, but Izzy ushered them both in, saying she had a new dessert to try out on them. Something she wanted to start serving at the deli.

Eli hadn't wanted to get the ice cream, and he didn't want any dessert now.

He signed something to his mother. No talking so Nate could be included. He didn't even glance in Nate's direction.

Izzy frowned. She both signed and spoke, "You didn't tell me you were seeing Trey tonight. I made dinner. I thought we could all eat and watch *Hotel Transylvania.* Do you know Nate likes that movie as much as we do?"

Eli did glance in his direction then, with an expression that approached a sneer. He signed again to his mother.

"Why?" she asked. "Don't you feel well? And, honey, remember that Nate doesn't know ASL, so you need to speak, too."

"Fine. I said, if I can't go to Trey's, then I'm going to my room. Okay?"

"No," Izzy said, "not okay." She looked at Nate. "What happened? What's wrong?"

Her question seemed to incense Eli. "What are you asking him for? He's not part of this family. He doesn't know anything about me."

"Eli—"

"He's not! Who is he? Some guy you're dating? Or not even dating? You want me to call him 'Uncle Nate'?"

"Hey!" Nate waded in. "Don't talk to your mother that way."

Eli turned on him. "Don't tell me what to do. Who are you? My life isn't any of your business. Neither is hers." He gestured to his mother. "Why are you hanging around all of a sudden? *Who are you?*"

Izzy and Nate did probably the worst thing they could have done at that point: they stared mutely at their son.

Eli shook his head, mumbled, "Never mind. I don't care!" and raced up the stairs to his attic bedroom.

Thunderstruck, Izzy looked at Nate. "Does he know? Did you—"

"No, of course not, not without telling you. I don't know what happened. Everything seemed great, and then—"

"What?"

Nate spread his hands. "I don't know. It changed." He felt like an ass for having no better explanation.

Seeing his frustration, she put a hand on his arm. "Teenagers are like that sometimes," she attempted to reassure, but it was obvious she wasn't reassured herself. "I'm going to go up and talk to him."

"I'll—" he shrugged, feeling impotent "—head back to the hotel."

"No. I've got iced tea and coffee cake, and... Stay," she said, looking at him imploringly. "It's time we started working through some of these parenting things together." She tried a smile. "Lord knows we need the practice."

Nate wanted to hold her. He wanted to give her strength. And get some for himself. He wanted to know how to do this, right damn now.

"I'll go up and talk to him first," she suggested. "See if I can find out what's really bothering him. You'll wait?"

He nodded. "I'll wait." *As long as it takes.*

When Izzy walked into her son's room, Eli was on his bed, throwing his basketball far too close to the ceiling. Because of her own background, Izzy had taken numerous parenting classes at community college and tried to balance firmness with empathy, which was often easier said than done. At this moment, she opted for firmness.

Stealing the basketball from midair before Eli could

catch it again, she shot it at the laundry hamper and scored. "You," she told her son, using voice and hands, "were rude. What's going on?"

Deliberately, Eli stared at the ceiling, ignoring her.

She thumped him on the shoulder. "Hey. Don't do that. Talk to me. What is going on?"

Using ASL only, he signed. *Maybe you should tell me what's going on. Why don't you talk to me?* His hands stabbed the air as he spoke.

There was only one person in the world Izzy felt she knew as well as herself. When Eli turned twelve, she'd had to amend that to *almost* as well as herself, because like most tween brains, Eli's could be a complete mystery at times. But, still, she knew her son.

She tapped his thigh so he'd scoot over, but he refused. And then he looked at her. His eyes were so much like hers. As a baby and toddler, they'd looked at her with a trust that had made her heart feel ten times bigger than it was. As he'd gotten older, his eyes had held fear, anger, hurt— all the emotions it took to grow up. But never, never had he looked at her with the resentment and fury and mistrust she saw now.

"Who is he?" Eli clamped down on each word as if he were tearing off bites of the toughest beef jerky. "Is he the man who— Is…is he…my father?"

An earthquake rolled through Izzy's body. Eli put his arm over his eyes, blocking her out, but not before she saw the glisten of tears.

"Eli. My boy," she whispered, reaching for his arm. He jerked it away. "I'm sorry," she said.

You said you always tell me the truth. He continued to sign only, reverting to the language they knew best.

Lying on his bed, he looked so young and so knowing and so afraid. Izzy felt as if he'd lassoed her heart and was squeezing. "I know," she said sadly. "I've been too scared. You never asked me much about your father," she began haltingly. "Not telling you was the easy way out, and I took it."

I was afraid he was a jerk. I didn't want to know about him. I thought I'd hate him.

ASL was a beautiful language, and Izzy had often thought it was particularly beautiful when used to express strong anger or grief or love. Now, as she watched her son's eloquent hands, she felt his emotions.

He's got the same birthmark I do. Over his ribs. I saw it when he took off his shirt.

Izzy closed her eyes. Lord, she'd forgotten. Over the years, she'd actually forgotten that Nate shared the same uniquely shaped birthmark that decorated Eli's skin. Nate's, she recalled now, had been lighter, less noticeable.

She had to restrain her impulse to take her son in her arms. Deep inside he must have wondered, must have sensed Nate's presence was something more than just a friend getting to know him.

He's never been around before. Ever, Eli signed strongly. *Why is he here now? How come he changed his mind?*

"Changed his mind?"

About wanting a kid.

This was the hard part, the part that would reveal her weaknesses—and Nate's—as much as their strengths. This was the part she couldn't put a good spin on, but their son was demanding the truth, and he deserved it.

"We were so young. Not much older than you are now. We weren't mature enough to handle a long-term relationship, much less a pregnancy. Nate already had a scholarship to a great college…" As succinctly as she could, trying her best not to blame anyone, she explained that Nate's parents wanted him to continue on his path, and then gently, so gently, she revealed that they'd talked about making an adoption plan. The wounded surprise on her son's face nearly sliced her in two.

"I don't know if you'll understand this until you're the parent of a teenager yourself. Nate's parents understood what it takes to raise a child, and they didn't think we were ready."

But you *kept me.*

"I did. I was selfish." She wanted so badly to touch him, to comfort him. But he was still too angry. "Nate went to college. He didn't know I changed my mind."

Why didn't you tell him? The question was punctuated with sharp, heated hand movements.

Omitting the part about his grandparents suggesting to Nate that she'd miscarried—because some truths could wait forever—Izzy tried to explain the feelings that had led her to raise Eli on her own.

"I was afraid. Afraid to be hurt. Afraid to risk being rejected by Nate or his parents. Afraid to have them reject you because of me. Eli, I love you more than anything." Spontaneously, she placed her hand on his arm. He reacted as if her touch burned. Swallowing the pain that caused, she continued, "What I didn't know then was that trying to avoid pain just prolongs it. I made mistakes. Nate… your father—"

Don't call him that.

Izzy lowered her head, took a breath, then continued. "He's a good man, Eli. I don't think I realized how good until I saw how much he wants to get to know you. How very much he wants to love you."

Tears filled her son's eyes. "I don't want to get to know him!" He used ASL and his voice this time. "And I want you to leave."

"Eli, we're human. Human beings blow it. Sometimes we blow it really badly."

He sat up, this time using his hands and shouting.

"That's your excuse?" Jumping from the bed, he stalked the room like a caged animal. "Great. So the next time I lie or do something I know is messed up, I can just say, 'Sorry, Mom, I'm human, so get off my case'?"

There had been so many parenting moments when she'd felt in over her head, but never like this. As hard as it was to let her child hurt, she could accept that pain was part of growing up. But this much pain?

"I love you. And when you're ready to forgive us, you're going to find out that you have *two* parents who love you and want the very best for you."

"I'm never going to be ready to forgive you for this. Go away!"

She stood her ground, matching his intensity. "I love you."

"Leave me alone, Mom."

I love you. She signed it, hard.

"Leave!"

The bedroom door swung open. Izzy hadn't heard footsteps and was caught by surprise when Nate appeared, filling the room with his tall, imposing, unapologetic presence. He looked like…a father. "Don't talk to your mother that way. If you want to blame someone, blame me, but she's earned your respect."

"You're telling me what to do? Seriously?" He turned to his mother and signed, *What a jerk.*

Eli, stop, Izzy signed back. For the first time in her life, she saw her son sneer.

Nate got right in the boy's face. "Your fight is with me. I left—she didn't."

"Fine. You both suck."

"Eli!" Izzy jumped between them. "Apologize."

Nate grabbed her arm, applying a gentle pressure while he addressed Eli. "No one's telling you you're not entitled to be angry. But your mother doesn't deserve to bear the brunt of it. No one has ever done more for you. She's worth ten of me." He paused briefly. "She's worth ten of anyone else."

Eli looked from Nate to his mother, then turned away, his expression still turbulent.

Izzy ached for her son. She ached for all three of them, but when she looked at Nate, she felt less alone than ever before.

Seated at the desk in his room at the inn, Nate attempted to concentrate on the plans Jax Stewart had asked him to draft for a green remodel of a sizable portion of the downtown area. Ordinarily, the project would easily claim his focus, but it had been two days since he'd left Izzy's after the confrontation with Eli, and he'd been jumpy as a cat ever since.

Izzy had encouraged him to give Eli some time. That might have been easier if he could have seen her in the interim, but she'd been sticking as close as possible to their son.

Closing the lid on his laptop with far too much force, Nate leaned back in the chair, tilting it on two legs. He was jealous.

Izzy had texted him an encouraging note this morning, urging him to be patient and have faith. Be patient? Picking up a pencil, he chucked it across the room. *There's your patience.*

Eli would be a man before they blinked. He wanted time with his son, damn it. He wanted…

Everything. Eli. Izzy. He wanted to know it wasn't too late. And he wanted to know it right now.

Picking up his cell phone, he tapped her number, waited one ring, hung up, tossed the phone onto his desk and dug his fingers into his hair. *Give it time…trust…*

Pushing his chair back, he rose, grabbed his room card

and headed for the door. Kissing Izzy—*that* was what he needed to do, because when he kissed her, then she felt as urgent as he did.

Flinging open the door, he headed down the hallway, arriving at the carpeted stairway in several giant strides and flying down the first flight until he reached the landing and stopped dead.

"Hi." The word was accompanied by a tip of four fingers moving from his son's forehead to form an arc in the air. In his other hand, Eli held a baseball and bat. "Are you heading out?" he asked.

"No." Nate's throat felt raw. His heart pumped like it had the first time he saw the ocean. "I mean, yeah, but… You want to come up? Or head outside? Whatever you want." *Calm down.*

Eli, looking about as comfortable as a colt in jeans, bounced the bat against his sneakers. "I play baseball."

Nate nodded. "Your mom says you're good."

"I want to pitch, but I throw too many balls. She said you pitched for the Huskies."

"I was a better football player, but, yeah, I managed to pitch the ball over home base a few times…" Emotion welled in Nate's chest. His son played on one of the same high school teams he'd played for. "I could give you a few pointers…if you want." *Don't say no.* When had he ever been this afraid of being rejected?

Eli shifted the baseball to his other hand and fingered it nervously. "If you've got time."

"Yeah." A smile began to grow in Nate's chest. "I've got all the time in the world."

Heaven on earth. That was what teaching his son to pitch a fastball felt like—heaven right here in Thunder Ridge. Now they were eating ice-cream cones—and he finally knew his son's favorite flavor: mint cookie dough—on a bench overlooking Long River.

I'm a dad, damn it. He had to keep from grinning. Eli was still a hard sell; they weren't as easy with each other as they'd been before the big reveal, but once Nate's pitching suggestions had helped put the ball into the strike zone, Eli had started to warm up again. Speaking of the big reveal...

"Hey, how did you know I'm your—" He stumbled.

"Father?" Eli supplied. The boy rubbed his eyes before he answered, a gesture that reminded Nate of himself. "I knew something was going on. My mom never invites guys over. And then the day we were on the river, you took off your shirt."

Nate looked at him quizzically.

"You have the Island of Manhattan. Like me."

"The what?"

Eli smiled. "It's what my mom calls my birthmark. Here." He pointed to his rib cage. "It's shaped like Manhattan."

Nate's jaw lowered. "We have the same birthmark?"

Eli took a couple of licks of his cone. "Pretty close. I never used to like it."

"Me, either," Nate related, feeling dazed. *We have the same birthmark.* It was one more awe-inspiring tie.

"Yours is paler. I don't mind mine so much anymore." He shrugged. "It's part of me."

"Yeah." Part of Eli. Part of Nate. "I don't mind mine, either." He went ahead and grinned. *My boy and I are a lot alike.* "I don't mind it one bit."

Chapter Seventeen

"'Happy Forty-Fifth Birthday, Pickle Jar,'" Derek read the sign Izzy had hung across the wall above a bank of booths in the deli. "Shouldn't that be 'Happy Anniversary'?"

From her vantage point behind the counter, where platters of smoked fish, trays of vegetables and mini brisket sandwiches tempted the guests, Izzy cocked her head at the sign. "Now that you mention it, probably. But Sam and Henry never had kids. The Pickle Jar really is their baby, so birthday seems apropos."

"I suppose." Derek finished a tea-sized corned beef on rye in two bites. "So, how's it going, Izz?"

Looking around at a deli filled with friends and neighbors, with her coworkers passing trays of knishes, bite-size kugels and other delights, Izzy answered honestly, "Good. I mean, we're still walking the line between red and black, but I've great promo ideas. I even think we can build an online presence. I'm thinking about starting a pickle blog."

"Wow. Subscribe me. But I wasn't talking about the

restaurant." He nodded to a booth where Nate and Eli sat on one side, talking to Sam and Henry, who were on the other. "I meant *that*."

She followed his gaze. "Oh." As usual when she talked to Derek about Eli lately, equal measures of pleasure and guilt washed through her. "Oh, you know. It's, uh, it's… nice."

"Nice." Derek scoffed. "You are so full of it. I see them biking all over town. It must be a lot better than nice."

"Well…" She shook her head. "Oh, Derek, I hope you know Eli loves you. I mean *loves* you. You're family, and no one is ever going to take your place—"

"Izz," he stopped her. "You've told me that forty-three times. Since this morning." Wiping his hands on a napkin, he put his palms companionably on her shoulders. "Eli and I hung out yesterday at the batting cage in Doc Howard Park."

"You did?"

"Yes. Got a soda afterward. We're good. He seems happy."

Izzy felt her stomach muscles relax. She nodded. "He is."

"All right, then." Derek let go of her to snag a passing knish. "What about you and Thayer?"

Oops, there went her stomach muscles again. "Nate and I?" Fiddling with the veggie tray, she shook her head. "We're focusing on Eli. On co-parenting. We're not really… you know, because there's so much work to be done to get everyone on the right track, and I've been so busy with the deli and putting together this party, and—"

"Is she talking about Nate again?" Holliday strolled up, parking herself on a counter stool in front of the lox on baby bagels. "*So* yummy," she purred, raising the hors d'oeuvre. "Nate *and* the food," she clarified. "You are talking about him, aren't you? It sounds like it. You hyper-babble when his name comes up."

"That's not true. I have nothing to hyper-babble about. There's nothing going on."

Derek smirked. Holliday laughed outright. "When was the last time you kissed him?"

"Last night around midnight," Derek supplied the requested information. "They were at the gazebo. Mrs. Kaminsky saw them."

"Really?" Holliday looked delighted.

"Mrs. Kaminsky saw us?" Izzy yelped, looking around to make sure nobody heard. "What was that old woman doing out at midnight?" she hissed.

"Walking Little Pete. He ate a triple-scoop waffle cone someone dropped on the sidewalk. That's a lot of dairy for a Chihuahua. Apparently, he had the trots all night."

"Aw," Holliday sympathized. "I love Little Pete."

"Yeah, he's a good dog."

"Will you two stop it," Izzy snapped, concerned about the gossip that must be swirling around town. "If Mrs. Kaminsky saw us and told you, then she probably told other people, too, right? Half the town must know by now."

"Half the town already knows you and Nate are sneaking around," Holliday said around another bite of mini bagel. They think it's cute."

"What?"

"That's not true," Derek scoffed.

"Thank goodness." Izzy sighed.

"The *whole* town knows. And they do think it's cute. Matter of fact, Mark Gooding, the sheriff over in Bristol—remember the one I tried to fix you up with?—he phoned this afternoon. Said to tell you good luck."

Izzy gasped. "No! You've got to be kidding."

"I am kidding," Derek assured her. "About Mark. But what's the big deal, Izz?"

"Yes. You're parents," Holliday pointed out. "Everyone will be thrilled for you. No one is judging."

"I'm sure some of them are, but I'm not worried about that," Izzy insisted. "I don't want Eli to get any ideas. To get his hopes up. You saw *The Parent Trap*," she said to Holly. "You know."

"The parents in that movie wind up together. It has a happy ending."

"But it's a movie!" She spread her hands. "Nate and I dating puts Eli in a very vulnerable position."

"So what are you doing? Waiting to see if it sticks before you tell anyone?" Holliday asked.

Izzy nodded. "Seems like a good plan."

"Well, I don't get it." Holly shook her head. Then she leaned close to Izzy and asked, her voice low, "Do you love him?"

Izzy figured she might as well answer that honestly, since everyone seemed to know her business anyway. She even opened her mouth to do it, but the musical tap of silverware on a water glass interrupted her.

"May I have your attention?" Henry Bernstein stood in front of the booth where he'd been talking to Sam and Nate and Eli. "I have a few things I'd like to say."

Izzy, Holliday and Derek cut their conversation short and faced their host.

"Forty-five years is a good long life for a restaurant," Henry continued. "Longer than some marriages, and definitely longer than I kept my hair." Laughter bubbled around the restaurant. "We couldn't have arrived at this place without help. Especially from wonderful, loyal employees, many of whom I've come to think of as family." He motioned for Sam to join him. Wiry and still spry, Sam slid out of the booth to stand beside his brother. "Sammy and I, we're about as lucky as two average Joes can get. We've had great lives. My brother pointed out recently that we're not getting any younger, and although I certainly think *I* am—"

There was more laughter and some applause. Derek whistled through his teeth and called out, "You're a pup!"

Izzy wanted to laugh along, but a strong foreboding crept into her.

Henry nodded impishly. "Yes, well, my brother also pointed out, quite wisely, that there really is a life beyond the walls of The Pickle Jar."

"That's only a rumor!" called Oliver.

Leon added, "Yeah, that's never been proven, boss."

Henry patted the air. "Okay, okay. What has been proven is that newer restaurants, owned by younger people, are doing better in this town than we are."

Izzy wanted to shout, *Stop!* She wanted this conversation, wherever it was heading, to happen in the office, not out here.

"What you don't know," Henry continued, "is that our building was purchased recently. The whole block was purchased, in fact, by someone young and energetic. Someone with a very good vision for change and for growth. Sammy and I want to step aside to make room for that change, that youthful spark, because, believe it or not, we were that spark once. We know it can be a powerful thing."

This can't be happening. It can't be. Not now. Izzy felt an urge to scream that felt very much like hysteria. *We need this restaurant. It's our home. We're family—*

"Nate, stand up with us," Henry requested. Appearing confident and so handsome that at any other time it would have taken Izzy's breath away, Nate rose from the booth, standing tall and square shouldered next to the Bernstein brothers. His gaze met Izzy's.

"This is an exciting time for our town," Henry said. He reached up to clamp a hand on Nate's shoulder. "And this is one of the people who is going to make it exciting. Nate

Thayer left here an eighteen-year-old boy with a dream to become an architect."

Was it Izzy's imagination or was Nate nervous beneath the calm and composed air?

"He has returned," Henry continued, "an architect of some renown, and it is his desire to contribute to the re-birth of Thunder Ridge. The town we all love should be a relevant player on the Oregon landscape."

Izzy stared, agape with an awful fascination, the way one would watch cars on an inevitable collision course.

"Nate will be working for the new owner of the building we are standing in. Together, they have plans to beau-tify the entire block. To bring in more business, which will mean more jobs and bigger paychecks. I'll let him say a few words about his plans. Plus, we have another surprise for you. I think I'll let him spill the beans on that one, too. Nate, it's your turn."

"Thanks, Henry."

Izzy couldn't hear. Literally could not hear. She plas-tered a smile on her face so no one would see the storm inside her. With all the attention at the front of the room, she backed up a few steps and then a few steps more until she was at the entrance to the kitchen. Grabbing an empty tray from the work counter, she turned and fled.

The building was sold. Nate was working with the new owner to "improve" the entire block, and Henry and Sam wanted to retire.

Tears filled her eyes. Anger, frustration, grief jumbled together.

How could Nate? How could he have known all this was coming and not said a word to her? No warning at all?

If the building was remodeled, the new owner would raise the rent—

Forget the rent, dummy. Henry and Sam are retiring. New businesses…new opportunities. The Pickle Jar had seen its heyday. And all her efforts to bring that heyday back had been for naught. They were going to close and make way for something shiny and new and "relevant."

Rushing to the back door, Izzy slipped into the alley and took deep gulps of the night air.

How could this be happening? Why hadn't she paid attention to the signs? There were always signs. Like Sam speaking so admiringly of the retirement home. And Henry talking about not visiting Hawaii since his honeymoon and wondering how it had changed. But Nate—

There hadn't been any signs to tell her that Nate was going to aid and abet in pulling the rug out from under her. Without a word. Without a warning.

Izzy pressed a hand to her forehead, which was starting to pound already. Every cell in her body seemed to be captured by fear and foreboding. It felt intolerable, and she started to walk. Fast and then faster.

She walked to her house, grabbed Latke, who was delighted to see her, got on her bike and pedaled in the dark, her dog trotting somewhat warily alongside. On the way, her phone buzzed. Pulling way off to the side of the road, she checked her messages while Latke sniffed the weeds. She had a text from Eli, one from Derek and another from Nate.

Eli's read: Mom, why rn't u here? This is so gr8!

Her son thought losing the deli was great? Maybe that was how everyone would feel about a modern, convenient, stupid new district that would look like a million other modern, convenient, stupid new shopping districts.

She looked at Derek's message: R U OK? TEXT OR I'LL PUT OUT AN APB.

And from Nate: Wanted to surprise you. I screwed up. Call me. Now.

Ignoring Nate, Izzy responded to Eli: Needed air and

breakfast 4 2morrow. U know me, always thinking food. BBL8R.

Then she reassured Derek: Am FINE. No APB. Thx, tho.

She slipped the phone into her pants pocket and resumed her ride.

Her body seemed to take over from her mind. She didn't so much *decide* where to go as she simply wound up there.

In the dark, the trailer she'd shared with Felicia looked more ominous than it did during the day, when it was mostly a pathetic, decrepit pile of junk. At night it seemed haunted, and the ghosts were all Izzy's.

Latke hung back, pulling on the leash as Izzy walked toward the broken front door. Giving in, she unclipped the leash to let Latke wander outside while she opened the rusted door and went in.

With the full moon as her only light source out here, she had to sense more than see the condition of the old place, but she wasn't interested in the aesthetics.

Tonight, she felt as though she were eight years old again, sitting on that lopsided sofa by the window, pretending that being alone didn't frighten her.

The only time she ever stepped foot inside this miserable place nowadays was when she needed to remind herself that she was no longer terrified, no longer desperate, no longer alone. Anytime she felt frightened or defeated as an adult, she promised herself she would never, ever feel as powerless as she'd felt as a child.

Except that now she did. It seemed that everything she'd worked so ferociously to build was falling apart.

Shaking, she wandered to the sofa, but memory hit so fast and so furiously that she stopped dead in her tracks.

There she was, at age eight, sitting on the couch, hopeful and frightened in the hand-me-down dress with a torn ruffle on the skirt that she thought was so fancy. Her mother showed up after the sky had already gone dark.

She had remembered it was Izzy's birthday and had come home, bringing a stuffed bunny for her daughter and a new boyfriend for herself. They threw Izzy a quick party by sticking a match in a Ding Dong and then put her to bed.

Her memories fast-forwarded to age twelve. On that birthday, she baked herself a pan of brownies and lit her own candles. Her mother didn't come home at all that night or the week after. Izzy had a contest going in her head, trying to see if she could outlast her mother's negligence by refusing to try to find Felicia or reminding her she'd missed her daughter's birthday. That was when Izzy promised herself she would never again beg for someone's love.

"And I didn't," she murmured, her legs so weak she felt as if she might crumple in a heap right there. She hadn't begged for Henry's and Sam's love or for her friends'; she didn't beg her coworkers to like her, and she certainly had never, ever begged for Nate's love.

The fact that she hadn't told him *I love you* in actual words had been a source of pride and comfort when she was seventeen.

Tears that were decades old got stuck in her throat, feeling like a lump of tar. She was afraid to cry, afraid she would be unable to stop, but it ceased to be her choice. Doubled over, as if protecting the little girl who'd refused to cry all those years ago, she sobbed, the sound echoing through the shell of a house that had heard much noise but little genuine emotion.

Responding to her mommy's crying, Latke braved the rusty steps and entered the trailer. Whining, she shoved her broad nose against Izzy's leg. Kneeling next to Latke, Izzy gathered her dog in a fierce hug as she wept in pain. She cried in recognition, too, because the truth was that she wasn't alone anymore. Henry, Sam, Eli and Derek and Holliday—they never missed her birthday, even when she told them not to bother.

She had learned to give her love to people who were capable of loving her back, and she'd come to trust that they weren't going to leave. Could she really choose to doubt all that now just because two wonderful men in their seventies had decided it was time to retire?

And what about Nate? She loved the way he looked at Eli when Eli wasn't looking. She loved the way he looked at her. When Nate grinned, she felt as light as down, and when he kissed her, the very last cracks in her heart knit together until she felt seamless, whole.

She'd thought refusing to be broken made her a winner. Maybe the willingness to be broken, knowing she would be put back together again, even stronger—maybe that was the real victory.

Trust beyond Izzy's understanding settled around her like a comforter, filling her with resolve. As the tears dried, she raised her head. Through the dark, she peered at the lifeless trailer, and the truth settled on her. *Izzy Lambert doesn't live here anymore.*

Pulling out her phone, she sent a text, then pocketed the cell again without waiting for a reply. Wiping her face, she rose and walked to the door, her loyal dog by her side. Heading out, they made their way down the steps and across the weeds to the spot where Izzy left her bike. Only then did she turn for one look at the trailer. The last look. She wouldn't need to come here again.

By the time she reached her house, Nate was there, pacing the porch. He bounded down the steps to meet her.

"Where's Eli?" she asked.

"Still at the party." He grabbed her arms. "I'm sorry. I wanted to surprise you. It was stupid. I should have realized that with all the secrets in our history—"

Izzy put her fingers on Nate's lips. "I don't want to talk about the past. Thank you for meeting me." She gazed into his worried features, so perfect, so intense. Taking his hand, she led him to the porch, but neither of them wanted to sit.

"I've already been here once," he said, "and to the grocery because of that cock-and-bull story you told Eli about needing breakfast foods, and to your favorite spot on the river. If you hadn't texted me—"

"I know. I'm sorry." She wasted no time with explanations about why she'd left the party. She didn't want to waste any more time at all. "I love you." Sounding breathless, she tried again. "I love you, and I loved you fifteen years ago, and maybe it wouldn't have mattered if I'd told you then, but I should have, just because it was the truth." The words emerged like a pent-up sigh, ready to be released at last. "We have a son, and I think we should finish raising him together— No. No, that's not right. It's not that I think we *should*, it's that I *want* to. I want to finish raising him as a team. I want us to be together." Her heart beat a mile a minute. Honesty felt dangerous and terrifying and absolutely right. "If you want us to be together, too, then great. And if you don't…" She was about to assure him they would work out the details of parenting from a distance, then shook her head. "You have to want us to be together, because this is right. This is whole. This is that thing you were talking about. It's what Henry means when he says *bashert*. You're my meant-to-be, Nate Thayer, and, darn it, I know it, and you should know it, too, and if you don't, well, then—"

Nate's kiss absorbed everything else she was going to say. A delightful dizziness replaced thoughts.

When they stopped kissing, she lowered her forehead to his shirt and breathed him in. "I can move to Chicago so you can be closer to Eli," she murmured. "I don't want you two to be apart again."

Nate held her face with one hand and kissed her forehead. "You can't come to Chicago." His response mirrored the look in his eyes—sweet and amused and loving. "You have obligations here."

"Only for a little while longer, apparently." She frowned. "Or would you rather that I not come to Chicago?"

He kissed her again, swift and hard this time, then said, "Hey, that bossy confidence thing is really sexy. Don't louse it up now."

Izzy pushed away from him. "All right, then tell me what you mean."

"That's better." He grinned. "I mean, you left the party too soon. And we were clumsy about the way we made the announcement. You, Isabelle Lambert—someday hopefully—Thayer, are the new co-owner of The Pickle Jar. Fifty-one percent interest with Henry and Sam as your mostly silent partners. The deli will have to close temporarily during the remodel, which you will work on with me, so that I understand your vision for the restaurant. Then The Pickle Jar will reopen as part of a green remodel of the downtown blocks. Jax inherited a couple buildings and bought quite a few others, but he isn't going to rent-gouge or squeeze people out. He's looking at a few-years-long project intended to make Thunder Ridge a more relevant tourist destination during ski season and in the summer. Too many people stay outside of town and come to the Ridge just to ski. Jax wants to keep them and their wallets right here. I've been looking for a project exactly like this. There'll be plenty more in Oregon, too."

Nate looked immensely pleased with himself. "And," he said, "your employees can temporarily go on unemployment or accept a stipend while the deli is closed. Jax found an anonymous donor to help out. Same for the other businesses that will be affected." He laughed. "You look stunned."

Izzy nodded. "Did you say Isabelle Lambert—someday hopefully—Thayer?"

It took Nate a second or two. "With everything I just told you, that's what you want to know?"

She nodded.

A slow smile spread across his face. "Good." He leaned close so close that no one, not even the crickets chirping all around them, could have heard him. "I want to stay in Thunder Ridge, with you and Eli. I feel better standing still right here than I ever felt chasing success anyplace else." Reaching into his pocket, he pulled out a dark blue velvet box, opened the lid and dropped to one knee before her. "Izzy Lambert, will you marry me? So that the rest of our lives can begin right now?"

Izzy couldn't believe what she was hearing. Or seeing. Nestled inside the jewelry box, a platinum ring with three diamonds sparkled beneath the porch lights. A family of multifaceted gems nestled together.

This was the life she hadn't dared dream about. "You're moving awfully quickly," she demurred, not meaning a word of it. "We've hardly dated, and you want to get married. What kind of example is that to set for our son?" Happy tears slipped down her cheeks.

Nate rose and gently thumbed the tears away. "I asked Eli for his blessing first. He gave it. We've waited fifteen years, Isabel. The way I felt with you—it was always there in the back of my mind, no matter what I was doing or whom I was with. I've been trying to recapture that feeling for half my life."

"What feeling would that be?"

Nate kissed her again, long and slow and thoroughly. "That one," he murmured when they parted. "The one that tells me there's nothing I need or want that I don't already have. The feeling that heaven is right here in my arms. That's the feeling I want every day for the rest of my life. Do you want it, too?"

"I do," Izzy agreed, feeling as if her heart might explode

with joy when he took her hand and placed his ring on her finger. The ring was exquisite, but nothing could match the beauty of Nate's expression when she looked into his eyes and vowed, "For better, for worse, for always. I definitely, definitely do."

Epilogue

Eli stood next to his dad, beneath the gazebo in Doc Howard Park. *You look nervous*, he signed to Nate. *You should
breathe or something.*

Not nervous, Nate signed back. *Excited.* He tugged his
tie as if it was way too tight, shrugged and signed again,
A little nervous, maybe.

Eli grinned. Smiling came easily around his dad. *His
dad.* Okay, it was still totally surreal to think those words,
much less say them.

In the four months since Nate had come back to town,
there had been a lot of changes in Thunder Ridge. Several of the stores, including The Pickle Jar, were closed
for renovations. With the deli dark, his mom had had a
lot of time on her hands, which had turned out to be a
giant pain. She fed everyone like every five minutes and
registered Uncle Derek on an internet dating site until he
told her to back off. Finally, Nate had suggested she stop

butting into everyone's business and start doing something useful, like plan their wedding.

His mom's face had gone through probably a thousand different expressions before she'd burst into tears. It had taken his dad a couple of minutes to figure out that all the blubbering meant "yes."

So, they were going to be a family—officially—in three... two...one...

Right now.

As LeeAnne Alves, the music teacher at the elementary school, played the wedding march on her flute, his mom walked toward the gazebo. Henry held one of her arms, and Sam held the other.

My grandpas. The thought came unbidden, surprising Eli and making him feel kinda weird. Sort of...sentimental about his whole life.

His grandmother—his dad's mom—was here, too. Eli didn't know her too well yet, and she seemed really awkward sometimes, but when he took a peek at her now, she was watching them and smiling as if she was really happy.

Everyone he and his mom knew was sitting in the folding chairs set up on the grass. Uncle Derek was in the front row. He made eye contact with Eli and signed, *Your mom and Nate look like they need oxygen.*

Eli nodded. *Scared of crowds.*

Wimps. Your mom looks pretty.

Eli looked at his mother. Wow. Yeah, she did.

Her dress was long with skinny straps on the shoulders, and the color was almost exactly the shade of pink in the sunset. Her gaze remained glued to his father, who walked down the gazebo steps to meet her. For just a second as they grasped each other's hands, a glow surrounded them, and they seemed to forget that anyone else was there, even Eli.

Suddenly, he felt nearly grown up and really, really

young again, all at once. His heart pinched in a not totally good way. But then his parents started toward the steps, and when his mother reached them, he saw tears sparkling in her eyes.

Letting go of Nate's hand, she passed her bouquet to Holliday and signed to Eli, *I love you so much. Ready, First Mate?*

Was he ready?

As Eli glanced at his dad, he remembered something. A couple of weeks ago, they'd been in this park, tossing a baseball around, and Eli had missed a catch. When he'd run to the bench where the ball had rolled, he had seen a guy with a real little baby in a stroller. That guy had been watching his baby just the way Nate was watching him and his mom now. Like he was sort of amazed by them and also determined to watch over them every day, forever.

Man, being on the receiving end of that kind of attention was going to get annoying.

This time Eli's smile began from deep inside, replacing the pinched feeling around his heart.

Meeting his mom's eyes, he signed back, *Ready, Skipper. Totally ready.*

He took her right arm and Nate took her left as they faced the minister—and their future—together.

* * * * *

Will Sheriff Neel find his perfect match?
Look for his story,
the next instalment in
Wendy Warren's new series
THE MEN OF THUNDER RIDGE

MILLS & BOON®

Cherish™

EXPERIENCE THE ULTIMATE RUSH OF FALLING IN LOVE

A sneak peek at next month's titles...

In stores from 14th July 2016:

- **An Unlikely Bride for the Billionaire** – Michelle Douglas *and* **Her Maverick M.D.** – Teresa Southwick
- **Falling for the Secret Millionaire** – Kate Hardy *and* **An Unlikely Daddy** – Rachel Lee

In stores from 28th July 2016:

- **Always the Best Man** – Michelle Major *and* **The Best Man's Guarded Heart** – Katrina Cudmore
- **His Badge, Her Baby...Their Family?** – Stella Bagwell *and* **The Forbidden Prince** – Alison Roberts

---

MILLS & BOON®

Mills & Boon have been at the heart of romance since 1908… and while the fashions may have changed, one thing remains the same: from pulse-pounding passion to the gentlest caress, we're always known how to bring romance alive.

Now, we're delighted to present you with these irresistible illustrations, inspired by the vintage glamour of our covers. So indulge your wildest dreams and unleash your imagination as we present the most iconic Mills & Boon moments of the last century.

Visit **www.millsandboon.co.uk/ArtofRomance** to order yours!

MILLS & BOON®

Why not subscribe?
Never miss a title and save money too!

Here is what's available to you if you join the
exclusive **Mills & Boon® Book Club** today:

* *Titles up to a month ahead of the shops*
* *Amazing discounts*
* *Free P&P*
* *Earn Bonus Book points that can be redeemed
  against other titles and gifts*
* *Choose from monthly or pre-paid plans*

Still want more?
Well, if you join today we'll even give you
50% OFF your first parcel!

So visit **www.millsandboon.co.uk/subscriptions**
or call **Customer Relations on 0844 844 1351***
to be a part of this exclusive Book Club!

**This call will cost you 7 pence per minute plus your
phone company's price per minute access charge.*